Praise for *The Place of the White Heron*

Alejandro Morales' novel, *The Place of the White Heron,* is a thrilling, action packed narrative in wealthy, glittering, but superficial Orange County, California. The cities of Tustin, Costa Mesa and Newport Beach are especially highlighted. The main character, Juana Inés Cruz, known by her initials, J. I., and later in the novel due to the miracles she performs as *la Santa Ilusa,* is born in the midst of a blinding coastal fog. Her parents are wealthy Mexican citizens traveling for business purposes. This is the first of future magical events that will transpire throughout the novel. Strong criticism is leveled at the wealth disparity found in Orange County and evident between the "glitterati," the immigrant working class, and other communities of color. Mexico City, the US - Mexican border, and its ever-present dangers are frequently depicted. Morales once again demonstrates his brilliance at creating a fictional universe at the center of Orange County, and the Aztlán U. S. Mexico Transborder Region, one of the wealthiest geographical areas in the world. I could not put it down!! It was a thriller!

—Maria Herrera-Sobek, Professor Emerita,
  University of California, Santa Barbara

Through a peaceful account of the experiences of artists, professors, bookstore keepers, detectives, and lawyers, native, visiting, exiled, and immigrant, we perceive the familiar view of Southern California landscape, typical taste of Latino-Latin American synthesis, and unique Moralesian sense of history & present, historiographizing a community beyond ethnicity, career, landmark, or even miracle, yet pulsating desire, passion, turmoil, struggle and strength, to present what is Aztlán, what is this country of white heron and what is the world, so different in appearance yet quite similar in essence.

—Dr. Baojie Li, Professor, Shandong University, China

Alejandro Morales' new novel, filled with drama and intrigue, offers a provocative view of Orange County (Orange Curtain) in Southern California as a distinct heterotopia: a multicultural space where the strange, mundane and paranormal coexist with the magical and the sacred. J. I. Cruz occupies the center of the narrative through her miracles, redefining herself as the people's *ilusa,* as she intimates crises and a prophecy of a borderized capitalism. Slowly, the psychological thriller echoes a gothic allegory of mystery and futuristic warnings mixed with myth and ancient spirits that inspire J. I. Cruz to transform an apocalyptic space into a promising and broader Aztlandia.

—Francisco A. Lomelí, Professor Emeritus, UCSB

The Place of the White Heron takes readers across the no-man's land of the U.S.-México transborder region into the cultural dynamics of Aztlán. And who better to navigate this heterotopia than J. I., *la Santa Ilusa?* Fluctuating between the grotesque and the sublime, and fuelled by enduring hope, the novel reads as a natural sequel that honors the standards of originality and relevance set out in the Morales trilogy, while promising much intrigue and climax for what is to come in the final installment.

—Adam Spires, Saint Mary's University, Canada

Set in Aztlandia, and more precisely in Orange County ("the fantasy world of hybridity and liminality,") *The Place of the White Heron* sums up all of Morales' previous literary interests, and it does so in a magnificent and intriguing way. Literary theory, metaliterature, medicine, the indigenous past and present, the grotesque, violence, gangs, urban renewal, the history of California, and the supernatural are just some of the main elements that conform this important new novel. Morales is in full command of his narrative powers. A must read.

—Manuel M. Martín-Rodríguez, Distinguished Professor
of Literature, University of California, Merced

The Place of the White Heron

Alejandro
Morales

TIA CHUCHA PRESS

ACKNOWLEDGMENTS

I wish to thank Luis J. Rodriguez for selecting *The Place of the White Heron* as the inaugural novel for the Tía Chucha Press new novel series. I hope it will inspire a plethora of Latinx writers to produce more literary narratives to add to this special collection.

I want to recognize the excellent editing, both critical and creative of *The Place of the White Heron* done by Margarita López López, my editor and friend.

Thanks to publicist Roxy Runyan, for teaching me the technology to connect to future readers.

My gratitude to Tía Chucha Centro Cultural & Bookstore staff for organizing readings and discussions for the presentation of my books.

It is with great appreciation that I thank my wife, Rohde Morales Teaze for her constant support of my writing endeavors, especially during those times when I couldn't find the correct path to continue the narrative.

To the readers, if you read this book like a work of history, you are reading fiction; if you read this book like a work of fiction, you are reading history.

ISBN 978-1-882688-63-0
Library of Congress Catalog Card Number:

Book Design: Jane Brunette
Artwork: Rosa M
Photography: Jacob Hernández
Editor: Margarita López López

PUBLISHED BY:
Tía Chucha Press
A Project of Tía Chucha's Centro Cultural, Inc.
PO Box 328
San Fernando CA 91341
www.tiachucha.org

DISTRIBUTED BY:
Northwestern University Press
Chicago Distribution Center
11030 South Langley Avenue
Chicago IL 60628

One class of women *offered a real challenge to colonial society—those denounced to the Holy Office as ilusas, that is, as deluded women. The ilusas were a threat to society for several reasons—they often defied or eluded the control of confessors, inventing their own religious myths, and they generally lived outside the recognized "estates," that is, they were neither enclosed in convents nor under the care of father or husband. Though colonial society did its best to hide this floating population in recogimientos (that is, special asylums), it was not always successful. They were not witches and had not made pacts with the devil, so that the Church had to find other ways of disqualifying their discourse, defining it as "illusion" or deception by the devil. The ilusas shared a common language with the mystical nuns, but unlike the latter they often "performed" rapture and ecstasy in public and exhibited their "grotesque" bodies, which they claimed bore the signs of God's special favor.*

—PLOTTING WOMEN: GENDER AND REPRESENTATION
  IN MÉXICO, Jean Franco

Past, Present, Future: Transborder Aztlán

In *The Place of the White Heron*, author Alejandro Morales propels a tour de force—a deliverance for both neophytes and veterans of Aztlán. The mythical home of the *mexicas*—the land of origin of the *aztecas* who journeyed south and founded ancestral México, *la gran Tenochtitlán*—is to become again, centuries later, a homeland for present-time *mexicas* and numerous newcomers. In this "place of herons," a "place of whiteness," a woman, J. I. Cruz, assumes an imminent protagonist role and renders a co-existence of many possibilities.

This central character, who makes a break from Mexico City as exiled *Santa Ilusa de las Grietas* in Morales' novel *Waiting to Happen*, now flourishes in *The Place of the White Heron*, revived with strength and introspection, and seasoned by a wisdom available from her ancestral and co-existing cohort of feminine figures from pre-Columbian to modern-day México. Amidst a span of human relations—from personal to global, as well as spiritual—Morales' modern-day *ilusa* conveys an analytical, yet direct, witty discourse of society's problems. Characters, such as the Maya immigrant family and the Anglo matriarch, Mrs. Dougherty, live happily together, help and understand each other and, eventually, own the same home and land, regardless of the fact that one is White and mute, and the others are Indigenous and do not speak English. The hidden, powerful, denigrating, and long-lasting attitudes, policies, and injustices, compelled on both sides of the border exist in the same plane of communication as the multicultural candidness of multilingualism and racial and ethnic diversity of a transborder ideology.

The backdrop of 21st century *Aztlandia* facilitates the allegorical completion of J. I. Cruz's prophetic return. As she descends "into the

Southern California urban galaxy" Orange County embodies, she is introduced in "a time of accelerations" to this cultural megalopolis where she is to become "alive to the world." An Ivy-league education provides her with some consciousness of Aztlán, but her existence in this polyethnic sphere is what drives her recurring ancestry, determines her present actions, and redefines her impending future. Leafing through the novel and journeying along with J. I. Cruz through her many experiences, enables an understanding, a follow-through, of this mythical return—a past, present, and future combined— to result in an enhanced co-existence in *The Place of the White Heron*. Events, such as Endriago's continuous letters revealing the Mexican Indigenous struggles, J. I.'s search for meaningful employment, and her growth in her interpersonal relationships, elucidate her present and future role. Both of her worlds, Mexico City and Southern California, which in essence are one and the same homeland for the *mexicas*, symbolize ill societies in need of a miraculous change.

J. I. Cruz's transcultural empowered vision and actions highlight her essential purpose. Her return to Aztlán is a sine qua non for her maturity as *ilusa*. However, will this development bring an end to the cross spatial-temporal experiences with Coatlicue, Malintzin Tenepal, *la Virgen de Guadalupe*, Sor Juana, Frida, and Comandanta Ramona? Is she to rise alone as a modern-day *ilusa*? Is society ready for her, or will the witch-hunt continue? Is the good news she magically offers enough to mend the besieged spaces of her present? Will her *facultad* help heal a globalized society, unbalanced with biases and injustice, and where books, weapons, drugs, big pharma, *maquiladoras*, and a patriarchal establishment appear so entwined they ensue but one deleterious outcome? Certainly, J. I. Cruz's miraculous encounters pervade *The Place of the White Heron*. They also stimulate curiosity, enrich the imagination, and incite courageous actions. All the while, the parable of Aztlán continues with the white heron on guard ... "It had traveled for thousands of years to rest here and watch over *la Santa Ilusa de las Grietas*."

—*Margarita López López*

The Place of the White Heron

PRELUDE

J. I. DESCENDED into the Southern California urban galaxy, the fastest-growing, industrial, cultural megalopolis in the world, where approximately twenty-three million people lived in the cultural vortex from Santa Barbara to the U.S. Mexican border. Prophesied to grow to over twenty-nine million, most residents are expected to be non-Anglos, further sliding the ethnic scales toward a polyethnic world. She entered a constantly changing, never-finished, directionless multiplicity of places, where people supposedly progressed, dodged lethal randomness, and evolved into fluctuating and adaptable poly-identities. J. I. stepped off the plane and walked through Orange County, not far from the Mexican farmworkers' housing where she was born years ago. Her mother delighted in telling the story of J. I.'s conception and birth; she told it as if she experienced a miracle of sorts.

Doña Gloria always started the story the same way: "*Siempre pedíamos la misma habitación en el Hotel del Coronado. Te concebimos en un cuarto maravilloso que daba al patio interior.* Doña Gloria and don Celerino often flew to Tijuana and regularly stayed in San Diego. "*Cuando yo tenía casi ocho meses de embarazada recibimos una invitación para visitar a un socio de tu padre que vivía en Beverly Hills*".

Don Celerino and doña Gloria rented a car and drove north. They had been traveling more than an hour when fog came off the ocean and made it almost impossible to see anything. They argued about getting off the freeway.

"*Salte del camino. Los coches vienen demasiado rápido. ¡Celerino!*"

"*¡Cómo puedo salir si no veo nada!*" don Celerino replied with a slight desperation in his voice.

In the excitement of the argument doña Gloria broke water somewhere north of San Juan Capistrano. She cracked like a fragile egg and screamed as if she had given birth at that instant. Don Celerino looked at her and almost ran off the road. He hugged the shoulder hoping to see the exit ramp.

"Dios estaba con nosotros esa noche, hija de mi corazón, porque tu papá pudo salir de la carretera y entró en una blancura milagrosa," doña Gloria said dramatically. Don Celerino slowly drove up a hill to a large house with a circular driveway. He ran to the entrance but was stopped by a man who suddenly appeared from the fog.

"Don't go to that house. The owner will have you arrested."

"My wife is having a baby in the car!"

"Get in your car and follow me."

"¿Adónde vamos?"

"Con alguien que le puede ayudar a su mujer".

The man walked in front of the car. For ten long minutes he led them down a road lined with fruit trees until, finally, they reached a house brightly lit.

"En la niebla la casa brillaba como un enorme diamante".

Several women came to doña Gloria's aid and, immediately, carried her into a common house where they helped her deliver an enchanting baby girl. *"¡Una niña de la niebla!"* a woman called out when the baby cried. The fog came in under the doors, through the windowsills, and every open seam and crack. Within minutes the dwelling was taken over by the fog. Doña Gloria could barely make out the women. Her eyes frantically searched to see her baby. Two hands emerged from the fog and placed the child in her arms.

"Fue la mayor felicidad de mi vida tenerte entre mis brazos y sentirte contra mi pecho".

The next morning, in the middle of a perfumed orange orchard, don Celerino and doña Gloria awoke to a beautiful, sunny day and with their new baby. By bad calculation on the part of doña Gloria's doctor, her baby was born in Orange County, California, in a migrant workers' agricultural camp on the Irvine Ranch, one of the largest in the Southwest. The women who helped doña Gloria give birth were the wives, sisters, and daughters of the farmworkers: these were warm, hospitable people who, although poor, provided all she and don Celerino needed during the few days they remained in the camp.

During their stay they were offered many suggestions for a name; one in particular was very popular—Niebla. Doña Gloria, however, already had a name for her baby girl. She had not consulted with don Celerino, who had selected the name of Andrea Franca. After a short discussion, doña Gloria announced to all that her daughter would not be Niebla, nor Andrea Franca, instead she would be named after doña Gloria's favorite poet. *"Nacida en la casa de luz brillante, en una noche de espesa niebla,* a night when her father and mother lost their way on the road north, *esta niña radiante se llamará Juana Inés Cruz."*

In the speed of flight from México, in route to LAX, and then on to Orange County, J. I. refused to remain immersed in the comfort of her birth story. In this transitional space, her uncontainable memories spilled out, swirling in a spiral of re-memories. Her mind gyrated into overload, transmitting a jumble of competing images. Flying in space disassembled her chronology, as companions of the past re-occupied her present. She thought about this and asked herself: How do I live my hybrid culture and identity as the Mexicanized Juana Inés Cruz with the Americanized J. I. Cruz? She felt a gentle nudge from the stewardess.

A group of excited Japanese students, with surgical facemasks, broke her reverie, and the image of doña Gloria and don Celerino handing over her documents faded from her mind. She gathered her tickets, cash, and U.S. passport, pushed her way through the group who were absorbed in texting and taking photos, and stepped onto the descending escalator heading to the baggage-claim area. There she waited and looked around in hopes that Mark would recognize her. Suddenly, like déjà vu she heard, "Where were you, J. I.? I love you, J. I. Cruz!"

Delivered from her immediate past, from the megalopolis of México—an order of disordered logic, a fragmented dimension of imposing realities—J. I. looked at the man who ached to love her in Southern California, the fantasy world of hybridity and liminality.

They embraced. Oh boy, she thought, two more emerging souls in bizarre CaliAztlán.

1 | The Age of Acceleration

Friedman's thesis: *To understand the twenty-first century you need to understand that the planet's three largest forces: Moore's law (technology), the Market (globalization), and Mother Nature (climate change and biodiversity loss) are accelerating all at once. These accelerations are transforming five key realms: the workplace, politics, geopolitics, ethics, and community.*

—THANK YOU FOR BEING LATE: AN OPTIMIST'S GUIDE TO THRIVING
IN THE AGE OF ACCELERATIONS, Thomas L. Friedman

Innovation happens faster than ever. *Huge companies and start-ups are eager to revolutionize small or large segments of medicine (...) What is still missing is a comprehensive, extensive, and public discussion that includes ethicists and representatives of all groups in order to cover the major issues about to shape the future of healthcare and medicine.*

—THE GUIDE TO THE FUTURE OF MEDICINE: TECHNOLOGY
AND THE HUMAN TOUCH, Bertalan Meskó

"J. I. Cruz!" Mark Forbes called from the driveway.

I looked down from the balcony to find Mark waving the contract for the one-year lease he and I had just signed. We rented a townhouse, not in Los Angeles, Beverly Hills, or Westwood, but in Newport Beach, California: three bedrooms, family and living area, good-sized kitchen, plenty of space to live and never feel confined. Mark commented on the view of Fashion Island, one of Orange County's elegant shopping destinations. There, people always had a destination, whether the law offices in tall towers, Disneyland, investment companies, restaurants, banks, tennis clubs, Joan Irvine Smith's offices, Laguna Beach galleries, Jalapeño's, the movies, or the Back Bay teeming with gleaming figures who walked, jogged, or rode bicycles in a bold effort to get that body fat down to a penis-raising and tit-tingling percentage. Health, youth, body fitness, and money—or the appearance of such—were the Orange County subconscious mottos, and surreptitiously lapping, licking, and slurping at it all was the glittering Pacific Ocean. We expected to live a fashionable modern life in a spacious white townhouse, with a magnificent view and an outlandish rent, even in a depressed economy. "We'll manage," Mark said. "We'll eat on credit cards."

On our front lawn, a friendly, good-natured golden retriever pranced around chasing a ball. I walked downstairs to join Mark playing with the puppy. Dogs had an odor that always bothered me, but this animal smelled perfumed. "*Hasta los perros son hedonistas*," I thought. Its right back leg shook uncontrollably from pleasure. I scratched the pet. The dog lay on its back, tongue out, satisfied, panting for more. It was a fun-loving, pleasure-seeking Newport Beach canine. This animal, with a perfumed body, was a black hole for love and attention.

A man and a woman came out of the nearby townhouse. When the woman clapped her hands, the dog ran to her and jumped up to lick her face. They approached Mark and me and tried to calm the dog with loud kisses, hand commands, and soft, soothing words. She finally picked up their pet and held it like a child perfectly comfortable in his mother's cozy arms. The man placed his arm around her shoulder. They both smiled and waited on the lush Saint Augustin lawn, well cared for by Asian and Latino gardeners. I knew from my Harvard and Princeton days that old stereotypes didn't hold anymore; that is to say they might not be Japanese or Mexican. Frankly, I don't think anybody cared, just as long as the grass was kept neat and green, and the common-area maintenance fees didn't go up. On this manicured carpet of grass in Aztlandia we shared a few seconds of silence.

"We're the J. E.s of Newport Beach," the man said. She laughed as if she understood that anybody might find the statement odd.

"Jack Ekkerson," he said.

"I'm Jill. And this is Chucho." Jill hugged the dog and put it down. "It loves people!"

We gave them our names and shook hands. They were certainly friendly, and I decided I had better take them seriously since they were our neighbors. "*A los vecinos hay que cuidarlos*," I heard an echo of my parents' advice. I thought of family often. I missed my two daughters, Sara and Jennie, and Endriago, my dear friend. In Mexico City, Coyoacán in particular, there were strange and wonderful neighbors, but I never had met a couple whose names and appearances conformed to my images of nursery-rhyme characters. Jack and Jill, cute and amiable, matched in my imagination, "Jack and Jill who went up the hill to fetch a pail of water."

It was a warm, breezy day in April. Jack wore tight, white jeans, a snug-fitting, short-sleeve shirt (I bet he lifted weights), loafers, and a wide leather belt with a big silver buckle. He combed his thick, straight, light-brown hair from left to right, and sported a curious mustache that sort of hung around his boyish smile. Jack was kind of cute in a funny, bashful way and so was Jill. *Jack y Jill eran curiositos y parecían ser verdaderamente buena gente.*

Jill wore black, tight jeans, and a black jersey. Her blonde hair was long, heavy, and parted in the middle, with bangs falling to her eyebrows. Jill's neck, arms, and legs were strong and well defined. By her appearance she probably lifted weights with Jack, perhaps much more than he did. It was my impression she competed with Jack as to the amount they lifted. She had an attractive, petite mouth and a bit more than a Mona Lisa smile that didn't reveal her teeth. Jack had a space between his two front teeth, one of which was chipped.

Jack handed me a camera while Jill still held Chucho. "Hey, how about a photo?" Jack put a leash on it and held its paw. He placed his right arm around Jill's shoulders. They made a wonderful photo of a handsome couple, with a good-looking, content, tongue-hanging-out dog.

I focused and took the shot. I liked them. They were different; yet they were a happy and nice couple, a family. In California or, better yet, in Orange County, two people, or two people and a dog, constitute a family, an Anglo family.

Jack kissed Jill, said polite goodbyes to us, and drove off in a van with signs painted on the side panels that said, "EKKERSON'S BOOKSHOP" and "Orange County's Oldest Surviving Independent Bookshop" right below. The backdoor of the van read, "Support your Independent Bookstore."

"Bookshop?" Mark asked. He hadn't said much until now: he had smiled and was nice enough, but didn't get into a conversation with our—or my—new friends. Mark had always been quiet with people. I found that to be an odd trait for a professor since all of my professors were talkative, sometimes downright discourteous. Others were even silly and obnoxious, but maybe those were just the Harvard and Princeton types.

"Uh, we own it."

"Who'd want to own a bookstore?" Mark asked. "Especially now when the giant chains are warehousing books and have the public convinced they get a great deal and the best literature from them. The monopoly of books in huge stores is the curse of small bookstores, giving customers this false sense of security. Big discount stores make customers think that they have it under control when they buy on credit. Worst of all, they eliminate customers' thinking, making informed choices, and problem solving." Mark stopped, realizing he was on a professorial roll. He knew I despised lecturing or, what I considered, preaching.

"Jack agrees with you. That's why he wanted to buy the store. It's been a dream." Jill tugged at Chucho's leash. "Come by and take a look. Jack likes to search for hard-to-find books." Jill pushed her bangs out of her eyes and allowed her dog to go to a tall palm tree at the edge of the manicured lawn.

"Sure. I will," Mark responded with a derisive smile. Jill was far enough not to notice Mark's mocking attitude.

"Will you both run the store?" I asked.

"Just Jack. I'm a med lab tech at Hoag Hospital. One of us has to make money to keep us going."

Money is what keeps everybody in Orange County oiled up. It's the fuel that keeps moving, and movement is the great archetype of Southern California, in every conceivable physical, metaphorical, and spiritual way.

Contrary to the liberal, anti-capitalistic ideas Mark had been vocalizing and defending ever since I had known him, he had changed jobs for more money! I didn't blame him, but, for some reason, he held this against himself. He went from a private Catholic university to a fast-growing, prestigious, rich, charismatic southern Baptist college in Orange County that catered to wealthy international students. Holy Spirit College, impressed with his academic credentials and his teaching evaluations, offered him $10,000 more a year, one less class, and a small research and travel fund, which he would never get from the Catholics.

Mark sold himself to the southern Baptists. He even offered to attend Sunday services. However, this wasn't really a choice, since faculty had to be seen overcome, deeply moved, in stunning ways, by the Lord's spirit, at least once a month. Mark felt he should have held out for more money. After speaking with another recently hired professor who was offered three times as much as he had been, he was convinced he could have made more. It truly bothered him that foreign scholars and writers hired by the university were getting six-figure salaries to come directly to newly established research centers. These intellectuals were famous for their once-political stance in their country. He considered them great hypocrites. Holy Spirit had hired two: one from Africa and another from Latin America. Both had lived in the United States for at least thirty years, but they still considered themselves exiles and always put a distance between their countries of birth and the U.S. The two professors claimed to speak for the oppressed in their respective countries and represented themselves as national voices. They made it a point to return to their motherland at least once a year to give lectures and readings at universities, about the terrible inhumane conditions their compatriots still suffered. At the end of their tour to open people's eyes, the perpetual exiles returned to the leisure and luxury of living the life of a six-figure-salary university professor. Here, in Orange County, they lived in expensive large houses; drove their children to soccer practice in pricey cars and SUVs; sent their kids to the best public or private schools; ate lavishly; and, of course, continued to claim they were living in forced exile. The African professor still wore her native garb, and the Latin American professor spoke with a heavy accent and sported long hair and a beard to remind everyone that he resembled Che. For these perpetual exiles, expatriation would never end. They in fact had turned it into a professional career. After thirty years both were able to return to live in their countries. However, being a political exile was too lucrative to abandon and return to what they claimed was still home. Mark insisted that after these many years they are no longer African or Latin American. Living successfully in the United States had, without a doubt, distorted their thinking, their vision of the world, and their individual consciousness. They lived like middle- to upper-class locals. After joining the university, they had become institutionalized and could depend on the support of administrators, in particular the dean of humanities whom Mark described as an arrogant, anguished Joycean stump. These African and Latin American exiles had sold their souls and were consequently part of the problem. In the meantime, their countries still lived in inhumane poverty, plagued by malaria, cholera, tuberculosis, AIDS, and starvation; they lacked education and struggled with horrible genocidal wars. Why aren't these expats back home leading the charge for change? At least I'm honest about it. I'm not a hypocrite, Mark thought.

"I did it for the money. What they offered was as good as or better than what the University of California proposed. I have a price. Doesn't everybody? I'll sell myself to the highest bidder. I am not ashamed." He mimicked himself as well as the president of Holy Spirit College.

I decided to take some time to settle and get to know Southern California. For many years, my father had worked here and in Tijuana with his Southern California business partners, establishing *maquiladoras* on the border. While I had my opinions about this area, I still needed to experience it first hand, drive around, explore, and feel more comfortable.

The day I arrived in Orange County I thought I had landed in Asia. There were hundreds, I thought maybe thousands, of Asian people walking through the airport. I remember that I held onto Mark. I was a little afraid, not of them but of whether I had done right by leaving Mexico City, my daughters, my parents, and Endriago.

"This place is being taken over by Asians," Mark commented.

"Are they on vacation?"

"No, I doubt it, probably going to UCI, the university that didn't give me a job," Mark said.

I hadn't experienced a religious trance for about two months and didn't want one either. I was afraid that Mark wouldn't understand what had happened to me in México. Maybe he would see me as mentally ill.

It was strange how my personality changed when I came to the United States. I had noticed the transformation ever since I had attended Harvard. Upon entering the U.S., I immediately became very Americanized; when I returned to México, I became Mexicanized. My tone of voice, way with people, gestures, just about my whole character was transformed into my *norteamericana* personality. Maybe it was the language, the psychology of changing from Spanish to English.

Each language required its own behavior, its particular manner of interpreting the world.

Often I found it awkward to speak English and to live or act that "American" way of life this language required. I struggled to suppress the Spanish vision, thinking I could not mix it with its English counterpart. It wasn't really me whom I saw dancing out there before me in spotless English, like a hologram, resembling a baffled, hypocritical, contrived white heron searching for a cultural body of water.

Certainly, this perpetual identity crisis was not odd in this place. Southern California was an endless spectacle of this institutionalized dilemma. The stars were the people who suffered from it, in every possible form, from gender, sexual, athletic, religious, social, linguistic, border, to meaningful or meaningless issues of "Where shall I shop?" to "Who am I?" Identity meant sameness to me, the condition of being the same, of desiring to be the same, like everybody else, recognizing that it was impossible.

Why are Chicanos and Mexicans, or Anglos and Asians, made to believe they are to have an identity crisis? I thought they prided themselves on being unique, different. The concept of identity should be swept into the Los Angeles or the Santa Ana Rivers; this conflicting concept has been misleading us, both Mexicans and Chicanos, long enough to make us believe that our identity is ambiguous, a blur, that we don't know who fathered us or our nation. This kind of thinking demeans Mexicans, perpetuating a victim mentality. Octavio Paz, Mexico's Nobel laureate, didn't do his country any favors by saying to the world Mexicans don't know their father. I bet Octavio knew his. Identity crisis ... my calloused running feet! I sure as hell didn't want to be like anyone or any group. That ideological trap is not odd in Southern California. Sane and demented people appear on television every afternoon. From four to eight, the TV anchor-news heroes and heroines of lucidity narrate the stories of the anti-heroes and anti-heroines of derangement who get their faces shown and their stories told in prime time.

Everybody watches! A few listen! Nobody reads! The image and the sound bite provide the faith that entities and events have meaning and can be comprehended by the viewers. Southern Californians expect to find in the image, in the motion, and in the sound, a rhythm that communicates to them the minimal information they require about their own experience. Feeling the beat, corporations were beginning to invest large research and development sums to supply an ever-changing and ever-profitable technology of access intended to keep the populace dancing to the tunes and glued to the screens of the coming electronic age. In this virtual reality, books, too, would soon become technologized.

Jack and Jill loved books. They enjoyed reading and handling them. Jack seemed happier when the Ekkerson's Bookshop inventory was high, when stacks of books on the floor would take over the store. Towers of knowledge were scattered strategically in the eight-hundred square feet of retail space of Ekkerson's Bookshop. Jack wanted to collect books—old, rare, out-of-print, and first editions. He had a good-sized collection of first edition, cloth-bound, popular writers' volumes, which he sold for at least triple the original price. He prided himself on this section. Jack claimed he could buy any work available, and, from what I saw, I bet the collectors were impressed by his collection and self-confidence.

"I hate the superstores that control and manipulate knowledge. These shops are situated next to multiplex cinemas. Their formula is obvious: the moving image is memorialized in a theater, and the unopened book is sepulchered in a warehouse. People attend the cinema for about two-and-a-half hours to gain life experience; they also buy books to possess and consult, and to become "one-book experts." They don't read them necessarily, but they know where to go where they'll get a great 20% to 40% discount deal on knowledge and intelligence."

Jack tended to price so that only the hard-core collectors bought from his rare collection. Yet, he often argued that his overpriced collector's editions didn't move fast enough to justify the space they took up.

The first time I entered their house for a short visit to give them their gun magazines that were being mis-delivered to us, I noticed books, cluttered and unorganized, mirrored the bookshop. Similar to a squirrel gathering nuts for the winter, Jack hoarded hundreds of books at home, no matter the season. Along with creative artifacts, they packed the natural pine shelves that lined every available wall space in their condo. Books became a point of conflict, of intangible anguish with the happy couple, the J. E.s.

Later I learned that Jack had started school young and intellectually excelled beyond his parents' expectations. Although photos may deceive, Jack had been a physical wimp until high school, where he entered weightlifting and self-defense programs he followed faithfully through college. He often mentioned he had never left school from kindergarten to college. At the University of Chicago he earned a degree in English and, like thousands of students from Generation X to the Border Generation, he didn't have a job when he graduated. Overly qualified for most jobs, he hated the idea of working his way up; he wanted it all now. Probably being more intelligent than most people made him stand out with his sense of history and his critical attitude about housing and control of knowledge.

Jack tried to find a job, but nobody ever called back after the first interview. He cut his hair short, shaved, and bought a suit, white shirt, tie, and wingtip shoes. Although he hated the masquerade, he had to dance and pretend to enjoy the party. Discouraged and about ready to give up, Jack finally found work. He started to bus dishes at Warm Meadows Retirement Home in Tustin. As a result, and according to Jill, Jack's life became the nightmare he had dreaded.

The retirement facility where he worked was a dingy, dreary warehouse for terminally ill, bedridden, senile, demented, and abandoned old folks. Its management kept them alive as long as possible to collect checks either from relatives who refused to deal with the patients, or from the Social Security Administration that sent them monthly. The facility was never inspected. The Warm Meadows' owner always had a little roll of money for the Orange County health inspector who frequently dropped by unannounced.

One day, on his way home from work, Jack did the unexplicable, to him, to Jill, or to me: in Newport Beach, he stopped at the small bookshop that he had passed so many times. Seniors, with their pungent odors of vitamins B, C, E, urine, excrement, and vomit, propelled Jack into the bookshop, literally running into the owner.

"What is this? The older you get, the harder it is to see where you're going? Your age is no excuse!" said an old man carrying a stack of books. "You should watch your path, young fellow-traveler, and clean up, 'cause you stink!" The senior balanced the load in his arms. "No, better you should help me with these!" Placing the pile on the counter, he shook Jack's hand for a long time as he talked about how tough it was being a small-business owner. Jack listened and noticed the elder's jet-black hair.

"Hey!" Jack yelled, finally and forcibly pulling his hand away.

"You should be kind," the old man said.

I had heard several times the story of Jack's meeting with Mr. Schwartz, a gentleman in his immediate eighties, and I enjoyed imagining their encounter. Inevitably, Mr. Schwartz took a liking to Jack and vice-versa. Jack frequented the store three to five times a week. He always had a compliment for Old Man Schwartz, who complained and cursed unceasingly, but that uniqueness was what made him different and attracted customers who respected him.

I remember Jill saying that, one day, the old fellow was not behind the register nagging and cussing about customers who "practically read the whole damn book in the store and walked out with not even a 'thank you'!"

He was not there whining that not one customer had made a purchase since he opened that morning. "This is a bookshop where you come to buy books! This is not a public library!" Framed by collectable leather-bound volumes, Mr. Schwartz urged his customers, "Buy a book, keep an independent bookstore from going down, and keep an old man from starving. You should understand, my friend."

On that day, Mr. Schwartz was not behind the counter greeting those who ventured into his store for the first time, or his regular customers who expected some kind of an insult and then a smile. Instead, his son managed the business.

"My dad, he's ill. I don't think he'll make it. He's lived a long, good life. Ever since Mother died, about a year and half ago, Dad hasn't been the same. They were together for almost sixty years. Long time, huh?" his son asked.

Jack nodded. "The store?"

"If I find a buyer, I'll sell it. If not, I'll close it down."

"How much?"

"The last inventory statement was valued at $75,000."

"I don't have $75,000."

"Then make an offer," the son said and shook Jack's hand. "Make an offer, Jack." He greeted like his father, holding on with both hands for an extended period of time.

Jill liked the idea from the start. She worked at Hoag Hospital, earned about $54,000 a year and had $20,000 in the bank from wedding presents, the sale of her parents' stock gifts, and her own savings. The frugal one of the two, she managed to set aside money from every paycheck. Purchasing the bookshop excited her and, to Jack's surprise, suggested, "Offer the owner $10,000."

The very next morning Jack asked permission from Warm Meadows to take two hours off to meet an obligation. With no hesitation his boss responded, "Be back by twelve and be sure to work through lunch."

Jack went to the bookshop with Jill and his offer.

"Sorry, that's not enough. By the way, I found the most recent inventory statement, which puts the books at $55,000. You've got to do better than $10,000, Jack."

That afternoon, I saw Jill, briefcase and white lab-tech smock in hand. The weather, the drive home, and the trivial chitchat made up a conversation between two people who had recently met for the first time, yet understood that they would see each other often.

Jill's smile had an innocent, quirky quality that I found warm and caring. She went into the condo. I lingered in the strong radiance that Jill had left, one with which I was familiar, a woman's luminosity passed to me from Coatlicue, Malintzin Tenepal, *la Virgen de Guadalupe*, Sor Juana Inés de la Cruz, Frida, Comandanta Ramona, and now Jill.

In late April, the sun sets on the Southern California beaches with an intense emotional power. Mark headed home from Holy Spirit College. He went north on Pacific Coast Highway savoring the glistening ocean under a reddish-orange, passionate, western sky. Mark dwelled on magnificence sharp enough to slice through the heart. I had lived sunsets like these on Mexican coasts: on the Pacific, the Gulf and the Caribbean.

Mark's new teaching schedule allowed him plenty of time to write. He was satisfied that he had made the right choice; his new job might even turn out better than he had expected.

The door closed and I waited for him to join me in the kitchen. He kissed and held me for a while. As he took a lusty, hard-on, deep breath, I pushed myself out of his embrace. Disappointed, he took off his shirt and asked, "Well, what's new, J. I.?"

"I placed applications at several companies. Now it's wait and see."

"Good luck. It's tough to get a job in Orange County."

"Maybe I'll clean houses, like many of my female compatriots."

"I wonder how many Mexican housekeepers have a degree in economics from Harvard and Princeton. You're screwed, destined to bus tables, scrub toilets, or collect tickets at the movies. You've educated yourself out of the job market, J. I., and you can't ask for references from AmerMex. Your history is just too colorful, too fantastic. Ah, don't worry; you'll find employment. I have faith in you, J. I."

He had practiced at home, at work, and in the car until finally Jack made the offer: "Fifteen thousand, that's all I've got, $15,000 for inventory and fixtures. You pay some of your debts. I start out clean."

Mr. Schwartz's son shook his head and said, "I accept. My father will be pleased about your taking over his store."

Jack had made the offer believing that the owner would not accept. Bewildered at what was happening, he wondered where he would get the money. Jill would put up $10,000; they didn't have the remainder.

So, as I understand the story, Jack and Jill bought a small, financially treading-water, independent bookstore, while three miles to the south and to the north two super-mega discount bookstores opened. One advertised a promise to deliver every book published in the United States along with the Sun and the Moon, and the other boasted that it carried every volume that one would ever need to read. The latter idea was scary since people in Southern California more than likely had no more than one or two titles, if any at all, on their "need to read" list.

Jill, I recall, thought that to invest thousands of dollars in the purchase of the bookshop, a business that in six months or a year might fail, was more than a gamble: although, on the other hand, the risk attracted her. In the bookstore she saw a beautiful opportunity that offered a worthwhile, needed service and that brought the best of national, multiethnic, and international literature to the community. These were Jack's ideas, and she adopted them. What she didn't want was to see the store taken over by somebody else and, a year later, say "That could have been mine." Seeing this as an opportunity, although the odds were against them, she decided to invest the money.

For Jack it was a better job fit and also a matter of furthering freedom of expression. Big bookstore chains owned by New York publishers or managed by Texas retailers were willingly shaping the country's reading tastes and censoring certain authors and independent small publishers. They wantonly excluded from their warehousing of books the majority of women, gay, lesbian, Black, Latino, Asian American, and Native American writers.

Jack believed what he had said to Jill and anyone who would listen: "Ethnic writers who break into the major presses pay a high cost culturally. They've been co-opted, shaped and made to fit a mold. Filtered through literary agents and editors before publication, their works are made culturally exotic, unthreatening and palatable for the dominant readership, and then sold in the giant book warehouses. Worse is what happens to the authors themselves: They are made into literary clowns, colorfully repackaged to look like authentic ethnics, or made to cry, sing, cuss, and perform like forever-wounded racial victims, or raging, ethnic donkeys."

Jack believed that an ongoing technological struggle of freedom of expression ensued nationwide between the written word, the cinematic image, and virtualization, the latter a recent entry to the entertainment market that rings the death knell of reading. A virtual-reality addictive experience will eclipse the practicality of film, television, and the written word.

"Notice how the large bookstores are situated next to multi-theater complexes. There the main attraction is the movies, where people spend nine or more dollars to see a film. They kill time by browsing in the bookstore before and maybe after the show. The ritual is made into a seemingly intellectual exercise. But it is the moving image that comes out ahead. Customers will come back to see a picture, not to buy a book to read, because it's easier. In two to two-and-a-half hours they're finished viewing, then they can sit down at dinner and have a discussion with their friends; family, and even kids like to participate. But buy a book and discuss it over dinner with friends, family, or kids? That's tough to do. Yet, in my mind, the greatest danger, the new addiction, will be virtual reality in practically every aspect of life.

"For now, the culture industry, the symbol makers, are weaning the people off the literary tit, giving them the big cinematic hole and cock, the eyes of the camera. Someday the bookstore and movie houses shall be gone, and the cinema and the moving image and television rendered relics, as virtualization will dominate our living experience. Written instructions shall cease. The sentient apparati we will constantly desire to integrate into our bodies will provide the majority of our knowledge and pleasures. It will convince us that we are learning, choosing, and thinking. We will believe that we are free."

Jack worked himself into a frenzy as he told his beliefs to Jill, Mark, and me.

"If no one stands up to these pseudo-bibliophiles, mad technos, then America is lost, and we are doomed to become brainless virtual-reality-addicted freaks!"

Then, Jack said, probably to draw me into the discussion: "It's like the Indigenous people in Chiapas. They're fighting for better living conditions and for the right to be heard. For centuries the landowners have tried to keep them silent by threatening to take land away, by enslaving the men, by violating the women, and by torturing and murdering the original dwellers of those lands. The natives resisted living like muzzled dogs. Our worst nightmares are not comparable to their life."

Jack paused and threw a tennis ball for Chucho to retrieve. I knew what Jack had described was true. In México I had probably abused them myself. It was as if Jack had read a novel about their exploitation at the early part of the twentieth century, but the horrifying fact was that their treatment in México, in Latin America, and in the United States for centuries had not changed. The racist concepts about the Indigenous communities had not differed. The majority of these people were still at the bottom of the social ladder: the men, dispensable beasts of burden; the women, expendable concubines; and the children, ragged, dirty pets. They were confined to suffer horrible poverty, rounded up on reservations or government-designated territories.

"Today, to protect their land, this Indigenous people are locked in an armed conflict against the government, the cartels, local police, and large landholders who form para-military squads. The native population wants a guarantee of their human rights, protection of their land, education for their children, and freedom of expression. Their leader, *subcomandante Marcos*, is an UNAM graduate who recruits United States-trained mercenaries." Jack was always for *los de abajo*.

I knew that his last comment was not an exaggeration. In México, ranking Army officers are West-Point graduates or trainees from The Western Hemisphere Institute for Security Cooperation—the old School of the Americas. Furthermore, numerous top intellectuals and politicians are especially proud to be alumni of the United States Ivy League universities. The rich educate their kids in the best schools, through *la preparatoria*. Then they send them to Europe or the United States, to what they consider the best universities. My parents had no doubt that their only daughter would attend the Ivy League.

I heard one of the President's aides speak on NAFTA. I remember thinking that the great gulf between the Indigenous, the poor, and the rich is symbolized by the fact that this man could pronounce "Mexico" in perfect American English and "México" in perfect Spanish. That man's pronunciation required centuries of history.

Mark listened to Jack's tirade, waved his hand in disgust, and said, "It's the same story I've heard before. Who is concerned about the Indigenous people in Chiapas? Shit, I could care less. Let's figure out a way to survive here and now. Save this country from the invading Asians, Mexicans, and Muslims! To me there is no difference between them. They are all related. They are all the same." Retreating inside his study to prepare his classes, Mark was unhappy and frustrated. Although he had just started at Holy Spirit College, he was already thinking about having to go through the tenure process.

Jill, on the other hand, seemed less spontaneous and more analytical and systematic before reaching any conclusion. She was good for Jack; she slowed him down. Above all, she loved and cared for him. This man was unduly vulnerable and more sensitive than Jill. She was the one to live with the pain.

Jack understood and worshiped Jill, whom he considered a superior person in mind and body. Her life, her being, according to Jack, was more significant, an infinite amount of times more important than his.

The Hotel Majestic had a quaint, open-air balcony overlooking the Zócalo. It was demarcated by the seventeenth-century National Palace, the sinking, tilted, sixteenth-century cathedral, and the excavated ruins of Tenochtitlan's Templo Mayor settling twenty-five feet below the *plaza*. At its center waved a huge Mexican flag. The esplanade often served as the rallying and meeting point for anti-government protests and demonstrations.

That day, as J. I. looked over the ancient magnificent square and watched a massive march of teachers opposing a shipment of nuclear waste to México, she and Carlos began to learn more of each other's habits. It surprised her to find that he had stopped drinking.

"Too many responsibilities. Besides, alcohol is reserved for our *ancianos*," Carlos explained.

It was one of those rare, abnormally clear afternoons when the sharpness of the light in the valley danced at the foot of the two great sacred volcanoes—Popocatépetl, *el hombre que fuma*, and Iztaccíhuatl, *la mujer de hielo*—more than seventeen thousand feet high formed a timeless crown of love that towered over the vibrant single CDMX, the capital, *el corazón de la nación mexicana*.

That afternoon Carlos told her that he worked for the President's Anti-Narcotic Brigade. J. I. sensed that he felt that this information might make a difference in their relationship, yet he had to tell her sooner or later. The Anti-Narcotic Brigade had not received flattering press. Newspapers reported abuses and violations of human rights by the federal police, including Carlos' group.

Carlos' entourage was made up of agents under his command. The malformed one was his personal guard, assistant, and brother, who also lived with him. Although curious, J. I. held back her questions about Endriago.

"I want our friendship to continue. Don't be afraid of Endriago. You'll someday realize that he is an intelligent, loyal man."

"Endriago."

"It means mythical monster, dragon, devourer of virgins," Carlos explained. J. I. quickly suppressed her astonishment and desire to laugh.

 Often, I thought of Los Angeles and Orange counties as places where a building could swallow a person whole. I was not thinking metaphorically here. Buildings came to life, had a nervous and physical breakdown, and devoured thousands of people during the 1985 Mexico City earthquake. In Southern California, in addition to seismic activity, there are strong winds, landslides, wildfires, floods, droughts, and random unrelenting violence. The unexpected is expected. People can count on the unanticipated to affect their life sooner or later. A dreadful, mutable movement supported this condition.

Early Sunday morning, Mark and I sat on the condo balcony to enjoy the warm sun, a true Southern California activity. Below, Jack and Jill locked the door to their place.

"Hello up there. Going to church," Jack yelled up to us.

It was nice to know they attended church. Nice clean-cut folks, I thought.

"Which church?" Mark asked, as if he cared.

"Saint Thaddaeus Catholic Church."

"Good Catholics," I said to myself.

Mark rolled to one side of the lounge chair. The warmth of the sun, Coatlicue's son, offered a motherly caress while shining on México, Coyoacán, my parents, my daughters, and my Endriago. But those people I had to forget, at least for the moment, until I established myself here in multidimensional Southern California or Aztlandia, as a UNAM professor described it. I waved to Jack and Jill as they drove away.

This is the third time these thoughts had invaded my mind,

causing a severe sense of uneasiness because they flower from my blood re-memories, remembrances I can't recall at will. Our ancestors are submerged there, waiting to be beckoned. They dwelled in a fortunate, prosperous and happy site they named Aztlán. There, in the middle of a body of water stood a grand disfigured hill they called the Squinted-Eye Hill. On it, there were large crevices and caves that our predecessors inhabited for many years. They enjoyed the abundant varieties of ducks and herons, and the wonderful songs and melodies of other enchanted birds. They benefitted from the coolness of the forest and the freshness and generosity of fruit orchards. But in time, families started heading in all directions, searching, they said, for a better location. As their journeys took them farther away, the energies of the cosmos turned against them: The plants spat and bit them; the rocks flung themselves at them; the water pricked and made them itch; the places they settled were infested with poisonous snakes and nasty, filthy, crawling animals that sought their anuses in order to infect them with disease.

Newport Beach boasts vast sands, good eateries, colorful boardwalks, and Fashion Island, a modern mall with exclusive stores and restaurants. Farther south is Laguna Beach, an artists' colony with quaint shops, exquisite food, and a significant gay population, notorious during the 1970s for wild free-love parties. South Coast Plaza is Mark's and my favorite shopping center. Here, too, people can find continental and international cuisine, all the major quality retail outlets, and Sears. This mall reflects what Orange County desires to be: a more democratic constituency, with people attempting to fit in and adjust to its diverse cultures. Across the street from the plaza are located the South Coast Repertory Theater and the Orange County Performing Arts Center. I especially like strolling among the parks, cafes, and postmodern buildings adjacent to the Performing Arts Center. There is a skyscraper by local standards. The shine from the edifice radiates elegance and class, the cliché that captures the essence of yuppie existence in the OC: life and style. Everybody races to achieve the highest level of affluence, and no obstacle better be shoved in the way, or else it will be trampled. Of particular danger is organic matter in the form of drug addicts, jobless nomads, homeless, victims of the greatest country in the world who are considered by a waning Anglo hegemony as taking up space in the Southern California borderlands.

Places in Orange County are inviting, rich, and comfortable, but the feeling, the emotion from them is ephemeral, like going to the San Angel Inn, *el Restaurante del Lago*, the fashionable shops in Polanco, Presidente Mosarique, an elite opening at Palacio de Bellas Artes, or a select art exhibit at a rich galleria in the Zona Rosa. The emotions, the sensations are the same as here, and as fleeting. There really is no difference. In these places, the attitude of being rich, or almost rich, or appearing to be rich, is the same as in Mexico City, and not much different in Orange County. A feeling of wealth remains but dissipates upon leaving. People know they can't live there. They can't stay. It's not home. Once they're out of the cathedrals of successful religious commercialization and drive away, the mask of sophistication quietly and distressingly peels away, as they deal with the speed of the rushing ceaseless freeways and the mesmerizing diligent humming of their cars' engines.

Late at night, in the stillness of the dark, I hear the copulation of the pressure of sameness in Orange County grinding against other powerful growing cultural forces of difference struggling to find a process, a way to fit in, to be comfortable, to be a part of ancient, elegant Aztlandia, the place of the white heron.

My father became a wealthy man by forming partner-ships with U.S. companies that wanted to build *ma-quiladoras* on the California-México border. To Father, México was absolutely the leader of the Latino and so-called Third World countries. Because of the country's geographic situation, he was convinced it had the capacity to become one of the wealthiest and most powerful countries in the Western Hemisphere. Yet he always talked about a contradiction in its development. México, he said, was being technologized faster than being industrialized. That duality caused many remarkable cultural incidents.

Father attempted to guide his business life based on the theories of Octavio Paz, who declared in his writings that there existed two Méxicos: One was cosmopolitan and modern with a *nouveau riche* pop-ulation that imposed foreign models on the country, making the other México—the underdeveloped, the folkloric, the religious and the tra-ditional—disappear. These two ideological lines of thought were the nation's motivating cultural and economic tensions. But unlike Paz, Father believed that the multicultural situation offered great opportu-nities to make money from both Méxicos, especially in the commercial base of the region where Mexicans resided in both sides of the border.

During my parents' trips back and forth from Tijuana to Los Ángeles they would visit with my deliverers, my emancipators into life. It gave me an odd feeling to hear Mother speak about Orange County as a place where people never get old. She often reminded me that I was born on a hill that was in the middle of a sea of fog, and that the entire place was white and brilliant. The farmworkers believed that people who considered themselves aged could climb that hill and return as young as they desired. My parents enjoyed their vacations in the zone where, in their minds, they would never grow old.

After two days of cool dewy overcast mornings, the weather turned muggy and the temperature climbed to ninety-five degrees.

"Now the seasons are so unstable."

"The weather has changed." That phrase announced the opening of the apocalypse, as if a strange, almost evil, event was occurring, as if the world had lost a part of itself.

"It's not the same anymore!" they repeated.

I didn't understand it. Why shouldn't the climate be unpredictable? I thought I heard statements like these in a movie, a play, or a Broadway show.

Mark and I had driven through the Irvine Ranch several times, trying to find the house of my birth. But the ranch had changed radically from what my parents had described. Homes had replaced thousands of acres of citrus orchards along Irvine Boulevard. The mansion that Mother had detailed, that belonged to *los dueños*, no longer stood; only the gardens and cement and brick walkways hinted that it once existed. There were a few wood frame dwellings remaining where farmworkers still lived. Perhaps I was born in one of them.

We walked the beach and the river trail, hiked the rolling hills often, and explored the ranch near my birthplace. There the earth was always damp, hidden fields were continuously planted with cauliflower, green peppers, asparagus, tomatoes, strawberries, and wildflowers—thousands of these. All this had been a desert. "The meek shall inherit the Earth," I thought.

Mark belonged to a running club, and I often ran with them to a small reservoir overlooking the ranch. Once in a while we socialized with some of the members: hard-drinking, party-hardy, young Orange County professionals. The group never failed to enter at least three people in the Southern California 10Ks. No matter where the race was held, there was always a Runners Club entry.

Once they took Mark to a hockey game at the Anaheim Pond. A stretch limousine drove up and the boys' night out began. They were out until four in the morning and the next day he had to run in the city of Tustin 10K.

I enjoyed sprinting alone to that reservoir at my fastest pace. The speed reminded me of my runs in college, in Amecameca, on the Popo, in Mexico City; although, when I ran with Mark, I did it at a slower pace. It was exhilarating to see the Pacific Ocean and bluish Catalina Island from that viewpoint. I remembered that years ago I had told him that I would never love him in the cancerated throat of Los Angeles, but now, *a la aurora del día*, engrossed in the beauty of Southern California nature, I thought that maybe this was the place for which I was destined. It offered all I desired.

 At approximately three in the morning, I heard the high-pitched ring of the delicate Japanese bird chimes that hung on the balcony. It wasn't an earthquake nor the strong Santa Ana winds that caused the havoc, but a gentle wind of life and freedom playing with and teasing the Japanese sculptured eaves. I had fallen asleep on the couch reading the *Los Angeles Times*, echoing its favorite, hackneyed theme about the Latino community in Orange County: a rash of drive-by gang killings that were horribly commonplace in the barrios of Aztlandia. I'm so weary of Mexicans killing our own. Those damn gang members don't deserve any publicity. By the time these boys and girls are out of their teens it will be too late for them to be saved or rehabilitated. They're a lost cause, no matter the prayers of their *madrecitas. Son jóvenes perdidos a las pandillas, institucionalizados por la sociedad en las cárceles y las prisiones de California.* Not even *Jesucristo* or *la Virgen de Guadalupe* can save them. Sadly, Catholicism has done more harm than good by teaching its faithful the discourse of victimization, of suffering and hoping. Worst of all, the Church has permitted and tolerated their failure. The Catholic Church—like the newspapers, television, movies, and the police— glorifies and makes heroes out of gangs and their crimes. Crime does pay; it represents billions of dollars in police investigations, incarceration companies, the law profession, the entertainment industry, and much more.

I read in the *Orange County Register* an article on a writer who published a novel about a young Latino who became a sociopath as a result of incarceration in the prison system. After his release, he killed a priest and burned down his church. Maybe that would be a viable plan: Declare war on the institution that educates Mexican people and demands that they think like children! War on Catholicism: The very establishment that had saved my life in México and allowed me to go free in Southern California. Because of my social and religious activism as an *ilusa* in the *colonias perdidas* in Mexico City, the government, the Church, the police, and even the Army declared me a persona non grata and wanted me arrested. Father Cristóbal de Lugo convinced his order to smuggle me out of México and into Orange County.

Algo más que me molesta is that the images of Mexicans the *Los Angeles Times* publishes are always the same: gang members and good Catholics, "illegal aliens" and migrants. Repeatedly the newspapers publish photographs of Mexicans either following a cross on a long staff, walking behind priests, kneeling in church with hands clasped in prayer; or as frail old people, praying to their *santito,* their *diosito* or *virgencita.* These old men and women are quoted speaking in the diminutive form like little children, like God's most innocent. They are portrayed as Mexicans who not only believe that the meek and the humble shall inherit the Earth, but who also act out this idea.

"Somos pobres".

"Somos gente trabajadora".

"Somos gente humilde".

These are the pictures and the dialogue of victimization the *Los Angeles Times* and others push on the entire Southern California community, representations many believe and accept as perfect depictions of Mexicans.

Outside on the balcony the wind felt warm. No loud music, no parties. An unusually quiet Saturday night for Newport Beach! From where I stood, I saw Mark reading and writing his class lectures for Holy Spirit College. He was a lonely, ignored howl in the American academic wilderness. There were instances when he seemed pitiful to me, but maybe that's why I loved him.

The lights were still on at the J. E.s' condo. There seemed to be a lot of movement over there. This leitmotif of Southern California was dominant even at three forty-five in the morning. Through the J. E.s' slightly opened blinds I distinguished activity. I could see that

 Two weeks later, on a Saturday, Mark and I met the J. E.s at their bookstore, which, surprisingly, was much bigger than I had imagined. Pine fixtures, white walls, and a balcony gave the store a warm, cozy feeling. Customers walked in as if they had entered a friend's house. They said hello and went directly to a specific section. Others browsed the shelves; some thumbed through a hardcover or sat in one of the few chairs for which Jack had found space amongst the stacks. The place smelled of fresh wood and of old and new books. It was more than a business, more than a library; it was a source to a mad oracle. Its chaotic overflow of volumes somehow accommodated the foot traffic. People passing by looked in, resisted for a few moments, and then stepped into Jack's literary web.

Jack's inventory reflected his interest in multicultural literature and issues. Acculturation, hybridization, and border and dynamic cultural expression were key organizing concepts for Ekkerson's Bookshop. Jill had added Women's Studies, which had become a best-selling section. National and international newspapers brought people in early in the morning. Folks bought the *Wall Street Journal*, the *New York Times*, others came in for the special-ordered British, Spanish, French, and German versions, and still others wanted their news from Tokyo, Hong Kong, and Australia. People actually purchased one-week-old papers. Jack had commented that it was not uncommon to enter the store and see five or more customers standing just beyond the coffee machine reading their wide-open, old, foreign newspapers. Orange County high rollers bought them, probably because it was the anti-native trend and it was a pricey and exotic experience.

At least when we were present, the bookstore was frequented by people waiting for tables at the many restaurants in the shopping center and by what I surmised to be the store regulars, Jack's literary armada, who came in faithfully to pick up their reading materials. It was evident that these customers were attracted to Jack. As the exchange was being made, they talked to him about Europe, Latin America, or the deterioration of morals and values in this country, whatever consumed them at the moment. From the international to the personal, they found it easy to talk to him. Always, Jack listened and carefully paraphrased what his patrons had said; he understood them perfectly.

On Saturday, Jack worked the store alone until three, when a high-school-student employee relieved him. In the silence, Jack seemed only occasionally lost in the realm of literary worlds of great writers, as competition from powerful international publishing conglomerates most of the time held him captive to the invoice, the phone, the register, or the calculator. He had declared war on behalf of the written word, to wake it up and to save it from extinction. He believed that the act of writing had become increasingly oppressive. Once the author fell into the hands of the aggressive New York or West Coast agents, the flashy Hollywood playwrights or the giant publishing companies, their texts became controlled and their freedom of expression lost. The fictional characters residing on the shelves were repressed and enslaved by their muzzled creators.

"Literature no longer brings joy by provocation, but by commercialism," said a customer who had purchased *Forever Amber*.

"A fifth-grade reading level and mediocrity are the measure of excellence on the American literary scene," said another customer at the counter.

"And we're buying it!" rejoined an anonymous voice from somewhere in the stacks.

"It's infecting the world," Jack agreed.

Mark approached the counter and handed Jack a list of five books that the warehouse bookstores had refused to order even after he had argued, insisted, and offered to pay in advance. One of the managers explained, "If they're not with our distributor we can't order them. The research requires too much of our time. They take too long to get. Sorry, it's not worth it for us."

The value of literature was based on the chain bookstore's time and space, and on the cavalier decision by managers ignorant of the content of their merchandise. In this marketplace of ideas, their attention was focused on how many units sold per square feet.

Jill walked in wearing her lab technician uniform. She disappeared to the back of the store and returned sporting tight jeans, a polo top, and a white lightweight-canvas windbreaker with a "CHOC Tennis Tournament" insignia. I brushed off some long black hairs from the white jacket. As I did, I noticed that Jack's white shirt bore the same black curly strands.

"I'm hungry. Let's go!" Jill said and grabbed my arm, and the four of us walked to a nearby seafood restaurant for dinner. Orange County had thousands of places to eat. Most of the eateries were clean and served well-prepared foods, but that bargain seekers, some of whom had no choice, favored them was not enough of an allure for me. I found the strip malls of Orange and Los Angeles counties repulsively grotesque. Mexico City was also plagued by these prefabricated instant commercial centers and, just about every street had a store offering a service or a product that could be consumed or bought. It was horrible to see that even the sacred residential areas were marred by weekend commercialism. Garage sales cluttered up the driveways with bargain seekers, some of whom had no choice but to buy used while others were trying to out-commercialize the vendors by buying low one day and selling high another day.

That evening Jack, Jill, Mark, and I went for dessert at an ice cream shop that specialized in exotic flavors. The owner was a Mexican man who must have known about an *heladería* I had frequented in Coyoacán. Photos of the streets, the *plazas* and Frida's blue house in Coyoacán hung on the wall. With each taste of the mango *paleta*, the images of Sara, Jennie, my parents, and Endriago rushed into my head.

A famous Mexican scholar once wrote that re-memories swelled so large that eventually they would not fit in the brain, and that people were forced, like Coatlicue, to carry each remembrance dangling on a necklace. J. I. wore one decorated with a throng of meaningful recollections. She was never without it.

J. I.'s first vivid re-memory as a child was the entry to her parents' new house on calle Abasolo in Coyoacán. Don Celerino and doña Gloria Cruz achieved what few people dared dream about during the 1970s. On three acres they built, with their own sweat and joy, a home that was their crowning accomplishment, a symbol of their great success. J. I.'s father and mother, besides being *hipitecas*, had become wealthy by purchasing properties on Mexico's border with California and Texas. Investing shrewdly the inheritance money from J. I.'s grandfather, they established *maquiladoras* on the Mexican side of the border.

J. I. had stood proud and poised, ready to walk into the purity of her naked, unlandscaped, unfurnished house. Her mother brought a potted hydrangea that she had purchased from the flower vendors on Revolución and placed it at the entrance.

Señora Cruz, the keeper of history of J. I.'s maternal and fraternal ancestors, waited outside the new house, holding a cardboard box full of precious photographs that had been in the family for generations. They included pictures and paintings of uncles, aunts, grandparents, and great-grandparents. Except for her grandmother's portrait, which would occupy a special place on the fireplace mantel, J. I never paid much attention to them.

Her mother called her to watch señor Cruz, with arms wide, gracefully bow and beckon his wife and only child to enter. J. I. walked along touching the white walls and found the kitchen with its shiny faucets. Señora Cruz opened a cabinet. It was bare.

"Empty. But not for long," señor Cruz said.

In a few minutes, men and women began to arrive with groceries, lamps, chairs, couches, beds, drapes, towels, and books. By early evening, their new house was filled with food, new and old furniture, antique-framed family photographs, and crucifixes that artisans had made especially for señora Cruz's new home.

J. I. sat in the middle of the living room and observed her mother sharing her happiness. She revealed her joy in her tone of voice and particularly in the manner in which she moved her body freely, effortlessly, as if dancing. Over the years, the house that J. I.'s parents constructed became adorned with gifts from Mexican and U.S. business associates. As the home filled and the garden grew, their property escalated in value.

 "Thai chicken and spareribs. How does that sound?" Mark asked, as Jack was barbecuing. He had been reading midterm papers outside on the small patio and ran to answer the phone. I was in the yard with Jill, selecting outfits from J. Crew, The J. Peterman Company Owner's Manual No. 47a, Eddie Bauer and Tweeds catalogues. Jill avoided the malls and did most of her clothes shopping by mail order. She dog-eared pages displaying vests, sweaters, jeans, tank tops, and a flax linen dress.

"Credit card, put it on a credit card," Jill said.

Suddenly, Chucho dashed out of the entrance of our condo. Papers flew as it scrambled happily around the grass. "Damn dog!" Mark yelled. "Come back here!" He chased his pet in a circle. Chucho wagged its tail and challenged Mark to make his move. "Shit! It ate my exams."

"What?" we asked.

"The midterms I was reading. When I was on the phone, the dog came in and ate them, shredded them all over the patio. It chewed them all up."

"Sorry I didn't warn you. It's into documents. It loves paperwork. It'll get into any pile of paper, except newspapers, and chew it up. I'm sorry, Mark," Jill repeated.

"Chicken and spare ribs are ready!" Jack called from the door. "What happened out here? Damn, Chucho!"

From that day on, all our documents were placed up high, away from the dog. No longer could Mark have his novel, short story, article manuscripts, and reading and lecture notes on the floor. A beast had changed our lifestyle. Chucho had the run of both condominiums, greeting us in the morning and afternoon as it fetched the newspaper, and barked to wake us up and to warn us when somebody approached. It became a buddy. Although annoying, it made us laugh. Chucho was happy wagging its tail and always so pleased to see us.

A few days after we discovered Chucho's proclivities to chewing documents, the Dean of Humanities of Holy Spirit College called Mark in and warned him that he should never again give all his class "A's" when term-papers were destroyed by a dog. "At Holy Spirit College, our students must be taught that God works in mysterious ways. When He sent a messenger to let us know that we must test ourselves again, then we must oblige His command. Professor Forbes, give your students another opportunity. It is God's will, and His will be done!"

It was miraculous! A minister from Holy Spirit College pronounced Chucho a messenger of God. I often thought how much Jennie and Sara would like this funny wonder dog.

I drove through Santa Ana and Placentia. I wanted to know more about those areas. Barrios of Orange County were exciting to me. I parked Mark's car and enjoyed strolling along the residential streets. I searched out the corner grocery stores, usually attached to a house, and I bought *pan dulce*. Aromas of Mexican food mingled in the air and followed me as I walked. These were not the dishes that I had been served as a child and that I was taught to make by my mother and her help. In México, food varied from region to region. Wherever one went, the cuisine was never the same. A taco in Mexico City was different from one in Veracruz, Mérida, Chetumal, Acapulco, Irapuato, Guadalajara, Hermosillo, Ensenada, or Los Ángeles. A taco was complex and carried with it the history of its creator and a regional context. Sounds of families gathering for dinner in the early evening, people working in their garden or sitting on the porch, watching, and waiting, led me to enjoy memories of Coyoacán. People smiled, waved, and said hello while I worried in silence about not having a job.

I had tried to find employment, but the interviews led to dead ends and once to a sexual proposition. The response was always the same.

"You're overly qualified. We want a more junior person."

But wasn't this the land of opportunity, Southern California, Orange County, the richest in the state, the country, the world? Although I didn't want to owe anybody, and even though it was against my better judgment, my desperate situation called for drastic action. Ultimately, I decided to use my Harvard alumni connections.

Mark suggested I contact one of my Harvard cross-country teammates, Rebecca Carter, who specialized in immigration and tax law and had a successful law firm in Santa Ana. I had mentioned her to him on several occasions, but I never wanted to make my friend feel obligated to help. Nonetheless, it was time I swallowed my pride, because soon there would be nothing else to swallow. Mark finally convinced me to talk to Rebecca. So I did. I called to request an appointment for later in the week, but she came on the phone and insisted that I see her after lunch.

Her firm was located on Fourth Street in Santa Ana, a part of town people consider run-down, lost to gangs and undocumented immigrants. As I drove slowly, I expected to find her address on a large professional office building, like the hundreds sitting vacant, rotting, and getting occupied by rodents and homeless people. To my surprise the numbers matched an old stately residence that had been gentrified. I guessed from the French baroque *façade* of the entrance that the creamy white house with an archway entrance and two big engraved beveled-glass windows was circa 1900. Five nearby homes had been restored and converted into sites for various kinds of businesses. Others remained residential. Even after rejuvenation, some were badly maintained and constituted an eyesore.

Rebecca Carter, a tall slim woman with an extremely professional, conservative look and demeanor, was all business, no doubt a good attitude to have in Orange County. She had straight brown hair, sleepy eyes, a straight sharp nose, thin tense lips, a slight double chin, and deep dimples before and when she smiled. I remembered her as a warm, hardworking Harvard student, a plain woman to whom nobody paid much attention, a brilliant individual, short on social skills, but likeable . . . very amiable, and brimming with contradictions and surprises.

She gave me a tour of the office.

"We made sure to maintain the dignity of the house," she said.

Outside in a brick patio, I noticed a block with "SIMONS" stamped on it. We drank tea under a white veranda when she asked, "Would you like to work for me?"

I was completely caught by surprise. At that instant I was so happy I could have hugged her, kissed her, danced. But I had to restrain my joy. I couldn't let on that I was desperate.

"I'm not sure, Rebecca," I said.

"Let me tell you what I have in mind, J. I. I know that you're a trained economist who did graduate work at Princeton. You also landed employment with AmerMex dealing with international banking between Mexico and the United States. For many people yours was a dream job."

Rebecca paused to sip tea and to study my reaction. She knew more about me than I did about her. I was at a disadvantage, vulnerable, a little uneasy. The young woman journalist, Cassandra Arenal Coe, who had stalked me in Mexico City and who knew every detail of my life came to mind. She was assassinated at *la Torre Latinoamericana*. I wanted Rebecca to continue.

"What I propose, J. I., is that you learn our accounting system, develop business plans and projections for our clients, our Mexican interest. Use your expertise and knowledge to help us, and my clients, make money in Mexico, in the United States, and on the border."

Rebecca paused, watched me for a moment and then dropped a bombshell.

"I don't wish to know why you left AmerMex or about your religious experiences. What I want is for you to produce. Help me! What you earn depends entirely on your performance. I'll start you with a good training wage. After six months I'll see how you're doing. Are you in the least bit interested?"

Before I responded, I filled our cups with more tea.

"Yes, it sounds fair," I responded in a detached manner, fighting to suppress my enthusiasm, my happiness.

Dimples filled her cheeks. She beamed and offered her hand, and I walked out of that gentrified office with a job.

That evening Mark and Jack had sushi, chicken, and ribs on the table. Jill opened a bottle of wine to celebrate my good fortune. I was so excited that I had to go to the bathroom. Jack pointed straight down the hall.

On my way I noticed a gold sharp object lying on the shaggy rug against the wall. Terrible carpet for dogs . . . fleas . . . an ink pen, I thought. Chucho sniffed at it and wagged its tail. I picked up a high-caliber bullet and saved it in my pocket. I returned to the table and toasted to my new job. We drank several bottles of dry fruity Chardonnay and talked about Latin American history and literature. Jack's knowledge about the subject impressed Mark and me. We enjoyed our evening with them. Jack and Jill were becoming our friends.

Later that night Mark held and kissed me. "No, it's too soon," I said. He was disappointed. My mind was preoccupied with the bullet I had found at the J. E.s'. I placed it in my purse.

At approximately four in the morning I was awakened by a voice. Knowing that it was only a matter of time before Coatlicue, Malintzin, *la Virgen de Guadalupe*, Sor Juana, Frida, and Comandanta Ramona returned, I listened carefully and heard only their silence.

Shortly after my job offer, Mark fell into a critical and theoretical writing trance. He prepared classes and lectures that he hoped to develop into chapter-length papers, honing his efforts down to a comparative study of the multidimensional ontologies in the writings of Julio Cortázar, Ana Castillo, T. Coraghesson Boyle, Carmen Boullosa, Alejandro Morales, Toni Morrison, Jeffrey Eugenides, Isabel Allende, Haruki Murakami, Karen Tei Yamashita, Benjamín Alire Sáenz, Leslie Marmon Silko, Marc Petrie, and Cormac McCarthy. Mark became obsessed with this project. There were times when he hardly spoke to me, and others when I don't think he even saw me. A different Mark began to reveal himself, with a side I never knew.

Mark had fallen into a hideous routine of getting up early in the morning, writing for three hours, teaching, returning home by five in the afternoon, eating, writing a few more hours, and by twelve midnight going to bed for a fidgety rest. To give himself incentive to finish his book, he withdrew from activities and foods that he enjoyed.

"I won't shave until I complete three chapters."

"I'll stop drinking wine until I finish the first draft."

"I won't sleep unless I finish the introduction."

"I'm not taking a shower until I've rewritten the first five chapters."

After one week without him shaving or bathing, I kicked him out of our bed. "You're crazy! You're going to get sick!"

Mark shaved and showered and then, still exhausted, sat on the edge of the bed. "I'm sorry, J. I., but I can't let go of this book." He looked desperate.

"You shouldn't let the writing drive you crazy. I thought you enjoyed it. Why don't you sleep? Get some rest, Mark!"

"I can't sleep now. I'll just work for an hour, and then I'll try."

It was Saturday morning: no classes, no Holy Spirit College obligations, but Mark was still working.

"*Te vas a matar,*" I whispered.

A magazine about Southern California had a feature article on Orange County: "Big Bucks Cruising the MacArthur Corridor." The region was founded in 1889 and had become one of the largest and richest economies in the world. Commercial firms promised, developed and built utopia; they constructed clean, planned communities. Like Satélite in Mexico City, OC offered a trouble-free, nonviolent, healthy lifestyle in modern housing surrounded by rural open space, greenbelts and trails to walk, run, and cycle in a temperate climate. The area attracted immigrants not only from Latin America and Asia but also from other counties and states. Thousands worked in the counties of Los Angeles, Riverside, and San Diego but lived in the OC. Monday through Friday they drove the freeways to labor somewhere else and sustain their OC utopia, their home in the planned community. They seldom ventured outside those work-home parameters. Living in the planburbs meant a non-confrontational life. The staring down of Blacks, Chicanos, Asians, and women was reserved for the professional arena. Every last one of the people who cohabited these areas was a professional, or so they claimed. There was barely enough space for a few low-income housing projects. Inviting K-Mart to build a store on the border between Tustin and Irvine caused a scandal. The planburb folks didn't want *chusma* near their homes. Other than for maids, gardeners, and handymen, "the mob" would remain outside the invisibly guarded boundaries of the planned communities.

By way of the freeways in relentless construction, I crossed a variety of urban, suburban, and rural turfs. Large impoverished neighborhoods, including Mexican barrios, were located next to middle- and upper-class vicinities spread out below the Anaheim and the Tustin Hills. Along the Pacific coastline, which nestled exclusive residential areas, I began to explore. As I ventured in I understood that affluent Orange County residents made great efforts to insulate themselves with a respectful indifference. Middle- and upper-class Orangecountians conjured up the image of a handful of poor people living between the cracks. In Mexico City these indigent people were called *gente de las grietas*. No matter how much effort they made to separate themselves from Mexicans or the undocumented, the well to do in OC were hopelessly entangled with them because they needed their labor. I don't think Mexicans paid much attention: they just worked. They always searched for a path, making their way forward, no matter what direction that might be. Rich, poor Anglos, Mexicans, Asians, and Blacks lived together because they had no choice: they were in close proximity behind the Orange Curtain. *La gente pobre de aquí son como la gente de las grietas en Coyoacán.* Mexicans constituted the familiar who coexisted in a space where we were taken for granted. Thus, we turned and twisted in a limitless number of ways to become for an instant the unfamiliar, in an unsuspected sense, and produce an unexpected, sometimes magical, heterotopia.

It was a beautiful morning. I slipped into one of my running outfits and quietly grabbed the keys to Mark's car. I parked at the Tustin Hills Racquet Club, an exclusive tennis establishment. Its newsletter indicated the monthly family dues were $400. Who had that much to spend on court time when there were beautiful public tennis spots everywhere in the planburbs? Only the rich could afford it. Why am I such a hypocritical bitch? My parents could send me all the money I need. Why should I criticize these people?

At seven in the morning the area was beautiful. A side entrance was unlocked and I walked through the courts to view the vast fields in the back. Orchards of fragrant citrus trees covered the hills to the south. Moist, dark, cultivated soil rested in the dawning sun. Suddenly, as I stretched, a man wearing white and blue running clothes jogged out through the back gate. I ran with him, from court number seven all the way to a small freshwater reservoir overlooking Orange County. At the summit a statue of Jesus Christ crucified stepped on the expanse. Below His pierced feet pulsated postmodern heterotopia and, as a heterotopian, I was learning how to live like the rest of my fellows in this ever-changing cultural zone. Hey, I ran from under the feet of Jesus. Like in México, I wouldn't let Him and His collaborators crucify me. Mexicans deserve better than the humble, self-sacrificing, superstitious, emotional, icon-worshiping, phallus-centered, failure-oriented Catholicism that has tracked us for centuries. Living *en los Estados Unidos* has improved my vocabulary. I studied English all my life and, just like Spanish, it is also my language.

My legs felt good. I broke into a six-minute speed and left behind the man jogging in his white and angel-blue outfit. I sprinted down a gradual slope toward Catalina. The island was bigger than I had imagined. No one could stop or catch me. Even though the five-minute mile was within reach, I slowed down and settled for my pace.

I remembered running the hills of México, on the skirt of *el Popocatépetl*, faithful Aztec warrior, my volcanic lover. How I wished you to erupt in me. You always offered an alternative, an unknown path. Here in the ancient place of the white heron, the trails are marked or painted. I follow them. If I deviate from their direction, I may suffer peculiar consequences.

Manuel Arias, slim, tall, well dressed, teeny-tiny-line mustachioed professional Chicano accountant/legal assistant—a future Chicano Lawyers of America success story from a gang-infested barrio to the hallways of the law courts of the land, dedicated and able to defend his community—placed a stack of files on the desk.

"Some of your accounts. Just hit the magic keyboard and more will appear. Millions of numbers are in there waiting for you."

I wasn't sure how to take this manicured guy: funny, serious, or . . . did he really take himself seriously?

This job required more desk time than I wanted, but I had no choice, and I wouldn't disappoint a fellow Harvard woman and hard-training cross-country warrior, even if it meant working with Manuel. He had bottles of Joop!, Azzaro, Armani, Obsession, and Brute aftershave lotions and colognes in one of his desk drawers. I couldn't help but wonder if he applied these potions to different parts of his body. Faithfully, he took bottles of Old Spice and Rogue Passion to the bathroom. Like a dog, everywhere he was, he left his mark, yet maybe with a different scent emanating from hand, arm, leg, face, and hair. Well-perfumed Manuel was a superior accountant/legal assistant, and it was clear that Rebecca had absolute confidence in him.

Rebecca, dressed like one of the congresswomen whom I saw on television listening to the President's State of the Union message, *el día de los millones en México*, walked by the office but didn't stop.

"Court in an hour for her. Rush, rush. She's got a tough one today," Manuel informed me.

"What's a tough one?"

"She's defending a Mexican national accused of participating in a drive-by. At the time of the killing he was in the hospital with a broken leg he suffered playing in a high-school soccer game."

"Well, what's the problem?"

"The parents were hysterical. The mother came into the office screaming that the police came into the house and took her son out of bed! Everybody in the office listened to them. His father, crying, described how *¡a media noche tumbaron la puerta, entraron y lo arrastraron! Mijo no podía hablar por el dolor de la pierna'.*"

"How can they do that?" My question was a self-reminder of the police abuses in México. I didn't actually believe that the United States was any different, especially when it came to Mexicans.

"Why not? The kid's undocumented. He sat in county jail for almost three months until Rebecca heard about his case. She sued and brought in the news media. The community went up in arms and now the boss and her permanently physically challenged client are TV stars. Right, the boy was never treated for the injury. He never complained, but when they got him to a doctor, his leg had atrophied horribly."

Manuel's words followed Rebecca and the boy, who soon became surrounded by thirty or more family members and community activists protesting the police injustice.

"Wow, big crowd outside."

Rebecca worked with grass-root folks, movers of the community. This group marched to the courthouse in downtown Santa Ana. I watched them move on when Manuel tapped me on the shoulder and directed me to my desk, the computer, and hundreds of financial histories and accounting records. *Mierda.* But I had found the right job. Rebecca's actions fostered pride in my work. She made me want to help those people. The office became quiet and I settled down to learning the financial histories of Rebecca's clients. People she represented varied in economic status and came from all walks of life. Days went by, Mark taught and wrote, the J. E.s worked their jobs, and I was learning mine.

I became routine, but life wasn't. One day, I delivered papers to the courthouse and witnessed photographers and a TV camera crew running alongside a large group of smiling, well-dressed individuals carrying a black casket. They were sure happy, for mourners. At one corner, under the box, a woman who looked like Frida Kahlo saw me and waved. She had found me. Frida was nearby. I searched for her but lost her in the congregation.

"Who died?" I asked a man standing and watching the bearers as they put the casket down in the middle of the *plaza*.

"They're trying to bury Progress," the man said and walked away.

The crowd spoke to reporters about slow growth and petitions of some sort while the casket sat on the pavement, unprotected from the hot sun. Mister Progress was embalmed but, even so, he should have been moved out of the sun or he would become heavier, emanating an odor. After the crowd picked up their dead-weight box and moved down the *plaza* in search of a cemetery or a hearse for Mister Progress, I made my way back to the office. No news reached the papers about Mister Progress. He wasn't as important as I thought.

The heavy oak front door to Rebecca's office shut quietly. On the center couch of the reception area, a woman sat perfectly still and straight, sobbing. It was ten thirty in the morning and nobody was at work. They had left her to tend to her anguish alone.

I offered the woman a glass of water, sat next to her, and watched her imbibe. The cold drink calmed her. She pushed her black hair away from her face, smiled, and took my hand. *"Eres una santa. ¡Qué preciosa mano tienes! Gracias"*.

The *anciana* could have been my mother. Suddenly, I wanted to embrace her but held back. A devastating event lined her face with a deep, inescapable fatigue. She breathed deeply, crying softly, peacefully. She was a saintly woman with an aura about her. Like Coatlicue, Frida, and *la Virgen*, she too had found me. Grief made her appear humble. Meek and holy meet the image and the condition that the Catholic Church demands of women. Obedience and silent suffering made her miserable and pathetic. Where are the news media, the photographers for the newspaper, to reinforce the controllable, childlike, and good Catholic Mexican image?

"Señora, ¿en qué le puedo ayudar?" I heard myself whisper. I didn't have the answer to alleviate her hardship, the burden of *la Virgen de Guadalupe*. I fought off a trace of pretentiousness and superiority. Embarrassed, I remained silent.

"Gracias, muchas gracias, hija. You cannot help me. *Como todas las mujeres*, I carry my burden alone."

"Perdóneme, señora, pero ¿me puede decir qué le pasa? ¿Por qué está aquí?"

"*La señora Rebecca* brought me to this country *como una* guest worker. I left my daughter *con mi mamá en Chiapas* to come to work in the *fábrica de camisas.* I make shirts for many years. I stay *más tiempo de mi contrato y de mi visa* and I settle in California. I do not want cross again the border. *Es demasiado peligroso, especialmente para una mujer.* At night men they wait for women who cross the border. They rob, beat, and violate them. Many women die and many suffer a fate more horrible than death. *Se las llevan* and keep them slaves *como concubinas de las pandillas de la frontera.* I was very much afraid to get deported and cross again the border. *La señora Rebecca me ayudó a arreglar mis* papers. When my daughter had thirteen years, my mother died. I was forced to return to México and bring my daughter. Here in this country, she would have better life, better chance, *educarse, llegar a ser alguien. No como su mamá que no sabe leer ni escribir.* My daughter would be educated woman, *lo juré en la sepultura de mi madre que trabajó para cuidarla, vestirla y educarla. Mi mamá se sacrificó para su nieta. Mija Carmen fue a* high school and she make all 'A' grades. *Recibió una beca y préstamos. Le encantaba* to study. She tell to me she never wanted stop her study, *¡nunca! Carmen quería ser profesora* in the university. I watch my daughter *convertirse en una mujer inteligente y hermosa. No tengo por qué no decirlo, era una mujer joven y bella.* She was my gift that God sent to me, for to take care and protect her, *pero, fracasé,* I failed."

'Señora Estrada, I'm sorry but señora Rebecca will not return until very late. She can't see you today," Manuel informed señora Estrada, as he went in a rush to his office.

"*¿Cómo fracasó, señora?* I'm sure you are a very good mother."

I tried to comfort the woman by offering more water. Talking was helping her to relieve anger, frustration, and anguish.

"*Mija* could go to one of best colleges in the United States *pero decidió quedarse conmigo.* She went to Holy Spirit College in Irvine. *No le dieron toda la ayuda que necesitaba,* but she did get work in the bank. *Y luego voy con el doctor,* and he tell me I have cancer. I have no insurance. I cannot pay for treatment. Carmen says she will quit school. *¡Ave María purísima! ¡De ninguna manera!* No way, *muchacha!* We get in big fight, and she leave the house. One week later she tell me that she find small apartment and that the bank give her a more better job. She was very happy and she also said she was still *en colegio*. She give me the name of a doctor to treat my illness. Carmen say she pay for it. *Pero, ¿cómo, hija? Le preguntaba y ella sonreía y me decía que* 'things are getting better, *mamá*. The bank and the college are helping us.' For six months we live apart. I beg her to return home. She refuse. *'Soy feliz, mamá', me decía. Desde cuando el banco le dio su* promotion I suspicious of her work. Once I go to the bank. There she work counting money and cashing checks. *¡Oh, qué orgullo! Mija la banquera* have much responsibility. I quit my suspicions and decide to work hard *para curarme del cáncer.* Carmen, my daughter, my little girl, give to me the miracle. The doctors say the lymph node cancer *desapareció.* I get better because of *mija."*

Señora Estrada paused to drink water. When she finished and had placed the glass on the table, a grievous sigh came from her. I comforted her. She calmed down and spoke again.

"Hablar de esto y decirlo todo me ayuda mucho. Tú eres una santa por escucharme. Le pido a Dios que me ayude a continuar. I tell you whole story. *Hace un mes* police come to my place and tell me Carmen commit suicide."

Mark used the University of California, Irvine library at least once a week. Holy Spirit College, although a highly endowed private institution, did not have access to the UCI collections nor to the entire University of California library system. His teaching went well, yet he was depressed about his writing and suffered nightly battles with insomnia.

Even though I knew it bothered him, I kept on referring to his writing. I would say "... but you love to write," or "Keep writing. Someday it'll pay off." The J. E.s joked with him: "Think of yourself as a big-league ballplayer. You're getting paid for what you love to do!" Finally Mark had had enough and blew up in a strange way.

"I'm going to the UCI library!" he yelled.

"Good, you need to take it out on more books. What's wrong with you, Mark?"

"Something happened. It keeps gnawing on me and it won't let go."

"Come on. Tell me what's wrong."

"No, I'm in a hurry! I have an appointment with a student. I'll be back at around seven. Let's talk then."

And so it was that afternoon, as I made coffee and waited for Mark to return, I recalled *la señora Estrada*: her immigrating to the United States, bringing her daughter Carmen here, and finally Carmen's careful premeditated death. Señora Estrada's version of the events, her struggle to make her life better, struck deep into my heart.

A difficult situation drove Carmen to take her own life, so horrible in her eyes that it made death easier, preferable to life. In señora Estrada's story there was an element missing. Hardly anyone talked about student suicide. Carmen's fatal end was only briefly mentioned in the school newspaper at Holy Spirit College. According to señora

Estrada, her daughter was liked by classmates and professors.

Mark came home at the beginning of one of those beautiful Southern California sunsets, the kind that convinces people to come to the West. He suggested a walk on the beach to relax, easier to talk in the beauty of the horizon. We strolled on the sand for about half an hour when he finally started to tell me his story.

"I don't think what I did was wrong. This girl . . . she came to me. Stood at the entrance for a while. I always keep my office wide open. On my desk I have a small lamp with a low, soft, calming glow. I prefer to work in peaceful light. I don't like the high-intensity fluorescent brightness. We have enough pressure without hysterical lighting. She entered and left the door halfway open, then sat in the corner chair looking down at her knees. I asked who she was. I'm terrible with names. This girl, Carmen, had beautiful, brown curly hair. She fumbled with some papers in her notebook and finally placed the midterm before me and said she never had gotten such a low grade. I heard this story before. Then she explained that her other professors tell her that she has great ideas and give her an 'A'.

"I told her that they were doing her a disservice. Rewrite the paper. She was profusely thankful and surprised. This doesn't mean you're going to get an 'A'. She told me how difficult school was for her. She had two jobs. I'm sure she didn't like my response. I simply pointed out that this was her choice, that many students work a lot. Suddenly, she blurted out that she lived alone, had her own apartment, and needed the money. I was getting tired of this conversation. Frankly, I wanted her out of my office. Look, rewrite the exam and bring it to me in a week. Why not live at home? No, I can't stay there. Then I noticed tears down her face. I asked her to tell me about her work. That question bothered her, I remember. She didn't answer, just looked out into the bright light of the hall.

"Carmen wanted to do well in school. She was concerned about her grades. But what stuck with me was that she lived alone, had her own apartment, and supported herself. Crazy thoughts and scenes of her and me formed in my mind. Carmen rewrote the midterm paper, continued to attend class for a while, and then she stopped. She never came back."

Several people ran along the beach, getting into their aerobic exercise. Orange County was a fitness freak's ideal habitat, a place where staying fit generated a lot of money. I was amazed at the number of overweight people that lived here, in this fat-free, health-frenzied environment. Another chubby jogger lumbered by with agony on his face, pushing himself to the limit. No pain, no gain, gotta lose that tonnage, that *extra lonja*, that extra flab roll that hides the bellybutton. Mark laughed at that poor guy.

Mark stretched his arms to catch his breath to calm himself. "I like to think that I'm good as a writer and as a runner. You know I run as much as I can. It's getting more difficult. You are aware of that, J. I. Usually my competition is younger. I've been a member of the Runners Club since my return to California. You realize that I run for you, J. I. . . ."

"She never came back?"

"Carmen's story . . . it doesn't end when I last saw her at school.

"On a Saturday when the guys from the club had tickets to a hockey game at the Pond, they invited me to go with them. They got a limo, stocked it with the best hard stuff, plenty of beer and snacks, and they wanted me to come along. They said in unison, 'You're it!' I, of course, said no, told them that I had papers to correct, but they already had the admissions, and had scheduled the transportation to pick us up at our condo.

"I remember you were out that night. They arrived exactly at six in the prettiest limo you ever saw. That was my first ride in one. It had everything. The guys started right in on the hard liquor, and by the time we arrived at the game a couple of my running buddies were pretty much feeling no pain.

"We had seats just above the penalty box. I got a kick out of the mascot, a wild duck flying down to the arena floor. The game was exciting, a real spectacle. When the cheerleaders came on, my buddies went wild, drinking and screaming as if they were celebrating a victory —but no matter, the Anaheim team lost.

"As we drove out of the arena parking lot they announced 'Dinner Time! We're taking the professor for an exciting meal!'

"I hadn't expected dinner. At that moment I gave up. I realized

70

that it was going to be a long night, so I resigned myself to their plan. About twenty minutes later we walked into the Scheherazade Entertainment and Diners Club: live adult entertainment, showgirls seven days a week, all day, all night.

"At first the fact that the women were mostly naked bothered me, but after a while I began to enjoy the nudity. They walked in high-heel shoes, bent their bodies in provocative ways. While serving me a drink, a waitress wore only a purse for change and tips. My psychological checks and balances, and my inhibitions slowly melted.

"How could I save one of these girls from having to expose herself to strangers? I think that's how the movie went. And so, as I ate filet mignon, I carefully watched the women, studied their bodies, their faces, and selected one. I imagined her happy with me, imagined myself being ever so tender as she happily held her legs wide . . . and why not, I had saved her from this fate. My girl brought me another drink and I placed a twenty in her little tip bag, and she cuddled her breasts against my cheek.

"There was a voice way in the back of my brain that tried to tell me to walk out of there. But it was soon gone, J. I., it was gone. Suddenly my girl escorted me to a room. As she walked, my eyes raced over her legs, her small waist, and her back. With a smile she kept me at arm's length."

Mark stopped. I'm sure he thought that the details of what he was describing might be offensive to me. I considered him such a stupid naive man. *"¡Todos son iguales! ¡Hombres necios que cargan el cerebro entre las piernas!"* Sor Juana screamed from a mutual women's ancient site.

"'Hands to yourself, no touching, and enjoy!' I heard as my girl's voice faded away and she closed the door. I sat in a pitch-black room. Light filtered from the edges of the entrance. I heard the guys outside laughing and talking. You're a lucky professor. Watch your nose. Nothing made sense. When a woman appeared in dim light and pulled a round three-foot-high platform near the tips of my shoes, I could not see her face, only her silhouette. Music began softly as she came to my side, held my shoulder, and stepped up onto the stand. She danced and removed her clothes piece by piece and never looked down. I didn't blink. I took deep breaths, felt anxious.

71

"The lights brightened slightly to reveal the splendid nudity of a young woman dancing. I couldn't keep my eyes off her. Above me, she arched her back, never looked at me. Her brown skin was clean of obvious blemishes except for a slight flaw, a round purplish shape on her upper thigh. She had not looked at me nor had I seen her face. Her body moved with the music, and slowly she bent her legs and squatted in an ancient way. With the dancer's back to me, I watched as she undulated her hips, moved her body up and down, again, and again. Then I felt my subconscious ugliness entrenched inside of me, a horrid, loathsome being . . . I felt painful shame. Don't touch, I reminded myself.

"I wanted to stroke her back as the young woman dancer raised her arms toward the ceiling, spread open, and gradually touched her toes. Then, with her head between her legs for a long instant, we gazed into each other's eyes and knew each other's face. At once she stopped, jumped off the platform, ran out the door, and turned, unexpectedly, to look at me. Then and only then was I sure that it was Carmen. I called after her, but she had run out.

"Outside in the hall a commotion broke out. My buddies argued with Carmen and the bouncer. I could hear him screaming, 'Did he touch you?' If she had answered yes, the guards were ready and eager to break every bone in my body . . . 'You know him! He's your professor!'

"In the midst of guards, Carmen Estrada leaned against the wall. Clients and some women walked by, yet nobody thought to bring something to cover Carmen, my student, the girl who had come to me, the one who confided in me, who sought counsel and help from me, her professor. As Carmen raised her face to look back at me, she struggled to get away from a bouncer who pulled her violently and asked once more if I had touched her. Carmen shook her head and tried to pry his hands from her. As I was pushed away and restrained, I could hear his mocking tone: 'This guy's your professor!' His grip tightened around Carmen's arm and neck. 'Yes!' She ran into a dressing room. By this time, three security men surrounded me. It seemed a long wait to hear what my fate would be.

"The guard in charge told me not to worry, she was probably an illegal. As he escorted us to the exit he followed us. 'Can't return your money, you got credit for a lap dance for the next time you're here, I'll remember you and give you a girl who's not your student.' He was teasing, but it sounded more like ridicule. The bouncer walked behind me out to where the limo was parked and continued deriding me, the fool I was. In the parking lot I recall him definitely speaking to me more as a threat than as a consolation.

"I was helpless. I didn't know what to do, whether I should try to see Carmen or not. What would I say? Me, her professor, in a topless bar, leering at naked women. What could she utter after I had observed her nude? From that moment on, fear became my companion.

"Days went by, from what I heard, they found washed, ironed, and folded clothes neatly stored in drawers, checks written for unpaid bills. The apartment was immaculate, clean dishes were stacked on the counter. She put a roast in the oven and left three letters: two to friends and one to her mother. And maybe she studied for some time, leaving her books and her notebook opened.

"She took time to feed the cat before she took a rope and hung herself from the patio post. A neighbor's dog barked insistently, until Carmen's friends went to the apartment for dinner at about five forty-five, just in time to turn off the oven timer for the roast. The two girls found Carmen facing a beautiful Southern California sunset.

"J. I., I didn't go to the wake or the funeral. I spoke to her mother once. I don't know whether she was told about the incident at the strip club. She never revealed any anger toward me, only a kind of empathy, a kind of regard as if she was aware of an intimacy about me that I didn't know."

Carmen's suicide was kept out of the major papers. I guess a young Chicana student's death was just not considered worthy-enough news.

I lived with the man whose stupid macho actions and lust probably drove Carmen Estrada to end her life. Mark was fast becoming someone I didn't know.

I saw Sara, Jennie, Endriago, and my parents, but I was not with them, not even in the images in my mind. Even with Mark, the sense of loneliness was overwhelming because lately he hadn't been paying much attention to anything except his classes and his writing.

I concentrated on work and learned the accounting system and codes used in the office. Not wanting to disappoint Rebecca, staying late became commonplace for me. Mark didn't seem to notice, and he enjoyed working alone in an empty house.

One evening I arrived late and found the J. E.s unloading heavy wooden boxes. "More books," Jack said. "You wanna help?" I waved good night and went inside. Unpacking books at this late hour, actually morning? Who were they kidding? I wondered why they were bringing so many deliveries to their condo and not the bookshop.

My sinuses hurt, I was probably running a fever, and I had a terrible runny nose and cough. I was miserable and my routine became work. Mark continued to be fixated to his novel. He reminded me of another obsessed writer, the Mexican woman journalist who lost her life for what she published and knew. She reported about out-of-bounds people and hidden events.

The other night, I started perusing a manuscript titled *The Stories of GA* that Mark had written, perhaps for the child he yearned to have, or maybe because he was in a weird mood—I suspect the latter. Mark was not in danger of losing his life, but he did seem to be obsessed, like the Mexican woman journalist. I took Mark's stories to bed but didn't get beyond the first page of the one I wanted to read.

At the doctor's office the next morning, I read some of Mark's manuscript and thought maybe he should write children's stories. She gave me antibiotics for a severe sinus infection. Must have been the different Southern California contamination to which my body hadn't adjusted quite yet. I remember about not loving Mark in the cancerous throat of Los Ángeles.

Images that appeared on television, billboards, magazines, films, and walls created the spectacle in which Americans wanted to live. Not being able to do it is a failure to achieve satisfaction in Southern California life. To rise above the crowd, here, people had to participate in an original form. To be the best meant to be original.

Newer cities in Orange County try to offer an original lifestyle by creating non-centered planburbs. Their founders build marketplaces with behemoth stores that warehouse every imaginable product. These commercial centers are usually located on the outskirts and, on the weekends, they draw thousands of people. Historic old towns, their main streets, and the businesses that have served the residents for decades, die.

Many independent small businesses closed because the baby boomers, yuppies, X- Generation, Rap-Generation, No-Religion Generation, and the Planburb-Generation overwhelmed others with their desire for instant purchase, information, and gratification. Too busy working hard at making money and partying, to waste time not getting immediate satisfaction in stores. No misuse of time in the now. OC dwellers, like other folks of Southern California, operate in a blur in the planburbs and are content. Development of these areas is a direct result of millions of people attempting to avoid undesirable elements they find themselves rubbing against, in schools, supermarkets, churches, shopping centers, and parks.

Planburb dwellers want a plain prose life, distant and separate from the undesirables, in a neighborhood based on moral goodness, respect, and politeness. Their goal is to live in a controlled community to promote the positive values of hard work, intelligence, and the golden rule, a place where people don't call attention to themselves but to the environment and the world they create and guard.

Typical creators and supporters of originality and community unity eat at the best restaurants in Orange County: Rov's Place, Rasco's, Pierre, Gorgiano's, and the Bull's Eye Club. Mark finally took a break from his sad novel and we went to Rov's Place. Great food and wine! According to Mark, we sat next to a writer who cut off three of his fingers to buy a computer and became a famous millionaire mystery author.

"His fingers look normal to me," I said to Mark.

"They're fake. See how they shake when he picks up the wine glass."

"The Chiapas revolution is directed and supported by Maoist *guerrillas*."

A dark-skinned woman talked loudly, as if she were competing with other loud patrons for "The Most Interesting Conversation of the Evening" award.

"And what's the result, honey? Thousands more Mexicans crossing the border and stealing our money."

"We must stabilize our borders, our language, and our culture."

"Oh, please, we want to buy what they need in the kitchen. No trouble now that they're living in Brentwood."

"Well, your daughter has great choices, Meg: Harvard, Columbia, Yale, and the Air Force Academy."

These types of conversations were anachronistic verbiage that I had heard many times before—in México, at Harvard and Princeton, and now Orange County. Values and views of the people with the money don't seem to change. As for the Mexican waiter, maybe his children had a better chance at changing.

"John, did you read the morning newspaper? The article on four bank robberies that have occurred in the last couple of weeks."

"The Tustin Wells Fargo Bank was robbed a few days ago."

"That's one of our banks, honey!"

"Yeah, by some desperate, fat, bearded asshole," concluded a man dining at the table in front of me.

"Mark, a few days ago Jack and Jill had a fight. They were violent. I think the quarrel was over money and the bookstore."

"And . . ." Mark offered and cut into his rack of lamb.

"I think they hit each other. I didn't go over. I didn't want to get involved."

 From inside Jack and Jill's condo, I heard loud thumping sounds, as if they were breaking down walls. Chucho barked and growled in an angry and not playful manner, and the banging increased in volume.

"Oh, God, they're fighting again." I decided to go over to stop them from hurting one another. In their arguments, Jack and Jill physically attacked. On most occasions the wrestling turned into a love-making match, but once in a while they would draw blood.

Noise intensified. The hammering splintering, of what I thought was dry wood falling onto the floor, urged me to ring the doorbell. Chucho continued to bark and, through the window, I saw him darting in and out of the hall. Jack grabbed Jill in a headlock. She responded by reaching and viciously yanking his hair and head back. They fell to the ground. That's when I noticed blood on Jack's neck and right ear.

"Jack, let her go!"

I slammed my fist on the door. They looked up and saw me at the window.

"Stop the fighting!"

"What the hell's wrong?" Jill asked, annoyed, and wiped the sweat from her face.

"Oh, shit! You're bleeding, Jack."

They smiled. Between breaths, Jill moved his hair, trying to find the cut on his head. Indirectly, they waited for my answer.

"You OK, Jill?"

"Yeah, we're playing. I was kicking this guy's skinny ass!" Squarely, at the end of her sentence, Jill unexpectedly jumped Jack and wrestled him down and squeezed his neck painfully. Jack bled faster now. The blood spread over his shoulders and onto the wooden floor.

"Say 'I give!'" Jill screamed in a fierce, loud voice.

"OK, OK, I give! You don't have to break my fucking neck. Fuck! You busted my skull." Jack's hands were covered with blood.

A pile of splintered wood lay in the hall. On a shattered piece I managed to read "caliber."

"Don't screw with me, buddy. Take a warning from an Orange County amazon."

Jill searched, trying to find the cut on Jack's scalp.

"Here it is! Ice that cut," she teased Jack, who went to the kitchen and wrapped cubes in a towel.

"I smashed a couple of heavy book boxes on his head. He got what he deserved and got a little upset. So I kicked his ass, but he still loves me, don't *ya* Jack?"

She kissed him and helped him adjust the ice pack over the wound. "Nice deep gash, my love. Should we go to the hospital and have it sewn up?"

"Shit no!"

"Well, I tried." Jill shrugged her shoulders.

They started caressing, wrestling, and finally drew blood and beat each other to submission. Love, violence, love, violence . . . not too hard to figure out.

Jill went outside with Chucho to enjoy a beautiful western beach sunset. I followed, and I saw all four of them. Jill sat calmly on the curb, looking toward the sea, petting her dog curled up beside her. Jack, in the kitchen, pressed a makeshift icepack on his torn scalp. Mark was in his study writing. What could you do with people like my friends? They were possessed. Like Cassandra, the dead woman journalist in México, their flaw, like hers, was that they were cursed or blessed by a passion that moved them to the brink of triumph or disaster. I guess I could just live with them, help them to succeed, hope for the best, and, above all else, love them.

Mark talked about his class, the books, and papers he read. He had the habit of speaking about the novels he wanted to write. Holding listeners' attention for as long as they could stand his telling stories was some self-evaluation and critique of his ability with readers. Mark did this to build his self-confidence.

Once he began to tell his stories, whether short or long, he could not stop. To be rich and famous, Mark wrote about the experiences of his life. This became a fixation that he could not leave alone. Every chance he had, he took notes, like the dead young woman journalist in México. Until now, Mark had not revealed this idiosyncrasy, this passion that drove him to act in an eccentric manner, with the talent or the bad taste to narrate for hours, on and on, word after word, at times laughing, crying or not making sense to anybody but himself, like in a trance. He would not stop.

I missed the other Mark, the funny, silly, "Freedom is just another word for having nothing left to lose" Mark, the Mark I loved in Princeton, the Mark who wrote to me in México begging me to come surf and love in the time of now in Aztlandia.

Teaching, creating, responsibility had all covered his mind with seriousness and professionalism. His fear of not getting tenure and losing his job overwhelmed him. This Mark took himself so very seriously now, so much so that there was no time to play or sleep. "After tenure, relax," he mumbled while sleeping, which he did very little, and when he did it was always briefly, restlessly, and sporadically. Academics had made him an insomniac.

In this Mark, there was no crazy love like the one we shared in Princeton. A touching, hugging, caressing of bodies was Mark's love-making now. Intimacy consisted of sensations and not penetrations; he had become almost celibate. If it sounded poetic, it was, and I enjoyed it, but I missed my passionate Mark. Now I wanted him to respond to me, to open me up, and devour me.

"Get some sleep, busy day tomorrow," the academic Mark whispered. He turned his body away and journeyed into the night, into a short fitful nap.

I got out of bed. Lights were on in Jack and Jill's condo. Three thirty in the morning, and still Jack and Jill worked and played. They didn't rest, charged up on beer and speed. In the kitchen I opened the shutters and looked up at the night sky. The silver moon Coyolxauhqui and Coatlicue descended into the house. Coatlicue took me back to bed and lulled me to sleep.

On Saturday, Rebecca arrived at our condo exactly at six in the evening. Wearing a casual elegant white jumpsuit, she walked to the back patio where Jack poked at steak and chicken on the grill. We practiced a favorite Southern California social ritual—cooking in the backyard with neighbors and friends. Well, with whom else would we barbecue? The unknown, unwanted derelicts, out-of-a-job homeless people of Orange County? Jill poured Chardonnay and I whipped up a spicy guacamole to add to the appetizers.

Soon after the introductions, the what-do-you-dos, and our first glass of wine, we relaxed. Jack immediately started in on Rebecca. He was concerned that immigration lawyers took advantage of undocumented people and sucked their money with promises of legalization.

"I have customers in my bookshop who will spend their last penny trying to achieve the dream of either becoming a documented resident or a citizen of the United States. Lead them on, promise them legalization, but that never happens. Some lawyers drag on the process for years, all the while getting paid for appearing proficient, yet doing nothing."

Rebecca, enjoying the wine, sat quietly, bemused by Jack, as if she had heard this harangue before. Jack's political diatribe attacked those who had the power to effect change for individuals, and for doing their job they got criticized. Rebecca knew this and was comfortable with it, so she listened to Jack's socio-political monologue.

". . . and why do you do it?"

"Do what?"

"Exploit the illegals."

"I make lots of money helping them." Rebecca smiled, lifted her glass, and toasted all of us.

 Later that week, on Wednesday, I arrived at work tired. The night before, Mark and I had attended a concert at the Orange County Performing Arts Center, a recently built theater with a sculpture of a huge thunderbird as the trademark-featured masterpiece for the main entrance. It was Orange County's monument to the arts. I wore a black evening dress with a white, red, green, and blue shawl.

That evening, a Taiwanese guest conductor was directing the Orange County Philharmonic. We had been invited by Mark's department head, whose parents had immigrated to the United States from Taiwan and had made a fortune by setting up *maquiladoras* in Anaheim and Tijuana to produce radio technology to sell to the United States. Mark's department head knew the conductor and had organized the tour.

As I took my seat between Mark and his boss, I remembered a night in Bellas Artes when Endriago had been honored. That night I had suffered the first spiritual trance. I tried not to recall those events but, lately, recollections were coming back stronger. Those unexplained energies that haunted me then were finding me here in Aztlandia. In the rows ahead of us, Coatlicue, Malintzin Tenepal, *la Virgen de Guadalupe*, Sor Juana, Frida, and Comandanta Ramona sat together. They turned and acknowledged me.

During intermission, Mark and I drank wine and chatted with other guests. I found it strange that people seemed to be commenting on my dress. It was, after all, a plain black evening gown.

"How did you do it?" Mark asked startled.

"Do what?"

"Change your dress without me seeing you do it?"

81

I didn't quite understand. Wasn't I wearing a black dress? I excused myself and went into the ladies room, where the mirror reflected an image of a woman wearing a white, red, green, and blue evening gown. The shawl that I wore had added black to its original colors. The people in the center, the few who sat around me, were perplexed by the transfiguration of my outfit. Amongst the crowd returning to their seats I searched for Coatlicue and friends, but they were nowhere to be seen.

After the performance, we returned to the Philharmonic's Circle Club for a reception featuring a variety of wines and desserts.

"That's quite a dress," remarked Mark's boss.

"Your dress is stunning. There is a radiance about you!" the boss' wife commented.

At about one in the morning, we said goodbye to our host. The department head's wife couldn't stop touching my dress. "Magnificent," she repeated.

Mark's boss, his wife, the guest conductor, and one hundred others— including Coatlicue and my women friends from México— kept on partying. That morning newspaper's first page reported *guerrilla* attacks in México and, in the Calendar section of the *Los Angeles Times*, a triumph for the conductor and for the opening-night party.

Nonetheless, Mark and I had abandoned the good times that were had by all and had arrived home at about one thirty in the morning. Typically, after a late night of academic political socializing, I felt restless. Mark was the same way. I longed for the happy Mark, but he didn't come forth; instead, the nervous professor Mark suggested, "Go to sleep. You need it, J. I." He got up and went to work on his manuscript. I joined Coatlicue and her entourage hovering over the bed. I was happy the women had found me, but I was fearful of the events that might occur.

 In Rebecca's office reception area, about a dozen uniformed Immigration and Customs Enforcement agents and Santa Ana police stood over a man, a woman holding a boy, and a girl, all seated on the couch. Mrs. Dougherty sat in Manuel's office. Two bewildered ICE employees argued with Rebecca.

"They have to go. No chance," they insisted.

"No, they don't understand Chinese!" an Asian agent explained to the others. "They're not Chinese!" he raised his voice. "You didn't need me!" He waived the group off and walked out, disgusted.

"What are they? They're not Chinese coming in through México? They don't talk Spanish. We got to take them." The agent reached for the man, who resisted by clinging to the woman and the children.

The lady sat serenely. With her arm, hand, body, she blocked the immigration officer. *La indígena* who carried a bundle of *alcatraces* on her back, who pursued me in my visions, now sat in Rebecca's reception room in Santa Ana, California. Of course they didn't understand Spanish or Chinese. They were Mayan and spoke Mayan! My eyes welled with pride watching her protect her family.

The ICE had found these people potting tiny orchids in the greenhouse of a small nursery in Santa Ana. The owner, an eighty-year-old woman who could not hear or speak, sensed what was happening. She ran to her kitchen and sent a fax to Rebecca, and we arrived in ten minutes. Rebecca identified herself as the couple's lawyer.

Rebecca produced photo identification, Mexican passports and U.S. work permits proving the couple's legal guest-worker status, and shared official letters and documents requesting political asylum. The couple came from Chiapas and left México because the man had been threatened by the Mexican military. He was accused of being a *guerrillero*, a Maoist proselytizer trained in Perú by the Sendero Luminoso, and a recruiter for the *guerillero* movement.

"Why raid the house?" Mrs. Dougherty wrote on her notepad, asking the ICE agent in charge.

"Come on, you should know better than that. Maybe someone reported them as suspected undocumented."

The Mayan family remained silent while Rebecca and I calmed the kids down.

"Yes, yes, yes," Mrs. Dougherty said, and escorted the Mayan family into the house. We were left standing in the cement driveway next to a large deep-green lawn. As I got in Rebecca's Land Rover, through the living room window I could see the children inside playing on a floral-patterned couch. They seemed happy in Mrs. Dougherty's home.

J. I. asked Rebecca, "How did you get this family together with Mrs. Dougherty?"

"Mrs. Dougherty came to my office and asked me to put together legal paperwork for Mexican workers. I did. I set up a guest-worker contract and, in two months, Ray, May, Jay, and Fay Maya arrived."

"Ray, May, Jay, and Fay Maya?" I remember laughing for some time. I hadn't laughed like that for a while.

"When they first arrived I didn't understand a word they said. So I gave them names. I made up easy names for Mrs. Dougherty to remember."

I listened in disbelief.

"You see, J. I., Mrs. Dougherty wanted somebody completely dependable and dependent. She wanted people who would rely on her, to live with her for the last years of her life. Mrs. Dougherty doesn't have to worry about finances. She is willing to support a family for the rest of their lives just as long as they stay with her. I had explained in detail what I needed to my contact in the U.S. Embassy in Mexico, and he sent Mr. and Mrs. Maya and family—a perfect match. They don't speak a word of English. They're afraid to return because they truly are condemned to die by the Mexican Army."

Rebecca pulled into the driveway at her Fourth Street office. Across the street, three men, probably Mexicans, walked slowly down the sidewalk. They looked dirty and tired; probably, they had just returned from working on crops in the Irvine fields, what remained of them. I wondered when they'd get stopped by *la migra*. I drove home thinking about those men and Rebecca, who probably got more than a usual fee for fixing the Mayas' immigration status for Mrs. Dougherty.

Wide face, broad forehead, full mustache, bushy beard, a mop of stringy, curly, Jimmy Hendrix-style black hair, wide dark sunglasses, long black winter scarf, white T-shirt or sweater and a large open beige trench coat composed the image of a corpulent Caucasian man.

Light fell from the right and highlighted part of his face. The side that remained in the shadow especially caught my eye. For a second or two I fixated on the man's nose, the bridge, the skin falling to the tip and rolling over and under to form the flaring contour of the left nostril of the image.

"They haven't caught that guy yet!" said Jack.

"He gets away every time. Why can't the cops get that son-of-a-bitch?" Jill lowered the television volume and returned to count out the cash, checks, and charges for the day, while Jack unloaded a box of books onto a cart.

"Now here's a great book!" Jack exclaimed. He slammed a copy of B. Traven's *Government* on the cart. "A forgotten novel, more relevant today than ever before."

Texts about México, Latin America and Chicanos, literature, history, economics, politics and titles that dealt with the border—the line on the map between México and the United States—filled a box that I opened.

"Beautiful books." Jack caressed one and placed it in the Chicano/Latin American Studies section. He held up another entitled *The New Millennium and Mexico's Multiparty Democratic System*.

"We are selling a lot of this stuff. We are Latin America and they are the United States. They are here and we are there. That's what makes this country squirm, especially here in California. You know what I'm talking about, J. I. What's happening now in Mexico reveals the noisy pangs of modernism, capitalism. That is a modern capitalist country trying to break through to become a multi-political democratic system. If you succeed, J. I., if Mexicans succeed, you will have a more representative and, therefore, a more democratic system than the United States. Mexico will become the world's model for democracy and an economic powerhouse of the new millennium! And that's a great accomplishment to look forward to, J. I.!"

"Well, Mr. *Político*, we had a $45 day. That's not going to pay for the rent, bills, and books. If it keeps going like this, we're not going to be around for the new millennium. We'll have to shut down," Jill said emphatically. She placed the day's receipts into a cloth bag and stuck it into her sweat suit jacket.

"I'm not going to let it die! We've got to buy more inventory!" Jack responded.

"With what money? Be realistic. We just about tapped out our savings!"

Jack was perturbed with the thought of closing Ekkerson's Bookshop.

"Hey, we're a real independent bookstore, struggling every Goddamn day to survive, and we should, we will survive, God damn it! Fuck! That pisses me off! Forty-five fuckin' dollars!

I'll never forget his reaction, the muscles in his face contracted with a cool rage.

"It's the damn big chains that are out to destroy the small independents. Most folks believe that what is sold in those outlets is what they should buy, that it's quality literature. They don't see that the savings of 20%, 30%, or 40% is at the cost of freedom of expression. The fact is these monopolizers shape, control, and provide their reading habits by slowly weaning them away from reading and shaping their minds. Don't they wonder why the Book Barnes, King's, G. Bolton, and Book Emporium are right next to the movie theaters? They're just an extension of the fantasy. In reality, each time people buy what they think is a great deal, they participate in censorship; they smash another nail into the coffin of indie bookstores, and finance the gagging of the masses and their freedom to write. Just look at the classifieds of the ABA newsletter: every month more independents go out of business. All the while more outlets continue to be built. Fuck! We should burn those ugly warehouses down."

I enjoyed the giant bookstores before or after a movie. Nonetheless, I always did my purchases at independent stores. In México, I preferred them also. Jack opened another box. He paused to make sure he caught our eye before he continued his diatribe on the chains.

"In this case, capitalism creates many monopolies and eliminates small independent competition. Doesn't anybody get it, J. I.? How can we compete? Giant stores are in control of knowledge. They buy books by the thousands while we can only afford one at a time. An intellectual cancer is killing the thinking around it; it's growing, but we keep feeding it. We should burn the fucker out!" Jack searched for us. We stood at the door waiting to go to dinner. "Hey, I really flipped out, huh? Oh, shit! You never listen to me anyway."

"We're too hungry," I said, and walked Jack out of Ekkerson's Bookshop. At the exit, Jack switched on the small door lamp. The light fell on one side of his face.

It does rain in Southern California, and that afternoon was between storms. The night before, Tláloc had fallen apart into millions of multiplying liquid splinters. Tláloc's spiritual body parts weighing tons crashed onto Orange County.

Flash floods, mudslides, and high surf devastated the Laguna Beach area; the mountains and canyons were flushed out by roaring torrents. Cliff dwellers had to evacuate as Tláloc's power undercut the support structures of their homes. Sides of foothills slid into small valleys, cliffs fell face first onto roads. From the heights, where the views were the best, million-dollar houses were thrust down onto those below.

Tláloc fell from the sky that night, saturated the soil and, through underground arteries, it swept, pushed, dragged from inside out whatever obstacles—from ants to mountains—remained in its moist silver path. The earth gave birth to itself and burst out of its skin.

On Friday morning, the sun shivered and shined a magnificent day. Coatlicue, Malintzin Tenepal, *la Virgen de Guadalupe*, Sor Juana, Frida, and Comandanta Ramona: their faces greeted me in the ancient fresh silver dew. The meteorologists predicted a second storm, heavier than last night's, due to reach Orange County by early evening.

I parked my car at the curb in front of Mrs. Dougherty's lawn. Water and more water made the patches of well-tended grass along Mrs. Dougherty's street a deep Kelly green. She lived in an old exclusive part of Santa Ana where, in former times, individually designed homes were constructed by wealthy residents of the area and, today, were sold to young professional families wanting an old California classic. Majestic palms, a reminder that this was once a desert, lined the wide streets, emerald turfs, and brick-trimmed adobes. Historical character was the selling point for these houses. Mrs. Dougherty was the senior, both in age and in ownership, and she made it a point to let everybody know that she was the neighborhood resident emeritus.

Jay Maya raked leaves and collected twigs and piled them atop a large canvas. His mother, May, wrapped the bundles and stacked them on the curb. All the while she spoke to her son, who nodded, seemingly agreeing with what she said. From the car, I watched for a half hour, fascinated by her lesson. In that time at work together, she had offered to him an oral teaching of some kind. Suddenly, May flung the largest pile over her back without any strain. She turned to find me now standing before her. Her eyes were the same as those of the Indigenous woman who carried a huge bundle of *alcatraces* on her back and who had accepted me in México, but here she quickly stepped aside, avoided me, and took her child by the hand as they walked to the backyard. I followed her to the greenhouse.

Mrs. Dougherty approached, placed her hands on her hips, and said, "Yes, yes, yes." She wore a long flowered pattern dress, loose at the waist, long sleeves, and Panama hat. "Yes, yes, yes?" she asked.

"Hello, Mrs. Dougherty. Rebecca told me to visit, to see if you need help."

She studied my lips. "Yes." All the time nodding her head, she waved her hand, indicating I should follow her to where the Mayas worked in different areas of the hothouse. The children, Jay and Fay, cleaned plastic pots. May had thrown the leaves and sticks into a compost pile isolated by a wooden frame. Ray and Mrs. Dougherty watered thousands of orchids of distinct colors, sizes, and delicate velvet leaves thirsting on white tables.

Mrs. Dougherty waved May to the table, who plucked one of the flowers and took a tiny bite. She tasted, smiled, and spoke Mayan to Ray. He laughed and placed the rest of the flower in her mouth.

"Are these for a medicinal purpose?" I asked. Nobody paid any attention. Mrs. Dougherty didn't hear me, and the Mayas didn't understand. Frustrated and in a loud voice, I asked, "*¿Las flores son para medicamentos?*"

The Mayas looked at one another.

"*Señor Maya, ¡yo sé que usted entiende español!*"

I faced him. He shook his head violently and pointed to May. There was a long silence during which time the children gathered next to their parents. They all suddenly took on a serious demeanor as if they were about to confess a secret, a sin. I decided to press on with my suspicion.

"*Señor Maya, ¡usted habla español!*"

"*No, el señor entiende muy poco, y habla menos, señorita,*" May responded, again taking on a defensive posture that I had seen her take before.

"*May, ¿español?*"

Ray pointed to May, somewhat startled by her revelation. I moved closer to her. She took a few steps back, still pushing her children behind her and taking Ray's hand.

"*Señora Maya,*" I practically begged, "*¿habla español?*"

She focused on me. The corners of her black, almond eyes sharpened with a little bit of tension against the white opaque glass wood-framed walls of the hothouse.

"*¡Sí!*" May answered.

Upon hearing that one syllable pronounced by her, for reasons I can't explain, tears came to my eyes. I resisted a sudden need to embrace her, but I dared not take one step toward her. My hunch was right; I knew that at least one of them spoke Spanish. It was usually the kids, the youngest generation, who interpreted the world for their parents.

"*¡Muchas gracias, señora!, ¡muchísimas gracias!*" I wiped tears from my face.

Mrs. Dougherty at my side, somewhat alarmed, repeated, "Yes, yes, yes."

Mrs. Maya made signs with her hands as if she scooped food in her mouth and then pointed to me.

"Yes, yes, yes," Mrs. Dougherty replied and went on watering her orchids.

That evening I didn't say much. I was happy to have been invited to dinner. I smiled and nodded a lot. The food that May and her daughter Fay prepared tasted delicious. Mrs. Dougherty approved; she had three servings. I was comfortable with these people. After eating, Mrs. Dougherty sat on the sofa and watched Jeopardy with the children. By the end of Alex Trebek's goodbye to the audience and a congratulatory handshake to the day's champion, she was sound asleep.

The children sat, fascinated by television. The elders moved about cleaning and putting dishes and leftovers away. The Mayas, I thought, had emigrated for political reasons. They accepted Rebecca's friend's offer because they had to escape a future that they had been born into. Ray and May's prospects would be the same as their parents: Ray would be the same cockled slave that his father had been—May would eventually be raped by the *patrón*. Most Mexicans follow the belief that *los nativos* multiply like rabbits and the blame rests on the female victims.

"Solo hay que calentarle el lomo a una india y se abre para coger. Así son, por eso me gustan".

I could hear the *patrón* bragging to the native leaders at the ranch *pulquería*. On Saturdays he drank with these men.

"Pero mañana domingo, tempranito, los quiero ver a todos en la iglesia de la Virgencita de Guadalupe".

And the *patrón* ordered more *pulque* for everyone. He insisted that the men drink until they dropped. And, after they fell, he would ask them to stand. They tried and collapsed. He declared that the *indio* who could get up and walk to the bar would earn enough for more liquor for everyone.

"¡Qué viva el patrón!" He laughed at the efforts of his workers struggling to stand and get to the bar. One always made it, and then the *patrón* gladly put up more *pulque* for his men. The men drank until they fell into a profound stupor from which, once in a while, one of them never awoke. While the leaders slept off their drunken numbness, their *cacique* went in search of their wives and their daughters. The women never resisted physically.

 *Mi mamá y mi papá*, Sara, Jennie, and Endriago were on my mind as I drove away from the house, thinking of how the Mayas and I were similar: We both had to save ourselves; we both were political exiles. Somewhere in our experience we had to stop and await the right moment for an opportunity to escape and, for May and me, it came. For her, it was a Mexican lawyer who offered her and her family a contract for work in the USA; for me, it was a lecherous priest who owed me a miracle. Father Cristóbal had arranged for me to leave Mexico City.

Now the Mayas and I moved through a transitional period: May, with her family in Mrs. Dougherty's house; me, with my past and memories, Cassandra, and her journal in Mark's house. We waited to enter an unknown space, one we desired in order to participate in its creation, one into which we wanted to be incorporated. That space, that experience, was not utopia.

Most people living in Aztlandia search and attempt to build utopia. It is a false concept, a frustrating journey that leads only to disappointment. Immigrants, like the Mayas, unknowingly construct heterotopia. I had heard this word in a lecture presented at the Newport Museum of Art. A broad-faced, big-eared bald man described Southern California as a heterotopia.

The Mayas and I affirm heterotopia. We confirm Southern California as a space of the multicultural, multi-dimensional real. I remember the big-eared professor saying, "We Mexicans stay to protect, develop, and better our neighborhoods. While the Anglos run from non-White racial and ethnic families who buy a house in their community, and search for utopia somewhere further south or east.

Please don't run away; don't allow White flight to continue. Please stay and help us construct heterotopia, for it is inherently an inescapable border zone, impossible to escape. So, why not stay, and we can learn to live in it together."

The professor spoke for forty-five minutes. I paraphrased his talk and drove home. I figured I'd get to the condo in twenty minutes if I took the 55 freeway. But I went northbound. I didn't pay attention to what I was doing. I thought I was driving home on the Newport freeway, but didn't realize that I was heading in the wrong direction.

The sign indicated Newport, north and south, but I was preoccupied with my friends, the Mayas. Their skin color was not dark or brown, but alive, their bodies were truncated and stocky and their faces shaped like long ovals. They were classic Mayans brought to the modern world with an F2 Guest Worker legal trans-border mechanism controlled by a legal pilot in Mexico City and by the master of the game, my friend Rebecca in Santa Ana, California.

Night had fallen upon my journey home. More than twenty minutes had flashed by and I was not recognizing any landmarks. I hadn't seen the MacArthur off-ramp, the Santa Ana Airport exit; the 405 freeway never came. As the 91 Los Angeles/Riverside freeway sign appeared, I glued on to the arrow pointing to Los Ángeles. The gas gauge read full. I squirmed comfortably into the bucket seat. Mark was probably home writing, studying, eating a TV dinner, oblivious to my situation, thinking it was another late night working with Rebecca, working with Mexicans.

"Buena Park," "Knott's Berry Farm" I whizzed by at seventy miles per hour, racing on with cars advancing in an orderly fashion. The United States excels in organization. *"Todo está muy ordenado. Todo tiene su lugar en los Estados Unidos,"* Endriago, my beloved Endriago, had said the last time I saw him. I missed him, Sara, and Jennie. I had received a letter, addressed to Mark at Holy Spirit College, from Endriago. Mexico City seemed to have gone back to normal after the assassination and the miracles. Nobody thought about me, only a few of my faithful gathered in Coyoacán in a vigil for my return. Events that had occurred to me were signs of an imminent *apertura* for more to evolve in México and the United States.

"Los Angeles city limits, Population 3,500,000." I zoomed, passing cars faster and faster. I slowed down to sixty. The dancing lights of Los Ángeles loomed to the right. Shortly I would drive over and into the heart of LAMEXICO, LAMEXICANGLASIA, AZTLAN ANGLO ASIA . . .

It had been a while since I had read Cassandra's journal. What would be the next entry?

"Take the road to San Pedro," Frida said.

Without hesitation, I took Frida's advice. San Pedro was west and that meant the beach, and Newport was there.

The traffic abruptly slowed to twenty miles per hour and came to a crawl. Cars streamed off at "Coliseum," "USC," "Natural History Museum," and "California Science Center" exits.

Frida smiled. She placed her hand on my right leg. Her lips glowed bright orange. I was just beginning to respond when her face splintered into the red stoplights ahead. Traffic didn't move. The drivers around me were Black. They were stopped, honking their horns at some homeless up ahead. Suddenly, a Black man casually pushed a grocery cart across the freeway. "Oh, my God," I whispered from the bucket seat of Mark's car.

A naked woman zigzagged behind him. She seemed to be trying to catch up to him. But she couldn't walk straight. She would stop and start, trying to make her way across the freeway. The man with the cart stopped directly before me. He looked at me and nodded his head. The lady caught up to him and they both darted across the last lane and rambled along the side screaming at each other. Cars honked and drivers yelled,

"Get your nigger ass off the road!"

"I'll take her, boy."

The passenger-side door of a car opened. The man and the naked woman argued with the driver as we all moved along the freeway at a snail's pace.

"Come on baby, come over here!" Two men in a truck laughed and waved to the couple.

Soon, the man with the grocery cart and the naked woman had disappeared into the green shrubbery along the embankment. The men in the truck looked over at me and moved ahead.

Cars began to move faster and, shortly, Frida and I were going at seventy-five miles per hour. Speed counts in America. Inglewood, Hawthorne, Gardena, Compton, the inner city, urban-mesh Black, Latino, Asian, Anglo lost cities abandoned long ago by disillusioned White people who ran away to secure the American dream, stabilize utopia in the surrounding counties. However, in reality, how many times can utopia be constructed in a lifetime? Utopia, a concept fated to instant and eternal failure. In México we have *las ciudades perdidas*, the lost cities created from naught and continually improved by the ingenuity of Mexicans. Here in Los Ángeles, the opposite transpires. Once the models of White urbanism, the inner cities are now the forsaken citadels of deterioration, abdicated to the colored and ethnic poor. *"Estoy pensando como socióloga"*.

Frida and I passed the connection to the 91 freeway, east.

"Oh, shit! *¿Ahora qué?*"

Frida shrugged her shoulders, *"¿Yo que sé? Este mundo tuyo lo encuentro algo aburrido. Un poco como los murales de mi querido Diego. La misma historia que se repite, de un lado a otro. Sólo hay que ver la totalidad para saber dónde nos encontramos"*.

"¡*El 405* San Diego South!" I shouted. That freeway would get us home to Newport. There were fewer cars, more space. Our speed was eighty miles. I slowed to seventy, and still, others sped ahead. The "SPEED LIMIT 55" signs were only warnings, reminders of the danger of speed. But seventy was too slow, and that was going to get us killed! Well, at least one of us. In twenty minutes we zoomed by Fountain Valley, South Coast Plaza, and then a welcome sight: the 55 to Riverside or Costa Mesa and then further south to Newport Beach. In a few minutes I would park, and as I took the exit, Frida tactfully vanished. I was confident she would return.

I quietly entered the condo. The kitchen clock read eleven thirty in the morning. I opened the *Thomas Guide for Los Angeles & Orange Counties,* which I had studied a few times. Los Angeles County looked like a profile photograph of an infected breast, a deformed protruding testicle, a truncated and stubbed maimed penis, with red freeway arteries forming a web through and above the flesh just under the skin of the counties. I poured a glass of water from the faucet. I had traveled some of those veins, kind of a voyage through the center of the body, through what a TV news program described as "the killing fields of America."

Mark worked in the study completely oblivious to my arrival. I wondered how long he had been writing. He suffered and tortured himself by writing, in hopes of hitting the big novel, like winning *el premio gordo* in the lottery. Some folks enjoy pain—I know that for a fact.

He turned toward me and, while I was seated, he put his arms around my waist, moaned like a child, and kissed my tummy.

"Where have you been?"

I turned the lights off and coaxed him down to the rug.

A crash woke us at two in the morning. Then another loud bang came a few minutes after, and screaming confirmed that our neighbors Jack and Jill were in a fight.

"Why at this hour? Now is a terrible time to have a fight," Mark whined. He rolled over and cuddled around me on the rug of the study.

After a hard slam against the wall, a dull heavy thud on the floor, and silence, I then heard a painful groan and the sound of someone crawling. I threw a blanket over Mark, slid into my jeans, and went to my neighbors.

The door was open. I walked into the living room from where I could see Jill sitting on the bedroom floor against the wall, her blouse covered in blood. She held her nose. Her hands concealed most of her face.

"Why can't you understand? We have very little money. We can't put more into the bookstore and expect to keep the condo or to eat, Jack!"

Jack walked into view with a bloody wet towel over his mouth. "Fuck! Why did you throw that damn hardback dictionary? Why not a paperback?" Jack smiled and dabbed at his split lip.

"*¿Por qué?* Why do you do this?" I asked, frustrated and angry. On the dresser next to Jill, I noticed two stacks of about twenty-five boxes of ammunition. I got closer to Jill and confirmed that they were .38 and .45 cartridges. I helped Jill stand.

"Did he hit you?"

"No, we were in a talking-cure mode, arguing and wrestling, and I flew into the wall. It's a damn game that our psychoanalyst, Jack Lacan, prescribes," Jill said.

"Careful, not too much pressure," I said.

She toweled her nose and mouth, cleaning the blood.

"Psychoanalyst treatment?"

"Yep. If we didn't play the game, we'd probably kill one another," Jill said looking into a mirror.

"Shit! I think it's broken, Jack!"

"Well, we'll just do what we did last time. Here, let me have a look at that cute nose of yours." Jack walked Jill to the wall. He made her sit with her back against it. With his left hand, he pushed her head and proceeded to stick his pinky finger up her nostril.

"That should fix it."

"Crap! That hurt! Damn it, Jack, did Chucho go out?"

I followed Jill into the kitchen.

"Do you want a drink, J. I.?" Jill asked as she handed a beer to Jack, who had returned from outside with their dog.

"I'm not going to give up the store. I'm not going to close it down."

"How are you going to keep it open or buy books? It's a lost cause, Jack."

"No, I'm not going to fail. Not yet. There's got to be a way." Jack popped open a beer and said, "J. I., you want to invest in a struggling bookstore?"

"I don't have money."

"How about Rebecca? She's rolling in the money she makes from Mexicans."

"I don't have money, Jack."

"Well, shit, you're no help. Then why don't you go and leave us alone." Jack gulped his beer and grabbed another out of the refrigerator.

"Come on, Jack, knock that off. Don't you see? J. I. cares about us!"

Jill hugged me as I started for the door. She whispered, "Don't go. Stay."

"It's late. I must go. Please keep it down and don't hurt yourselves."

That morning I got up again at four thirty, and the Ekkersons' lights were still on. I saw them going in and out of the bedroom. After breakfast, which Mark made, I walked outside. Jack and Jill were in the front playing with Chucho. Jack went inside and came out with two large boxes to load into the truck. They took Chucho and drove off, not noticing me.

I checked their door to make sure it was locked and found a cloth tag that seemed to have been torn away from a garment. I could barely make out the name "Don" in the trademark.

Mrs. Dougherty, the Mayas, and I drove on Silverado Canyon Road and almost to the end we came to a dirt path marked by a battered iron sign that was placed there, according to Mrs. Dougherty's notepad, at the turn of the century. The Mayas' excited children seemed to know where we were headed. An old sign had its share of bullet holes but even so the words appeared clearly: "The Dougherty's Twist."

We turned and followed a twisting dirt road around the mountain to an isolated valley, where we stopped before an oddly shaped house made of stone, adobe, brick, and wood. The style of the building had a sense of grandeur, formality, and genius.

Far off, at the vortex of the valley, an imposing modern greenhouse, a cabin, and, at the base of the mountain stood what looked like a chapel. As soon as the car stopped, Jay and Fay ran to the corrals for five horses. The children were thrilled and spoke to Ray, who then asked May a question. May made signs to Mrs. Dougherty. "Yes, yes, yes," she said and made a galloping gesture. "Yes. Yes." The children ran to the corral.

Mrs. Dougherty wrote:

My husband and I built this place, a long time ago. There is no sweeter sound than children's voices at play, even if you can't hear or understand them. It's just a delight to share in their joy.

Mrs. Dougherty pointed to the greenhouse: "Yes, yes, yes."

"Vamos a la casa de vidrio," May said.

We all walked behind Mrs. Dougherty, like a line of ducks. She led us by a well-organized vegetable garden, and a dilapidated chicken coop filled with a variety of hens and roosters. I laughed at the noisy ducks, the squabbling geese, and the proper quail crossing our path on our way to the greenhouse.

The sun reflected sharply off the large aluminum tank. An encased motor's sound caught my attention. "Well Pump" was written in red lettering on the bright container's padlocked door.

Suddenly the greenhouse's two doors flung open. A tall woman came out to embrace Mrs. Dougherty.

"Hello, Mrs. Dougherty!" the woman yelled.

"Yes, yes." Mrs. Dougherty was all smiles.

"May! How's the English coming? Not good, huh?" She shook her head in disapproval. "Keep trying. Don't give up!"

The woman acknowledged me with a smile.

The children on horseback came towards us. They were guided by Ray and a man wearing a black cowboy hat. Each had his or her own horse. Jay and Fay grinned from ear to ear and rode proudly by us.

"You guys look great. Pretty soon you'll have those horses galloping. Be careful, and listen to Rufino." The woman glanced at me again.

"Mrs. D, you brought a friend. Hi, I'm Lea, Lea Durk. I've worked for the Doughertys for years. When Mr. Dougherty passed away, I stayed here at Dougherty's Twist. This is the main operation. From here we distribute orchids all over California."

Lea and I were alone. Mrs. Dougherty and May were inside the greenhouse.

"Come on, I'll show you the ranch. Mrs. D doesn't bring people around here unless she really likes them."

Lea walked me to the back of the greenhouse. "Twist's Nursery" and several orchids were painted on the sides of three vans and on a pickup truck parked in a garage connected to the structure.

From a rise, in a field of wild flowers, Lea pointed to the chapel. "Right over there, Mr. Dougherty and Twist are buried. Well, not exactly buried."

"Twist?"

"Yea, Twist, their daughter. She and Mr. Dougherty drowned right back there, behind the chapel, in the creek, about thirty years ago now.

It rained like hell. The water rose to about ten feet and overflowed the area where they had built their first home. Mrs. Dougherty was at the Santa Ana house and couldn't get in; the road washed away, flooded out. The current was so strong that it took the house, Mr. Dougherty, and Twist. They found his jacket, a shoe, and a doll that Twist always carried. Those objects are buried right here."

Lea pointed to two simple gravestones, the only evidence that Mr. Dougherty and Twist had lived and died nearby.

"Their bodies were not recovered. The Natives and Mexicans believe their souls roam the valley trying to attract people's attention to their remains. If they are never found, their spirits will wander the area for eternity."

My sight roamed the valley into the sporadic patches of wild oak trees, over the fields of grass and shrubs and wild flowers on the hills. Along the creek, I kicked over stones hoping that maybe I would find a bone to give their spirits a little peace.

"Right there is Rufino's cabin. Mr. Dougherty hired him about forty years ago. His wife, Chac, takes care of the house, and she cooks. You'll taste her gourmet feast shortly."

Lea's muscular arms opened a heavy fence gate.

"Milking cows, steer. Over there in that corral we keep two bulls. Grazing on the other side of the hill we have horses. We used to forage a lot more animals, but the damn county politicians are cutting back what we can raise out here. Even so, they still leave us pretty much alone. Nobody comes out here, not even the county sheriff.

"A while back, I shot at one of Orange County's fine sheriffs. It was dusk. I was rounding up some cattle. Came over the hill there and saw this fellow, all curled up with some gal in the backseat of the police car. She was crying and moaning and he was working away at her. I sat there on top of my horse, and watched them for some time. Their wet arms, legs, and bodies moved and moved. They made me think of two fat rattlesnakes sliding round and over one another. It was the noisiest and funniest maneuvering I've ever seen and heard.

"I fired twice to get their attention and fired twice more to scare the passion out of them. That sheriff fellow rolled out of his police car, his pants around his ankles. Before he realized what had happened, I took his gun from the front seat. The woman ran away towards the main road. I fired at his feet. I noticed then that the man was petrified standing there with his hands high, his shorts and khakis at his feet. He had shriveled down to a scared little peanut. All I could see move were the tears streaming down his cheeks. With the rifle barrel I nudged him into the car, made him unlock and give up the shotgun, and pointed to the road he patrolled. I fired twice more just to remind him where I was. I expected the whole Orange County Sheriff's Department here in a matter of hours, but no one ever returned. The next day came and went, and still no sheriff. Funny thing, I never said a word to him. There's the rifle right up there on the rack."

The sheriff's county-issued shotgun rested on the wall with Lea's collection of assorted weapons. In Lea's gunroom I counted at least one hundred rifles and shotguns, and about fifty handguns.

"I added this special room to the house myself."

We had not gone in the front entrance but a side door. I followed her through a series of hallways. Finally, we came to a living area at the center of which was a massive brown and gray stone fireplace. Mrs. Dougherty and May folded "Twist's Orchids and Nursery" newsletters and placed them into catalogues.

"We'll have dinner as soon as Rufino, Ray, and the kids come back. They're great kids, aren't they? I'm hungry, aren't you? I'm sorry, I've been talking all this time and I didn't get your name."

"J. I., J. I. Cruz."

Lea reached for a magazine and said confidentially, "Make yourself at home, J. I. Towels and toiletries you might need are in that bathroom right over there, J. I. I'll see you shortly."

Outside, Rufino, Ray, Jay, and Fay rode at full gallop toward the corral. Mrs. Dougherty came to the window. "Yes, yes, yes," Mrs. Dougherty repeated approvingly of what she saw.

White, lavender, red orchids in a bouquet bound by a woman's hands; an image transfigured white, yellow, green *alcatraces* tied to a woman who laid gifts of love on my grandfather's tomb. Mrs. Dougherty arranged an array of orchids around her husband and her daughter's graves. Lea sat with me and May as we watched the Earth turn away from the Sun, and into darkness. The rocks on the face of the mountain shifted. Coatlicue, our mother, before *la Virgen de Guadalupe*, moved her massive body, knelt, and prayed that her son would not forsake her people, that he would help the Earth return with splinters of light to push away the darkness.

May seemed to enjoy the moment observing and assisting Mrs. Dougherty. She stood up and sighed, then came over to me. In a matter-of-fact voice and in an ironically comical way, May recounted a solemn ritual, as if it unfolded before us, creating a very funny image and situation in my mind. I could not hold back the laughter that rushed to my mouth. She made an effort to speak English and I tried to understand her.

"*Nuestra costumbre es que,* after five years, *la familia* take remains of our loved ones *a la casa de Dios.* We go, *el padrecito o los ancianos del pueblo también,* and dig up the box from the cemetery. *Primero,* the village undertaker ask the family '*¿Cómo quiere al difunto? ¿Cremado, en cachos, o en huesos enteros? Si la familia pide cenizas, el funerario lo crema allí mismito y coloca* the ashes *en una cajita de puros bonita.* If they want *cachos,* he chops bones and flesh and puts pieces in a box. *Si piden huesos enteros con carne,* they get bones *en una caja hecha para el* loved one, *pero así es más* expensive.

"*Mi familia siempre pedía cachos* because only a little left *de nuestros difuntos venerables, casi nunca con carnita.* My father only pay for *servicios mínimos.* No pay for the smoking of the dead, *ni por* little box, *ni la caja de madera.* My mother make a bag, *decorada con la imagen de nuestro Señor para los cachos de hombre, y otra con nuestra Señora para los cachos de mujer.* After the undertaker make a few cuts on the longest bones, *en esta* bag he put *cachos de mi querido abuelito.*

"*El funerario siempre estaba enfadado cuando venía* to our house. *Mi padre le decía que la iglesia es carita y que nuestros huesitos nos piden que ahorremos para la fiesta en casita. Queda usted invitado. Que Dios le pague con salud, larga vida y felicidad. El* undertaker *nunca se quedaba para la celebración y tampoco le daba las gracias a nadie. Montaba su caballo y se iba en dirección del pueblito.*

"*Tomábamos toda la mañana para llegar a la santa iglesia en una colina muy bonita* overlooking *el pueblo. Todos querían sus* ancestors' remains *adentro, cerca del altar,* close to God *mejor* for giving the family more respect *y prestigio* in the Church and the village. It depend on our donation and how the priest consider our family. *Cuando llegamos* we find my *abuelito* is not inside. *El padrecito* choose a place under the rock wall of the fountain in the garden. My grandfather's *cachos* would be there for always. *Yo consideraba el lugar fresco y muy bonito. '¡Se van a sentar sobre él!' protestó mi madre. 'El abuelito tiene espalda y aguante para todo el mundo. Es bonito el lugar', concluyó mi padre. 'Este jardín siempre está en la gloria de florecimiento. ¡Está harto de flores!' aclaró el padrecito.*"

Mr. Dougherty and Twist's objects rested in a well-tended garden.

May looked at the graves and said, "*Aquí no hay* bodies, *no hay cachos,* no spirits." She raised her eyes and looked toward Santiago Creek.

"Yes, yes, yes."

May's "*Aquí no hay* bodies, *no hay cachos*, no spirits" statement slammed into my memory when I found Mark slumped over his desk snoring. He caught me walking out of his study.

"I didn't want to wake you."

"It's OK, I wasn't sleeping, just resting my mind."

I hesitated before I asked, "How's the writing going?" I tried to encourage him all I could.

"I can't get beyond *The First Chapter*. It keeps repeating itself; it comes back to me always the same way." Mark smiled under a tired and desperate gaze.

"The first chapter? All these months and you only have the first chapter?"

"But every word must have a meaning!"

"Let me see that chapter."

From the top drawer Mark pulled out a manuscript that was four hundred pages.

"What's this?"

"*The First Chapter*," Mark said confidently.

"But you said you couldn't get beyond the first chapter."

"That's the title of the novel. I'm trying to get started on a damn sequel, find an incident, a place, a person who will be the center story. Maybe I'll base it on you, J. I., on your life." Mark gave me an inquiring look.

One too many books have been written about me already, I thought. I had never shown Cassandra's journal to Mark, nor any of my writing. I wanted to forget a lot of that life in México, including Burciaga, and my beloved Carlos who disappeared and whom I never saw again. The home of my parents, Jennie and Sara, Endriago and Frida—that México I never wished to forget, but I needed it there, in Coyoacán. Here I longed for it in memories only.

For now, Mark was my lover, but that was as far as the feelings went. I didn't love Mark like I did Carlos. I would tear my heart out for Carlos if only I could hear, touch, taste him. The desire to eat, to devour Carlos, I didn't have for Mark. What Mark and I had in Princeton did not re-kindle here in Aztlandia; instead, the feelings I had for him slowly turned to pity. Methodically, Mark taught me how to leave him.

He had his hands on my waist. He reached up to my breasts. I let my pants slip away. For the first time, we understood completely that we shared our bodies like good friends shared two bottles of sublime wine.

Mark was my friend whom I pitied. Rebecca was my boss whom I admired. The Mayas were my people whom I respected and loved. Jack and Jill were random individuals who loved and battered one another. Mrs. Dougherty, Lea, Rufino were wonderful, kind, and truly interesting inhabitants of the peripheral world of Orange County, California.

This world was not only the world of the poor and the rich but also of the strange, normal, and paranormal. It was a place from which emerged a new lifestyle, a new culture, a space divided up into cultural niches, safe and unsafe zones from which and to which people run or avoid ever entering. Aztlandia, Orange County, an ambiguous area where movement and change were infinite—never quite finished, arrived, still, or complete; a point where the natural and the supernatural impinged into the happenings of everyday; somewhere in which borders were physical and figurative, and not only ran between countries, counties, cities, neighborhoods, but through the mind, heart, and vision. The Aztlandia borderlines had made its inhabitants into chameleons.

"There's a certain light shining in your eyes, in love, with your perfect smile . . ." The international beat of Shakatak moved me, dancing, twirling through space early in the morning in Rebecca's office. I had finished drafting several Guest Worker F2 contracts. What's-his-name had gone, and I listened to Shakatak and several other CDs from Rebecca's collection. I found a rhythm for different aspects of my life: Mark's love turned to friendship; Rebecca's immigration law contracts became

money; the Mayas displaced but adjusting, surviving; Jack and Jill late at night collecting and storing books . . . and guns in their apartment?

I acquired the habit of living between worlds, existing in a border zone that was radically incongruous, and ran through my language, music, food, dress, architecture, life, mine and everybody else's. Here in Orange County, in Southern California, in México, in the United States, what better place for a stranger? There are millions of frontier strangers living in the borderlines.

All the inhabitants of Southern California have become migrants just like the people, documented or not, who come from Latin America, Asia, Africa, Europe. They experience the same fear, uneasiness, and pass through the process of separation, transition, incorporation, and settlement that recent immigrants endure. The *gringo*, for example, who has to drive through a barrio, may feel afraid, unwanted, never really a part of the place, and often avoids it. We are all migrants in Aztlandia. We cross a multitude of borders every day of our lives. My God, Frida, you must be the one who puts these thoughts in my mind!

Mark puts on the radio and hums a tune in bed. He sleeps naked. I enjoy his warm skin pressing against me; he cradles me and always cups a breast, to assure himself that I am there next to him, my breast his security; I enjoy his feet warming mine. He runs his hands down my thighs and between my legs, slowly making sure that I am there next to him, my body his safety. We listen to two, three songs; he turns the light and radio off, and soon we slumber apart, cradled in Mark's lullaby.

Ekkerson's Bookshop had more volumes on the shelves, on the floor, and in boxes than ever before. It felt like a sort of refuge for those for whom books represented tangible proof of respect for higher culture. This association of texts with knowledge attracted shoppers who wished to own them to match their aspirations for a richer life. Jack unloaded two large packages of what he called special orders. Customers in search of intellectual companionship seemed to have discovered the bookshop. Jack struck up a conversation on just about any topic the clients wanted to discuss and always had a title to suggest; he treated them with great respect and acknowledged their intelligence. Whenever they made a purchase at Ekkerson's, they left the store feeling that they had found a friend in Jack Ekkerson.

Not far away, large warehouses, like Book Barnes and the other giant discount stores, boasted a coffee shop and restaurant and, yet, Ekkerson's Bookshop survived. Big chains wanted to destroy the independents and probably each other. That was capitalism. But Jack often said, "When the dust clears, Ekkerson's will still be selling books."

I jogged the bike trails, the river run, and the Newport Beach Back Bay: dreams come true for a runner who had contended with Mexico City streets and traffic, and the hills of Amecameca. When I ran to Ekkerson's Bookshop, I always stopped at the Daily Grind to have some cappuccino and talk with the folks who operated the coffee shop. I enjoyed the clientele there, but I especially looked forward to seeing a friend from college days, Alessandra Morales, my competition from Columbia when I was at Harvard. She was the first person I saw when I walked in soaking wet.

"The world is truly a small place, Alessandra," I clichéd. She was teaching intermediate school and incorporating film into her classroom lessons. She loved film, and we often discussed the latest movies and her independent projects, and, of course, I told her about what I was doing.

Occasionally we ran together and finished at the Daily Grind.

"Hey, maybe we've started a novel Newport Beach tradition," I remember Alessandra saying the last time we ran. She reminded me of Sister Antonieta, always one step ahead.

It was late in the afternoon when I had left Alessandra enjoying a *café au lait* at the Daily Grind, debating vegetarianism with Ms. and Mr. Generation X, Jane Kim, and Chad Lavin, real-life Douglas Coupland characters.

I ran the Back Bay, heading for the condo when I saw Jill walking her dog. Her face was flush and her eyes puffy. No question, she was crying.

"Nothing," she said, "nothing that you can help with, so please, I don't want to talk about it. I'm fine."

Jill and I were alone. Chucho wagged its tail, tugged at the leash, and sniffed home. We walked in silence for a long time. I was lonely with her. Jill's smile, her face, made me want to hug her. There was disharmony in her life, in her world, and I was challenged by it.

Late that night Jack and Jill had a fight about the bookstore. It was over finances again.

"There's no more money," Jill yelled.

"Don't give me that shit! There's always money to be had!" Jack screamed and walked out the door. I quietly went outside and stayed out there in the shadows, undecided on whether or not to go to Jill. Jack threw a briefcase and a canvas coat in the back of the truck and drove off.

I found Jill sobbing desperately, uncontrollably. I made tea and calmed her down. "What's the matter?"

"I love him and I don't want him to get hurt," was all that Jill answered.

I didn't know why I checked, but while she sat in the kitchen I went back to the bedroom and found nothing. The study was full of books. I noticed that scattered on the desk were invoices, credit card receipts, delinquent bills. I pushed the closet door open and found an arsenal of handguns, rifles, and boxes of ammunition.

I put Jill to bed and waited until she was fast asleep. At one in the morning, after Saturday Night Live, I checked the closet once more. I counted seventy-five boxes of bullets, seventeen handguns, and fifteen rifles. Chucho came, sniffed at the boxes of ammunition, and ran out. It jumped on the bed and curled up at Jill's feet. When I left, Jack had not returned.

Jack and Jill truly loved each other, certainly more than I loved Mark. With Mark's arms around my shoulders, I thought about Jack and Jill. They were rushing toward an occurrence, a great moment in their lives that I failed to distinguish. I didn't know what it might be, but what worried me more was that I didn't know whether I should get out of the way or not. We were all running, rushing to a cosmic meeting. It didn't make sense—cosmic meeting, *baloney*! Guns and ammunition didn't make sense in the Ekkersons' life.

2 | Prophecy

When Europeans arrived, the Maya, Azteca, Inca cultures had already built great cities and vast networks of roads. Ancient prophecies foretold the arrival of Europeans in the Americas. The ancient prophecies also foretell the disappearance of all things European.

—THE ALMANAC OF THE DEAD, Leslie Marmon Silko

Mrs. Dougherty, May, Ray, Jay, Fay, and I entered the Ralph's supermarket. May grabbed a shopping cart, and we marched down the aisles of food and household supplies to the soaps, detergents, disinfectants—Lysol, Ajax, and other liquid cleansers. Mrs. Dougherty refused to buy any kind of food from the grocery store. At the check stand, Mrs. Dougherty placed her cleaning products on the black rubber conveyor belt. The clerk kept looking at May, Ray, and the children, who spoke in Mayan.

Ahead of Mrs. Dougherty, a customer slipped her card through the cash register credit card machine. She turned and smiled at Mrs. Dougherty, who said, "Yes, yes, yes." The woman nodded her head, agreeing politely.

The Mayas were ahead of me and kept chatting in their native language. I noticed people looking over to where we were.

"What language is that?" I heard a man ask the clerk next to us.

"Sounds like Chinese to me," she answered and counted out cash onto the man's open palm.

I reminded myself that I was in Orange County, in a crowded supermarket, standing in line waiting to check out, listening to a Mexican native language, and watching people react to it.

The clerk who helped us kept looking at the Mayas as they talked among themselves while Mrs. Dougherty repeated, "Yes, yes, yes" with every coupon she placed on the counter. I simply observed and waited to offer any needed assistance to Mrs. Dougherty, but the opportunity never came.

From a thick roll of money she paid with a hundred-dollar bill. The clerk called the manager to look at the bill.

"It's fine," he said.

"You sure?" The clerk was skeptical and pushed the bill in his face once more. The manager nodded his head and waved to the children, oblivious to the loud language they spoke. May and Ray continued talking, and Mrs. Dougherty repeated, "Yes, yes, yes."

The clerk punched in the one hundred dollars and gave Mrs. Dougherty her change. "Yes, yes, yes," she said, and pushed the cart filled with cleaning products out into the exit aisle. The Mayas followed out of the check stand. Not knowing that I was with the group, the checker looked down while crediting the coupons and unwittingly shared a thought: "Wonder where those Neanderthals came from?"

I wanted to respond, but I simply walked behind the Mayas. I was not offended by her comment. Instead, I felt proud that I knew the answer to her question, which reflected her fear, and that I wasn't afraid because I possessed the knowledge she desired. I walked by with an I-pity-you smile. The checker was not a happy person.

Outside, Mrs. Dougherty had stopped her entourage and waited for the cars to let her cross. Many different racial and ethnic groups shopped at the market: Anglos, Asians, Latinos, Indians or Pakistanis, and Blacks strolled by me. Standing there I heard three different languages.

For Mrs. Dougherty the supermarket was not for buying food. Meats, poultry, fish, milk, fruits, vegetables, food products came from Dougherty's Twist. We all stretched our necks trying to locate my car.

Before us a parade of automobiles waited in front of Ralph's: in a British Racing Green Morgan, a senior citizen couple listened to Bob Marley's reggae music; in a Toyota pickup truck, five dusty farm workers listened to talk radio in Spanish. While Asian, Anglo, African, and Latino high-school kids in prom attire turned up Vivaldi on their limousine's speakers, a Black couple and an Asian Latino couple listened to *mariachis* atop a hugely raised four-wheel-drive vehicle.

As we watched the Ralph's parade of cars and culture, a low white convertible drove by slowly with speakers booming so that no one would miss Cold Mad Rat rapping. The deep sound penetrated my body. Mrs. Dougherty sensed the rhythm and moved to the beat. "Yes, yes, yes," she said. The Mayas mimicked what she did. We were a dance line heading toward my battered car.

The children laughed as they followed their parents following Mrs. Dougherty. May and Ray were being silly. A few people looked toward us, smiled, and then shook their heads. What's Orange County coming to? They probably thought.

Mrs. Dougherty tossed a city newspaper on the driver's seat. I glanced at a headline: "Wells Fargo Bank, Coast Federal Savings Bank Robbed at Gunpoint."

I remembered the heated Harvard classroom discussions about White flight, Anglos running scared when a Black or Latino moved into the neighborhood. I recalled the professor's lecture at the library: people shouldn't abandon their homes, communities, and cities; they should stay, guard their turf, and help create the world evolving around them. Don't be afraid, I thought as I smiled at some folks watching us pile into my car, stacked bags of cleaning materials on our laps.

As I slowly drove out of the shopping center, I mused that the checker was right: We were a band of postmodern border-region Neanderthals, just like everybody else.

A few days later the *Los Angeles Times* and the *Orange County Register* ran several articles on a series of bank robberies. I recalled the headline on that city newspaper that Mrs. Dougherty had tossed on my car seat. They published a photograph of the "Black Beard Robber."

The photo revealed a heavy-set man, black long bushy hair and full black beard, large thick dark glasses, wearing a black scarf, white heavy-knit sweater, and what appeared to be a London Fog raincoat. I zeroed in on the man's nose and lower lip, carefully inspecting the contour of every facial curve. The image of the Black Beard Robber stayed in my mind all morning until I got to Dougherty's Twist.

There's a certain life or level of life that exists, or coexists, with one's immediate world: it's kind of in-between the cracks, not completely public, nor private. If given an opportunity to observe, to meet the dwellers of that space, one will be tempted, if not enchanted, by them and their life. Lea was one of those inhabitants of the in-between who enchanted me. I wanted to see her again, her face up close, touch her arms and hair. It had not hit me until many days and weeks after I met her.

During this time I inquired about her repeatedly. I asked May how Lea was, and each day May's answer was different.

"*Está bien*. Lea says hello."

"*Me dijo que usted* go for to visit her."

"*Dice que* no forget her."

"Lea like you, go for to see her."

Lea's replies planted temptation and chipped away at my resistance to my desire for her. The sounds of her responses were coated with the promise of excitement and a tinge of lust.

Slowly, I drove by the place where Lea had witnessed a cop raping a woman. I wanted to get a good look at this spot of violation. Here, one of my sisters was penetrated by undesired flesh, forced to take into her body slimy semen. I marked the place with memories of violent defilements in Mexico City.

Lea's account of the incident hologrammed in my mind. I drove in the solitude of my body, entranced, while I followed a well-paved road. Screaming yellow lines sped to a dream world of isolation and peace, existing unknown, in-between the common lives of the majority. Getting closer all the time to Dougherty's Twist, to Lea's world, her house, I was drawn to her garden.

As I entered the ranch, Rufino waved. In his dark face he didn't carry a sense of newness, of present, but of a past, a history of colonialism. He and I dragged with us an ancient chronology.

Rufino, like Lea, was in a comfortable anachronism. They were unique curious folks living between the spaces of hegemonic existence. Their choice to forsake the newness of Southern California was the vanguard idea.

I parked before Lea's special entrance to her room of arms and munitions. Rufino worked in a cornfield about a quarter of a mile away. He had waved twice. I waited, walked around my car several times, and knocked on the special entrance door, but no Lea. His shrill whistle called my attention toward and beyond him to see Lea coming out of the canyon, riding a horse at full stride and waving her hat.

In the early evening Chac cleared the table and, about a half hour later, returned to see what else we needed. Lea excused her with a nod and we were alone. I was in the middle of the answer to why I had come to Dougherty's Twist. She stirred the fire and sat next to me on the couch. I was warm, apprehensively waiting next to her. I took a deep breath and a kind of relaxing fear exhaled from my lungs. I came here. I had instigated this situation, and was willing to respond positively to whatever she would say or do.

I wanted to be Lea's, like I had been Linda's confidante and lover in Mexico City before I was transformed into a saint. But it had to be her choice.

For a long while, we sat silently watching the dancing and sensing the warmth of the fire, and finally Lea said, "So, tell me about yourself." We talked late into the evening. In the early-morning hours we went into the kitchen, made cookies, and drank warm milk.

"You can sleep on the couch, or with me if you want."

At dawn at Dougherty's Twist in a warm, comfortable bed, Lea and I spooned like sisters.

My contact with Mexico City was sporadic. Once in a great while I called my parents. I asked how they were getting along and, of course, I asked about Jennie and Sara. The last time I spoke with them, my father said that Endriago had become a recluse in my house in Coyoacán. He refused to go out of his room or to the street. He ate alone and no longer wanted to help the girls with their school projects. The greatest worry to my mother and father was his health: he dangerously and progressively lost weight. A letter from Endriago that had arrived in the afternoon mail confirmed their concerns:

After my parents found out about Carlos' disappearance, they were told at first that he was killed. Once they knew of my involvement, they shunned me. They called me terrible names and expelled me from Carlos' house in Coyoacán. I have been living in your place. Since your miraculous departure, it is haunted by your voice, your footsteps, and your perfume. Your presence is there. I cannot live at your home any longer. Your mother and father, Jennie and Sara have been more than generous, but I do not want to depend on them nor be a financial burden. They offered your home for as long as I needed it, but I refused. Your father is the legal owner. It will be maintained in good condition until your return.

As for me, I must go back to where I originated. There I can live in peace, do penance for my terrible deeds of knowledge. By the time you read this letter I hope to be deep in the jungle of Chiapas. I am returning to the land of your grandfather. I will be with him.

Love forever,
Endriago

In the envelope, Endriago included an old photograph of a fellow holding the reins of a black horse. The man seemed to be smiling and waving. This picture was similar to ones my mother and father had scattered throughout the house. Photos! I had grown up with them but never asked about them. Images of ancient relatives whose lives, in my hurried day, amounted to a glimpse of a knocked-over unframed snapshot. I placed the photograph between the pages of Cassandra Arenal Coe's journal containing suppressed evidence.

 "Chicanos are discovered every seven years," stated the professor from the University of California, Berkeley, at a lecture on his theory of border metaphors as archetypes.

"Engage the border as a lived reality," he declared. "It is the daily relationship between you and the other; it is actualized as an everyday archetypical experience. Erase it and we will discover that it is hilarious and serious; it is what we make it." I remembered how he paused, looked around, and assessed the audience.

"Border is not a Chicano, *mexicano*, or government issue . . ." The professor's lecture began fading back into my memory while I walked into my office. Somehow that talk fit into the recent job that Rebecca had me doing. Rebecca, who was involved with several grassroots community organizations, the real-McCoy, gave me the task of contacting public leaders. Through my work, I had met many of the founders of these groups, or the followers who labored long hours to keep their groups above water.

Several parents who had filed for citizenship had saddened looks about them, worried, and with swollen eyes. In their interviews, I discovered two had lost a child to gang violence. One lost a seventeen-year-old son who had been in and out of incarceration since he was ten years old.

"*No me prestaba atención,*" the mother said.

By the time he was twelve, the boy had become a hard-core gang member.

"I lost control of him. He never was a little boy," the father said.

My feelings for their seventeen-year-old son were that I was glad he was gone. He had become a hardened warrior who lived by his gang code: "For my homies and for my barrio or die." This was the life the famous graffiti artist wanted us to condone. In the short time I had been in Southern California, hundreds of children and adults had died from drive-by shootings or gang-related assaults. They were not gang members. I had ceased to care about understanding the cruel homeboys and homegirls who killed in the streets of Los Angeles. Let the artist exploit the *pachuco*, the *cholo* and their victims, and make money from their misery and concoct a career in their image. Gangs, like drug traffickers, dealers, and junkies were all blight parasites, carriers of a disease that had to be stopped, cured, or eliminated.

I worked with the mothers, *veteranas* of violence, to try to save their babies, the preschoolers and elementary school kids, from drugs and gangs. Among these there were children who did well in school and were not affiliated with cliques. I realized this was the vast majority of the barrio residents, but the news media exaggerated the problem. Repeatedly, journalists implied that all barrio youth were involved. This stereotypical image of the Latino exacerbated already tense and racist attitudes in Southern California.

"Hey, come on, J. I., crime sells! Commercialism, that's the name of the game, that's what people want to see from Latinos around here. It makes money for everybody," said Manuel Arias, soaked with a variety of men's colognes and aftershave lotions, as he stared into my computer in my office on Fourth Street, in Santa Ana, California.

"Criminality at all levels of society supports jobs, police, prison guards, lawyers, courts, incarceration corporations, social workers, academics, and food, medical, religious, construction, education, film and TV, political systems and many more. Did I miss anybody? Along with violence, it represents billions of business dollars. We need the lumpen to justify our employment. Without gangbangers or immigrants, where would we be? We lie when we say we want to eliminate crime." Manuel Arias went back to work. He understood nobody listened to him.

Rebecca, hoping for more clients, encouraged me to establish relations with school, parent, and community organizations. I broke bread with Los Amigos, La Hermandad Mexicana, Alianza para la Juventud Latina, Parent Teacher Organizations, Mothers Against Barrio Slaughter, Hispanic Chamber of Commerce and, sure enough, Rebecca's hunch paid off: Her practice tripled. She named me her community liaison with a salary almost equal to Mark's. He couldn't believe what I was offered.

"It's because you Harvard types stick together, like leeches to skin!"

"No, it's because I'm worth every penny."

Keep moving and working, because if you don't, you will break down, cry, feel sorry for yourself. Remember there is nobody else to protect you: no daddy, no mommy, no Carlos, no Endriago, and no Mark to shelter you from rushing life. Time seems to go by too fast. I can't slow it down. I dare not stop to think about my condition because I'll feel the weight, the tightness in my heart.

This morning is cold. May in Southern California should be warm but, for the past week, clouds and rain have persisted. On the East Coast it has been the same: ice and snow. I read in the *New York Times* that Harvard, Princeton, and Columbia graduated on rain-soaked mornings. I've been chilly for three days. The dampness had covered and permeated completely my physical being and the world that surrounded me. I was afraid that I never would feel warm again.

 I parked my car in a sloping driveway at a home in Cowan Heights built along the edge of Santiago Oaks Regional Park. Plentiful rain made the grass exceptionally green and flowers abundant. The minister of a nomadic, nondenominational group had invited me to attend their meeting away from the Catholic Church where they usually met. They were considered by the local newspapers as a politically active community organization. I had met with them twice before at different churches in Orange County. One of their main concerns was how to counter the anti-immigrant campaigns directed against Mexicans. The vicious attack organized by Californians for Immigration Reform, which plotted for stricter laws, had intensified the xenophobic fear in the county and the potential for more hate crimes.

Those present I had never seen at any other meetings. These folks drove expensive cars, were successful business and professional leaders, the cream of the crop of Orange County Latino money. They desired to finance a counter-attack, to organize an oppositional dialogue to a racist strategy for the eventual and complete abolishment of Mexican immigration. Highly successful, they considered the growing Latino populations a potential market and financial source. According to Manuel's analysis, the majority of the activists here had made their wealth from the Mexicans in food, medical services, cleaning services, legal services, bail bonds, construction and education. At this casual gathering, everybody wore name and company tags. While we enjoyed a California Chardonnay, a woman dressed in a tennis warm-up suit said, "The more we prosper, the more the Hispanic population will benefit." I nodded yes and circulated through the group.

"No sabía que eras mexicana".

"Oh gee, I didn't know you're Mexican," a man said, with a tone of voice from which I inferred that to be Mexican was a disadvantage.

"They're having such a rough time down there, aren't they?"

I heard several times that evening: "You're from Rebecca's office! She does a great job helping our people."

A man, surrounded by male and female professional types who wore dark suits, spoke loudly and aggressively: "We don't talk the talk of victimization. We act from a position of power. Organize and act. No more asking permission from authorities. We tell them what we want, and we respond to achieve our goals."

The man paused while more people gathered around him. He continued to speak in an assertive manner.

"With all due respect to the Catholic Church, I'm getting tired of the newspapers, movies, and television presenting us Mexicans as a priest-and-prayer-ridden, idol-worshiping little saintly childlike people. Prayers don't define or defend us—money and resolution do. I don't wish to be a member of a church that asks me to pray to *la Virgen* and give her money. I want a church that gets things done for us. No more false hope and stagnation. Prayer gets in the way. It gets us sore knees and a bad back. *¡Y eso ya no lo aguantamos!*"

The man was yelling at two priests and three nuns who stood silently, filling crystal goblets full of fine California Napa Valley Cabernet Sauvignon.

Weeks later in La Guadalupe Catholic Church, a few blocks from Rebecca's office, I stared into the oblique desperate gaze of ten undocumented migrants pleading for sanctuary, terrorized at the thought that we might push aside their request for political asylum.

"Si me regresan a México, estoy muerto. Prefiero arriesgarme la vida aquí".

The man scratched below his right red-hued eye. His fingertip moved over his shiny face, the ridge of the nose, the slender mustache, the thin-lipped mouth, and the chin, his Indigenous features. His finger migrated through his countenance, recognizable in a changing, foreign place. Yet he could never control his visage totally; he could only give it up, make it not his, not anyone's. His native face a territory, his finger migrated that familiar and yet unfamiliar terrain.

I was a nomad, a migrant journeying across a constantly changing territory too great to belong to me, but which had consumed me and involved me thoroughly, making me cross a wealth of borders, making me live, develop skills of resistance, of survival. Yet, I always remembered México, my parents, Sara, Jennie, and Endriago, and especially Carlos. I existed with one foot in the Mexican culture, in the memories of México, and the other dancing elsewhere, tiptoeing, straddling frontiers like a teeter-totter. I should not desire a unilateral, unicultural, univision of the world, but a cosmopolitan, multiculturated, poly-identity nationalism. I ran with the latter, for in it resided my strength. Frida stood amongst those men; she claimed them as her lost children. It was Frida who dialogued with me.

It was Frida who made me realize now that I was, we all were, destined to live in a border condition. Now, I understood it as a magical space where the familiar, the undocumented Indigenous' face made an unexpected twist and became the unfamiliar, producing a strange magic space and experience which became more and more ordinary every day.

For months, I worked with this sanctuary organization, bringing in labor from México sponsored and supported by Rebecca's law firm. We were like highly educated coyotes, forming immigration law to fit our needs: the more she managed it, the more it became profitable for ourselves and for others; and the more flexible it turned, the more it functioned for our benefit. We were true effective cultural smugglers, law and economic shamans, multidimensional migrants who crossed every conceivable border in Southern California and made money by performing miracles in this habitually magical space.

Mark's office at Holy Spirit College lacked borders. It was a workplace of chaos and inaction. There were a few dictionaries and a thesaurus on his desk. That was all. He compensated for the lack of completion, the failure of bringing a project to fruition, to a publishable end, by having thousands of pages of his writing on the floor: mounds of research notes, chapters of novels, short stories, academic essays and memos, books, and articles everywhere. The walls were plastered with posters and reminders to himself, many entitled "Things to Do Today."

Journals, unopened mail, and uncorrected papers were stacked on his desk. He worked in a small square in the middle of destroyed trees, a forest transfigured into white sheets covered with lines of words.

"Rambling sentences. It's just a pile of beginnings!"

Mark placed a red pen on top of several midterms he had been reading and philosophically declared, "But I found the right one."

"The right what?"

"For my novel. My novel has the right start. The beginning of a story is crucial. You need a hook. You gotta hook the reader, J. I.!"

"You're nuts. You've been working on the same novel since we met. You're never going to finish. Let it go, Mark, let it go!"

He stood up. I knew he was angry.

"No, you let it go! What right do . . . do you have telling me what to do with my work? You don't know my work, and you don't care. You just fake caring. You're good at that, J. I. Why don't you just leave? Get out of here. Go home."

"Mark, I didn't mean . . ."

"Go home, J. I.! Go home!" he pleaded. Mark's anger was more of a prayer now. He grabbed the exams and threw them at me.

"If you screw those up, you'll have to give a remake—that or all A's." I tried to make a joke.

"Go home. You fucked up our relationship. Don't you understand? I don't need you here. Thank you!"

"Mark, calm down!"

"I will, as soon as you leave."

"I'll leave, but I'm not going home. I'm not ready."

"That's OK, J. I., you can do whatever-the-fuck you want. Just go for now!"

 Driving had become therapy. I drove for a while, sailing the freeway concrete transportation currents. Moving constantly at variable rates of speed towards Riverside, Los Ángeles, San Pedro, Anaheim, Santa Ana. I finally ended up in Tustin, in a Catholic church on Sycamore Street. The place was empty. I sat with my friends, the holy icons. I must have prayed; it was automatic for me to do it when I was down.

Next I drove to Santa Ana, to the Guadalupe Church. *La Virgen de Guadalupe*, Jesus crucified, the Immaculate Heart of Jesus, and statues of saints were placed strategically in the old sanctuary. *Ancianos* prayed at pews. Some did the Stations of the Cross, and others prepared to go into the confessional. They practiced archaic rituals.

Hope and prayer endured in church, while outside in the barrios they tore each other up. Young men and women shooting each other for the pride of their gangs. To hope and to pray were all they knew how to do. I had tried to organize them, teach them that along with prayer they had to act, question why the gangs grew more powerful. I tried to explain that with hope they should have action. Themselves, people of the neighborhoods, had to stand up to the violence. It was only a few who were responsible for the random violence.

The police were perfectly happy to watch the young people kill each other. The police were perfectly happy to exaggerate statistics, making it seem like the neighborhoods were infested with thousands of gang members and encouraging the belief that every Latino youth should be suspected of being a dangerous, potentially lethal gang-banger. The police were perfectly happy to keep Latinos in their place, in the barrios, out of school, unemployed, drunk, drugged-up, abusing and murdering each other. The police were perfectly happy to convince Latinos that they were victims of each other. The police were perfectly happy to offer modern stations for interrogation and detention, like the Catholic Church offering magnificent churches and altars for prayer and hope. For hundreds of years this alliance has not changed. It was time to stop praying and cuddling the gangbangers, the police, and the Catholic Church.

I thought of . . . no . . . I prayed for Mark and myself and for Endriago, and I hoped that he was healthy and safe in Chiapas. While the great star set behind the sea, I drove to Lea's house at Dougherty's Twist. I couldn't explain Mark's reactions toward me, but I didn't care anymore. Lea offered the house to me. She also extended her bed. Frida and *la Virgen* watched but refused to participate. For that night, I was Lea's sweet fortune.

 "One of the first expeditions to explore the Southern California area, led by Captain Gaspar de Portolá and Father Junípero Serra, camped near a river they named *El Río de Nuestra Señora la Reina de los Ángeles de Porciúncula*. One month later, in 1781, a group of forty-four original settlers and four soldiers founded their community there, naming it *El Pueblo de Nuestra Señora la Reina de los Ángeles de Porciúncula*.

"The first eleven families were described as persons whose blood was a mixture of Native and Negro with traces of Spanish. Some historians gave a more detailed racial census of these early pioneers, recording that the *pobladores* of Los Ángeles included one *peninsular*, one *criollo*, one *mestizo*, two *negros*, eight *mulatos*, nine *indios*.

"History recorded the establishment of a demographic pattern. Among these original founders of Los Ángeles came representatives of the ethnic and racial populations that would compete for the land and eventually have great impact, if not eventual dominance, on Southern California's culture. These settlers of Los Ángeles were an appropriate prototype and metaphor for the future, extending now into the twenty-first century.

"Chicano students searched for their roots starting from Mesoamerican civilizations and mythologies, and the Spanish-Colonial period. In their twentieth-century historical quest, they found Aztlán, in the northwestern Mexican territory, and declared it their sacred place of origin and source of their indigenous identity. From the time of the Spanish colonization, they saw themselves as *un pueblo mestizo*. Yet, understanding contemporary Chicano identity remains a psychological conundrum, a complex cultural mystery, a dynamic enigma that cannot be stable, resolved, much less understood.

"Defining one's culture, in the midst of a multi-cultural milieu, challenges us continuously as we Chicanos do a dance with one foot in the strongest part of our being, while the other foot steps into the coexisting diversity. By fixing ourselves securely in our mother culture, some in the first generation try to keep their balance. Living in the U.S. will dynamically assimilate the descendants.

"We Chicanos tended, in the past, to imagine ourselves as complete, possessing a clearly defined identity. Now, in the heterotopian cities in which most of us live, we are slowly beginning to understand the complexity of our contemporary struggle to maintain our membership in an ever-changing uniquely multifaceted group that includes our families' names.

"Regardless of our geographical location in the contemporary diaspora, Aztlán, where we live today, is our ancestral homeland that exponentially expands naturally to the north and to the east as our population increases. Aztlán offers us the comfort of a secure zone, an ever-present unbreakable bond, a steadfast touchstone embedded in our collective unconscious, in our shared psyche."

The professor closed his notebook and walked off the stage.

I had come to see Mark at his office but, at the last minute, decided against it and, instead, went into that Chicano Studies class. The students walked out of the small lecture hall where I had been thinking about my situation with Mark and listening to the professor.

No one smiled.

They entered a dynamic life, a constantly changing, never-able-to-catch-up culture in Southern California, where there is a sense of difference that makes the past and present the same. Sometimes events, experiences, and persons come back from the past to become strong in the contemporary moment. This coexistence, this multi-dimensionality of time, place, and people creates a magic-like space.

Like the first settlers of Los Ángeles, Latinos have returned, they have been reborn with their families. They have been a historical constant for more than two hundred years: always present, never recognized.

At the condo, I gathered my clothes and packed some books. Mark and I agreed that I should gradually move out. I didn't care much to fight over the place. I never considered it mine. It was Mark's, and I didn't really like it. His was just another one of the thousands of cloned condominiums and apartments in Orange County. Cloning was what made Orange County repeat, burp, or throw itself up daily!

Mark and I lived in a strongly cloned zone. From Irvine through South Orange County to San Diego and Tijuana, there percolated a replicated corridor that seemed to come from the same architectural gene pool. For miles upon miles, the inhabitants lived in buildings that were all alike: same shape and identical front doors. Often parents, and especially grandparents, were lost in the yuppie two-hundred-plus duplicated housing projects. The worst scares were when latchkey kids became confused and failed to locate their own homes.

In the midst of floating masses, rootless yuppies ran from growing ethnic populations and abandoned old Orange County boroughs to reside in exclusive fenced and often guarded planned communities, representations of utopian desires and ideal imagined worlds. They settled in created strange residential newness that, from certain streets in the southern area and from sections of the Interstate 5 freeway heading south or north, appeared like seas of tiny Lego blocks, repeated identical house boxes, covered with Spanish red-tile roofs. This was the fabricated, fabulated, constructed version of yuppie Aztlán's White-edge cities. They failed, also, to be amazed by the paranormal place they called community where they escaped to live. Satellite bedroom communities sprang up like shiny new hopeful stars just far enough from and around the ethnic and racial concentrations in the old Orange County towns.

But people penetrated the in-between places, all of the livable cracks in the clone communities. The poor found spaces here to live, like in Coyoacán, Mexico City, in *las grietas*, the cavern spaces that the yuppies, not even in their highest efforts at imagination, wouldn't consider habitable.

I stacked three boxes next to the door and closed my suitcase. I had what I needed for the week. Mark handed me three envelopes, including a letter from Endriago:

Chiapas es una zona preciosa. La selva es verde y libre y soy feliz en ella. Chiapas tiene mucho dolor. Los indígenas han sufrido aquí por muchos siglos.

Ahora, I have found the place where your grandfather rests. I am with him now. The people in the villages are growing angrier with the owners of the big haciendas. What the revolution promised to destroy still exists. The government does not help either. The Army makes accords to protect the hacendados' property. *Los indígenas* are abused daily. They have nobody to turn to.

They demand education, electricity, access to fresh water, medical care, and land. They want the simple basic necessities to exist, to survive, to be able to raise their children. The jungle is deeply magnificent and marvelous, but it is also dangerous and savagely cruel. I have found peace here, and every day I save a little for you. Please come when you decide.

Forever faithful,
Endriago

Chucho had barked for at least half an hour. I listened intently for a while and thought that there was urgency in its tone. Mark probably thought the same, since I found him in the living room quietly looking out the window. Chucho exited from the entrance of the Ekkerson's condo to the three Newport Beach patrols parked at the curb. The animal didn't threaten, yet seemed frantic. As it continued to run in a circle from the front door to the police cars, several officers attempted but failed to catch it. Its bark was persistent and loud.

As Mark and I observed through the window, more police gathered. In a few minutes, cars literally barricaded the street. It was strange watching red, yellow, bright silver flashing lights flood the area. I dared not try to estimate the number of cops that moved about in the front lawn. They were everywhere. A sickening feeling pounded at the pit of my stomach, a tension clenched my heart, fear seized my eyes, and I knew where they were going. Chucho barked urgently. I had the silly thought that it might hurt its throat. Mark grabbed my arm.

"The police will take care of the dog." He resumed his observation out the window as I phoned Rebecca and Lea to report what was happening. About one hour went by and they had not yet arrived. Probably they were unable to get through the blockade.

"What the hell is going on?" Mark appeared at the door. Immediately, one of the Newport Beach police officers, with shotgun in hand, responded.

"Don't come out, sir. Please stay inside. Get away from the windows." The officer was insistent and pushed Mark back inside the condo.

"All right. But what's happening?" Mark yelled.

"Police investigation, sir. Please stay inside." The officer closed the door.

We ran to Mark's study. From there we had a clear view of the Ekkerson's main door. There was no doubt that the police were planning to enter Jack and Jill's condo. It was only a matter of getting the SWAT team in position.

"Are they there?" I asked.

"Haven't seen them for days." Mark sat on the floor against the side of his desk. "They've gotten a lot stranger. Jack dresses weird. I've seen him, late at night, parading around in a beard, long hair. I think he even dresses as a woman sometimes. Jill yells at him and makes him walk in an odd way. He's nuts; she's nuts. Jack's gone crazy over that bookstore."

The orange-red shimmer of the sunset blended with the whipping and pulsating patrol lights. I went to the entrance and pretended that it was another peaceful sundown in Newport Beach, California. I walked out. As usual, nobody was around: no neighbors, no police. Ours was a quiet street. I found Chucho running to the edge of the grass and back to its door. It barked and seemed to be near exhaustion. I was able to calm it down and coax it into our condo where Mark waited. He let the animal in and, just before he closed the door, he muttered, "Be careful out there, J. I."

For I had entered into a zone of high tension, a magic space where overwhelming energies seduce and make people act in strange and unpredictable ways. I stood behind a tree a short distance from the Ekkersons' entrance. I was either invisible or the police chose to ignore me. Slowly, from the side of the tree there seemed to emerge a woman dressed in a black painter's smock and pants. She spoke to me: "It's me, Frida." She took out an enormous brush and painted dozens of officers and civilians watching the Ekkersons' front door. The SWAT team made final adjustments, put on their bulletproof vests, drew their guns, and set up their sharpshooter rifles. Two took several practice swings of the battering ram to knock down Jack and Jill's planburb entrance. At seven that evening, Newport Beach police silently took final positions before ramming the door down.

Abruptly, the shattering of the door blasted the peaceful evening as if a stereo were turned on full blast; shouting started at full-volume.

"Police. Search warrant!"

"Drop to the floor!"

"Get back!"

I thought I heard Jill.

"Let him go!"

Shots were fired; several officers stumbled out of the condo. Three of them came out dragging Jack by the arms. They struck him repeatedly with batons. Jack didn't move; he barely lifted his head to see me.

He moved his head once more, looked my way, and called out to Jill, who at that instant, with gun in hand, at the entrance to the condo, in plain view, heard the police officer order: "Put the gun down!" Upon hearing that combination of sounds, all the violence that had been written in Cassandra Coe's journal splattered from Frida's paintbrush. And between the memories and the images that came to mind, I witnessed Jill confidently and quickly aim the weapon to her temple and pull the trigger. I screamed as a cornucopia—a horn of plenty formed by blood, flesh, and bone—shot out from the side of Jill's head.

Bright red color formed a large Rorschach stain on the white entranceway and spread on the brick porch. Slung against the wall, Jill sat with one eye open looking toward Jack and me and, again, I gazed into the deepest terror. One member of the SWAT team grabbed Jack by the hair and deliberately turned him to face Jill, with half her head on the wall and the gun still in her hand. In the backseat of the police car, Frida painted Jack's face a deep pale gray, as if his heart had ceased beating but his mind and body lived on.

Police officers raced in all directions, pushing onlookers back away from the suicide scene. But they had lost control of the crowd, which numbered in the hundreds, nudging its way to catch a glimpse of the Frida Kahlo painting that surfaced on Jack and Jill Ekkerson's front door. It wasn't *la Virgen* or *Jesús* who appeared, but Jill Ekkerson who had technically and viciously blown herself out of her brain, out of paradise.

Photographers had not yet finished with Jill's body. Flashes of light revealed the faces of the people who stood around amazed by the carnage. Hundreds of oglers came to see Jill, who continued to sit for almost two hours until, finally, the snapshots ceased and several officers came carrying official Newport Beach Police Department blankets.

While the police carefully covered Jill's body, Rebecca, Mrs. Dougherty, Ray, and May came to my side. That night I was taken to Dougherty's Twist, where I slept peacefully in Lea's bed.

It was the third heat wave, when the temperature teased the 102 mark for three to four days, and, at night, it roamed the high seventies. Rebecca had not wanted to install an air conditioning system.

"The heat is going to last only a couple of days."

I remember her saying this, but Manuel, who was convinced that the hot weather would continue, persuaded her to install the unit. On one of those heat wave afternoons, I parked the car in the office driveway, sat for a few minutes, and saw Manuel through the arched bay window playing with Chucho. On the night of the day Jill died, Rebecca agreed to take their dog. It had now been seven months that it lived in the backyard of Rebecca's office. Manuel liked it at first sight. When they first met, he bought food and went to Home Depot for wood, nails and tools to build a sturdy doghouse. Chucho seemed content in Rebecca's garden with its new companion. Manuel took care of the four-legged friend like he took care of himself. Concerned with its hygiene, he bathed it twice a week and always made sure that his Chuchito smelled good. Manuel provided the animal with his own bottles of colognes and aftershave lotions, and applied them, like he did to himself, to different parts of the body. I don't know why he became so possessive of Chucho. Maybe it was because it was the Ekkersons' abandoned pet. Did Chucho remember, miss them?

From the day Jill died, seven months ago, Jack had been in jail. Newspapers informed that they had been suspected of eight robberies. The media dubbed them the bloodthirsty Bonnie and Clyde of Orange County. One reporter wrote that Jack and Jill had supposedly stolen over $200,000.

"They were fanatics, obsessed, but with what? Jack was driven by the fear of failure of the bookstore. He felt that the government only helped big business and ignored the small entrepreneur. They both seemed to like weapons, but why did they arm themselves to the teeth?"

Jack had the answers, but he refused to talk to the media: He shunned, despised, cursed, and deeply hated the buzzard-like reporters, the vulture-like camera crew waiting to pick a photo chunk from the dead and the condemned. Journalists hovered, in anticipation of any sound or movement, or a view of the cadaver. They waited for their juicy morsel of information or show of emotion. Jack resented how the news media glorified the criminal, and he wanted no part of that. Although he had no money for an attorney, he refused a public defender. Jack considered court-appointed lawyers incompetent paper-stampers who moved lives through the judicial system as quickly as they could sign the documents. Finally, Rebecca stood up for him.

Jack and Jill Ekkerson, the fairy-tale couple that did everything together and were never apart for more than the hours they spent at work. They were obsessed with each other, never wanting to be far apart. After the day's toil they rushed back into each other's arms. Sweethearts since high school, they were forever lovers. Whatever they did was for the other's happiness. Often seen working out in their Newport Beach condo, locals described them as an athletic couple that loved to run the Back Bay with their dog. What they enjoyed was bodybuilding, although, according to neighbors, Jack and Jill never tried to become muscle-bound but merely slim and strong.

Police discovered many photographs of them standing in body-builders' poses. In each snapshot Jack and Jill smiled. They were a young, happy, up-and-coming Orange County couple. Several enlarged images made the front page of the Orange County section of the *Los Angeles Times* and of the Metro section of the *Register*. One photo revealed them naked and smeared with what appeared to be blood. Another enlarged image showed a cut on Jack's forehead, and another featured Jill with a bloody nose. She leaned her head backwards in an attempt to stop the hemorrhage. In another picture, perhaps the oddest, Jack and Jill sat undressed, with blood on their faces and necks, and both touched a gun lying between them on the kitchen table. Their dog, Chucho, was in most of the snapshots.

Several TV news programs changed them from Bonnie and Clyde to Robin Hoods of Orange County, who stole from the rich institutions to protect freedom of expression for the people. This story was broadcast from Ekkerson's Bookshop as the reporter read from Jack's notes found in his desk: "The bookshop stands against the giant bookstore chains that ironically and subliminally smother out free thinking, freedom of choice, and freedom of expression."

"Jack Ekkerson," concluded the *Right-Wing-of-a-Dove* editoial author, "was an extremist, atheist, political intellectual, a throwback to the radical Marxist who believed and supported the overthrow of the United States government. Ekkerson's Bookshop served as a front, a means of laundering drug monies for the purchase of weapons."

The Ekkersons' condo was sealed off and searched meticulously by Newport Beach detectives. FBI and DEA investigators stripped the wallpaper and the drywall from the wood framing. They found guns, ammunition, $8,000 in cash, thousands of books, and a trace of marijuana.

I began to hear a ceaseless rumble beneath and between the great lifestyle of Orange County. It wasn't the Mezzacorona Trentino Pinot Grigio that I was drinking for early brunch, lunch, dinner, nightcap, and between three thirty and four in the morning, when I sat up in bed, out of breath, hoping that my next breath would come easily, afraid that my effort would be stopped at my throat, and I would wait for the panic to set in, and then I would pass out from exhaustion to wake up at six, looking forward to early brunch at eight, nine or nine thirty, shaky, struggling to uncork the Pinot Grigio, or a California Chardonnay, or any other that I or Mark had bought. I purchased cases of these, lots of them, drank, and pretended that Orange County was the same as before Jill went away.

Blood and chunks of flesh covered the wall. Jill's gaze saw me from beyond and her open hand tenderly rested on her upper thigh. She was gone, but I still saw how she had left. Daily, unexpectedly, her gaze produced the image of her death. The smell of her pain created the form of her body. Jill smiled beyond her coagulated face, teasing Jack and nobody else, and screamed: "Money wasn't the problem! It was just damn hard to be happy around here! If I tried, it got worse! It comes or it doesn't!"

At night the rumble beneath subsided, while periodically it was shattered by horrible screams, sirens, and mournful prayer chants. Mark slept, snored softly. I opened my eyes and found a mist floating in the house. A dank, musty odor of ancient stone filled my nostrils. A loud clatter approached and the intruder broke into my view as I whispered, *"Gracias a Dios, eres tú."*

"¿Quién más podría ser, niña?"

Frida's face stared down from above the bed after she emerged out of the rubble beneath. Draped with what seemed to be human organs and limbs, she moved closer and roared, "*Vengo de una carnicería en el* swap meet."

Laden from her neck down, she moved heavily and peered into my eyes and spoke again: "Mexican gangs, Asian gangs, and White supremacists, lots of slaughter everywhere I turned. Look at this big hand, see how well it fits your breast."

I sat up and moved away from Mark.

"I don't want those organs to go to waste. This liver is gorgeous. Look at these lungs—amazingly they're clean! This offal, these body parts are wonderful models for my art. If you want one, I'll paint it in for you."

"*No es nada más que un aviso de un difunto. Tú verás,* soon it will be clear as water," May added as a conclusion to her analysis. She opened the door to Mrs. Dougherty's house. Inside, the children ate a snack that Mrs. Dougherty made for them. "Yes, yes, yes," she pointed to a chair at the table. A collection of white chicken wishbones stacked on a plate caught my attention for a moment. I waited for some kind of sign that explained my dreams and inability to sleep.

The children stared at me as if they saw or understood what I was unable to fathom. They ate and looked up at me, as if they waited for the unexpected to occur. I always considered them to be strange, possessing a different . . . an extra sense, with which they observed, surpassing adults, unable to explain in words, only in looks or odd gestures.

I parked the car in Rebecca's driveway. Manuel and Chucho played in the front yard, on the green well-kept lawn. He tossed the ball, and Chucho fetched. Jack and Jill enjoyed the same game with their pet. Jack had sent a letter to me in which he repeated how painful his existence without Jill had become, how the loneliness was changing his insides.

"It's like my insides are growing and my heart will soon burst through my chest. I miss Jill. Help her. Bring her closer to me. Only you can do this, J. I."

I thought of this last statement while I petted the dog. The different colognes that Manuel sprayed on the animal were overwhelming.

"It's beginning to smell like you, Manuel. Why do you put so much men's junk on it?"

Manuel never answered.

"Her body is still at the morgue. Nobody has claimed it. They will burn it."

"*¿Cómo quiere al difunto? ¿Cremado, en cachos, en huesos enteros, o el cuerpo entero?*"

Nobody came to claim Jill's corpse. The police had held it for as long as needed, for autopsy, evidence, and tests. But no one, not even after her face and Jack's appeared in the front page of the newspapers; not a soul stepped forward, not even after Jill's body was televised in the local news minutes after the shooting. She had become fatherless, motherless, brotherless, sisterless, relativeless, and friendless: not one person came to cry over her.

"Don't touch her!" I screamed at Frida.

She had come for Jill's organs and limbs.

"For art!" she said.

That morning, after a restless, sleepless night, I heard Jill's voice. Her body had rested in the county morgue for months. Jack didn't have the money to buy his wife back. A letter explained that if he didn't make other arrangements, Jill was scheduled for cremation. The police and a chaplain asked Jack for information about her family. He refused to divulge their identities. Even Rebecca pleaded with him to tell her about her parents. He simply said no.

"You find out!" he insisted. "You and all your modern fucking technology can find her parents."

He abused Rebecca, but she still stuck with him.

"I don't want to get them involved. They haven't come for her. They don't want her dead. As it was, Jill's mother and father weren't too happy when she married me. Now look what I have brought her to. Look at what I have made her do. Nobody wants us or wishes to be with us. Only I miss her, only I can be with her! I want to be with her!"

"*¿Cómo quiere a la difunta? ¿Cremada, en cachos, en huesos enteros, o el cuerpo entero?*"

May's words returned on a very windy day while Rebecca and I waited for Jill's ashes.

Word by word, the story began to be told. In a time and county of all possibilities, the Ekkerson's tale amazed Southern California. For about a year, the police had been following a series of bank robberies occurring in Newport Beach, Costa Mesa, Irvine, Tustin, and Santa Ana. The Orange County BRAT team headed the investigation. The BRAT crew was like the Anti-Narcotic Brigade that my beloved Carlos had headed in Mexico City.

Lately, I had thought much more about my parents, my girls Sara and Jennie, and Endriago, but it was difficult to remember their physicality. In Orange County, like in Southern California, memories were produced continuously and pushed in competition for space in my brain. Remembrances were so plentiful that it became impossible to hold the important events and people in my life. Recollections were everywhere in what I saw, heard, touched, smelled, and sensed. Television, the movies, the ugly signs and billboards along the streets and freeways slammed memories into my brain. I tried to recall Jill's face, but I only had her ashes.

An avid book reader by the name of Rodelo, who frequented Ekkerson's Bookshop, had overheard a loud and angry telephone conversation that Jack had with a bank officer about a loan payment. The detailed discussion had gone on for over twenty minutes while Rodelo browsed. It was clear that Jack Ekkerson had to come up with $5,000.

Rodelo, who happened to be a police detective, remembered Jack saying, "You'll get paid! Since when do you worry where I get the money?"

Finally, Rodelo walked over to Jack and placed a book on the counter. Jack slammed down the phone.

"Hi Jack, how's business going?"

"Just great! I only had the giant book chains, and now I have to worry about the retailers like K-Mart and Costco that sell books."

Rodelo reported that Jack went into a tirade about the big chain stores killing the small independent bookstores.

"How do you survive?"

Jack ignored the question, placed Rodelo's book in a brown bag and handed it to him. The counter lamp highlighted Jack's mouth and chin. Taking his book, Rodelo noticed his nose. From that moment on, Detective Vince Rodelo started to search for an answer to his question.

Vince Rodelo was a local cop who had worked his way up to detective by working hard, testing well, and capitalizing on every advantage the job and society offered. The Tustin police chief described Vince as an intellectually curious cat who, once interested, never let go until he found the explanation that satisfied him. Because of his persistence to get to the truth, Vince had more enemies than he had friends. But none of these mattered much to him, because Vince Rodelo was always buried in his work or in a book of some kind. Vince told a local reporter that "enemies, friends, and holidays just got in the way of finishing a job."

An odd sort who kept to himself, Vince didn't have much of a social life: no girlfriend; a legal address still at his ninety-year-old mother's in Montebello. He stayed with her at least two to three nights and drove to work at five thirty in the morning. Also, he rented a small apartment in Old Tustin. The rooms, according to the local *Tustin News* reporter who wrote the story, were packed with books. "There was hardly anywhere to sit in Detective Rodelo's place."

Vince Rodelo wanted to help Jack. He didn't want to see the Ekkerson's bookshop fold. He began to trace its history up to the time that Jack bought it. Jack and Jill's financial and credit records were easily available to him, who discovered that they had reached the limit, maxed out, on two $10,000 and five $7,000 credit cards. They had $55,000 in credit-card debt alone. Just this fact sparked his interest in the Ekkersons. He followed Jack to his bank and, after Jack left, Vince showed his badge and inquired about the status of the Ekkerson's accounts. The bank was threatening to foreclose not only on the business but on the couple's condo as well. Vince had to find out the source of money keeping the bookshop afloat. He took it upon himself to watch and follow Jack. One day Detective Vince Rodelo got lucky.

Vince was alone when he watched Jack Ekkerson leave his condo at eight in the morning. He followed him to UC Irvine, saw him buy an hourly ticket and drive into parking lot seven. Jack got out of the van carrying a shoulder bag and walked to a men's washroom located in a portable trailer unit next to the School of Humanities' administration building. Vince waited outside for twenty minutes. Hardly anyone walked near the restroom.

Vince sat on a bench, fifty feet away from the restroom entrance. The person who emerged was not Jack Ekkerson but a much taller heavy-set man, with black curly shaggy hair and a thick beard. He wore thick dark glasses and a trench coat. He carried no shoulder bag but a notebook and a book. Vince had to decide on whether to follow the bearded man or wait to see if Jack came out of the restroom later. He opted to pursue him. He noticed that the fellow wore thick-heeled shoes adding about two inches to his height. Gotcha, Vince must have thought, but his hunch faded away momentarily when the individual reached the parking lot and did not get into Jack's van. Instead, he strolled down the hill to Bridge Road and got on to a Number 60 Orange County bus. Vince ran back to his car and caught up on College Avenue.

The bearded man got off at First Street in front of Larwin Square, bought coffee and a donut at Foster's, and ate and drank calmly. Vince began to have his doubts if this person was Jack Ekkerson. The man bought the newspaper and started to walk through the shopping center. Vince followed slowly in the car as the mysterious Black Beard, a possible student from UCI who had emerged from an isolated men's restroom, headed directly toward a Wells Fargo Bank located on the Newport Avenue side of Tustin's Larwin Square. Vince told the reporter, "I thought that this was it! I watched the bearded man go into the bank."

Detective Rodelo was able to observe both entrances to the bank. With his engine running, Vince waited and, sure enough, in less than five minutes the bearded man walked out the opposite entrance and got into a slowly-moving automobile, which he followed as it moved down Newport Avenue, turned right on McFadden and eventually onto the Newport Freeway heading south. The car sped up and went directly to UCI, to parking lot seven. It was Jack Ekkerson who got out, went into his van, and drove to Ekkerson's Bookshop. Vince followed Jack and walked up to the store at eleven in the morning just as Jack opened the front door. Vince went in and purchased *River Town* by Thomas Keneally and said, "I got here just in time, Jack."

"Sorry, I usually open at 10:00, but had some errands to run this morning."

Vince and Jack knew each other by name, but Jack never found out that Vince was a detective until it was too late. Vince walked out of Ekkerson's Bookshop, elated. He had found the answer to his question. He knew where Jack was getting money to support the bookstore. That morning, on his day off, he went into the Tustin Police Station, to the radio dispatcher and asked about any robberies. "Wells Fargo Bank around 10:05 a.m. today." Upon hearing the confirmation he needed, he jumped up and came down with clinched victory fists and immediately requested an emergency meeting with his commanding officer, the Bank Robbery Apprehension Team and the BRAT commander.

I never really wanted to meet Detective Vince Rodelo, but reading the articles, talking with the reporter who interviewed him several times and listening to Rebecca talk about the man, I couldn't avoid him in court. When we did meet, we both recognized each other as *gente con facultad*. I didn't necessarily consider him a traitor who betrayed a friend. He pursued a hunch, wanted an answer to a question. Rebecca thought of him as a detective of the old school, a decent old-fashioned cop. I saw Vince Rodelo as a curious person blessed with *la facultad*.

To visit Jack, I went through a series of screenings and a battery of questions. I saw Jack twice, and after that I was denied entrance because, according to the psychiatrist who assessed Jack, his state of mind worsened daily. Finally, he was put under constant surveillance in a suicide-watch cell. Soon it would be only Rebecca with access to him.

When I saw him for the second time, he seemed very nervous and jittery; although I didn't know how I could help him, the least I could do was to listen. Maybe out of pity, I attended to Jack, a man who about a year ago I didn't even know existed and who spoke in a language I thought I understood. Now I was completely involved and enthralled with his predicament. He spoke with the way he pushed his hair back, with his eyes, with the tone of his voice, with the luscious little smile he formed on his lips, those lips that Jill had, with tender unfathomed desire, kissed not often enough. Without words, he conveyed that he could not go on, and that he was resigned.

He explained repeatedly how happy he was that Rebecca was representing him. "Thank God she's defending me. The lawyers from the DA's office want me to plead guilty to the robberies and to say that I drove Jill to kill herself."

Jack, chained and cuffed, sat in a chair with his hands on the table, his fingers making circles on a piece of paper. We were never left alone; one officer was always near.

"Nobody ever came for Jill. No family ever claimed her body. No one will come for me either. I miss her so much. Please, J. I., do what you must with the store. Give the money to Rebecca. I doubt if you'll get what you ask for it, but try. Do what you have to do, please."

Jack wrote letters to Rebecca, giving her instructions as to what he wanted her to do. He never asked her to argue for the lightest sentence. It was as if he had lost the will to continue living outside prison. He had resigned himself to his isolated condition.

He described in detail the few objects in the cell, explained how the guards checked on him even when he was sitting on the pot.

Jack wrote me a letter:

In life we never stop shitting or pissing. Isn't that strange? You can lose what you love most; the most precious person in your existence, and still you will not stop shitting. You can lose weight, hair, you can cry for days, you can fall into deep depression, become hysterical, not eat nor drink water, and still your bowels will move. When it comes right down to the essence of life, it seems to be crap.

The guard often walked over to check on Jack, making sure that he was coherent and wasn't getting out of hand with his visitor. I reassured the guard that all was well. At times, clarity came to Jack's mind and he remembered Jill.

"I miss her so much," Jack repeated.

I tried to convince Jack to cooperate, to help Rebecca prepare his defense. Curiously, he never admitted to committing any bank robberies. Also, he blamed the police for Jill's death.

"If it wasn't for the cops, Jill and me, we would be fine right now. They killed her. They made her shoot herself. Jill couldn't, she didn't have it in her to do that."

Toward the end of the time allotted, he became weird and rambled on about Chucho: "My dog's a mutt . . . my dog's name is Chucho, . . . my dog never fails to wag its tail . . . my dog drinks beer . . . it drinks beer because . . . I feel bad for it . . . I never take it for a walk . . . I never take it for a run . . . I just don't have time for my dog . . . my dog drinks beer . . . it stinks because I don't bathe it . . . sometimes it doesn't eat, because I forget to feed it . . . I can go for days without talking to my dog . . . when I remember to take it to the vet, to avoid a fine, I give my dog the works, all the shots it needs, a flea dip, a bath, an anal squeeze . . . my dog, Chucho the mutt, wags its tail and drinks beer with me to celebrate . . . my dog drinks another beer . . . my dog's face is turning white because of my guilt." Jack smiled at me and waved to the jailor to come and get him.

"God, how I miss Jill" were Jack's departing words.

 *La vida sigue. Nadie y nada puede detenerla. Tanta gente vive ignorante de los sufrimientos y alegrías de los demás.* Life goes on and so does work. I was amazed that I finished what I needed to do. Rebecca leased a new vehicle for me. I selected a nice, practical four-wheel-drive utility truck. Lea took me off-roading at Dougherty's Twist. She was a remarkable driver. My relationship with her, Mrs. Dougherty, and the Mayas grew stronger and more enjoyable. They, in fact, were becoming my family away from my family, my parents, Sara, Jennie, and Endriago. I knew the girls were fine with my mother and father, but I often worried how Endriago was doing in Chiapas.

I continued working with several churches, community organizations, people and families who were going through court proceedings, and still my top priority was Jack, who sat in the suicide-watch cell waiting for the legal process to move forward. Outside, life progressed at different speeds, but inside, a snail's pace was considered fast.

Ekkerson's Bookshop remained cordoned off by police. All this time some young people, in their early twenties, had been inquiring about the bookstore. They wanted to know why it closed, how much was the lease, and they expressed an interest in purchasing the inventory and taking over the space.

Five young people and their friends waited to see the store on the first day the police barrier tapes came down and the first day I was able to enter. These youth called the landlord and by three that afternoon he and the new entrepreneurs had struck a deal.

Rebecca had warned me that the landlord had rights to the entire inventory since Jack owed rent and could not meet these obligations.

The young folks signed a one-year lease, with a two- or three-year option, plus a possibility to purchase the building, with no personal guarantee required. In two weeks those new owners transformed Ekkerson's Bookshop into Newport Beach Books and Java.

Rebecca explained to Jack the fate of the store.

"A group of entrepreneurs, very young, took over your store and made it into a coffee-shop bookstore."

Jack seemed content with the news.

"At least it didn't disappear. All that work was worth something. Young people are smart nowadays; if they can't get a job in the field they're trained for, they create their own work. Jill, I'm sure, is happy. How I wish I could be with her to tell her the good news."

"Jack has become more obsessed with Jill's death; that's all he wants to talk about. I explained to him that they want to file accessory charges against him, but he doesn't seem to care what they do against him and made no effort on his own behalf. He just wants me to know how much he misses Jill. No, I didn't tell him that after speaking to him I was going to the grand opening of his former store."

Rebecca and I walked into Newport Beach Books and Java. I didn't feel guilty. Sitting at one of the tables was Frida, being worshiped by some artistic movie types. *Querido Diego* waved from a cameo portrait in a hole in the middle of Frida's forehead. Frida waved at me while all her groupies smiled.

You can worship Frida
put her on a pedestal
tattoo her on your body
I worship nobody
I acknowledge the Mexican
or Central American working woman
sitting on the bus bench
at five in the morning
who cleans your house
who mends your expensive
department-store clothes
who takes care of your child

or your grandparent
I praise the Mexican
or Central American woman
who waits at six thirty
in the afternoon
for bus Number 67
I offer a smile
to a tired face
who nods to sleep
during the hour-and-a half ride
to a corner in Santa Ana
where she gets off
to walk a half hour
to her sister's apartment
I offer respect to that woman
who survives low pay
dirty words
pawing at her body
lustful looks
racist opinions
ugly gestures
empty nights
heart-felt loneliness
she is not afraid of you
she is the unseen
unrecognized crucial link
to your economic backbone
that you lean against
in the seat of your luxury vehicle
she is not afraid of you
no se raja
from her tumultuous
and burning dreams
she will rise again
never rested

with the dawn
to look you in the eye
mark your mind
and remind you
of your fear of her
leaving.

Marina, the Newport Beach poet, lifted her arms and applauded with the crowd. I was surprised how the people liked this *poeta comprometida*. The young proprietors worked hard preparing complimentary coffee, drinks, and desserts. I have not mentioned their names purposely because these youngsters are a story themselves. They had accomplished what Jack dreamed of doing. I wished them all the success, grabbed my coffee and pastry, and went to a table as far away from Frida as possible.

Rebecca and I were just about to sit down when a man holding a cappuccino and what appeared to be a tiramisu stepped into my field of vision. Vince Rodelo sort of smiled and without saying a word asked to share the table.

Rebecca and I shrugged our shoulders. "Sure."

It had been a four-middle-finger afternoon driving to Mark's condo in Newport Beach. Maybe it's the way I drive, but on some days I often have people give me the universal Orange County opinion sign. They reveal it through the car windows, others stick their arm out and extend the finger out in public; some maneuver their automobiles right next to others, make sure they're being looking at, and then flip the bird accompanied by a litany of the choicest words in the English language. I interpreted all this attention as good luck, sort of like finding a four-leaf clover.

Jack and Jill's apartment still had the crime-scene tag posted on the entrance and windows. Mark sat on the front steps reading the mail and, as soon as he saw me drive up, went inside, leaving the door open.

Mark had gone to his study. I heard noises as if he were dropping books and papers on the floor. "Look, five more rejection letters from publishers and agents! How can I get a damn manuscript published?"

Pages were scattered everywhere. I started picking them up.

"Leave them alone! The pages are worthless!"

"No they're not," I said softly, trying to keep him calm.

"What the fuck do you know about writing and publishing, J. I.?"

"I know that it can be dangerous. Look at the way you are acting now, Mark."

Mark sat down looking across the lawn toward the Ekkersons' condo.

"Two people have died, both committed suicide, and they were so close to me. You know, J. I., I keep seeing my student dancing nude on the tabletop. I can't shake her image from my mind at night, in my dreams, during the day in front of a class, in the shower. What I hate the most is that I think of her, and I get aroused. What a waste, a beautiful girl lost, and I look up and there she is offering herself with every movement of her body. Why did she do it? It was because of me that Carmen Estrada killed herself."

"Mark, it wasn't you. There were so many factors."

"Right, I was the stupid asshole that brought her to the brink, and it was me who pushed her off; it was me who hung her after that night at the bar, who sat on that chair and looked up at her nakedness. What did she think? That I was going to report her?"

"Mark, let's go for a walk."

Ever since Jill's death Mark continually talked about Carmen Estrada. He wasn't sleeping at night, and he asked me repeatedly for her mother's address—to see her, to atone for his terrible sin—but I refused to give him the information he wanted.

I didn't want to hear more of his self-torture. I needed him in a better mood because, ironically, I had come home that afternoon to let him know that I was leaving, and I wasn't going to wait much longer.

"No, I got too much work to do. I need to fill out these credit card applications and work on my book."

Mark spoke rapidly with a slight slur. I went to my room, packed my last suitcase. I had contemplated this change for some time now. I considered moving to Dougherty's Twist, but it was too far of a drive to work. Mrs. Dougherty offered a room in her house, but I wanted more privacy than the children allowed.

It was Manuel who gave me the idea to move to the office. There were several back rooms that were used for guests. The converted house had what I needed, and Rebecca thought the plan was great. In fact, she had been thinking of moving there herself. But, since I had asked, the place was mine.

There was also the matter of Detective Vince Rodelo, who had called the office and asked me to lunch several times now. Not a very handsome man. He was stocky, balding and had an odd sense of humor. Not good-looking Carlos, or tall blue-eyed Mark, but kind of short and heavy-set. Yet, more important than looks was that I felt happy and secure with him. Our togetherness was odd, sufficient, and fulfilling. What most attracted me about Vince was that he lived an uncomplicated life. No psychological hang-ups. His life was relatively simple and content.

My hands picked up the same outfits that I had packed when I left Mexico City. For those who saw me in Southern California my clothes had a different meaning than for those who saw me when I wore them in Mexico City. My wardrobe knew my history, who I was, what I had done, and that afternoon my garb reminded me of *la Santa Ilusa de las Grietas*. My garments resisted, begged to remain in a permanent place. Not on your dirty threads, I mused.

Endriago came to mind. I was about to walk out of the house, but I was unsure of Mark's reaction. If only Endriago were here, I would not hesitate an instant. *¿Qué me importa cómo reaccione este hombre incapaz de vivir? Me voy y ¡ya!*

"What are you doing?" Mark yelled. He suddenly broke out of his remorse for the dead student. "I need you now more than before!"

"I don't need you." I was out the door.

"J. I., I love you!"

Mark ran to the door of the truck. I locked it and rolled up the window. My final image of Mark Forbes was his face of disbelief wet with tears, his desperate hands clawing the glass as I started the engine. As I pulled away from the condo, he screamed once more, "I love you, J. I.! Don't leave me, please! I know who you are!"

I stopped the truck and answered, "And since you know who I am, don't you dare come after me."

I looked in the rearview mirror and saw Mark sitting in the middle of the street, sobbing. A sad sight indeed, but I didn't really give a damn.

Suddenly I remembered that I forgot . . . my mail . . . I made a U-turn, Mark's eyes brightened, his mouth dropped open and broke into a smile, his arms joyfully reached for me. I passed right by him, stopped in front of the condo, ran to the kitchen and back out the front door to my truck.

"I forgot my mail!" I yelled as I departed for the second time. I looked back again and saw Mark collapsed head down, like a child in a tantrum, slapping the pavement with hands and feet.

This time I couldn't help but laugh at the professor.

From the belly button of the universe, Endriago wrote:

I've come to Mexico City for a day and a night. Long enough to see Jennie and Sara early in the morning on their way to school. I looked at them from a distance. They never knew I was there. They are with your parents and seem to be doing well. How I miss helping them with their homework. The situation here appears to have calmed down. For a while there was turmoil after you disappeared from the public. Many investigators came to interrogate your mother and father. Today I watched people go right by your house, and they didn't even slow down.

My house in Chiapas is very simple: one room, a clay oven built into the wall. Many indios come by on their way to San Cristóbal. They say it is a shortcut to the city, but I think they come to see me, and they want me to see them too. I was told they considered me un fenómeno sagrado and felt blessed just by my being near them. I don't want this attention, but I can't refuse them. They are very sincere and reverent. I survive because they teach me how to live in this dense, green area. My home is like a cave of a hermit.

Day after day, I explore the jungle, its vegetation, trees, and flowers, its sounds beneath my feet, above my head, and beyond the treetops. I move through its ever-changing cool fog, warm mist, and astounding sources of steam; water runs everywhere here sprouting and maintaining life; animals, insects of every imaginable species are my neighbors. They appear unexpectedly at any place or at any turn. I once stared into an ocean of deep brown and green trees and leaves to discover suddenly that a large snake politely watched me. When the serpent sensed that I knew it was there, it slowly slithered away. The hardest inconvenience to get adjusted to is the bugs: great and minuscule, they can surprise you at any time or place. Some are grotesquely attractive and others are terrifying to wake up to. The indios have shown me how to keep the house clean of them, but still, once in a while, they come in to startle your Endriago. It's funny how I can't even scare away the tiniest of them. They surely are mightier than me, and I have learned how to live with them and not destroy them.

I have great news for you. The indios have taken me to where your grandfather resides. I am now his servant. Come and you will be surprised and joyful. I have learned to feel the jungle breathe around me, for I survive in its lungs, travel through its heart, see with its eyes. It offers peace: I accept and know that it will not devour me.

When you read this letter, envision that I walk the valleys and climb the mountains of the jungle, and I dare not imagine what wonder may lie beyond my gaze.

We wait for you.

Endriago

Manuel tossed a ball to Chucho and it ran happily about the yard. The animal had adjusted well to its new home and wagged its tail at the sight of a new master. I observed it from one of the back rooms that I had converted into a place to sleep and work. My move to the Fourth Street house and office space was therapeutic for me. It gave me my own private realm in which to think and write. Rebecca stuck her head in my room and said, "I envy you and your life. You really don't have any responsibility, you know."

Out in the garden, Manuel rubbed perfume into Chucho's back, powdered its rear and testicles, and scratched the dog's chest until Chucho got an erection.

"Good boy!"

Manuel gave Chucho a biscuit. He more than enjoyed Chucho following its new master into the office.

Mark had not tried to see me but called several times, and we talked. He had located Carmen's mother's address and said that he was going to see her.

"You should leave her alone, Mark. She can report you to the police," I warned him.

"She will see me, and she will forgive me, I'm sure she will."

I hadn't heard from Mark since that conversation.

I made a cup of coffee and walked to the front of the house. Cars rushed up and down Fourth Street to Grand Avenue, to the Newport freeway. In Orange County, the population never rested, always rushing to or away from a place or a person; folks feared the in-between because it was the place of the uncanny, the marvelous, the spiritual, where loving cherubs and fearful, terrifying creatures resided.

While I sipped my coffee, Rebecca stepped into a monitored meeting room with Jack. His eyes were swollen, as if he had cried for days.

"I miss her. I can't help it!" he cried.

"Here's the list of what's in the condo."

"Sell it all, give it away, burn it if you must. I don't need it anymore." He spoke with tears running down his face.

"Of course, just as you instructed. The estate sale is set for tomorrow."

"Jill and I were married at the end of this month," Jack mumbled, stood up, and shuffled away.

"Don't you want to talk about the court appearance?"

"Not today, maybe next week."

"We don't have much time."

"I'm sure."

Children walked home from Remington Elementary School, only a block away. They were so funny. Sara and Jennie were older than these kids. The Mayas' teens, Jay and Fay, were closer to Sara and Jennie's age. Mrs. Dougherty still refused to let them attend the local school. She insisted on a home-teaching program, but didn't want a teacher. She demanded that May educate them on the basic skills.

But, materials were written in English. May asked for these in Spanish. Mrs. Dougherty wrote on her notepad: "English Only! English Only!" So, that was that.

May called me. I gave her reading, math, and social studies books that I got from a teacher at Remington School. I took Jay and Fay there to see Mrs. Morales, a pretty, warm, silver-blond woman whom the children liked immediately. I explained the situation to the teacher.

"They should be in school," she said, as she handed me five books written in Spanish. She accompanied us to the parking lot.

"Goodbye, children. You can come visit whenever you want. *Por favor, no se olviden de mí. Vengan a visitarme cuando quieran.*"

Mrs. Morales smiled and waved. There was a tone of concern in her voice, a slight gesture of melancholy in her eye contact with me.

Ray had completely taken over the operation of the greenhouse. Mrs. Dougherty oversaw him continuously, but as the months went by and he learned, she gave him more responsibility. Finally, she didn't have to instruct him anymore. To her delight, the day came when Ray rose and took over the orchid business.

To be sold at Jack and Jill's estate sale, Lea had sent Rufino with an old saddle, two pairs of boots, three hats, and jeans and shirts to be added to Mrs. Dougherty's two armchairs, one small sofa, knitted white-linen tablecloths, place settings, and napkins.

Vince and I arrived at seven in the morning. People had already parked their cars along the street, waiting for us to open the doors. Rebecca had coffee and pastries, and waited in the kitchen. She heard us walk in. "Can you believe that folks are out there this early?" she said and offered us doughnuts.

"It's the Orange County vulture mentality. Estate sales are always like this. They are not like garage sales, with odds and ends. In these sales, furniture, dishes, whatever is in the house is up for grabs. Orange-countians are always looking for a damn good deal. Some of my best books, first editions, I've found in these sales. Many times the relatives of the deceased don't know what's in the house; don't realize the value of antiques. What they want to do is, get rid of it all, out of their way; they don't need one more piece of junk from Aunt or Uncle Milly."

As Vince and I carried the furniture outside, people began to make offers. By nine we had sold every furnishing in the house, as well as dishes, pots and pans, small rugs, towels, blankets and bedspreads. At noon we sold Mrs. Dougherty's chairs and every one of her embroidered linens. Lea's saddle didn't sell, but her boots, hats, and clothes went one by one in the afternoon. Throughout the day the house was being stripped to the bare walls. Framed paintings, thousands of books, shelves, light fixtures were carried off along with even a few photographs of relatives who had never appeared nor come to claim Jack or Jill.

"Why do you want that photograph?" I asked a woman.

"The wooden frame is exquisite," she said.

Jack and Jill's clothing sold slowly, but by three we were making deals. All these objects offered up in an estate sale where nobody asked who died, who lived here, or why they moved. It wasn't a concern for the people who came. If they cared, they probably wouldn't buy anything. They were there to find a real bargain, a steal. Our objective was to get rid of the material goods as quickly as possible and to try to make a little money.

A young blonde woman bought all of Jill's new and worn jersey shirts for twenty-five cents each. She tried on a sweater that fit nicely. Jill's face, her strong muscular body came to mind, but only for a short while. The lady paid me and drove off in a new Porsche Carrera. Two others picked through the clothes: T-shirts, shirts, blouses, pants, dresses, and coats. They selected a large amount of clothing, some of which seemed new.

"How about $50 for all of that."

The two women laughed loudly.

"I'll give you $10, *ni un centavo más*," she slipped into Spanish.

"Take it for $50," Rebecca offered.

The woman and her friend looked over toward the two men who waited by their car. They seemed impatient.

"I'll give you $7 for what we have selected."

"But you did offer $10."

"We're in a hurry!" And they started to put clothes down.

"OK, $7," I called to them.

At four we decided that the sale had finished. We had sold all items except the saddle and a box of coats. Rebecca counted almost $3,000. That was the total worth of Jack and Jill's fallen household.

"Jack's defense fund," Vince said.

I was surprised that Mark had not appeared. We went back into the sacked condo for cold drinks and coffee, but somebody had taken the ice chest and the electric coffee maker with a full pot of coffee.

Eminent domain was the phrase used to frighten the elderly survivors of the old, upper-class neighborhood in Santa Ana where Mrs. Dougherty lived. The average age of the property owners was seventy-five years. Most had remained in their homes after their sons and daughters had graduated from college, married, and moved away. On her block there were five non-Anglo families—three Black, and two Latino families—who had bought houses within the last two years. Their moving into the area caused negative reactions from the older folks; some had even put their properties up for sale. Racism and economic prejudice was alive and well behind the Orange Curtain in Santa Ana, California.

"Once those low-class minorities start taking over, it's downhill. Schools, neighborhoods, parks, property values go down. I'm leaving while the going's good!" I remember hearing one of Mrs. Dougherty's neighbors yell out at one of the meetings Manuel and I organized.

According to the city of Santa Ana, they were all in danger of losing their properties to freeway construction. Now everybody—Anglo, Black, Asian, and Latino residents—had been threatened, and they had all come together to fight a common enemy: the Santa Ana City Council, the Orange County Board of Supervisors, as the State of California had declared eminent domain over their property.

The *politicos* had walked the neighborhood and discovered a well-organized group of senior, fixed-income property owners who lived in some of the most beautiful houses in Orange County. The politicians included the mayor of Santa Ana, several city council members, two supervisors—among them the fence-sitter Matty

Vasca—three reporters and a female note-taker for the mayor. The group started to walk with their civil engineer aides measuring sidewalks, the width of the street, and noting trees at different points. The Mayas waited and waved, motioning for them to stop.

According to May, the entourage stopped a short distance from them, consulted with each other, and then waved and waited for a response.

The Mayas waved to indicate they should not step on Mrs. Dougherty's property. The officials talked amongst themselves, then waved again. The Mayas responded by waving their index finger and yelling "¡No!" Finally, after ten minutes or so, two men walked toward the Mayas while the others watched.

A movie camera was pointed at the Mayas. Several people took snapshots of them as the group started to approach very carefully behind the first two men. They seemed to study the Mayas' every move. May looked back to see if Mrs. Dougherty was coming. She was afraid because of what Mrs. Dougherty would do. These people didn't know whom they were about to face.

The two men were five arms' lengths away when one of them called to the Mayas, "Hello, we are friends. Do you speak English?"

The Mayas, of course, didn't understand, but they waved back.

"Do you speak English? Where is your boss? *¿Su jefe?*"

"*Entendí que querían hablar con la jefa. Yo, para evitarles la batalla que les tenía preparada la señora, les indiqué con las manos que no*".

"Please, we want to talk to your boss."

At that moment Mrs. Dougherty came out of the house. She scribbled a message on her note pad and gave it to Jay to give to the leader of the group.

Matty Vasca read the message: "The only way you can take my land is over my dead body!"

Meanwhile, Mrs. Dougherty stepped forward. She reached under her apron, raised a heavy twelve-gauge shotgun, pointed it directly at the group and screamed, "Yes, yes, yes!"

The official entourage ran for cover. Matty Vasca and the mayor ended up face-down in the mud in the middle of a rose garden while some people stood behind trees and others ran to the back of the neighbors' houses, screaming for help and begging Mrs. Dougherty not to shoot. The cameraman was the only person who held his ground and continued to record the incident.

"Yes, yes, yes!" Mrs. Dougherty replied.

From where they hid in the mud or from behind the trees, from under cars, from behind houses, the *políticos* shouted.

"Don't shoot! We come in peace!"

Mrs. Dougherty and the Mayas marched in front of the house, repeating Mrs. Dougherty's only words: "Yes, yes, yes!"

A standoff ensued and nobody dared to move. Finally, one of the neighbors, who found one of the Orange County supervisors cowering in her backyard, called the police.

The historic floral park section of Santa Ana was surrounded by cops in a few minutes. The *políticos* scolded Mrs. Dougherty and asked her to give up the weapon. The Mayas, who were now in the house, could not respond to their questions and insults. The police wanted the shotgun, and Mrs. Dougherty responded with a note saying that, like her land, she would not give up her gun because she had a legal right to both.

Rebecca, Vince Rodelo, and I arrived shortly after the *políticos* and the police had created a SWAT team incident, a situation similar to the one that had killed Jill. After informing the officers who we were, they allowed us to enter the house. By nightfall Mrs. Dougherty still had her shotgun, and the *políticos* and the cops had retreated. It seemed as if the battle had been won.

While Rebecca introduced Vince, May placed a plate of cookies in the middle of the kitchen table, and just like on any other evening, the Mayas and Mrs. Dougherty sat around, enjoying *café con leche*.

I walked the house, checking doors and windows. When I returned to the living room, I found Frida tossing paints and brushes into a box. She grabbed the canvas and smashed her fist through it.

"*¡Cabrones, esperaba por lo menos un destripado para pintar!*" With her artist box and easel, Frida walked out the door.

As the days went by, Matty Vasca, the mayor, and the *políticos'* entourage showed up on the other side of the Santa Ana freeway with their tape measure and notebooks to walk the streets of an old Mexican barrio.

Eminent domain was the phrase pronounced to frighten the elderly survivors of one of Santa Ana's oldest barrios. Seventy-five to eighty was the average age of the fixed-income folks, longtime laboring residents of Santa Ana. The engineers measured and photographed the entire five-mile section leaning against the freeway. In that neighborhood the residents knew that they were going to lose their homes.

The *políticos* had come to walk the neighborhood to discover economically and physically vulnerable Mexicans who had resided in the barrio since the late 1800s. These old- timers had lived through the glory days when the men worked for the Irvine Ranch or the Santa Ana Sugar Factory.

Eminent domain, the threat brandished by the city council, pointed at the residents like a legal shotgun. In hopes that history, at least for a while longer, would not repeat itself, the old-timers of this Santa Ana barrio called me to organize them, to fight for their land and their homes.

These barrio dwellers, like *la gente de las grietas* in Mexico City, lived in peaceful social and historical obscurity. Folks like octogenarians *güero* and Carmen Muñoz, who built in 1947, were considered owners of newer homes, in comparison to houses constructed in the early 1920s. As they continued to toil with life's pleasures and agonies, to the Muñoz family eminent domain meant life or death. They promised to fight to the end. Prepared to shoot it out with the authorities, unwilling to run, they were prepared to protect their hard-earned land. To God and to themselves they promised that their residence, their neighborhood—where they had raised their five children—would not be another Chavez Ravine or Barrio Margarito.

They promised that there would be bloodshed here, that if they had to they would make a stand and die. They were eager for the opportunity to put an end to the legal pilfering of land from *mexicanos*. Alive or dead, the old-timers would be victorious over eminent domain.

Disappointingly, violence was avoided. Frida again left the scene angered at the lost opportunity to paint exposed blood vessels, organs, and flesh shredded by bullets. The battle was avoided by clandestine negotiations carried out by the city, county, and state with the old-timers' children. Matty Vasca benevolently allowed the barrio dwellers to remain in their homes for as long as they lived. Meanwhile the progenies convinced their parents to sign over the rights to their property. Almost everyone did sign. In a matter of less than eight months, it happened amazingly fast, the senior owners were relocated to retirement institutions, and the families who rented were moved to other comparable houses in the area. Eminent domain was swift and legal. In order to widen the freeway, *mexicanos* of one of the oldest barrios in Santa Ana had lost their land and dwellings: another sacrifice, another contribution to the progress of Orange County and Southern California. Rebecca and I had failed miserably.

"What do the *políticos* know? They are blind, ignorant of our historical and personal significance. They have all forgotten what we did here in our barrio: how we worked, how we formed our families, how we reared our kids, how we cared for each other, how we resolved disputes, how we made a community. To us this was not an ugly place to be condemned, but a neighborhood we loved and called home," Mrs. Muñoz said the day the bulldozers came to crush her house. With noise of shattering wood and pulverized cement that sounded like gunshots, *güero* and Carmen Muñoz hesitated a little before allowing their children to take them to a retirement home in Tustin.

As they drove away, in the middle of the Muñoz house I saw Frida standing with her easel, canvas, brush, and paint box, disappointed that another opportunity to capture her carnage images had not developed.

Vince Rodelo's apartment in Tustin was very much like Jack and Jill's bookstore. Books were stacked on every available space. I moved volumes of history, psychology, anthropology, myth, and culture, clearing a wider path to the bedroom, kitchenette and bathroom. Walls were completely covered with shelves. Vince had volumes on top of tables, chairs, sofas, bed, around the sinks, and on top of the refrigerator. It was unbelievable how he could live like this. I later learned that there was a somewhat standing joke at the Tustin Police Department that, out of his apartment, Vince Rodelo was operating not a bordello, but a bookdello. Witticism never bothered him. He kept reading as an act of revenge on those who teased him.

Vince Rodelo took copious notes about what he read, what he saw, people he met; he wrote about his impressions, attitudes, ideas about his experiences, his life. He was a clandestine, silent philosopher obsessed with contemporary life and culture, and he was also a poet. In one of his notebooks, open on the floor, I read:

Most Anglo Americans believe that it is a plain historical fact that the American nation has always had a specific ethnic core and that it has continuously been White. Immigration was bringing about a radical change in the country without precedent. The recent influx was much larger, less skilled, and more different from the American majority than what was anticipated or desired. The consequence of these new arrivals is that the population is rapidly moving away from that traditional White-racial and ethnic core.

White Americans identify ethnic groups as high and low minorities. In a popular coffee shop in Tustin, I have often heard them say they don't want their children to attend a school where there are low minorities—Mexicans and Blacks. These folks say they prefer their kids go to schools where there are predominantly high minorities and they can associate with them, meaning Asian or European Americans.

Vince ended this page with a final note:

This White ethnic-core theory reminds me of the Aryan race concept. We all know its deadly consequences. By the way, what happened to the Native Americans in this White-core theory? The author does not consider Native Americans as original settlers of America. He does not include Natives or Mexicans in his imagined community. The man's somewhat of a Walt Whitman, calling everyone south of the border "Spanish stock." Boy, is he running scared.

Finally, a poem:
Los Angeles County
Orange County
Two similar worlds
Like México and the
United States like
family members
who have interchanged
the future and
made it one

I placed the notebook down as Vince came into the room. I had gone out with him for six months, and each time we were together we found out more about each other. Slowly, with eagerness, we gave up pieces of ourselves. We surrendered parts a little at a time, a bit of my family history, a chunk of his, a tad of my psychology, my attitudes, some of his thinking, his ideas, a touch of my body, a part of his. When I told a secret, he responded with "I am a monster, too." I laughed and embraced him.

Paperbacks fell around us. Sitting on his couch, separated by books, I saw his mouth; he leaned toward my lips, a kiss. We fought each other with our mouths, hoping to sense a vulnerable sigh, a deep breath, a moan. We began to give our organs to each other.

Frida watched lustfully. I heard her make grunting sounds as if she were reaching orgasm. Oh, how she exaggerated! She moaned from behind the couch, from the bedroom, from near the kitchenette. *"Tú verás, es una verdadera bestia, un animal, un monstruo que como todos los hombres piensa en solo una cosa. Así era mi querido Diego. ¡Gracias a Dios!"* she mocked.

She started panting again as if she participated in a pornographic film.

Frida soon gave way to passion. That night Vince and I struggled with our mouths, hands, and legs. He removed his shirt, and to my astonishment he revealed a chest and stomach thick with hair. I never imagined a man could be so beastly.

"J. I., it gets worse."

Vince sat up.

"My stomach, my thighs, my entire lower body is covered with long hair."

Frida was right: *un lobo o un centauro.* I kissed him and placed my arms around his back, and ran my fingers through his hair. Soon it was a matter of completely removing our clothes. I volunteered mine and stood before him only in my body. I noticed that he was pleased. Vince stood up and shyly removed his pants. I immediately understood. His thighs and buttocks were layered with curls. Uncommonly thick in diameter and crowned with an anomaly of a large head, Vince's penis had a long mane. Vince turned and started to walk away. I brought him to the couch, held him against my breast, and soon Frida's moans and grunts blended with my own.

At least once—before or after work, breakfast, lunch, or dinner—I kissed him or slept with him; at least once a day or night, at his place or mine, Vince became a daily part of my life. There were a few days when I tried to pick up his apartment; it wasn't dirty, but there were just too many books. He kept bringing more: "For my research," he said. He placed them on a stack leaning against the wall.

I had often heard people talking about how the violence in Orange County grew. Tustin, a town of about 75,350 people, recently divided into the north and the south, the rich and the poor, the white and brown, the black and the yellow on both sides, into the high minorities and the low minorities, the thriving Market Place with a large discount warehouse, retail stores, restaurants and cinemas, and the withering Old Town vicinity with unique "ma and pa" boutiques offering personal-oriented private services. The city had its share of violent crime, but the worst, according to Vince, was the recent murder of a fourteen-year-old teen, shot in the side of the head for some stereo equipment. Vince was involved in the investigation from the very beginning; from the time the boy was reported missing, to the funeral, to the first and last arrest of the youths charged with the murder.

Vince investigated the boy's interest in disc jockeys, music, and dancing. His investigation took him right to the accused murderers. Pathetically, the pattern was the same as in other youth-killing-youth cases: senseless deaths over material objects that one child had and another wanted. Objects, in the value system of these children, were worth more than life.

The murder took place in the rich, exclusive North Tustin community. On a hilly trail that meanders through the backyards of a group of secluded, peaceful, custom homes, a group of boys ambled together late at night. At this point, what they said to each other doesn't matter. One of the boys took a small handgun out of his coat pocket and fired point blank into the back of the head of another child. The sound of the gunshot did upset people in the neighborhood but, even if they had called the police immediately, it would have been too late, for the first and only shot was fatal. The teen-agers walked up the hill to their car and drove for some fast food. For some, killing stimulates the appetite.

"It was a senseless murder. Killing of a child for some pieces of electronic equipment, absurd! Incomprehensible what these children were thinking," Vince said. He jotted notes in his notebook.

Vince and I chatted with Hak Francis, the manager of the Red Hill Tennis Club, snuggled into the hills of Alta Limón. A couple had gotten off the courts, toweled off, and sat next to us. The man drank a beer, the woman a glass of wine.

"Sorry, but I heard you mention that kid's murder. You know that killing has really distressed me. The homicide of a boy over stereo equipment!"

"In our backyard, honey."

"It's just getting too close to home."

"We moved here to get away from that, and look what happens." The woman shook her head in disgust.

"Hak, you won't believe this, but I think I saw that kid walking, wandering up here just the other night."

"No, I won't believe it." Hak said.

"You don't believe in lost souls, Hak?"

"Hey, I refuse to believe in ghosts and, as for lost souls, we have a lot of lost living ones around here."

"I'm serious, Hak."

"Ah, ignore him. He's lost and is oblivious to it. Please, tell me about it," Vince said.

"OK," the man said. He finished his beer and waved at Hak for another.

The whole scene reminded me of a gothic novel with people sitting in a pub somewhere in the Irish backcountry, drinking whisky, and getting ready to listen to a hair-raising tale; or in the Mexican countryside, drinking *pulque* in a cantina, listening to a man who had witnessed an *alma en pena*, a wondering soul, searching for somebody who would listen.

"We finished playing about nine in the evening. I stayed to have a couple of beers with the guys. Just about everyone had left when I grabbed my bag and headed out to my truck. The night was clear and the wind suddenly had stopped. That sort of bothered me, made me feel weird. The parking lot out there is about two football fields long. On both sides of me, I saw the bushes and trees being moved by the gust, but where I stood, the wind had stopped. I couldn't feel the blowing. I started to walk up to my truck and looked around. It was silent, but on both sides of me, the shrubs kept swaying violently. My skin and the hair at the back of my neck became cold and created a sensation of wanting to run back into the club, but Hak had already closed the door. I opened the truck door and hoisted my bag, which felt heavier than normal. God I can't be having a heart attack. Just let me get home and I'll be all right, just got to get out of here. I fumbled with my keys, tried three times to crack the engine. Finally it started. The hair on my arms was bristly, on my head, coarse. Get out of the parking lot, get out of the parking lot, I kept saying."

Several other members had gathered to listen. Hak poured more wine. The man, convinced that Vince took him seriously, started to speak again.

"I looked around, backed up, but quickly hit my brakes. I saw somebody behind me. I got out. There was nobody. I was in a deep silence. God, I wasn't sick, but maybe I was scared. I got back in the truck and started to drive to the exit that seemed farther than I had ever imagined. I drove on the upper side of the parking lot, along the palm trees and bushes. I stopped. Next to the palm trees, a person came towards me, kept coming closer. I recognized a kid. What the hell is he doing there at this hour? The boy was in my light, at my front fender. His lips moved, but I heard nothing. He reached for the truck door. His head was at the window; every muscle in my face tensed, and my neck ice cold, all my hair sharp as a needle. I hit the gas. He turned his head. I noticed a small hole at the base of his skull. His mouth moved again, but there was only heavy, slow-moving silence. I hit the gas again, looked back, and saw him following me, his jaw constantly moving. Finally, I passed the fenced area, and the wind struck my nose and I was able to breathe."

"Come on, Alex! It's your imagination getting away from you," Hak said.

"You saw the boy, the one who was killed?"

"I know it sounds crazy, but I believe I did."

Vince had been writing all along. He stopped and said, "I believe you, Alex."

"Oh boy, the club parking lot is haunted by a kid who was killed a month ago. That's all we need to attract members, a damn soul." Hak poured himself a glass of bourbon.

"I sensed that he was scared. I heard of these anxiety attacks happening, but I can't explain them," Alex said.

"I, uh, I think I know what you saw," Vince said. He looked at me and continued: "Maybe you know about this phenomenon, J. I. I learned about it from my parents, my grandparents. My grandmother survived a similar experience."

"What do you mean, Vince? You think Alex was in some sort of danger of being taken away by Casper?" Hak laughed loudly.

"No, only fright could have taken Alex away. That is, he might have died of terror," Vince said.

"Cut the scary crap, Vince. We're not anywhere near Halloween!" Hak shook his head.

"Alex, you had an encounter with an *alma en pena,* a lost soul, a wayward soul, a soul in agony; probably the boy was trying to find his way home, back to his mother's breast," I added to Vince's explanation.

"If a person's life is cut short by an accident, a terrible or unjust death, or if the individual left behind an untold secret, or a task that he or she was on the verge of completing, that person's soul may seek to communicate with the living to try to tell perhaps the cause of their undue demise, or seek help to return home, or try to reveal a secret. Unfortunately, these lost spirits are condemned to wander near the place they died. Until they reach their goal, they will never rest in peace. They will forever wander."

"I think I did see that boy. But what do you do in a situation like that?" Alex asked.

"Well, the experts, and there are some on these matters, say that when encountering these souls, some people die of fright, and others die because they react in the wrong way."

Vince took a little sip of my wine and continued: "When confronted with an *alma en pena*, people scream, cry for help, swear, run away. These are the worst actions you can do. All this does is to attract the soul closer to you, for it now believes that it has upset you and wants to make amends, so it naturally follows you, tries to get closer, to communicate, until either the living breaks away, which was what Alex did, or until he or she dies and essentially becomes one of them."

"Now he's giving an Introduction to Ghost Defense," Hak offered up and asked, "So what do you do? Call the Ghost Busters?"

"The experts say that when confronted by a lost soul, you must bless them, pray for them, tell them they are beautiful, that you love them, that you understand their plight, that you will always think of them, even invite them to join you wherever they confront you; then they will disengage, because they can never completely cross the line between life and death. They can hear you, but you can't hear them. That's why Alex only saw the boy's mouth move, but never heard a sound. They toil in a space, a dimension where the elements do not exist. Lovingly grieving and praying will make them fade away."

Vince sat back in his seat with a satisfied expression on his face.

"Hey, Vince, Alex, there's some kid out in the parking lot waiting for a ride home." Hak laughed and poured himself another bourbon. "I'm not kidding."

At that moment, a young boy walked into the clubhouse.

"Is my dad finished playing tennis?"

"He left about an hour ago," Hak replied.

"Didn't my mom call to let him know that he was supposed to take me home?"

"Here, call your parents. Don't they know where you are? And tell them to come get you quick. I'm closing up in ten minutes." Hak walked over to us.

"There's your ghost, Vince. Some kid forgotten by his parents. He's alive, Alex."

We drove down from the hills to Vince's apartment. On the Tustin streets, I couldn't help but compare the city to some of the cities in México. Tustin was becoming more and more a haunted city. Its tragedies roamed the roads and the public buildings and what was left of its pristine lands. Even though not everybody believed in *almas en pena*, there was a growing population who did and who affirmed their existence.

Vince had transformed his Tustin apartment into one of the best literary libraries in all of Orange County. In his bibliophile environment he spent long hours reading, researching, and writing in his notebooks. At times he slept only a few hours at night and, on his days off, if he didn't visit his mother, he sat at his desk reading. He ate very little, yet he was a little overweight; he drank even less; his only amusement was provided by me who insisted on going out to the beach, the park, and driving on Sunday afternoons with no particular destination in mind.

It was after one of these meditation drives that Vince and I read the news on a note on my office desk. We had returned to my place to pick up some clothes before going to his apartment. We had started our Sunday drive that day by exploring the corner of Myford Road and Irvine Boulevard.

"This corner is historical but, like many old sites in the State of California that pertain to the Mexicans' contributions to its economic development, there's no damn marker."

We walked along an old road, set off Irvine Boulevard, hidden by orange and palm trees, some figs that had been there since the turn of century. Several small, nicely painted wooden houses with well-kept gardens and expensive cars parked in narrow driveways stood in a row.

"James Irvine kept his favorite Mexican workers in these houses." Vince continued: "This novel I'm reading mentions that Irvine had a large family mansion somewhere on this road."

We came to a grove of tall palm trees and what looked like a vineyard, with grapevines entwined above long wood overhangs that covered three concrete paths to an open space. He crossed the road to get a better look at the sight.

"I bet this is where the house was. The book describes this vineyard, the palm trees, and the walkways leading to it. This must be the place," Vince called out to me.

"Yeah, I think you're right. I seem to remember this place as if I've been here before. Strange sensation."

I worried that I might break into an *ilusa* trance. Perhaps I came here with Mark and the Ekkersons, I thought. My memory failed to confirm my déjà vu, and in a short while we drove up Jamboree Road, to Chapman Boulevard, and into Irvine Park. We hiked up a trail to a view area looking out toward the Pacific. From this beautiful place, Catalina Island's silhouette waved to us over the ocean. We remained watching the sunset. Finally, with the disappearing reddish glimmer of the sun, we sped out of Irvine Park to a lookout spot high atop the Tustin Hills. There, we watched the Orange County lights and the stars on a clear Southern California night. Instinctively, we practiced the clichéd actions of passion. We were primordial lovers. It had been a long time since I laughed freely.

These were the California nights that attracted migrants from other states. How pleasant were the lingering aroma of a barbecue, music from a backyard party, kids playing in a pool, a dog barking. We listened to sounds floating in the twinkling night.

"Was this the hill?" I asked Vince.

"Uh huh, just below us they found the boy."

"Great view."

Vince maneuvered the curves down Skyline Drive, to Newport Boulevard and the Tustin flatlands.

"This land was once a series of large agricultural fields with immense orchards of fruit trees, broken up by windbreaks of rows of tall eucalyptus spaced a mile apart," Vince said. He turned south on Newport Boulevard.

"Now," he continued, "the land's covered by cement, asphalt, houses, and mini malls, one after another. Look at this over-built crap. We sure know how to ruin a beautiful place, huh?"

"It's not so bad."

Vince and I drove by more cluttered shopping centers. Tustin was congested with ugly buildings, thousands of signs, lights, and wires that didn't reflect a design of tranquility, architecture of peace. All of these will hardly survive. There was no place for the eye to rest in a space of chaos, continuous movement, and change.

"Tustin is like all the cities of Southern California: obsessed with destroying the old, the traditional, and all that's related to it, desperately wanting to be modern."

Vince turned right on Irvine Boulevard and soon crossed over the Newport freeway and, shortly after that, the Santa Ana freeway to, finally, turn into Rebecca's driveway on Fourth Street.

"Well, that can't happen in old México. We try to erase the past, and the next morning we discover a new museum dedicated to it. There, we are always standing on history, or it is only a few steps away, or a few feet below the surface. It runs in our blood, shows in our skin and face. It messes with our mind: History permeates space, waiting to rise, to express itself in the now."

"But it doesn't make you less modern."

It was right about the time of that thought that Chucho barked, Vince closed the door, and I walked by my office and saw the note propped up on my desk. I gave it to Vince.

"I'm taking my car in case they need me to stay."

"That's fine. I'll meet you there."

The dog barked as Vince's car drove away. I checked food and water for Chucho, played with it for a few minutes, grabbed some clothes, and went out to my car. Somewhere off in the distance a bell rang, children played and a *mariachi* band performed. I drove on Fourth Street, crossed Broadway and came to Main Street. That area was the administrative center and cultural heart of Santa Ana.

The natural horizon had been lost. At just about every intersection, I could not find it. Like in Mexico City: signs, buildings, pools, wires, asphalt, lights, cars, trucks, and humans cluttered my vision, tired my eyes. Distance had been destroyed by overbuilding. The peace of looking out toward the skyline had been abolished. There was no peace of mind here, only steady mental movement from one object to another. Southern California stirred tension that concentrated itself right in the back of the neck, a constant pressure numbed only by doses of alcohol, analgesics, or ibuprofens. Here, in the administrative center of Orange County, there was no horizon. People had to go to the ocean to rediscover it and experience a sense of tranquility.

Candlelight illuminated the room. Lea, Rufino, Chac, and the Mayas had hundreds of candles throughout the house. On the dining room, Chac's gourmet dishes invited visitors to help themselves. Refreshments, wine, beer, and coffee were also available. May had placed colorful rugs on the floors, sofas, and chairs. *Manteles* covered the tables and counters.

Vince and I walked into Mrs. Dougherty's room where an altar had been set up. Votive candles, in a variety of sizes and colors, warmed the space with the spectrum of the rainbow. Throughout the house, we walked through the energy and smell of floating color. In the middle of that illumination, May and Chac prayed at the side of Mrs. Dougherty's bed.

Rebecca found Mrs. Dougherty in bed surrounded by the Mayas, kneeling, and praying for her. From what she could understand from May, Rebecca deduced that Mrs. Dougherty had fallen ill that morning after breakfast. Rebecca arrived in the afternoon to tell Mrs. Dougherty that her land was out of danger of being claimed by the city. But she had arrived too late. Mrs. Dougherty lay in bed, with her eyes open, whispering her one and only word: "Yes."

Lea, who never left Dougherty's Twist, came immediately after Rebecca's call.

Rebecca followed the detailed instructions that her client had written. "She doesn't want the hospital, only a doctor to make her comfortable. She doesn't want to prolong life or hasten death. She wants to join her husband and daughter naturally. I believe this is the last poem she wrote:

My heart became so
heavy that my body
refuses to carry it
it is like an unwieldy
boulder of sorrow
that rolled to the
earth and took me
with it I was
lucky that I fell
near my bed my spirit
so weighty now it
will not let me stand
the weight is my
longing for my husband
and daughter it is
strong and pushes
my soul toward them
I can see them coming
for me from a great
distance these
years alone I thought
they forgot about me
but now that my life
changes to pure soul
my beloved are almost
here and finally I
will be with them.

Rebecca continued to speak about Mrs. Dougherty's obsession to die at home. "No hospital for Mrs. Dougherty, because she is afraid the city, the *políticos*, will return to take her property. She wants to stay to the end. This land is hers, and she will never give it up in her lifetime."

"She reminds me of Modesta Ávila, a woman who, at the end of the nineteenth century, defended her land against the big railroad interests coming into Orange County. When the Santa Fe Railroad was laid through Modesta Ávila's property and refused to compensate her for its use, she placed a couple of big fence posts across the railway and stopped the trains. Claiming 'this land belongs to me, and if they want to use it, they must pay me for it,' the railroad agreed to remunerate her for it, but her victory marked the beginning of her calamity. To celebrate her win, she rented a dance hall in Santa Ana. Modesta Ávila was defiant of the big companies and *políticos* who abused the poor, and she rubbed her defiance in their noses. A few minutes after the party ended, the men she hired to keep order arrested her for disturbing the peace. At her hearing she boasted about her triumph over the Santa Fe Railroad. The instant Modesta Ávila completed her statement to the court, the judge sentenced her to three years in prison. She died in San Quentin, resisting to the end. She was only twenty-seven years old."

At the moment that Vince Rodelo ended his story about Modesta Ávila, Mrs. Dougherty sighed and peacefully ceased. Courageous to her last breath, she died protecting her house and land from the forces of the big companies and the *políticos*.

 At Dougherty's Twist, Rebecca, Lea, and I fulfilled one of Mrs. Dougherty's last requests. We spread the wonderful old lady's ashes along the creek where Mr. Dougherty and Twist had disappeared many years ago. We were heading toward the family plot where the monuments to Mr. Dougherty and Twist had been placed and where Mrs. Dougherty wanted "just a bit of my remains snuggled next to my husband and daughter's places so that we could be together again."

That morning the Mayas, Rufino, Chac, Rebecca, Lea, Vince, and I had walked to each corner of Dougherty's Twist to sprinkle Mrs. Dougherty's ashes. According to May, Mr. Dougherty and Twist's souls would not wander now that Mrs. Dougherty was here near the creek that had taken them. They would finally be reunited, but they had to be guided back to the center, to the heart of their existence, to their love, to Mrs. Dougherty, who waited near the memorial site.

On that crisp late-May morning, we gathered and placed an urn containing a little bit of Mrs. Dougherty's ashes into the ground next to the memorials to Mr. Dougherty and Twist. Then we positioned a large stone marker there. While Rufino prayed, I looked at everyone around and wondered about what waited for us in the outside world. Out there, there was a force that summoned us.

One week later we gathered at Mrs. Dougherty's house in Santa Ana for the official reading of Mrs. Dougherty's living trust. Rebecca had asked everybody present at the funeral to attend. Rebecca, honoring Mrs. Dougherty's instructions, scheduled the meeting for ten in the morning, but she arrived a half hour late because Jack had been acting up in his jail cell and Rebecca had gone to see him at eight that morning.

Jack had become increasingly despondent and obsessed, unable to accept Jill's death. The court had granted Rebecca special permission to see her client earlier than the indicated time. One of the guards, who knew Rebecca well, simply warned, "Be careful with him. I don't know what he might do. I'll be watching." That morning, just before coming to Mrs. Dougherty's house, and hours before she got the first whiff of the aroma of May Maya's sweet *pan mexicano*, Rebecca heard the cries of Jack Ekkerson, who pleaded to see his dead wife.

When Rebecca walked into Mrs. Dougherty's kitchen, she immediately chose a seat next to mine. May served her coffee, Rebecca reached for sweet bread, and suddenly, as the aroma of the pastry and the warmth of the kitchen aroused an overpowering emotion in my friend Rebecca, she cried out to Mrs. Dougherty.

Nobody said a word. Rebecca, exhausted, put her head on the table while I massaged her shoulders. Lea, Rufino, Chac, and Ray gathered around her and waited.

"I'm fine. Let me wash my face!" Rebecca stood at the kitchen sink and splashed water on her eyes and cheeks. "It's been a rough morning."

In the living room, she whispered, "Jack's breaking down. I hope he makes the next court date."

"I hope *you* do," I said.

Lea, Rufino, Chac, the Mayas, and I watched Rebecca extract Mrs. Dougherty's trust from a sealed brown envelope. Lea inherited all of Dougherty's Twist, the business and Mrs. Dougherty's stock, bonds and mutual fund investments. Rufino and Chac received the house they inhabited, the acre of land that surrounded it, and $25,000. To my surprise, the Mayas were left with the home in Santa Ana and $25,000 for each of the children. However, Mrs. Dougherty added two stipulations: one was that the Mayas had to become citizens of the United States before they were awarded complete control of the house and property; and second, that Lea would have the right of first refusal if the Mayas ever decided to sell their inheritance. Rebecca was paid a salary to be the executrice of Mrs. Dougherty's legal and binding testament.

When Rebecca finished explaining the details, and I had interpreted for May Maya, May then told her family, and they jumped and danced. In their frenzy of happiness, they pulled us into their joyful circle, and we whirled and laughed until we collapsed onto the sofas and chairs. While the others were talking, or trying to talk to each other, Rebecca handed me an envelope. I recognized Mrs. Dougherty's handwriting, and I read the note:

To J. I. Cruz: I give you my deepest heartfelt thanks for your friendship. For I know that with this simple acknowledgment a magic woman-saint like you will be eternally content and happy.

Mrs. Margaret Dougherty

"Thanks?" I whispered to myself.

 In one of the oldest brick buildings in Old Town Tustin, Vince and I had lunch. From the Rutabagorz semi-vegetarian menu, we split an avocado sandwich and a chicken delight salad. That restaurant was one of Vince Rodelo's favorite places. Its interior walls reminded him of Simons Brick Company, where his father had worked for about twenty-five years before getting a job during the war at the Philips Dodge Copper Corporation. Along with local history, Vince was fascinated with brick. Whenever he came across a structure being demolished, he stopped to check if it had any brick. On several occasions he found some from Simons.

"Maybe my father touched this brick!"

He made an offer to the guy in charge of the demolition to buy a few bricks with the Simons trademark stamped on them. Vince always started to tell the history of the piece, but, as usual, the man in charge didn't have time to listen and walked away.

"Take some, but you have to clear the area."

Vince had collected, among his thousands of books, approximately one hundred Simons bricks and had stacked these in small piles throughout his apartment. But on that afternoon, brick was not the issue.

Earlier that day, the Santa Ana police had visited the Mayas and Rebecca. The police asked to see the room where Mrs. Dougherty died.

"They never showed a search warrant, but the Mayas didn't know any better, and they let them go inside. They walked in every room, and through the garden. May called Rebecca's office and, luckily, she was there. Rebecca kicked those men out. Those damn cops wanted an angle. They know about the trust and they'll try to challenge it. Rebecca noticed that outside, waiting in the car, was some sleazy lawsuit-crazed lawyer waiting to file some lawsuit against the Mayas. Why don't you tell your colleagues to leave this family alone. Mrs. Dougherty knew exactly what she was doing when she dictated and signed the document. She was perfectly sane and competent!"

I pushed my plate away.

"Please don't let this ruin our lunch."

"Call off those cops!"

"I don't know who they are. Don't worry; there's no question about the legality of the will. Rebecca is an honest person."

"Why are these cops harassing us?"

"I don't know. Don't get upset at me. I'm trying to help you. Come on, J. I., there's no need to argue."

"That lawyer can challenge Mrs. Dougherty's will!"

"He might. There are nativist groups challenging everyone nowadays. They're starting to throw it all at us again."

"They're what?"

"You know . . . How could these Natives and Mexicans, and Lea, a lesbian or bisexual . . . How can these people inherit Mrs. Dougherty's estate? Simple. They paid attention to her, they cared for the old lady, and they were rewarded. But you see that this is a time when the once-dominant culture is challenging what the minority, soon to be a majority, is doing—especially what makes the minority more powerful. They are afraid, and so they will throw everything at us again. Here's a piece I wrote in my journal. Here, read it."

Vince handed me a journal, not unlike the one that had exiled me from México. Its contents forged images that I tried to forget. But I carried Cassandra Arenal Coe's journal as if it were a kind of protection, an assurance against powerful forces that could snatch me back to México, where I wanted to be but was afraid to return.

to *"where we came from."* But, many of us were born in the United States, and México was a great distance from where our parents came. Operation Wetback offered us money like before, and herds of burros, because they said they were our favorite mode of transportation. They deported millions of us back to México: *"Don't need your help anymore. Go back to your mother country"* came off as an insult more than a destination. *¡Váyanse a la chingada! until we need you again.* They started their *"We'll Call You Policy."* The national political oratory calmed the American middle class, but then after a few years they started throwing everything at us again. *"Urban renewal,"* they shouted, and it translated to urban barrio removal, Mexican barrio eradication. Eminent domain demanded the destruction of our communities and homes. Early in the morning the bulldozers came, pushed into our neighborhoods by the legal system, by the great White fear that we were going to take over California. It meant Mexican diaspora in the late 1950s and the 1960s. La Raza spread through the Southwest and the rest of the country, all because the gringos se escamaron, and they're still scared of the brown faces walking into their world, but no one stops us. We mexicanos continue to return and to be born in our land of Aztlán: México and the United States are our countries. Even though we are occupied, we keep getting stronger, and they throw everything at us. In 1986, they tried to cut our tongues out. All over the state of California, we were chased down by Anglo American do-gooders, who grabbed us and cut out our Spanish with shiny new English-Only political-proposition knives. They gathered the quivering Spanish tongues into huge piles and danced around the mountains of castellano-articulating flesh and sang: *"English is the official language. Praise God, all born-again Christians."* But, Mexicans knew that, to succeed in the United States, we had to speak English. Now with our Spanish tongues with which we were going to learn English, we reverted back to our mother tongue, and in time we started to learn English but still kept our Spanish. The declarations started up again, and they threw everything at us again, including the Simpson-Mazzoli Bill to control us in 1982. And they threw everything at us in 1986 with the Rodino-Simpson Bill. They used political legislation like insecticide, spraying constantly the annoying cockroaches that bred too near them, and, when morning came, we opened their eyes and they discovered that we were still here in our Aztlán, and we keep coming and growing stronger. But they still keep throwing everything at us: multiplying the hatred, the paranoia, the fear, the accusation against us even from the Black population, producing Proposition

187, attacking not only the adults but our offspring, our right to an education, to medical services. They want to deport us again, they want to send the Army to the border, they want to brand us with a national identification card, they want to brand us with a Catholic stamp and condemn us to hell for not being saved. They want to control every aspect of our lives, mold us to be a fixed identity like a Rodin sculpture. They fear us because the demographics project that California will be a Latino-minority majority state by the turn of the century, by the turn of the millennium. They threw everything at us at the beginning of the twentieth century. The hegemonic leadership predicted that Los Ángeles, Southern California, would be a stronghold, a haven for the Arian race; they planned Los Ángeles to be like Europe, like Venice—like Venice, Italy—but thousands of Mexicans dug the Venice, California, canals, and hundreds of Mexicans were hired to be the gondoliers after the authentic Italians refused to work for such cheap wages. And all of a sudden, history and destiny cast their vision on México and all of Latin America. The xenophobia that resulted paralyzed their minds, fear gripped their throats, and they threw everything at us again by attacking and demolishing any and all mechanisms designed to assist Mexicans in creating a safe zone in Los Ángeles. They pointed to the Mexicans as the cause, the root of the problems in Southern California and the country; they recognized that La Raza's face appeared more and more in positions of power, when they would rather see us fill up the courts, the state prisons. They wanted us there in cages and then out of the country. Back to México—greaser, beaner, spic, cholo. Terror struck their hearts when they saw Mexicans sitting on the judge's bench, community councils, chambers of commerce, teaching in universities, gaining professional positions, moving to parts of the city where in the past Mexicans could not buy a house, taking over sections of cities once dominated by Anglo Americans, Asians, Blacks. They ran, they abandoned their land. We slowly got comfortable. They moved further away from the centers of the cities, holding on to several very rich areas like Brentwood, Hancock Park, Beverly Hills, La Cañada, or San Marino, but we'll soon be there, too. They still continue to throw everything at us, and they will continue. Under this heavy bombardment, do not be afraid. Stand tall, be proud! We're not the enemy or the victim. We Mexicans, we Latinos are on center stage, in the limelight, and we can only get stronger, but be assured that they will again and again throw everything at us.

In downtown Santa Ana, near the county library, the city hall, the federal court building, and the police station are two huge monolithic, multilevel, technologically advanced concrete warehouses where Jack Ekkerson, one of the few White men in a cellblock where the majority are Latino and Black men, waits for his next appearance. Both modern jails are monuments to Santa Ana's politically unconscious attitudes toward the fast-growing Latino population. Like Vince said, they're throwing everything at us, even building ultramodern jails for our benefit.

They're willing to spend many millions of dollars on jails, build them in the inner city, in barrios where they are championed by the *políticos*. Not in Newport Beach, near Laguna or Irvine, best to incarcerate where the criminal lives is the theory of California legislators. The barrios hate being converted into holding zones. Felons are let out early because of overcrowding, released into the inner-city blighted areas of the county. Once elected, politicians who promised to improve schools then spend far more money on imprisonment than on education.

Many schools are in terrible physical and spiritual condition. Classrooms are falling apart inside and out; bathrooms, science labs, athletic facilities are in complete disrepair; electrical and water systems are in shambles. Hey! But you always have jail, kids. Three square meals, a place to sleep, TV, daily exercise, and if you make it to the big house like Folsom, you might have permanent employment.

These thoughts meandered through my mind as I drove alone up Santiago Creek Road to the top of Saddleback Mountain, Orange

County's highest peak, overlooking the Pacific. I looked out toward the ocean, as maybe the Natives had done over two hundred or thousands of years ago, but could not imagine exclusive Pelican Hill, where the rich build their multi-million dollar houses, where famous mystery authors create a new personal aspect, surgically transfiguring their faces into living fiction by shaving off every facial hair, by getting the best hair implant, by nipping and tucking under the eyes and chin, hoping to achieve the young Orange-County look. The power of writing, I thought, can change appearances or can get you killed.

Fashion Island towers, Newport Harbor, and UC Irvine loomed ahead, silhouetted by radiant light from the setting California sun. A mingling red, orange, purple radiance warmed my face as I closed my eyes for a short while, relaxed, and slowly opened them to be awestruck. Before me, stationary and staring, attempting to configure whether I was danger or a plant rooted to the Earth, a brown golden fawn, with an obsidian gaze and a black moist nose, stood precariously at the edge of flight, sensing its predicament. A current of wind blew and the fawn broke away. In three leaps it had disappeared into the brush. I rose to chase the baby deer. Convinced that I had seen and experienced a prayer sent by God, I yearned to see it once more.

Names and faces I loved and cared for rushed by as I drove, as carefully and as fast as possible, down Saddleback Mountain. I exited the Newport freeway on Fourth Street, past my office where I noticed somebody working. I kept going west to Mrs. Dougherty's house, past Grand, in the old part of Santa Ana where most of the businesses were owned by Latinos and the area reminded me of areas in Mexico City.

In Mrs. Dougherty's kitchen, May, now more than when Mrs. Dougherty was alive, kept appliances, tables and chairs, windows and floors immaculate. Ray and May didn't want anybody accusing them of not being intelligent enough to keep a house, or claiming they were dirty, culturally deprived *indígenas*, ignorant Mexicans who didn't know how to operate the most basic modern domestic devices. Way ahead of the game, they had learned from Mrs. Dougherty to be well prepared for the attacks from envious conniving strangers. I could hear the Mayas working and talking in their native language in the greenhouse, in the backyard.

Out the front window I noticed that more cars than usual drove by slowly. Some passengers stopped and for a while stared at the house. I grabbed the newspaper and saw an article in the Metro section of the *Los Angeles Times:*

"Illegal Mexican Indians Inherit Fortune"

The headline brought to mind another *Los Angeles Times* article:

"Illegal Population in U.S. Now Tops 10 Million"

I had been peacefully enjoying a cup of coffee at the Infinite Bean and reading the paper in which the article appeared. At the next table sat a man and two women discussing the report.

"Why don't they close the border? Send the Army down there and keep those people out," the man reacted to the front-page headline: "Ten million illegal Mexicans, a sea of brown faces ripping off the system."

These kinds of comments were the body of their conversation. They became more agitated as they spoke. I took one last sip of coffee, folded the newspaper to leave.

"Did you see this article?" the man asked me and pointed to the headline that angered them.

I nodded.

"I just got started," the man emphasized.

As I walked out of the Infinite Bean, I realized that those people had been expressing opinions triggered by the headline and had probably not read the article. Words bring forth images, and the *Los Angeles Times*, like other major newspapers, communicates a subliminal message, even though that may contradict its editorial positions. Media language specifically chosen to describe an ethnic group has metaphorical powers. These words—taken from a source, a domain, that contains the names of all that is familiar to us the readers—are repeatedly used to refer to particular individuals. In doing so, I thought, a figurative relation is established. The allegory is accepted by the general public as are the characteristics related to a target group.

Hence, those coffee drinkers at the Infinite Bean read "Illegal Immigrant Population in U.S. Now Tops 10 Million" and immediately concluded that it referred to Mexicans. They didn't even bother to read the article. In reading the "10 Million" headline they saw

"drug dealers"   "dangerous waves"   "a desperate flood"
"ruining our schools"   "they bring gangs, drug cartel violence"
"a brown tide"   "ILLEGAL ALIENS   "murderers"
"drug smugglers"   "overrunning" "they only speak Spanish"
"rapists"   "criminals"   "inundating"
"they don't assimilate"   "porous borders" "flooding" threats
to the United States and understood only negative social, economic,
and political consequences.

Now the newspaper screamed: "Illegal Mexican Indians Inherit
Fortune."

Mrs. Dougherty's neighbors volunteered to the media a detailed
account of the relationship the late woman had with the Mayas. Some
of them said that Mexican Natives and a New York lawyer took advantage of the elder. These people were quoted: "Old lady Dougherty
couldn't talk or hear and probably was senile too." They added, "She
didn't know what she was doing when she gave the house away to
those ignorant low-life gardeners."

The article, from the neighbors' point of view, gave every detail
except for the address. Yet photographs of the house and surrounding
area made it easy for the public to find the street. Now there was a
parade of curious gawkers driving up and down out front. I drew the
drapes closed and sat quietly waiting in the living room. I recalled the
fawn bounding and disappearing into the high brush on Saddleback
Mountain.

After Mrs. Dougherty's death, life for me seemed to lose direction.
I had lived like this before, in Mexico City, and I prayed silently that
my spiritual trances would not return, but I left that up to God. That
evening, the Mayas invited me to stay for dinner. I sensed that they
were afraid of the print media and TV news publicity about them.

The Spanish news show *Primer Impacto* found the house that evening just before dinner. They arrived with a news van, asking for an interview. I told them the Mayas had no comment and asked them to
leave; yet they stayed parked out front and made several reports from
the scene. During dinner we ignored them.

After dinner May asked the children to go watch TV. For some reason, they seemed excited and wanted to stay, but May insisted that they go to the adjoining room. The kids went off and left May, Ray, and me alone.

"We want you to stay with us," May said.

"I can't tonight. I have too much work," I responded and peeked out the window. The cars still drove by, studying the house.

"No, not just tonight. We want you to live with us," Ray explained.

"You can have the room that faces the backyard." May got up and I followed her to what Mrs. Dougherty called the garden room. It was her guest room, decorated with antiques, colorful oriental rugs, and a mahogany four-post bed. French doors opened out to the patio, which brought to mind other gardens in my life: Endriago's, and my parents' in their house in Coyoacán. May must have sensed my feelings, my loneliness and melancholy and, when I turned toward her, she hugged me. It had been such a long time since I had experienced a mother's tender embrace.

That evening, from my room in Rebecca's office, I called Vince to let him know about my pending move.

We ate breakfast at
Baker's Square in Montebello.
The table next to the
window offered a gray
retirement hotel
for a view.
Mother held her gaze
across the street
on the medieval
apparatus connected
to a bed on the
second floor.
"Gracias a Dios que tengo
mi casa".
I nodded, smiled, where's
the waiter I wondered.
Service here had become slower
but most of the old folks
didn't mind,
they were never in a rush
nowhere to go but return
to a bleak smelly ancient cell
"Yo no quiero ser
molestia para nadie".
"Madre, ¿qué es lo que
más recuerdas?"
"A él".
"¿A mi papá?"

"Me acuerdo cuando
limpiaba la casa.
Ya no trabajaba
y me decía,
'Ahora me dejas la casa' .
Y la limpiaba".
"What would you like to drink?"
Finally the waiter said,
"¿Café?"
Mother nodded.
"Two coffees."
I made sure he understood.
"Be right back
to take your order."
"¿Te acuerdas mucho
de él, madre?"
"Sí, lo tengo
siempre en mis
recuerdos.
Pero no lo quiero ver".
She turned her head
toward the window.
An old woman slowly,
dangerously
made her way across
Beverly Boulevard.
Cars stopped abruptly,
impatient drivers honked,
shook their fists
at the oblivious woman
making her way to
Baker's Square where
I contemplated my
mother's beautiful
profile which made me
happy.

On the day that Vince wrote this poem he started to read about human sacrifice among the Mexica people in prehispanic México. Through his general reading about the country he had become aware of the practices related to religious or mystical needs and overtones. He purchased several tomes on ancient México at the large warehouse chain stores like Book Barnes and others that had recently, to the detriment of small independent bookstores, completely dominated sales, putting more and more independents out of business. Vince remembered Jack's store and how much he had enjoyed browsing in a place literally covered with books—that is, when Jack had the income for inventory. Then Vince recalled how Jack got his money to restock the store. Now, Jack waited in a cell, Jill gone from him forever. One's greatest sorrow is to know there's only one life on Earth. There are no do overs, Vince thought.

He hadn't been himself lately. He worried about the health of his ninety-year-old mother. In recent weeks, she had become lethargic, lost her spirit, and refused to eat. She claimed she wasn't hungry, or she would order food and either forget to eat it or say it didn't have any taste and would push the plate away.

Vince drove to Montebello, at least twice a week, to call on his mother and also talked to the woman who took care and accompanied her to the doctor to make sure she received the best tending. The idea that she, in her last days on Earth, had to be safe, comfortable, and relatively happy obsessed Vince Rodelo. Her mind was giving way to forgetfulness, to fits of anger, to throwing away photographs and important documents, including her green card. He worried that although she had been a legal resident since 1912, now she had no official papers to prove that she was lawfully in the United States.

He worried that the federal agents—building the triple fence, the triple barrier, the U.S.-México border wall like the ugly Berlin Wall— would come and take his mother away. He remembered news footage about East Germans attempting to scale the Berlin Wall, of people running across the neutral zone and being shot and left there lying in freezing temperatures, dead or dying. These images foretold the future of the triple U.S.-México border wall, where a blood bath awaited the right excuse to shred and scatter its victims' bodies. Vince wished that millions of Mexicans would climb the wall and occupy the space on each side and in between, like bees clustering into a hive, swarming, neutralizing the hideous and artificial division of the border, which should be one space not two, not a divided blood-stained international tumor.

My mother lost her
green card
she is ninety years old
has been in
United States
since nineteen hundred
and twelve
if the Immigration and
Customs Enforcement
doesn't believe she
lost her green card and
requires her to go
to México to reapply
to enter the
United States
a trip she won't
survive
I will arm myself
to prevent them
from taking her
if they take her it will be over
my
dead
body

His mother's physical condition and her immigrant limbo had pre-occupied Vince, but an occurrence on the job during these days made him more obsessive and ill tempered.

I had been concerned, but he kept insisting that only his mother's situation worried him. Vince placed a new book on the table and went to the refrigerator. I picked up *El sacrificio humano entre los mexicas.*

"Don't, you've lost my place!" he snapped.

"What's bothering you? It can't be that bad."

I tossed the book at him.

"Sorry, J. I., but I don't think you'll believe it, because I didn't until I saw it. This is so terrible that the department kept the media away for almost a month. We didn't want a panic."

What can be more terrifying than the imagination? I thought, as Vince began his tale. What he described was incredible, but now that a second victim had appeared, the department was having a difficult time keeping this out of the public eye. Several witnesses, two people who found the second fatality, had suffered severe shock and psychological trauma, and had spoken to reporters at the hospital. The FBI had also gotten involved, since the case dealt with several kidnappings.

Vince had been involved in the investigation since the night he was called to the Parker House, a local restaurant frequented by people in their fifties and above to dine, dance, and hook up. The place was a meat corral for the older generation, a legitimate establishment with no record of any major trouble. Vince received the call at approximately one thirty in the morning. It was a Friday night, yet, curiously, most clients had left the eatery. The parking lot, which wrapped around the building, was almost empty in the back. The owner—a tall and obese man—waited for the police in the front. Vince got out of the car and immediately noticed a strange odor. A squad patrol had just arrived ahead of him and the two officers were calming two women who cried hysterically.

"Detective Rodelo, these two, they're cracking up. I don't think it's drugs."

"What the hell smells?"

"They," the officer pointed to the women, "don't make much sense. It's the smell that got them crazy. I've called the paramedics."

Vince approached the car where the two women were seated, crying, attempting to talk.

"What's the problem, ladies?"

"Our car . . . back . . . with the smell . . . from that corpse . . . my car!"

He talked to the owner.

"The smell has grown worse. I sent some of the staff to investigate, but they found no body. These ladies," the owner pointed to the women, "came running into the restaurant screaming about a cadaver and the horrible odor. They asked me to call the police. Nobody had been back there. We all waited outside, here, for you to come. God, it's getting worse, the stench is awful!"

The paramedics arrived and attended to the women, who kept warning the officers not to go back there.

"Don't risk seeing it! You won't be able to get away from the smell!"

The odor had intensified and it circulated in the air, floated around objects, and clung to clothes, flesh, and hair. The cops consulted with the Fire Department's Hazardous Materials crew: three men wearing special protection garments and helmets. They moved a fire truck to the back of the restaurant. Two police cars drove in behind them.

"It smells like a bunch of dead animals. I bet that's what the fuck it is! Probably some wise guy dumped a dead dog," the officer walking with Vince declared. Then they stopped suddenly when they saw it.

"Hey, shine the light on the middle of the parking lot!" Vince ordered. Quickly, all lights fell upon the center of the black asphalt.

"What the fuck is that?" a fireman yelled.

"It's no stuffed turkey!" somebody nervously responded.

"Get in closer."

"Careful!"

"It's on a chair!"

"It's a person on a chair!"

"Hey, what's that on the ground?"

"Don't step on them, there's a lot of them!"

"Shit, they're like organs, intestines!"

"Oh, God!"

Several police and Vince reached the carcass sitting on the chair. It seemed to be human. The smell was unbearable. One officer turned away, vomited, and retreated to the front where more fire trucks and police cars had pulled in.

In fewer than fifteen minutes, the object was surrounded by thirty officers, detectives, fire personnel, and five investigators from the Orange County coroner's office. All, except the coroner's crew, held handkerchiefs over their noses and mouths.

The coroner's two principal investigators, as if fascinated by the smell of decomposing human tissue, quietly did their work. The two women now seemed attracted to the yet- indefinable other, sitting, installed on a chair as if it were listening to the cars rush by on the Newport Freeway.

"Push everybody back, away from this and the organs on the asphalt! Set up a perimeter! Throw up a ribbon! Cordon it off, God damn it!" Vince yelled at the officers to comply. He pushed a couple of officers to snap them out of their incredulous state.

Organs and pieces of organs had been thrown on the ground in four rows in front of the object. Vince identified parts of intestine, both small and large, lobs of liver, lungs and two kidneys.

"I guess these organs came from this poor devil?" he asked one of the two coroners.

"I think so. I think it's human. I think it's a guy who's been gutted, disemboweled. This fucking world has gone insane, Vince, just like in the movies, man. It's scary." She kept joking with the crew and working enthusiastically.

The coroner photographed each object on the ground three times. The whole scene was shot on pictures and film from different angles and positions around a circle.

By daybreak the remains and organs had not been removed. Daylight confirmed that the object was human and most likely a man. Vince stood, studying the scene.

"This is like an installation."

"An installation?" the coroner asked.

"Yes, like an artist's installation. It's an installation of art."

"This weirdo has a curious sense of humor, but you might be right. The way this whole performance is set up," the coroner agreed.

She waved Vince to come closer to the cadaver on the chair.

Vince covered his nose with a handkerchief, but it didn't impede the heavy, almost fatty smell of decomposing human flesh. He listened while the coroner explained what might have befallen this pitiful creature. The murderer had rearranged the face, replacing the eyes with the victim's testicles. The mouth had been forced open wider than usual and the heart had been stuffed into it. Starting directly below the chin an incision was made that went down the chest, abdomen, to the end of the penis. Daylight made these features clear and also revealed that the individual was Black.

The man had been gutted like a chicken. His thorax, his abdomen had been cleaned, and the offal scattered about the cadaver. However, the murderer had stuffed the cavity with inflatable objects filled with a liquid. The coroner pushed at the balloons, but stopped for fear of bursting them. The chest had been barely closed with a dark cord stitched wide and loosely through the black skin.

Even stranger were the parts of clothes with which the murderer had dressed the body. Around the thighs it had the leg portions of basketball shorts. On the back, the murderer had sewed on the flesh a part of a jersey with the number one. The body also had a large sneaker crammed up the anal canal, which had been cut open alongside the spine to accommodate the shoe.

"Can't tell you more 'til I get this baby to the lab. Have a good day, Vince." The coroner walked away from him to an organ on the ground. She laughed with the other coroner in charge of the forensic investigation, moved confidently through the crime scene. Vince suddenly felt alone, staring into the macabre face of this joke that some deranged person offered to him. Then, he also laughed.

At one in the afternoon the investigation continued. The restaurant was closed, and the parking lot completely cordoned off and made off-limits to the news media. Cleverly, Vince and the coroner ordered the placement of a tent over the spectacle to prevent news media helicopters from filming the victim. The horrendous odor was constant and heavy, like a hot, crawling, sticky humidity. The coroner instructed a large truck to transport the cadaver to the laboratory. Four men were carefully lifting the chair onto the electrical lift when suddenly a bursting sound made them drop it. Two of them screamed, wiping the red liquid from their faces and chests. Grinning with its heart in its mouth, from its testicles the cadaver squirted four streams of a putrid red liquid.

Vince sat in his car, wrote notes, and watched the now-congested Newport freeway. Police helicopters and cars, portable lights, the tent, and an army of officers searching the freeway embankment that led up to the restaurant created a spectacle attracting drivers and passengers to slow down and look up toward the Parker House. Vince retreated to the department office, wrote reports and, by seven in the evening, he had been up almost forty-eight hours. He went to his apartment and searched desperately for books in his library that dealt with disembowelment, human sacrifice, and performance artists.

As Vince finished telling me about the first victim, I had reached for *El sacrificio humano entre los mexicas*.

"And this? What's this about?"

"That has to do with the second victim."

Vince pushed several books to the side, sat next to me on the sofa, and kissed me.

 For days, I kept thinking about the Performance Art Murder. Vince's account was not as detailed or graphic as he was capable of narrating. He spared me those images, although I would not have been bothered by them. I drove to the top of the Tustin Hills, among the expensive homes of Cowan Heights, above the rich residences of Tustin Heights, near the place where the boy had been killed for stereo equipment. The *Los Angeles Times* and the *Orange County Register* described him as a victim of children killing children over material objects. Didn't his parents see this coming? I thought, as I parked the car looking out toward the Pacific. A windy, cool, clear day offered a view of Catalina Island and Saddleback Mountain. I opened Endriago's letter postmarked November 20.

We are starving and dying from the lack of food and medicine. It has happened again. They are killing our people. Carlos is here with me. We need you, J. I. A right-wing paramilitary group, with connections to PRI, known as Paz y Justicia, carried out a machine-gun attack against the Bishops Samuel Ruiz García and Raúl Vera López. Fortunately, nobody died. We take this as a warning. Harder times are coming and you must return. Allow your ilusa mind to emerge again and help your people.

Your faithful servant,
Endriago

I placed Endriago's letter back in the envelope and allowed my eyes to wander over the tile roofs of the pristine neighborhoods of the rich. What's wrong with being wealthy? I said to myself, and sensed that time and events were going to accelerate.

About this time, the Mayas had found Guadalupe Church, located just down the street from Rebecca's office on Fourth Street. They enjoyed attending morning masses because they had found a few people who spoke their Mayan native language, Tzotzil. To the children it didn't really matter if they spoke it. They were speaking English and Spanish. They and their parents were slowly forgetting Tzotzil. On that particular Sunday, the Mayas, Lea, Rufino, Chac, Vince, and I went to church together.

We attended the special morning nine-thirty *mariachi* mass, which attracted the faithful from the Santa Ana neighborhoods and elsewhere. *Mariachi* music and the pageantry of the mass lured many non-Catholics. Delicious food, homemade *tamales*, and *menudo* sold after the ceremonies appealed to people from outside the Santa Ana community. The *señora* who prepared the stew was repeatedly offered backing to open her own restaurant, but she laughed, and served a free bowl to any entrepreneur who wanted to set her up. On that Sunday after church, we went to the outside eating area to savor some of it.

We ordered bowls of *menudo* and reached for the *tortillas* on the table when, suddenly, a man, who stood behind me in line, carried a full dish and walked over to me. I placed a spoonful in my mouth and tasted the lemony, onion, spicy-red *caldo con chile*. Frozen with what seemed to be delight, he must like the Mexican stew, too, I thought, as he stood before me for a short while until the group noticed him. I raised my head and stared into his eyes. "Oh shit, here comes trouble," I mumbled to myself as he came closer to me. Vince enjoyed his bowl, oblivious to what happened, until the man dropped to his knees, placed the dish on the ground and, in a loud and clear voice, beseeched, "You're *la Santa Ilusa de las Grietas. Lo sé porque te he visto hacer milagros.*"

The man, emotionally charged, waited calmly for my reaction, which didn't come.

"I followed you from Mexico City to Amecameca. I know that you are holy and can perform miracles."

The man spoke loudly enough so that everybody in the serving area heard what he had said. His claims began to cause a commotion. Three ushers came forward and asked him not to disturb the parishioners. But, as they nicely escorted him away, he turned and yelled, "She is a saint, a woman of miracles!"

His shout, a sound between hysteria and joy, had identified me. In his emotion, he expressed hope as he was being dragged away, out of the serving area permeated with the aromas of *tamales, menudo, pozole, buñuelos, frijoles, arroz, chiles rellenos,* and *tortillas* warming on a special platter. I looked at the food and listened to the man on the street calling me to come outside. With his every scream, there came to my mind Endriago and Carlos in Chiapas, one of the poorest states in México. There, Mayans live in wood-slat-and-mud dwellings. Families of eight to ten people sleep in one room, three or four on a bed or on *petates* on the dirt floor. People drink from streams polluted by washing, cooking, and dumping of human waste. Children die from easily curable diseases or from malnutrition. Land, food, health, and freedom are controlled by *caciques* that for centuries have abused the *indígenas* mercilessly. The Mayas have been kicked off their territory, exploited with impunity by the *mestizos* of mixed Spanish and native ancestry. The Mayas found safety in Santa Ana after their escape from the unending and escalating violence in Chiapas.

For a while, outside, the religious fanatic continued to call out to people that *la Santa Ilusa de las Grietas* was inside eating. He did it in vain for nobody paid attention to him. He was just another homeless nut on the streets of Santa Ana. An usher picked up his bowl, poured the *menudo* into a trash barrel, and handed the dish to one of the cooks. Finally, the police came and took the screamer away by force. The sidewalk was peaceful. No more shouting absurdities about saints in our presence, I thought. But the shrieks from a distance of thousands of miles and hundreds of years came to my mind and remained there. Yet, nobody else received them. Here in this country, the cries of desperate communities under siege are only heard on the television for instant pathos, but most are ignored for us to live our comfortable daily lives, for us to understand that we, no matter what our economic condition, are better off than they are.

I recalled how I ran the paths of the volcano in Amecameca, how I cured the sick in the camps, how I defeated the Mexican Army. I remembered my parents, and Sara and Jennie. Those screams still stirred in my head. I felt faint, quickly pushed my plate away, and walked outside to the street from where I listened to the children's choir sing el Padre Nuestro. Outside on the sidewalk an old woman pushing a shopping cart handed me a card with the image of Saint Jude, the patron of impossible cases. Vince followed me there and asked what was wrong.

"I'm afraid."

He didn't bother asking me why. It didn't matter. He just held me until I stopped shivering.

3 | Alive to the World

Es en mí donde *se manifiesta la capacidad del milagro. En mi persona, más que en mi cuerpo, opera la posibilidad de lo imposible… Lo saben todos los que acuden para que a través de mí, o siendo yo el vehículo de lo que no puede ser, llegue a ellos un milagro.*

—LA MILAGROSA, Carmen Boullosa

La facultad *is the capacity to see in surface phenomena the meaning of deeper realities, to see the deep structure below the surface. It is an instant "sensing," a quick perception arrived at without conscious reasoning. It is an acute awareness mediated by the part of the psyche that does not speak, that communicates in images and symbols which are the faces of feelings, that is, behind which feelings reside/hide. The one possessing this sensitivity is excruciatingly alive to the world.*

—BORDERLANDS/LA FRONTERA: THE NEW MESTIZA, Gloria Anzaldúa

I held Saint Jude's card as I watched Jack Ekkerson enter the courtroom.

"I wish I could be with her," Jack Ekkerson said over and over again as he walked by Vince and me.

Rebecca had seen him two days before his court appearance. She described Jack as dejected, because nobody, not even his parents, came to visit him. He became obsessed and terrified by the thought of being alone. Jack had been isolated, on a cellblock where guards monitored the prisoner's every mood—where he slept, ate, crapped, pissed, masturbated. He was intensely aware that eyes constantly observed him. After months of life in a padded cell, he concluded that it was God who watched over him, that God and Jill were testing him.

"I wish I could be with her," he had repeated to Rebecca during her visit. During this intensely lonely time, the district attorney heaped charge upon charge upon Jack. If they were to give him the maximum sentence, it would add up to one hundred and twenty years in prison, but the good news was that he would be eligible for parole at ninety-five years of age. Jack read the Bible. He spent hours, during the day and at night even after the lights were dimmed, learning about the apocalypse, convinced that Jill and he would see Jerusalem. To Rebecca he explained that he was a child of the revelation, that Jill and he, as chosen, would guide the righteous to the doors and enter paradise on Earth.

Jack told Rebecca that he had seen visions of the events that must soon come to pass. In a whisper he told Rebecca that he had not forgotten from where he had fallen and caused the death of his beloved Jill.

218

"I have repented. Tell the judge I have repented," he cried to Rebecca. He sat with her for several hours describing images that haunted and terrorized him day and night. In the last ten days before his court appearance, Jack had been terrorized by a mouth that first appeared as a tiny spot on the wall and moved its way around, up and down, and onto the ceiling and the floor, all the while becoming larger, until it consumed him over and over again. A tongue of sharp swords painfully cut his flesh, and his blood flowed with Jill's on the day she died. "Bring me white pants, shirt, and tennis shoes, for all that I am worth," he sobbed to Rebecca.

That morning Rebecca requested a postponement. She pleaded with the judge that her client had difficulty concentrating due to physical and mental health deterioration, and she needed more time to prepare the best defense. Jack dressed in white, constantly mumbled and at times spoke out loud. He seemed to speak with Jill, to people who were not present; his eyes wandered; he was incoherent and weak.

"One week. We can't hold up the state's business, Ms. Carter!"

The judge slammed his gavel.

"Next!"

Two marshals stepped forward to escort Jack out of the courtroom. As they neared the transfer point at the door, two other marshals reached for Jack's arms. Rebecca spoke to him, tried to calm him down.

"I'll see you tomorrow, Jack."

As he turned to acknowledge Rebecca's advice, he lunged at the female marshal. Although manacled, Jack's hands had approximately six inches of slack, enough to allow him to grab at the marshal's holster and pull out the gun. Jack's feet were chained, but he was able to bend his knees and jump upwards. Tottering, regaining his balance, he stood with the weapon firmly in his grip, squeezed the butt, aimed at the marshal, and as she went for him, he focused just above and between her breasts, found the trigger and fired once. She collapsed, a bloody carnage at Jack's feet. A ringing whiz passed through her flesh and bone below her left armpit. A warm dampness slowly spread on the left side of her torso. Liquid ran quickly down her left leg as a second shot missed her head. Jack shot twice again, crushing the second marshal's head.

Suddenly, he saw Jill before him: Her right hand mimicked a pistol, and she pointed it to her head.

"It's our anniversary, and you want to be with me."

Jill smiled and opened her arms for her lover. In an eerie replay of his wife's last act at their condo in Newport Beach, a roar of memories reminded him of how cozily they had lived with his dog and the bookstore. Jack put the gun under his chin. "How I wish for some way I could be with her on our anniversary!" he screamed.

From behind the benches in the courtroom, Vince heard the blast and the impact of the bullet crashing through Jack's skull. Vince never considered himself a hero; he never, in reality, wanted to save anybody's life but his own; he never even carried a gun when he was off duty, and often was unarmed when he was on duty. He would rather talk to people, help them out of the bind in which they found themselves. Or, he would write a poem and save them in that way. His life was about salvation. One last gunshot rang toward the ceiling and, then, a dead, loud thud rose from the floor. Vince crawled out to the aisle and carefully peeked out to the open area where Jack, Rebecca, and two marshals had stood a few moments ago. In silence, he moved on his knees toward Jack's broken body.

"Rebecca?"

"I'm here with J. I."

Vince stood up. Already other officers and paramedics attended to two fallen marshals. Rebecca and J. I. had ripped off the woman's blouse, but the chest wound was hideously large and oozed blood. Rebecca had a chance at resuscitating her with external heart massage. After tearing the top, blood covered Rebecca's hands.

J. I. seemed to pray while she held the woman's feet. Vince came closer to the fallen marshal and saw directly into the hole between her breasts. A strange smell overwhelmed the courtroom. For a moment, the pandemonium ceased and people looked at each other, then, immediately, turned to their deceased comrades. J. I. stared down into the marshal's chest. She tenderly pushed Rebecca to the side.

"Rest," she said.

J. I. leaned closer to the open wound. She smiled.

"I can see it."

J. I. reached into the shattered chest and her finger meticulously extracted a bullet fragment.

"What have you done!" a guard screamed.

"Wait! The bleeding stopped!" a second guard said.

"It was only a thorn in her chest," J. I. said.

She got up and calmly walked toward the exit. Rebecca and Vince, awestruck and unbelieving, followed. Vince looked back and saw the seated female marshal talking to her fellow officers. As Vince and Rebecca fearfully escorted J. I. out to the parking structure, chaos had overcome the courthouse. Men and women ran out weeping and screaming. "Miracle" was repeated in the distance. As they drove out, spectators pointed to their car and several onlookers placed their hands on the window where J. I. sat.

Vince drove them to the Mayas' house, where they stayed all morning. In the evening, the TV news programs broadcast from the courthouse *plaza*.

"Miracle!"

"¡Santa mujer!"

Officers ran in all directions, police cars blocked the entrance to the *plaza*; city and county buildings emptied, and their workers amassed in the square. Some screamed and ran hysterically; others kneeled, held hands, and prayed.

On TV, several theories were put forth to explain what had occurred. A sociologist declared that it had been mass hysteria that made people believe that they had witnessed a miracle. On a different channel a doctor explained that the bullet had simply missed the vital organs and shattered a bone. The unidentified woman, who supposedly extracted the bullet or a piece of it, must have taken out only a fragment.

"The bleeding never stopped, only subsided, and slowed to a trickle. No phenomenon happened here." The doctor finished his expert commentary with a chuckle. However, on several other channels, including two Spanish-language stations, the reporters interviewed witnesses, several guards, and court spectators who swore that what they had witnessed was indeed a miracle.

"The marshal took a direct hit to the heart. She was bleeding to death, and the lady pulled the bullet out and, then, held up a thorn for all to see. It was a miracle!" a woman testified.

"I've seen gunshot punctures before. The marshal was shot through the heart. No doubt about it. This lady extracted the bullet, the bleeding ceased immediately, and the wound almost completely healed before my eyes. Hey, if that's not a miracle, I don't know what is." The guard continued: "I'm not a religious man, but, after what I saw today, I'm going to church on Sunday."

By two in the morning, Vince had taken me to his apartment. As we embraced in bed he seemed a little unsure of himself.

"What's the matter? Are you scared?" I whispered.

"Yes, I'm afraid. Am I really holding a saint who performs miracles?"

"You decide."

We made love several times until we fell into our lively dreams.

 The immediate aftermath of any major event is a moment of peace before related and unrelated reactions appear. A serene instant may translate into seconds or days. In Jack's case, it took longer than three weeks before the county morgue called Rebecca requesting instructions for the disposal of Jack's body. In the matter of my miracle, for a while afterwards, believers brought flowers, candles, and their sick loved ones in hopes of being touched by the power of the miracle that they trusted would linger for eternity in the building, at the center of the Federal Plaza, and extend to the surrounding area. Daily, the believers came to meditate and pray, and to ask for the Virgin's blessing. It was the touch of *la Virgen de Guadalupe* on that saintly woman that saved the marshal, they asserted time and again. In a little more than a week, the news turned the sacred shrine and the assembled praying, miracle-seeking people into a public spectacle.

The news media focused on the negative side. They interviewed police who worked overtime to guard the area, janitors and maintenance workers who had installed portable latrines, and lawyers who expressed anger at the community.

"It's absurd! They can't have that ragtag shrine next to the police memorial, a place of honor. It's insulting!"

"That crowd shouldn't be here; it's costing too much taxpayer money to keep order here. This superstition is interrupting the business of government."

The day after the interviews, the police moved in and removed the memorial and the faithful. Believers took *el altar* to a house on French Street to continue gathering for prayer. "If the lawyers and public employees are so afraid of the miracle and the shrine, then it must be powerful and true," the owner of the house declared. "I will not let *la Virgen* down. My home is her home." Faithful from as far north as Santa Barbara and as far south as Ensenada came to plead for a *milagro*. Santa Ana police and city council became alarmed when large pilgrimages arrived to hold vigils. Neighbors within a mile radius complained. Their streets were being taken over by cars and strangers who encamped there in order to visit *el lugar sagrado*. After crowds continued to gather and ignore the lawful warnings, a squadron moved to disperse them. Seeing their patrols roar into the neighborhood, *los fieles* of the shrine prepared for another confrontation with city politicians and cops.

On several occasions, the Mayas had attended the special masses sung at the shrine. I refused to accompany them for fear of being recognized. I sensed that this social, religious situation was becoming like previous manifestations in México. I didn't want to cause trouble for Rebecca or Vince. Rebecca had already been besieged by calls and visitors to her Fourth Street office. Her assistant, Manuel, had several altercations with individuals who barged in and demanded he tell them the name of the holy woman who performed the miracle. Jack and Jill's dog, Chucho, had bitten several trespassers who climbed the back fence looking for *la Santa Ilusa*.

I stayed with Vince most of the time. When I wanted to go to the Mayas', he drove me, always late at night because many in the community wanted to find "The Lady of the Miracle."

On a Sunday, the crazed man who had recognized me came after church and stood in front of Rebecca's office, screaming that *la Santa Ilusa de las Grietas* was "The Lady of the Miracle." I refused to acknowledge him. I was afraid of what might happen, that the trances, the religious unions with the Loved One would return. If the ecstasy materialized, I wasn't sure I would survive. I asked God for guidance. I prayed for a sign, and my request was answered with an abomination.

"*Yo los vi.* I saw them before they entered Acteal. They licked their fingertips with their long thick tongues and caressed their AK-47s. Their faces were just like mine: Indigenous."

"I know who sent them. I will avenge my parents, my brothers and sisters!"

At five in the morning the thirty paramilitary gunmen took a position outside the remote Chiapas mountain village of Acteal, located approximately four hundred fifty miles southeast of Mexico City. They took two hours to prepare their weapons, study maps, and review final instructions. In six groups of five, the marksmen moved quickly, unemotionally, in a highly organized manner. One band approached the community of six hundred people, by opening their own path through the rugged terrain. At approximately a mile away, they encountered a father and his two sons coming from the town. Upon seeing the paramilitary, the father froze, while his children walked a few steps ahead and looked back, puzzled. Turning toward the direction of their father's horrified expression, they felt several heavy blows to the chest from two different AK-47 assault rifles, and then they staggered back and collapsed at his feet. As their father fell to his knees and reached to embrace them, three spurts silenced his cry.

These were the first shots the residents heard that morning. Close to four hundred villagers gathered their children, grabbed food and water, and ran into the jungle toward the river, hoping to hide in the underbrush along a nearby steep shoreline. By eight thirty in the morning gunfire from two paramilitary groups, who had been following the stream, started and did not subside until nightfall.

"*A machetazos* they killed women who carried their infants wrapped in *rebozos*. When I arrived the next morning, the earth was still wet with blood."

The Red Cross calculated that approximately seventy-five *actealeños* went to the village church to hide and to pray. All morning the people asked for God's protection from the oncoming evil. At eleven in the morning, the villagers inside heard gunmen talking outside, joking, and laughing as they started to bang on the doors with their rifle butts. Several people started to scream, children cried, most continued to pray, and others escaped through the back entrance and side windows, leaving approximately fifty terrified persons inside. At exactly eleven forty-five in the morning, the paramilitary killers crashed into the place of worship and opened fire. Forty-five human beings were slaughtered: twenty-one women, fourteen children, one infant, and nine men.

Local authorities prevented Red Cross and human rights workers from entering Acteal until nearly midnight. Throughout the day, they contacted Chiapas state officials, urging them to come to the village to investigate the reports of gunfire, but the authorities ignored their pleas.

Evil had spread into the refugee camps where thousands of villagers from the surrounding areas set up tent camps to escape the malignant violence perpetrated by Mexican troops, state security forces, pro-PRI militia units, local community security forces, and land- baron paramilitary groups which operate inside and outside the law to target whoever disagrees or moves against them.

The apocalyptic abomination was this massacre in Chiapas where Endriago and Carlos beckoned. News reports flashed images of slaughtered Tzotzil women sprawled on the church floor, clinging to their murdered children.

"Whenever they heard children cry, they literally shot them out of their mothers' arms."

"Those young men acted like machines at work without feelings. I'll never forget their cold-blooded brutality, especially the evil in their youthful eyes."

This, I could not understand: the presence of a kind of evil invading Chiapas, spreading throughout México, akin to what developed throughout the world in many different ways. It made itself known in giant tsunami waves and horrible floods that drowned hundreds of innocent peasants and left their bodies to swell and putrefy the air with a thick stench, only to float back to the ocean. It appeared in the form of great earthquakes, striking in over-populated regions, burying thousands living in mud huts constructed one on top of the other. Drought and famine stretched the skin of starving human beings in Africa, Asia, and Latin America. These were God's natural disasters, a god unable to bridle iniquity. Sudden hideous diseases wiped out villages in Africa, ravaged the United States, foiled science and, meanwhile, the Almighty seemed to be unable to obliterate malignancy. It appeared repeatedly in the acts of individual human beings: serial killers multiplied and played hide-and-seek with police, leaving a trail of corpses in different parts of the United Sates. Violence claimed the victims of drive-by killings in gang-infested areas in the inner cities of America. Killing for a pair of tennis shoes, a stereo system, or a cap entertained children possessed by the global greed. Drugs and the drug lords and their corrupt lethal empire-like amoebas infected the great cities of the world, dragging children, young and old men and women to the depths of unimaginably horrific actions. Forces from beyond life overran zones of the human experience and manifested themselves in almost comic, horrible crimes. God's fallen angels declared a war of attrition on God's faithful angels, and on the battleground of God's creation, Earth, the Devil unleashed legions of evildoers into the realm of the logically possible, made his existence a resident component of God's spoiled paradise.

"We as [...] young Zapatista women of today, no longer know what a foreman is like, what a landowner or boss is like [...]. We now have the freedom and the right as women to give our opinion, to discuss, to analyze, not like before," Comandanta Ramona's words came to me as I pondered these thoughts, in the Mayas' backyard, watching them plant orchids in Mrs. Dougherty's hothouse. The Mexican political system, I thought, the same group that made Carlos disappear and Endriago retreat to Chiapas, had planted seeds that now developed into embryonic jungle wombs of rebellion. The corrupt system

had spawned violations of human rights, like thriving tumors that attached themselves onto the dominant political organizations.

Carlos has learned more about your grandfather Laurelio Cruz. He was an
unsung rebel who defended the chiapanecos. It is time you understand that your
maternal abuelo was a leader of the armed resurrection against the Army, land-
owners, and politicians. He worked diligently in the Chiapas region to insure basic
human rights for the indígenas. While Zapata, Villa, Carranza, Obregón licked
their fingers from eating the spoils of victory, Laurelio Cruz quietly and without
fanfare trained and guided his troops to fight the oppressors, the racists who, still
today, want to exterminate the totziles. Your tata loathed recognition and refused
titles like "hero." He despised brash men like Villa and Zapata, and he especially
found despicable intellectual warriors like subcomandante Marcos, and his E-Mail
America-On-Line fan club, his famous writer's Nobel Prize-dreaming discourse,
his Hollywood mega-media sharks, his gringo Halloween/Mexican Day-of-the-
Dead mysterious masked-super-hero disguise. Tu abuelo Laurelio Cruz considered
men who put themselves on a pedestal, seemingly in the name of the people, to be
abominations from the Book of Revelation. Now, J. I., in his name, to protect
their families from abuses, los Laurelios—men, women, and children—have risen,
arming themselves again, preparing to confront the authorities, by force and, at all
cost, to reclaim their human dignity and their land. There is great fear here now,
after the massacre. Now the peasants are split even more. Some support the priístas,
others the Zapatistas and their allies, Las Abejas, and now, every day, a few more
come to us, the Laurelios. Too many people have lost their lives, and now there is
no turning back. Our path, Santa Ilusa de las Grietas, leads only forward. Please
come when you decide to answer our plea.

Endriago

Orange County has a way of making even the most accompanied
person struggle with a heavy sense of loneliness. There are times that
I find myself crushed with the feeling that I am alone in this place,
inhabited by millions of people working to achieve their individual
utopias. There are thousands of homes of different sizes, styles, and
costs; there are various apartment complexes in rich and poor areas.
Different faces with diverse racial features look back through their

dissimilar eyes: some smile, others don't, and many just seem to stare beyond, reminding me of how unimportant I am to the majority of human beings in Orange County. Residents are usually in a hurry, always busy, trying to earn more money, add to the house, make a car payment, often preoccupied thinking of a restaurant for the evening dinner, the kid's baseball, soccer, football team, the coach who doesn't play little Junior, or a cute daughter as competition reigns overtly or discreetly, rush to the Nordstrom sale, make sure the cleaning lady doesn't wash the new Persian rug. For eating out with friends there are Chinese, Vietnamese, Mexican, Indian, Arab, Turkish, French, Greek, Korean, Italian, Tex-Mex, New Mexican, Japanese, fusion, In-and-Out, McDonald's, Carl's Jr. hamburgers and, of course, Taco Bell, a company that has reduced the identity of one-hundred-million Mexicans down to a heavily accented English-speaking Chihuahua that says, *"Yo quiero Taco Bell."* Then there is white-ball-clown Jack in The Box, who reminds the Chihuahua that he *is* a dog. Jack sniffs the air and says, "Who's been eating beans?" Still, with all this activity and special attention, I feel lonely living in this postcolonial rush. *"Para todos todo, para nosotros nada,"* I felt the Zapatista uplifting cry from beyond.

Postcolonial—a concept that I had discovered while reading about subjugation of Latin America, Africa, Asia, India, and the United States to European colonialism—defines a process that has a long history, and its practices and social mechanism still function today. I never thought of México or the United States as postcolonial countries, but I understood how the process has influenced—better yet, molded, enframed—our way of thinking.

No matter how many friends surrounded me, loneliness pushed against my heart. I imagined Jack, in the morgue, alone, rejected by every member of his family. Unwilling to be recognized as his relative, not even his father or mother came to claim his body.

Destiny came and tapped Rebecca and me on the shoulder and said, "It's up to you."

She went to Jack's parents and received permission to bury the body.

"All we want is to forget these last few years."

 Two neon crosses rose from the front entrance to Kiki Ramiro's El Mortuorio Que En Paz Descansen on Grand, between First and St. Andrews streets. In one of Santa Ana's older homes, his family had for generations been the main mortuary for the Mexican community. Many years ago, Kiki lost three children to drugs and violence. Ever since, people say, the Que En Paz Descansen specialized in providing wakes and funerals for the poor of Orange County. For several years now, his clientele consisted mostly of indigent gang-members' relatives who had nowhere to turn except to Kiki's funeral home to bury their heroic homies, shot defending their little nation. The homeboys and girls had been eulogized by Kiki Ramiro's speaking to a wordless small group of *familia y amigos*. According to him, the bereaved never had words to speak about their dead loved ones; in their anguish, they offered only sobs, tears, mucus, and gestures of love and revenge. He understood these silent clients, for they had embraced his own kids a while back and, one by one, brought other youths to him to cleanse, embalm, and dress for their wakes and funerals. He refused to blame or hate anyone for what had happened to his offspring but, at times, he repeated to his friend Vince Rodelo, who had often tried to help his sons and daughter, "I don't know where I went wrong or when it happened."

With a white damp linen cloth, in the embalming room, Kiki cleaned Jack's icy eyelids; he gently stroked down over his grayish cheeks, wiped behind the ears, and combed his thick hair from left to right. They say it keeps growing after death, just like the nails that Kiki had clipped from the hands and feet. With a white towel he cleansed the body, then covered the shriveled testicles and penis with the damp cloth. Bathed, Jack's body lay there waiting for makeup to take the gray anemia of death away from his countenance. Kiki painted Jack's lips, added reddish color on the cheekbones, powdered the face, and looked up at Vince and me.

"Ain't this little *gringo* homie pretty?"

Kiki smiled and proceeded to dress Jack in his navy blue high-school-graduation suit. He slipped the pants over the stiff legs.

"I don't cut the clothes. I dress them, give'm a little dignity, even though they are dead."

Kiki struggled with the shirt and the coat, and finally he tied a cheap blue tie. The suit sleeves and pant legs were too short.

"Let's have him hold a cross in his hands. These kids believe they're making a sacrifice, like Jesus on the cross."

Vince pushed a plain walnut-stained wooden coffin next to the slab table and slid Jack carefully into the box. He's all set to ride: Jack in a suit that was too tight, pants and sleeves too short, in a cheap indigent fake-wood box. Kiki, Vince, and I guided Jack into Kiki's Que en Paz Descansen Mortuary's 1939 black, lowered Plymouth hearse. Many a gangbanger had taken his last cruise to a final resting place in that super-fine *carroza*.

Rebecca had acquired the legal documentation to bury Jack out at Dougherty's Twist in an area adjacent to those marked for Mr. and Mrs. Dougherty, and their daughter, Twist. On the public health forms, Rebecca noted that the Doughertys had a family plot with seven burial vaults, one of which would be used to inter Jack Ekkerson. Kiki led the way there, followed by Rebecca and the Mayas in one car, and Vince and me in another. We followed Fourth Street south to Jamboree Road, turned left, up over the foothills leading to Chapman, and took a right on the canyon. Later, Kiki would comment to the funeral guests at Rufino and Chac's house how much the roads and the canyon had changed since the last time he had ventured out to them. He was amazed and saddened by the thousands of new houses that replaced the open fields and orchards that James Irvine had planted many years ago.

"The *gringos* still run away. They're creating these communities on the edge, far away from the central city where Mexicans live. But they can't stop us. Eventually we'll buy out here, too."

As Jack's caravan cruised toward the entrance to Dougherty's Twist, Kiki blasted Oldies but Goodies, Sancho tunes, and some *rancheras*. At stops, people in cars next to us gave us the strangest looks and stares. Some waved, thinking the hearse was nonfunctional and used as one of those low-rider wagons. As I saw the reactions of drivers passing us, I could only smile.

For a while, Vince and I drove in silence, evidently not wanting to ask any questions, or discuss any thoughts regarding what we were doing—not just now but in our lives. I thought about Jack's life. At the end, deemed worthless by his parents and family, they refused to claim his body or plan his burial, denying him their blessing, their recognition of his redemption. His own father wanted no contact whatsoever with his son's body.

"They had been possessed: Jack and Jill had been taken over by an evil that drove them away from what we taught them. Their acts were those of the Devil. Companies they fought against, like Book Barnes, who destroyed small businesses and ruined lives, are instruments of evil. The warehousing of knowledge, of books, is a wicked way to control the minds of human beings," Jack's father had declared to Rebecca during one of her last attempts to convince him to claim his body.

His mother meekly complied. Providing his blue high-school-graduation suit, she embraced her son for eternity. I thought I caught her cry three times on that day when we buried Jack. At the instant Lea waved to us, received us on her magnificent horse, I heard Jack's mother. Lea rode ahead slowly, leading us to the gravesite. When I saw Rufino and Chac—who had prepared a deep, wide and thick cement vault—greeting the Mayas and their children, I heard Jack's mother's weep again. Rufino and Chac embraced the Mayas and the kids; they were so happy to see them again. Jack's mother's lament became more distinct then, a wail of anguish and pain for not being there to return her son to the Earth.

Kiki backed the hearse into position, opened the back door, and men placed the coffin at the edge of the grave. We gathered around the opened pit and listened to him pray. He raised his arms to the heavens, beseeched God to open His divine kingdom.

"God forgive your wayward child. Forgive him for his errant ways. Cleanse him and welcome him to paradise. The books made him crazy, and the big chain stores drove him over the brink, and so, God, like books will surely turn to dust, so too must Jack return to Mother Earth's womb created by You, Lord. For those who remain above the ground, guide us, Lord, in your righteous paths. In God's many names, amen! Amen! Amen!"

Kiki, Vince, Rufino, and Lea secured the coffin at the opening of the cement volt and slid it into place, then walked out of the pit. Kiki grabbed a handful of moist earth and allowed it to fall onto the grave.

That afternoon there were plenty of shovels; even the kids got to dig earth to bury Jack Ekkerson. As each shovelful of soil covered Jack, his mother's cry echoed through the green canyon, over the hills and boulders and followed Santiago Creek, bumping into lovely Twist, the Doughertys, and Jill, who called to her beloved Jack. That day they rendezvoused at Dougherty's Twist, overjoyed that they were together again.

I heard Jack's mother's cry again. Her wailing slowly disappeared, fading into the sounds of the canyon. As I listened to the children playing, her hopeless lament was transfigured into a song of happiness and hope; she knew that her son was now with Jill, and at that moment she let go and ceased to weep. Dougherty's Twist had been changed into a place of blessed spirits accompanying us as we walked to Rufino and Chac's house.

After dinner, at sunset, when the animals started to sing to the coming night, Jack spoke through me. "That's not funny, J. I.!" Rebecca snapped at me as I coughed, clearing my throat, allowing Jack to come forth:

"I am with God and I have risen. I am with Jill. At last we can be together forever in peace. I love you . . ." The trance subsided, and I fainted.

234

Chac put a cool cloth on my forehead.

Vince was not surprised.

Rebecca no longer doubted.

Lea sat shaking her head, not quite sure what she had witnessed, or how to explain the voice that had spoken from my mouth.

"It was Jack," Rebecca said softly.

"It sure sounded like him," Vince agreed.

"I never heard his voice, but that sure sounded like a man speaking from way out there, man," Kiki responded. After I gained consciousness, she shook my hand and said, "That was pretty good, J. I."

Kiki drank a cup of coffee, asked if anybody wanted a ride and left, alone.

That night we decided to stay. The Mayas settled with Rufino and Chac. Rebecca, Vince, and I accepted Lea's hospitality in the big house. There wasn't much conversation that evening. We all retired early. I struggled to sleep, for in the back of my mind I was convinced that everybody believed they had witnessed a miracle from God by hearing Jack's voice. They went to bed certain that I was a blessed, saintly woman, through whom God spoke and performed His wonders. The worrying, of not knowing when the trances would come, intensified. However, I considered myself a worthy person who could rise to any challenge, and if God wanted me to be *la Santa Ilusa de las Grietas* in Southern California, I would not resist Him.

In the morning Chac served breakfast to all of us; then, early-risers Jay and Fay went quickly to help Lea saddle seven horses. The children had been excited about riding again. Lea, Rufino, Ray, Vince, the kids, and I gathered our steeds in Rufino's corral and set out to ride for an hour or two. Jay and Fay maneuvered ahead, leading the group toward Santiago Creek. They crossed it and picked up an ancient native trail that meandered for five miles to Lea's favorite watering hole. "It's beautiful up there. The view is spectacular," she offered to me.

In half an hour we came to a small stone altar that, according to Lea, had been built by missionaries in the eighteenth century. "Here they would rest and pray." Lea dismounted and showed Jay and Fay the mosaic image of *la Virgen de Guadalupe*. "It has stood here for over a century, and nobody has vandalized it because it is a sacred place. To the natives it was a place of great power and natural energy."

Lea waited for Rufino and Ray to finish their prayers to *la Virgen*.

As we headed to the top of a small hill, a cloud covered the sun, and for an instant it felt like the temperature had dropped ten degrees. For a moment the horses vacillated, resisted going forward. Lea spurred her horse to move up, urging the rest to follow, when Fay's mount neighed and went up on its hind legs and bolted through the group, knocking Vince off, startling the rest of the pack. Fay screamed as she galloped ahead toward rough ravines and rocky territory. Lea, Rufino, and Ray spurred their animals and tried to catch up. All the while Fay's screams and cries for help became more horrible. Everyone sensed that if nobody stopped her they would probably find her gravely injured or dead. After twenty minutes chasing her, Lea, Rufino, Ray, Jay, and Vince caught up to the breakaway beast and found Fay seated calmly, facing the ocean, observing the magnificent view. At her side J. I. knelt while, at her feet, both the runaway horse and J. I.'s steed bowed in reverential positions. For a long time the animals knelt before what appeared to be a sacred image of *la Virgen* communicated to the observers through me, *la Santa Ilusa de las Grietas*. Ray held his daughter, and asked her the inevitable questions, "Are you OK, *mija*? How did the horse stop?"

The child pointed to J. I. "She came on a cloud and grabbed the reins. Then my horse stopped and knelt in front of her, *papi*."

Lea and the rest of the group watched J. I. as she prayed and gave thanks to *la Virgen de Guadalupe* for saving beautiful Fay.

"*Papi*, she ran faster than the horse, on a cloud. She came on a white cloud, *papi!*"

Fay freed herself from her father's arms and ran to J. I. and embraced her.

Although the newspaper informs the public, at times its efforts create a fear that resides in the readers' hearts until it explodes. According to Vince, fear was one of the characteristics of life in Southern California. Fear of losing it all hummed below the surface of daily activity. Individuals worked to maintain and improve the economic and social circumstances they had attained; they struggled to protect the level of relative comfort achieved. People survived with the knowledge that, at any given time, their shopping cart filled with their worldly possessions, or their stock portfolio, or the little they owned could all disappear. Fear of losing the good life they had achieved constantly pressured the mind just underneath the smile of Southern California existence. Fear of losing a share of the American Dream to another person, in particular to a "non-American," "a foreigner," "an illegal alien," "a minority," "a low-life Anglo" compelled some to join radical groups and to commit extreme acts.

An expansive fear of information, of numbers, of multitudes, of percentages provided and inflamed by the newspaper—in the fast-evolving world of Orange County, where movement and change were daily constants—drove the fearful to actualize horrific crimes. About an article in the *Los Angeles Times* which led with "O.C. in 2040: Near-Majority of Latinos, Far Fewer Whites," Vince commented, "This headline only fuels the hatred of radical groups toward immigrants and minorities."

Vince continued: "J. I., in Orange County, the population changes as we speak. Look at these statistics! The county is moving fast from today's approximately 2.6 million, with an ethnic composition of 55%

White, 30% Latino, 13% Asian, and 2% Black, to almost 4.2 million in the year 2040, with 48% Latino, 27% White, 23% Asian, and 2% Black. Now, that's scary stuff. This kind of information just drives extreme right-wing groups and conservatives crazy."

"In Germany the Neo-Nazis are growing stronger. Just the other day the *Los Angeles Times* published an article describing how thousands of them demonstrated at a traveling exhibit about Hitler's military. The installation uses photographs and documents to show that ordinary German soldiers killed Jews and other civilians while under his rule. These xenophobic beliefs of the past still linger and grow in the minds of ignorant, unhappy Arians who are certain their country is being overrun by foreigners who steal jobs, education, medical care, homes, and opportunities from the 'native' population. Hatred and intolerance breeds there and here," I added.

I listened to myself and concluded that Vince and I had developed a pessimistic view of human nature reinforced by reports of a series of attacks perpetrated by Skin Heads and Neo-Nazis that had shocked the general population and contributed to the general public's negative view of humanity.

"How could one person be so cruel, heartless, and cold blooded toward another?"

Nobody had the appropriate answer.

Since the Performance Art Murder, six Blacks had been brutally beaten, shot, and left for dead by race-hate groups in Southern California. Skin Heads had pulverized, beyond recognition, the faces of several of their victims. In Orange County, not far from Vince's apartment in Old Town Tustin, a Vietnamese honor student was heinously murdered by two self-declared Neo-Nazis who systematically stabbed him well over thirty times. They left, then returned later to kick and to jab him again. The victim's last gasps were answered with more brutal kicks to the face.

However, these attacks, for the most part, are ignored by cops and the media. The district attorney's office and various city police departments choose to give the hate-crime problem lip service and not much more, refusing to admit that some cities, like Huntington

Beach, are infested with Neo-Nazi groups who teach and wage a low-intensity race war. Official groups in charge of recording these incidents report that they don't receive very many hate crimes. Social activists blame this banal reaction on the part of government agencies for the rise of open xenophobia. Racism of slogans has become racism of acts: violence has turned into a substitute for political action.

It had been three weeks since God had sent Jack to speak, through me, to the people he loved. Rebecca accepted a case in Los Angeles County, in City Terrace, where several women had founded a Federation of Women. This organization functioned as school, daycare center, and refuge for the battered and abandoned. It was run by three females who had become somewhat famous, having appeared on television several times defending women's rights to protect their neighborhood. Their methods were confrontational and had resulted in conflicts with gangs and cops in the area. The mass media had identified the leader of the group as Micaela Clemencia and described her as a religious advocate and social revolutionary. Rebecca had been called upon to visit the Federation Center and had begun to defend them against the police and government agencies that accused the Federation of hoarding guns, interfering with the Los Angeles County Sheriff's Department, obstructing the normal process of justice, and several other charges aired by the news media and published in the newspapers.

I thought the Federation had done a wonderful job organizing the women in the neighborhood to act against the gangs that had killed several innocent children. They practiced a kind of modern-day vigilantism that I considered very effectual. They considered cops as another violent gang and had twice stripped several policemen of their guns and clothes and sent them, naked, to the station. This daring action incensed elected officials and major donors. Rebecca would leave the office and not return for days. The case of the women of the Federation had taken some of the confidence from her demeanor, and her face appeared haggard and worried.

During this time, Vince started to go to the beach to read and write poetry. Often I would accompany him to pray, to think about my parents, my two girls in México, and Endriago and Carlos. How I missed them! I enjoyed walking on the sand, feeling its texture between my toes and the coolness of the water on my legs. I watched young people, lovers, families, and the reddish-lavender sunset. I pretended that the ocean I felt on my body brought messages from the Mexican shores I adored. I whispered to the deep-green salty sea and sent my love.

Vince and I took our dinner—usually fruit, cheese, and a bottle of wine—and a large heavy blanket. We arrived early at the Little Corona Park, a small grass area located at the foot of the rock jetty that ran out into the ocean. Just across the way, on the Newport side, was a parallel rock jetty that was world famous for the notorious body-surfing ultimate challenge, a place—the Wedge. These two quays created the path to exit and enter Newport Harbor and were popular for picnics and sailboat watching. People would walk out on the wharves and fishermen would often cast their lines from there. The Little Corona side had fire pits that were so popular that partygoers came very early in the morning to claim one.

We sat on the Little Corona side, on the hedge leading to the jetty, enjoyed an early picnic dinner and drank an excellent Merlot in paper cups. As I ate and sipped wine I watched strollers along the green garden parkway that overlooked the beach and ocean. They moved with a sense of ownership, maybe headed to a restaurant, to a coffee shop, to meet a friend. Others walked to their car and drove away, perhaps to the grocery store. While passing by, they stared at me eating next to the jetty wall. They looked beyond me and, for a second, lingered at the coming sunset, a glorious repetition in their lives.

On the street there were no more parking spots. While more people arrived to secure a place on the grass, seven couples with a variety of different-colored blankets had already claimed their sunset-viewing banquet venue. I watched as families with chairs, ice coolers, fire briquettes, covers, and towels rushed out to the fire pits. That day Latinos made up the majority, but Anglo families had claimed several of them before Vince and I arrived. Nearest the ocean, three had been taken by a large group of Asians celebrating several children's birthdays. Two young Black couples wove through the bonfires and headed toward a big party of high-school kids blasting music from boom boxes and dancing to rap tunes.

"Hope they don't get any louder," Vince said.

He emptied the wine into my paper cup, wrapped the bottle and what was left of our delicious morsels, and forced it all into an already-stuffed green trashcan. Vince wore a light white T-shirt that revealed the thick black hair on his back, chest, and arms. Passers-by turned quickly for a second look at the man with ape-like look.

"I'm going for a sweater." Vince went to the nearby car while I finished the wine.

When he returned, he found me walking carefully on the huge boulders that made up the jetty. Wind pushed the choppy water, creating white caps on the small waves. Sails were full on the boats that broke toward the open sea. I noticed at least twenty or more fishermen standing on the edge of rocks, casting their lures into the water.

Vince and I walked further out, almost to the point on the jetty where there was even a larger group of fishermen. The smell of the ocean, its life, grew thicker out nearer the point. There the wind was sharper and colder, but the sensation of being surrounded by sea almost made it warm. We stood at the highest spot. Below us, among the rocks, fellows drank beer, cleaned small fish, and threw the offal back to Neptune's watery womb.

On a round flat rock, casting its thick edge over the ocean, two men, one woman, and two children tended three rods as they laughed at the ongoing comments of an older lady—with long black hair, wearing a red, green, blue, purple, and white full skirt pushed high around her waist, and a thin, wet, cotton blouse that bared the imprint and the shadow of her ample, round, prickly nipples—who sat with her legs dangling over the rock's rim.

Vince and I agreed: "Definitely the featured spot!"

Approximately five feet above the round rock, he squatted and listened to the elder joke about the five little fish they had caught. He kissed the wind and the sun that made its way toward the west. I took three steps down toward a girl, roughly three years of age, who hugged the old woman. Still above them, I turned to face the sea, took a deep breath, and closed my eyes in the peace of the family and the happiness of the place.

I peered into an instant where movement had ceased. At the periphery of my right eye, dampness fell from above me and crashed, silently covering my body. Suddenly, still squatting, Vince floated before me and gently sat where the elder had been a moment ago. The child seemed to move rapidly away in a blue volume of moisture. The afternoon reddish light of sundown broke through the sea. Ancient screams of people in trouble splintered the peace and happiness of the place. From the highest point above, on the jetty, a woman cried out for her daughter. The old lady with the colorful skirt now stood on a swaying sailboat between the two jetties. I stood wet and erect on the round rock now, where I had been baptized again, and at my feet, without a shirt nor his sweater, Vince stood with salt water streaming from the mat of black glistening hair on his chest. At the boundaries of my sight, terrified bodies and arms pointed toward the center of the sunset, at a bobbing kid in the grip of the ocean. I held Vince back, stood at the edge of the happy round boulder, and stretched out my arms to the oncoming wave that surely would fall upon us. Shouts quickly drowned out the roar of the current, and the frenzy of Neptune's power calmly placed the girl in my arms. She smiled at me, snuggled in my embrace, turned to the retreating sea, and viewed the dazzling nightfall.

I climbed to the top of the jetty where the child's mother waited in silence: with her mouth open, and her eyes wide with happiness, she conveyed terror with no fear; in awe, she approached carefully, with arms stretched to receive her baby from my hands. The woman kneeled and touched my wet dress. On the sailboat, yards away, following me, the old lady's words made sense to the hundreds of people on the rocks: some knelt, prayed, and others reached to caress my soaked garments.

"Miracle!" they called out.

This word circulates, like an eggbeater, whirling around the beach. Translated and understood in many languages, it comes back to where I carefully make my way toward the small green park. Behind me a radiant sun disappears. The horizon's red, purple, lavender move through clouds while hundreds watch as Vince and I get into our car and drive away into the coming darkness.

That night, the sea retreated to its normal place and left Southern California talking about the astonishing event. After this, news was reported on television, reporters interviewed the rescued little girl, and believers placed flowers, candles, and crowns to create a shrine dedicated to the Lady and the Miracle of the Jetty at Little Corona. The memorial is continuously replenished by faithful who come from throughout the Southwest to pray at the site. Boaters passing through the breakwater between the jetties at the spot of the sacred flat rock toss a bouquet and say an orison for the Lady's protection. On a television report about the miracle, a sailor said, "I'm not a Catholic or a religious person, but I do believe that the sea has a soul, a mind and heart, and so I ask the Lady to bring me back from the waters to my family, like she did that child."

"It was the same lady who was at the courthouse and performed the miracle there. *Es una mujer santificada, una mujer de milagros,*" an onlooker claimed.

As the story spread throughout Southern California, the faithful organized pilgrimages to the sacred flat rock. On a daily basis, the ill, some raised from their wheelchairs and carried, struggled to get near the exact spot on the Corona side. Others went to the Newport edge of the channel, from where *la roca sagrada* was clearly visible. To touch or to see it brought on a surge of happiness that pushed the hearts, the limbs of the ailing, the crippled, made the infirm smile and wave at the worshipers praying on the jetty near the flat sacred rock, the holy place the Lady selected for her miracle. Like the incident at the county courthouse, this phenomenon brought many hundreds to the site. Little Corona requested assistance from its neighbor cities to assign extra police to control the crowds. Finally, the council approved a curfew and declared the area off limits, closed to visitors. Still, pilgrims came to stand or kneel before the police lines, hoping to capture a glimpse of the sacred rock. Again, it was believers, worshipers poised against authority.

"God is everywhere! Why are we being arrested?"

"We can worship the Lady anywhere we choose!"

Rebecca had been away for two weeks, working with the newly founded woman's organization that had received a lot of publicity for its community efforts to control gangs in the neighborhoods of East Los Angeles. Manuel, Chucho, and I took care of the office on Fourth Street. I alternated between my space there, the Mayas' house, and Vince's apartment in Old Town Tustin. The man who recognized me at Our Lady of Guadalupe Catholic Church camped himself, sometimes for days, in front of Rebecca's office, the Mayas', or Vince's. If I could deal with him on the sidewalk, where he only wanted me to recognize him and tell him he was right, that I was the woman from México; if I could invite him in and satisfy his obsession, maybe he would leave me alone. I understood, however, that it could only get worse and more intense. Reporters began to follow me wherever I went, jumping out of their van with a cameraperson right behind them.

"Are you the lady who they say performs miracles?"

"They say that you are *la Santa Ilusa de las Grietas* from Mexico."

When reporters started to pursue me, life in Orange County became increasingly unbearable. But what I feared most was what was happening to me again. The trances, the miracles, all this was coming back, and I knew it was not going to stop. This time my body seemed to be changing: I lost weight, and my hands seemed to be thinner, longer and more sensitive to the touch. I was afraid for the men, women, and children of all ages, ethnicities, races, and mixtures who came together around me, who cared for me, because terrible events were happening to them.

Jack's intellectual nightmare was becoming reality. Every three or four months, another small bookstore closed its doors for good. All the while, the big chains flexed their economic muscles and built bigger and better commercial venues, more warehouses, selling only their versions of literary excellence. They shaped the canon for the ordinary folk. This exclusive warehousing of knowledge chokes freedom of expression along with small independents, Jack used to say. When I read that Book Barnes had bought the largest United States distributor and declared that it would now aggressively help the independents, I imagined Jack rising acrimoniously from his grave.

Catastrophic events were striking down my friends. Mark Forbes came to a sudden but natural end: He was found in the same townhouse that we shared, slumped over his computer. In the middle of a sentence of his never-ending postmodern opus, his brain fried, heart cramped up like a prune, his body turned black, his mouth opened freakishly wide, and his nose fused straight down on the middle keys of the board. He was discovered five days later when the fire department responded to a call at the community. It seemed that his drool and mucus caused an electrical short in the keyboard sending a current into Mark's brain and heart? His corpse smoldered for several days until the neighbors reported a strange barbecue odor coming from his place. When the university called and asked me to clear out his place of work, I refused. Shortly after, an article appeared in the *Los Angeles Times*, giving a biography of Mark, a little about his career as a professor and writer. The newspaper also reported a cruel, anonymous note posted on his office door that read: *Guilty as charged, professorial topless watcher turned on and smoldered in his own words!*

At this time, Vince wrote a poem to his mother that described her in a battle to the death, a struggle with millions of beasts that haunted and finally actualized to devour her. During one of her worst bouts, Vince praised his mother in this poem:

When I went away to Tustin
minutes away from her
millions of beasts
invaded my mother's body
a woman of ninety-one years
of cultured survival experience
she knew the process, like water
she gave birth to herself
a border crosser
lived in Simons, and now in the same
house that my father built back
in Forty-Eight
nobody knows when
or how the beast came
to where she made her stand
the body plague came
one, or maybe one million
metastasize for enjoyment
in the heart of her being
the beast gave no mercy
my mother asked for none
she fought, her nails, her sight

her mind, the fiercest attacks
came at night, the beasts camouflaged
in a moment of physical peace when
she rested and breathed softly
the beasts cramped half her
loving heart
took her oxygen
smothered her flesh
turned her blood green
in veins like
transparent ferns
she screamed at night
she tore at her skin
blood streaked timeless
over her devoured flesh
no pain she said
only a heavy
debilitating anxiety
a desperation for life
she awoke and I found her
bathed in blood wrapped
in a stained white sheet
my father had not bitten her
the tips of her fingers
red with life
flesh lodged
under her fingernails
"¡Ay!" she exhaled
"¡No sé lo que tengo!"
She exposed her wounded
windowed heart and tried
to smile for me
"Las arañas del temor casi
me devoraron el corazón".

My mother needed more care
to fight off the spiders of fear
she lived in constant battle
she will leave only
rememories
like I will leave
rememories of me

Mark's demise and Vince's mother's death exhausted both of us. Vince even talked about getting away from work for a while; he had accumulated over one hundred days of vacation time. His captain informed him that if he didn't take them, he would lose them. But he didn't seem to be in a rush. He was too inspired by the "Performance Artist Killings," his title for the case, and by me, the lady who performed miracles.

"I know that you have special gifts," Vince would say. "I will protect you, whatever it takes." He didn't mean to shield me from those who would do harm to my person, but he referred to the constant stalkers with cameras and microphones, who followed me and waited for the next surprise. He and I often observed paparazzi or a crowd watching or anticipating for us to come out of his apartment, the Mayas' home, or Rebecca's office. One warm afternoon, we watched three men and five women waiting for me to exit Vince's apartment. Believers, reporters, photographers—whoever they were—milled around the sidewalk, leaned against the walls of the storefronts across the way. I observed from our bed, as we were lying on our tummies. We wore only T-shirts and commented on how nasty we were being, enjoying each other for hours, as those people wasted precious time expecting me to be saintly. All the while Vince traced my body with his hands. I reached back and felt the opulence of his hair. I slowly aroused my lover. In a short while I arched the small of my back and sensed the nearness of his rigid flesh. My eyes widened as the fullness of his mane came forth into me and as his desire worked its way deep into my heart.

On a sunny Saturday morning, I rolled over to listen to the news from the clock radio next to the bed in Vince's apartment. Mexico City had been blanketed with black soot from an eruption of the Popocatépetl. The situation in the ancient capital had become chaotic as smoke rose high above the mountain, blocking out the sun. According to the news reports, ash fell continuously, and there seemed no end in sight. Chaos and panic paralyzed the city. Millions, attempting to exit by car, created mammoth traffic jams that brought movement outbound to a horrifying halt. Many more, realizing that they could not escape by car, simply packed a bag and walked out and away from the city in the directions where the ash didn't seem to be falling. It was a catastrophic natural disaster in the making.

Throughout the morning, Vince and I listened to the radio and watched on TV the dark live images coming from Mexico City. I peered into the small television screen and witnessed thousands of people dead or dying on the streets, the highways, the parks, while others did not stop to help those gasping for breath but kept on walking to try to make it over the mountains, on the other side where the air was clear, where no black poison dust penetrated their clothes, seized their hair, and congested their lungs.

Although this footage from Mexico City was terrifying, I, J. I. Cruz, the saintly woman, *la Santa Ilusa de las Grietas*, unable to help, slowly shed tears, prayed, and watched. My daughters, Sara and Jennie, my parents, came to mind. Mother and Father knew what to do when it came to handling and protecting themselves and the children during situations of crisis. These were ancient major forces that stirred to affect modern Tenochtitlán. Tezcatlipoca, The Smoking Mirror, had entered the city and struck back at the Christian God who had ruled for hundreds of years.

Vince and I sat perplexed by the impossibility of escape from Tenochtitlán. We spoke not a word while we ate breakfast, not a word as he went off to shower, not a word as I stepped into the shower and he stepped out, not a word as the TV anchorwoman estimated 300,000 dead throughout the Capital, not a word spoken as my heart for an instant comprehended and staggered and cried out, not a word to crash the silence of the bright morning, as if the world, for a second, realized what was happening in the mighty and high capital of the *mexicas*. Fires broke out in the city, electrical shorts destroyed large sections; they would probably burn for days, the TV reporter hastily said through his gas mask, as sirens, fire trucks, ambulances, police cars attempted to traverse a main street.

"What the hell is going on out there?" Vince went to the window. The phone rang.

In five minutes we drove on Newport to South Tustin, turned right on McFadden and stopped at a barricade. I got out of the car to face an immense blaze, blocks of apartments burning to the ground. Fire, police, ambulances, city maintenance, water district units congregated there looking on, helplessly, as blocks of residences fell to the destructive power and intense heat of the blaze. In the street, down at Hank Lloyd's tennis shop and court, hundreds of residents, mostly Latino, watched calmly as their homes burned. Hundreds ran in and out of the fire zone, trying to save valuables and loved ones. Officers could not and did not try to control the crowd. There were simply too many people. Many others screamed at the firefighters for assistance.

"*¡Mis hijos están con mi esposo en el apartamento!*" a woman screamed directly into my face and knew that I would follow.

Without hesitation the woman stepped toward the blaze. For an instant she looked back to make sure that I was directly behind her, and Vince followed with two dozen neighbors ready to offer support. The deeper into the complex, the more intense the fire seemed to get. Flames leaped out from burning structures now charred and weakened

251

by powerful fire; the buildings cracked and popped, and still others caved into themselves. Everyone felt helpless. When the woman waved for me to get closer, and as I neared a green wooden gate that secured a back door entrance, I heard cries, an infant's cry, other children who called out and, what seemed to be, growling.

Vince and I moved closer and pulled the gate that collapsed with a thunderous crash. We froze and stared at two pit bulls that tore at a man on the ground.

"¡Los perros del vecino!" a woman screamed out, warning the four children huddling together under the burning apartment balcony that was about to collapse.

"¡Presciliano!" She ran to the man on the ground, and the dogs turned and went for her. By now, a few men had picked up pieces of wood, a chair, and they went for the dogs. Three children broke through their fear and ran into the crowd. The youngest rushed to the woman. One of the hounds wrapped its jaws onto the boy's head and dragged the two-year-old back under the balcony. At that moment, the veranda fell halfway and hung there, then collapsed upon the kid and the canine. Several people had clubbed the second animal, lying injured, panting desperately.

The whole second floor of the apartment came down. After the smoke cleared, the fire raged on, burning what was left of the standing structure. Vince and several men attempted to go in for J. I. and the child, but the intense fire easily repulsed them. He grabbed a blanket and rushed toward the flames, but several neighbors held him back. A silence—broken only by the crackling of wood, the whimpering of a dying dog and desperate voices in the distance—made the people stare into the fire and wait for what was coming from within that space. From deep within the fire, an object approached, and the on-lookers sensed it was for them.

"Viene un obsequio," a woman said.

"Una señal para su gente".

"Para nosotros," a man joyously declared. The man held his hands up and began to pray.

"J. I.," Vince cried out.

Finally, several firefighters and officers arrived and faced the fallen balcony. People pointed to the rising flames. They ignored the police who tried to push them back; they kept pointing to the center of the flames and stared into its warmth. From deep inside the conflagration, a blue bead rushed, forming a sapphire half-haloed glow arching a path for a pit bull to serenely come forth to the crowd. It emerged from the blaze with calm eyes and relaxed jaw, wagged its tail, lifted its head diagonally, and seemed to greet everybody. The first pit bull turned toward the fire and sat. At that instant, the second dog, which had been badly beaten, appeared whole and placed itself next to it. Both waited patiently. Nobody feared them now. Although the blaze raged like an immense snow-and-glacier-bound mountain struggling to tear itself from the earth that held it down, everybody waited and watched the constant azure glow from its heart. Movement slowed down as they saw a man heaved from the flames that lapped at his exit. He who had been attacked by the pit bull stood in ripped and bloodied clothes before the witnesses. He raised his hands to the crowd as if no harm had happened to him. His wounds healed. He walked up to the animals and patted them on the head, stood at their side, and looked into the fire.

"¡Presciliano! ¡Te han salvado Dios y sus ángeles!"

Presciliano's wife's declaration brought witnesses to their knees. The word "miracle," expressed in a murmur, circulated quickly through the crowd, when from the heart of blue flames came the child whose head had been pierced by the ferocious canine teeth only minutes before, and who had been buried by the burning balcony. He smiled as applause and cheers of joy greeted him. With no fear, he went to the dogs, knelt between them. The animals licked the boy's face. He, too, saw into the blue halo.

Hundreds attempted to squeeze closer to the blue aurora. The power of silence moved the crowd to kneel and pray. The number present staved off the police who, rendered ineffective and moved by the emotion of the events, stood witnessing, astounded and afraid. Many joined in the prayer, and others cautiously withdrew, stepped away from the religious fervor. Prayer competed with the loud sounds of crumbling charred buildings. Thirty minutes passed with no sign of life from what remained of the balcony. Suddenly, blessings came forth from the crowd that tried to get closer to witness the miracle of the flames. Screams broke out; cries of astonishment came, as slowly there emerged a woman whose image was focused on the eyes, on the gaze of all present who looked into the fire. They saw approach them a lady wrapped in eternal blue blaze with dancing gold fire stars, who calmly shook the soot from her hair, called the child, the man, and the pit bulls to her side and, together, along with Vince, walked away from their nearly fatal disaster.

That afternoon, in modern Tustin, California, while the apartments smoldered, talk began about two worlds coming together, concerning the existence of a profane and a sacred sphere coexisting and overlapping, forming spaces where they both communicated and affected one another. Tangible evidence, witnesses to the phenomenon, declared what they had seen and experienced. Religious intensity grew in the different sectors of Orange County society. The fervor and desire to have faith, in particular in the Anglo world, made pilgrimages to the churches located in the Latino community more popular, for its residents believed in miracles and, in their minds, these actually occurred. Like the courthouse and the jetty, the Tustin apartment fire site was converted into a sacred shrine devoted to another miracle by the holy woman now known in Southern California as *la Santa Ilusa de las Grietas*.

Along with the disastrous calamities played out in daily life throughout the world, people began to realize that happenings of kindness, love, and miracles appeared juxtaposed to the negative events; however, these incidents were never talked about behind the Orange Curtain until J. I.'s appearance in Santa Ana, California. The inexplicable events performed by J. I. Cruz attracted the faithful from diverse religions, races, and ethnic backgrounds. These actions were driven by a force that had rarely before expressed itself in this way to present-day humanity. It was God, it was many deities and, thus, they came and gathered to wait. With them came birds, and one stood out: a white heron that arrived to stand guard on the roof of Vince's apartment.

The rumor and the understanding spread that it had come from far away, not only in distance but also in time. It had traveled for thousands of years to rest here and watch over *la Santa Ilusa de las Grietas*.

The area around Vince's apartment had to be closed off from cars because the faithful came to worship where *la Santa Ilusa de las Grietas* lived. Merchants protested. At first they didn't complain, commerce improved but, then, the streets became intolerably congested with campers, mirroring what happened in México. The crowds choked access to the businesses, children played, rode their bicycles, jumped their skateboards, and ran about unsupervised.

Outside on the sidewalk, the man who recognized J. I. as *la Santa Ilusa de las Grietas* at Our Lady of Guadalupe Catholic Church in Santa Ana continued to camp out at the different sites where J. I. rested. At night, the man called out to her, beckoned her to reveal her state of grace.

"Yo sé quién eres. Santa Ilusa de las Grietas, ¡responde a mis plegarias!"

The man became a celebrity on the morning TV news programs. Interviewed by both Spanish- and English-speaking reporters, his exaggerated expressions and movements made him entertaining and even more popular. He began his descriptions of *la Santa Ilusa de las Grietas'* miracles in México in a calm low voice, progressively becoming more physically agitated and emotionally excited. Physical contortions and a variety of vocal tones hyperbolized his story. Yet, people who listened to him found him sincere and believable.

"How can people believe that crazy man?" I asked Rebecca as I watched three reporters with camera crews interviewing the man outside the Mayas' house.

"I have no idea and I don't care. All I know is that we can't continue like this much longer. Your followers are smothering our daily lives. Now there are more police patrolling the neighborhoods," Rebecca said.

"At times, you have a radiance emanating from your body. It will be impossible to hide you," Vince said in a saddened tone followed by a chuckle.

"It's harder now. I can't control it anymore. I must surrender to God's will now. That's my guide," I said.

Vince noticed the Tustin police cruiser drive by, observing and slowing down whenever they spotted a group of young Latinos. He knew this was the policy, to always make sure the Latinos and Blacks knew they were being watched and were constantly under surveillance: not only the individuals, but also their entire community. Police had partitioned the town into districts, and these into quarters, supervised by designated officers under whose command patrol cars were assigned to particular streets, and to monitor individuals and families intimately. Vince knew the theory: observe constantly, discipline and punish when necessary, mediate to civilize, educate to control, instill self-restrain. The barbarians had to learn how to act, to be what the authorities designated as productive, law-abiding citizens.

That night, Vince and I made love. I wanted him to touch me, to love me, but he refused. He had a difficult time sleeping because of the soft glow.

He looked down into the fifteen- to twenty-foot-deep trench the crew of five men and two women from the Santa Ana Water District had dug for three days on Fourth Street, just north of the railroad tracks. The furrow was about to be completed when one side of it, the one being reinforced, started to slide. Two workers at the bottom scrambled to get out. One had reached for a hand from above, and as he tried to pull himself out, the earth slipped, bringing with it the hand and its body. The man below started swimming up through the surging clay, and he stopped with his head and right arm above the surface. As they pulled him out to safety, the team looked around for each other. Someone was missing. Pangea helped her fellow laborers escape the cave-in, but she had fallen to the bottom. Immediately, they started rescue procedures, and, in a matter of minutes, the Orange County Fire Department and several construction companies working on the Santa Ana Freeway brought in cranes and other heavy equipment to assist. They had started at the moment they understood that Pangea was buried under tons of soil. Several of them panicked and, in a frenzy, started to excavate, wildly calling her name. Suddenly, they realized that the faster they dug, the quicker the dirt slid into the pit. They had to stop the sliding, reinforce the walls, bring in heavy iron sheets to place down the sides and prevent the slippage. They calculated where Pangea was and, at great risk, they sank a four-dimensional iron rectangle with a door six feet away from her. They extracted the earth from the plate, opened the door, and started plowing toward her direction. In the process, they introduced a five-foot pipe, creating a large tunnel to her. Over fifty men and women worked quickly, precisely, not a second to waste, not an inch to err; in half an

hour they had tunneled approximately to where they had calculated she would be, but Pangea was not there.

There are documented cases of survival of individuals buried in a landslide for more than half an hour. Experts have explained that it depends on the consistency of the material and on how the body comes to rest underneath it. In this case the engineers hoped that Pangea might have dug out air pockets as she struggled to survive. Vince had followed the fire trucks to help in whatever way he could. He had arrived there minutes after the cave-in and found himself handing shovels to the workmen and sensing the desperation of the situation. For an instant he thought of J. I., who had gone back to stay with Chucho and Manuel at Rebecca's office.

I returned to my room at the office hoping that the radiance that pursued me would subside. I knew that Manuel would not be overwhelmed by what he saw, by the strange glow emanating from my body. That morning of the cave-in, he and I had decided to sneak out and go for breakfast. He opened the door to the beautiful mansion of Fourth Street in Santa Ana and saw only approximately twenty people waiting to see *la Santa Ilusa de las Grietas*. The construction accident had occurred at nine in the morning and reporters, TV camera crews, and helicopters were on the scene almost immediately. Manuel drove down Fourth Street towards downtown Santa Ana and, upon crossing Grand, came to a stop. The scandalous yellow, orange, red, and blue lights of patrol cars, with fire trucks alongside, peppered the space ahead. Manuel turned into an alley, parked the car, and we walked toward the crowd that gathered around the trench. Police pushed people back away from the machines and workers trying to save Pangea.

"You still put on different lotions for each part of the body," I said, as Manuel and I walked toward the crowd. As we crossed the tracks, the signals went on. Soon after, a long freight train pounded by, making the earth shake from its weight.

I wore sneakers, jeans, a T-shirt, a loose-fitting black sweatshirt, and a baseball cap, trying to be as inconspicuous as possible. As we moved closer to the crowd, a few observers, alarmed about something, ran towards us, screaming.

"Water is coming in!"

"It's turning to mud!"

I walked alone now. Manuel had stopped his advance when he heard somebody yell, "The whole street is caving in!"

Manuel waved at me to come back. His mouth moved; he was yelling, but I could only hear the rumble of the railroad. Behind him the machine picked up speed; the clanking sound, iron upon iron, became louder. I could feel the vibration under my feet as it moved faster. I walked forward as the space before me cleared. To my right, a large crane started to teeter and, slowly, began to sink in what appeared to be liquefied asphalt. The workers left their shovels, threw down their ropes, and abandoned the pit that was filling with water and turning the soil into a thick sludge. Across, on the other side, I saw Vince, who slowly moved away. I waved and kept walking toward him. I could see people frantically waving their arms, their mouths open, surely screaming, but I could not hear. When I went forward toward the muddy liquid and, as I neared the site, my reflection glimmered, my glow beamed more radiantly, the roar of the train passed, a sudden silence overcame my few steps before and above the pit of mud, broken with screams.

"Go back!"

"Stop! It's quicksand."

At the last instant, I heard the warnings. For seconds, I stood on top of the mud, walked a few steps, sank quickly, and advanced to the other side.

In one of the ancient indigenous myths, it is recorded that the Great Energies of the Cosmos created humans from mud. "*Los hombres y las mujeres de barro,*" I whispered to myself as I roamed the liquid soil. The men and women of mud disappeared from the face of the Earth: when rain fell they melted away; when the sun beat down on them they baked and became dry and brittle; when cold arrived they froze and broke into thousands of pieces. Their world was destroyed to create another, a fifth world created by the Great Energies of the Cosmos, one in which I made my way through the mud, remembering the visions of the ancient past, guided by the beat of a child's strong heart and the clear sound of lungs respiring. The breathing and the thudding grew faster, louder, and older as I neared to them. I reached out and found the hand of a woman lost in this obscure space of brownness. When I opened a path toward the voices above, I noticed her eyes seeing, like mine, up above where Vince stood with many police officers and onlookers staring down into the dark, roiled terrain. She held on, didn't let go of my hand. I stepped on solid soil and pushed upward; my head broke the surface. We rose slowly and graciously from the mud, together, holding hands. I walked toward Vince until, finally, hard dry ground stabilized my body and hers.

"Pangea!" A woman and man hysterically ran to my mired fellow traveler. We had walked from the beginning through the evolution of life and, finally, humankind. There, Pangea stood wet and muddied but alive and smiling. She had been swallowed by the Earth, a sea of mud from which new life came.

"How did you do that?" Vince asked, not really expecting an answer.

Police officers, workers, and people who had seen what had happened silently watched me as I carefully removed the mud from my face. A slight glow, a soft, warm luminosity dried my clothes, baked the mud, and made it fall to the ground until I was clean.

"*¡Un milagro sin duda!*" an old Mexican woman said angrily.

"A miracle, but I still can't believe what I witnessed. She brought Pangea out of that muddy grave."

"She brought her back from the dead!" a young woman sobbed.

"Pangea was buried and this woman made her rise from the grave!" an officer blurted out, followed by a cry of great happiness.

The crowd gathered while I waited for my clothes to dry completely. Vince guided me slowly, deliberately, to his car. As we opened a space through the people, many fell to their knees and prayed. Some reached out to touch me. By the time Vince and I were in the car, I was dry and clean, not a wrinkle, not a stain on my clothes.

"*¡Otro milagro de la Santa Ilusa de las Grietas!*"

The words "miracle" and "*milagro*" began to circulate. Onlookers didn't know how to act, what to do. It had happened again, the unexpected, in their time, in their lifetime. Some cried, some laughed, others complained of chills, and a few simply smiled and roamed about, excited because of the new inexplicable event. Like in previous miraculous episodes, they came to pray at the sight, they brought flowers, created a shrine, and waited, hoping to see *la Santa Ilusa de las Grietas*, the saintly woman who performed these holy feats. However, in this case the city of Santa Ana completed its work on the street, repaired the damaged water lines, covered the pit and paved the street, then voted to make the site a communal space. For several months, thousands came from throughout Southern California to plead, make a special request, receive a mandate from *la Santa Ilusa de las Grietas*. As the crowds got bigger, police came only to help direct traffic, not to disband the believers. All the while, the city made plans to build a community area for families and children, a space that would attract residents from Santa Ana and from the outside vicinities as well, from the edge cities that had sprouted out on the rims of the metropolitan centers now abandoned to the poor Latino immigrants and impoverished Blacks. New rapid toll roads went directly to the edge cities, modern dreamlands where mostly White affluent middle-class couples created their personal utopias. Daily, men and women drove the freeway and looked down at paradise lost. They realized their parents had allowed themselves to be pushed out of heaven. They had not stayed to protect their turf, their utopias; they had not stayed to work with the new neighbors. Instead, because of fear and ignorance, they ran to new developments in Orange County, a county they were currently losing to new migrants. Today, new generations found themselves living farther away from what was once the heart of White hegemony; now they found themselves in the edge cities living in manicured neighborhoods or in gated private facilities, still afraid of the newcomers. These were the people the predominantly Latino city council wanted to allure. "Come and visit us. *No mordemos.* We don't bite!"

To welcome all, on the site of the Miracle of the Mud they constructed a magnificent commercial palace called El Palacio Real, an area where the Santa Ana City Council ordered the streets closed off to automobiles and motorcycles. They enticed the best restaurants in Orange County to open there. Many coffee houses served up a variety of exotic blends, teas, and delectable international pastries. Some of the celebrated attractions were the many independent presses and

Thousands of workers' labor and millions of dollars invested allowed the freeways and toll road to open. Again, Vince and I drove out to Dougherty's Twist to visit Lea, Rufino, and Chac. As we drove out to Santiago Canyon, I recalled Jack and Jill and wondered how they would have liked El Palacio Real, especially how people came to support the small businesses and, in particular, the independent publishers and bookshops. Most amazing of all was the dialogue that happened in El Palacio Real. I couldn't help but believe that Jack and Jill would have joined the forces of the Infant Idea, and I believed that, somehow, they were involved with its gestation and birth. Also, I thought of Chucho and how Manuel enjoyed taking it to the Miracle of the Mud Cafe.

I carried a letter from México, from Endriago. The letter had been in my backpack for several hours. Vince urged me to open it. I refused. I was worried. Lately, after the Popo eruption, the news from México never seemed to be good. For months I hadn't heard from my parents, and Sara and Jenny. I reached for my backpack and pulled the envelope out. Endriago wrote:

Your parents and Sara and Jennie were not in México when the Popo erupted. They had traveled to San Diego and Tijuana where your father has invested money in several new maquiladoras that promise to make millions. He told me he had to do it for the girls. His partner, a mechanical engineer, is a long-time friend from Orange County, California. They send their best and miss you very much. If you don't return soon, the children will forget your face.

Your parents' home and your house in Coyoacán had over a foot of soot and fine rock on the roof and inside the rooms that had windows open. The yard, it was horrible, the gardens were buried. The gardens were destroyed, even some old pine trees. Pompeii had died like this, I remembered reading in a National Geographic. It took weeks to clean the place, to replant and water. But now they are almost back to normal. They need you: la casa is empty, a void where only ancient spirits, weeping, roam in and out of the rooms. J. I., you give life to the house, to Sara and Jennie, to your parents, and to me.

I am writing this letter on a table that I made. I am sitting in front of my one-room house in the lush green jungle of Chiapas. It is afternoon and the sunlight streams through the trees, like a million strings from heaven to which lives are attached. What I will tell you now is about the power of God's light to resurrect the dead. The Laurelios, guided by God, beheld a sudden trembling shimmer in the middle of a forsaken milpa in a small flat valley farmed by Natives. The shimmer had been reflected off a gold wedding band freed from the earth by the caressing warm wind.

While Carlos inspected the ring, some men and I explored the milpa and discovered that, in sections, the soil had recently been turned. There was no odor, no smell. I resisted the thought, when Carlos screamed the order to dig. He was frantic, as if he believed that he could save lives. J. I., ironically there are times when rage and revenge seem to be the only relief from the injustice perpetrated by humans upon others.

Ten men from the troop ran through the ruins, found shovels, forks, picks, and hoes. They moved to the center of the milpa, formed an oval, and started to dig. The rest of the twenty-five-man squad kept watch from the perimeters of the field where it met the jungle. It wasn't difficult to cut into the soil. In less than a half hour, several men had dug pits five feet deep.

Rich brown, moist, soft soil did not resist the sharp slashing of the digging instruments; it seemed to give of itself, almost as if the Earth desired to reveal, obscenely expose, what it had hidden deep in its bowels. Carlos motioned to keep excavating. The men then dug faster until one found a shoe. It was Sunday footwear that indígenas might wear for a special occasion: a wedding, a baptism, or a funeral. The young soldier threw it up to the surface—his eyes, his face stunned at the newness of the item. He started to ascent, then he slipped and fell to the bottom of the pit; he now understood what the prize was. He struggled once more to climb out. Carlos struck him down and forced him to plow a little more.

J. I., a little more was all we needed for our most horrible thoughts and images to stand before us. The soldier suddenly screamed and tore at his face, cutting himself. I jumped in to grab his hands, to stop him from tearing at his eyes that beheld a countenance, with an open, distorted mouth, an exposed chest, and twisted legs that had been buried standing or who had been thrown into a mass grave against a pile of bodies half-covered with earth. I saw the blue in the child's eyes. He collapsed when he recognized hundreds of compressed arms, legs, heads of hair, a human mural of death composed of body parts.

We ordered the men to exhume the corpses. They excavated for hours and brought to the surface of the living two hundred twenty bodies and fifty dismembered limbs. Carlos organized the cadavers in rows of twenty-five. Even before we knew

for sure what we had found, we had sent for the International Red Cross represen-
tatives in San Juan de Cristóbal. We estimated their arrival by noon the next day.
The carcasses wouldn't last much longer; that is, because of the stench, we would
have to burn them. We wanted the agency's officials to film and photograph this
holocaust, document this proof of genocide against the indígenas.

Carlos and I, the whole troop, were excited because finally we had proof that
the Mexican military or paramilitary forces had slaughtered villagers for their land
and their women. Females to the military were worth their weight in gold; they
were just as important as weapons or land, because they would provide the future
labor. One healthy girl could produce ten or more children who would comfort the
patrón, protect him, and work his fields.

However, as this episode in the saga of Marcos and el señor Presidente grew
more critical, our discovery in a dense forest, a few days later, proved that the war
was one of racial survival. The Natives battled to escape extinction from deliberate
genocide practiced by the government and private interests, and from experimentation
practiced by large pharmaceutical companies in the region who beguile the indígenas
to ensure their participation. We found that two large clinics hidden away in the
jungle were estadounidenses, places where North American and British scientists
conducted tests on chimps and humans. Some of the results were horrible. I don't
know what disease they researched, or what they expected to get out of the experi-
ments, but several of the subjects were grotesque. A few of the mutated children
are gods now. I can't tell you more because in the camp an urgent call to arms has
just now reached me. Goodbye, Santa Ilusa de las Grietas. Please come to the aid
of these innocent people and of your most fervent servants.

Endriago

The wind in Southern California has many minds. It is fickle. Capriciously, it plays with nature and humans who live within it. Its eccentric demeanor is treacherous. It can caress nature, its earth, its flora and fauna, and its children. From one moment to another, like a psychopath, a criminal, it can also violently rip asunder. This gust takes no sides; it defends no material object and no individual person. It has no place. It originates from all places and goes everywhere. This current of air always has an edge and moves in its own timelessness within time. It is the first and last motion, circling the world and roaming the cosmos forever. It collects in itself every incident, every object in history. What has occurred, is occurring and will occur, is housed in its breath. It is the memory of memories that wander eternally on the rind of the globe and are heard by ancient and modern visionaries, the oracles who hear recollections transfigured into voices.

I listened to the many voices that inhabited Dougherty's Twist. They came plundering, insisting to be heard, like the strong Santa Ana wind that, according to the radio reports, gusted up to eighty miles per hour. Lea, Rufino, and Vince had gathered the horses, goats, and other animals in the barn, tied down the doors in hopes that the structure would hold up to gusts. With the warm air current blasting the brush, the wooden structures dried, making them kindling for any kind of odd spark. Hence Lea, Rufino, and Vince secured every shovel, pitchfork, pick, rake, axe, wrench, hammer, any object that if banged together could accidently create a flicker and ignite the fields, the sheds, the barn.

Sirens moaned in the distance as the horses, restless, bucked at the moving, creaky walls of the stables. I looked outside toward the barn, wondering how Vince was doing. I placed the plywood over the window just as a blast of wind slammed buckets and a few chickens against the outside walls of the house. I could hear the chickens desperately cackling to fight the wind. Suddenly two thuds slammed against another window, shattering the glass. Chac and I looked at each other and continued to fold clothes and blankets. We prepared a stew for dinner. It had been a while since I had prepared any kind of food. I was happy helping Chac. It was as if I was back home when I was a child. I walked to the screen where I had heard the thuds. I could hear birds' wings flailing hopelessly behind the plywood. I noticed blood trickling over the ledge, coming from underneath the plywood sheet. Chac immediately filled a large pot with water and put it on the stove to boil.

"Their time has come."

She smiled and carefully opened the front door. She stepped outside and untangled the two chickens from their fatal crash landing. She looked up to the sky, at the trees, and the bushes.

"The wind has stopped! It's gone," I said, amazed at the calmness of the canyon.

Dangling two bleeding chickens by the feet, Chac pushed me back into the house. Moments later, a horrendous gust roared through Santiago Canyon, taking trees, fences, tables, chairs, small boats, and dogs and cats, a myriad of unsecured objects. A burst of wind shook the structure and vibrated the walls. Making human squeals, the ceiling and roof clung by nails to the framing of the old building.

In the evening, the wind had settled down and the sky and stars were infinite. The five of us sat on Rufino and Chac's porch and stared up toward the milky white blanket scattered above us. Out in the canyon there was less artificial light, allowing for a spectacular show of celestial luminaries.

It was the same sky that Vince and I contemplated the following night from the window of his apartment. Nearby, the high school had an evening concert in the park where the high-school orchestra and choir performed. The student crew decorated the stage with strobe lighting, a variety of colorful spotlights, and they wrapped the trees with long cords of colorful illumination. The park was happier than a birthday at Christmas time. Children loved the flickering, flashing, throbbing colors. Tustin High School's orchestra, chorus, and teens brought out a real sense of community pride, belonging, friendliness, and happiness. People smiled, laughed, and talked to each other, asked, "How are you doing?" and meant it.

Vince and I decided to go to the park to listen to the orchestra and choir. It was a warm, fresh, exciting evening. Through the window I saw the faithful, now forced to stand up, clear a path, now scattered and lost, swallowed up by the hundreds of Tustin folks who made their way to the concert, hoping to get a space to open their blankets, to enjoy a family picnic dinner with their kids and friends. With the faithful distracted, Vince and I made our escape through the back of the apartment.

As we approached nearer to the park, the music and choir became louder, and everyone was so peaceful here on the grass and under the trees. Mothers sat with their children on blankets, young lovers sat holding hands and kissing, grandmas and grandpas observed approvingly this Orange County anachronistic small-town scene. A slight breeze meandered amongst the crowd, as the musicians and chorus performed popular movie themes. A low wind brought voices, not happy ones but terror-stricken, unintelligible, screaming shrieks of ancient people, struggling, clawing their way out of the automatic weapons' fire. After two hours of killing, the armed men inspected the bodies and with machetes split open their heads like coconuts. Gathering more villagers, the killers gathered more young men and women, and made them dig deep graves for their dead neighbors and for themselves. Exceptions were made for some of the prettiest girls of the village.

"*Pues, ¡qué lástima! Tan bella niña*".

"*¡Llévesela, mi general! Le dará placer,*" a mother begged.

Shots rang in my ears as the kettledrums roared and the people in Tustin applauded and cheered their young high-school musicians.

Under a large old oak tree, one of Tustin's landmarks according to Vince, I watched a pregnant woman give her elderly mother several pills. I thought of the hospitals in the wilderness where *indígenas* were made to believe they were receiving treatment for their illnesses and their children were injected with infections for the scientists to monitor. Once infected, they were made to return every day. There were potentially profitable projects carried out in the darkness of laboratory cells deep in the bowels of the family clinics in the jungles of Chiapas. As I picked up the business section of the *Los Angeles Times*, I read, "BioMedTec gets approval for three of its anti-rheumatoid arthritis drugs. Originally developed abroad and tested at several European universities, the United States and European pharmaceuticals announced approvals today. The drug, ARheuFreeTic, will be available in the United States in one month."

While the testing continued, it created horrible bone mutations in Native offspring. Once the doctors completed their experiments, the boys and girls were released into the jungle to survive on their own. If found by villagers and interpreted as good signs, the deformed children were praised as creatures, *criaturas*, of the natural energies of the cosmos, given a special god-like place, worshiped and consulted as oracles. Others, not so lucky: If not killed by residents, eventually they were devoured by the wilderness.

The elderly lady coughed. She choked on the pills. Her daughter made her drink more water. She seemed to be fine, her suffering over. She turned to face the stage, to enjoy the concert. One of her grandchildren jumped on her lap, nuzzled her head between grandma's warm breasts. Three more children gathered around her and sat at her feet. She drank more and held on tightly to her babies, as if they nurtured life in her.

Endriago's letter, genocide, Chiapas, Carlos, Sara and Jennie, *el Popo* in Mexico City—"What would make mountains move?" I queried, as I looked out toward Saddleback Mountain under a violet-red evening sky where I found a tall slender woman standing, hidden from the crowd, behind several large red camellia plants, painting. This elegant lady stood directly before the grandma, her daughter, and three children. Her gaze went to the family and returned to the canvas. Vince walked to the artist's side and waved me over. By the time I contemplated the portrait, he was listening to the smiling woman, who wore a brownish red-earth color long dress, a green bandana with small, delicate green feathers around her head. She stared into my eyes and gently placed her hand on my face.

"You have a beautiful, wonderful glow to your skin."

For a moment longer she touched my face, and then began to explain her work. She waved Vince and me closer, as if what she said was only for us to hear. She methodically pointed to the many figures and objects of the painting.

"It is a painting of the park, the people and, especially, that family."

The woman pointed to Grandma and her children. The portrait had two principal figures, one a tall, naked Indigenous woman. A crown of green feathers blended with her long, black hair. The female figure ran out the door carrying the second important person, a child wrapped in a blue blanket, taken from a crib, perhaps stolen away from a room, a dwelling inhabited by paranormal creatures. Outside, the Moon observed, and directly beneath it a fiery mountain smoked toward the dark night sky. Objects and beings in the house moved outwards. The painting was fascinating, and the Moon and the volcano drew in the spectator.

"The child is dying, and he is taken away by a *cihuatita*."

"This is what you see here? The park?" Vince asked incredulously.

"Yes, the park, that family, that old lady with the children, and the young pregnant woman. They are surrounded now by a variety of *cihuatitas*. There are several of them, naked, competing to take the child." The mother-to-be paused. She smiled at me.

"You understand, *cihuatitas* are energies of the cosmos that protect dying and dead children who come for them at any time. These are unpredictable forces that often steal living babies or take abused kids and protect them in death, transporting their souls to Xochitlalpan, the Land of the Gardens, where there is the Tree of Lactations under which they grow. The broods and the spirits that take them there are happy in their world of the dead."

"You say they are here now?" Vince asked.

"Yes, several are here, but these people have not learned to see them yet. They are always around young children, guarding their souls, ready to take them away to the place of the dead. That is their function in the order of the cosmos."

I pointed to the volcano in the painting.

"You know that volcano. Popo is the energy of eternal love."

"That just about buried Mexico City," Vince countered.

"Yes, because of love."

The woman nodded to confirm what she had just said. She brushed with the moon's glow a little white and blue on the brilliantly snowcapped Popo.

"Popocatépetl, Smoking Mountain, and Iztaccíhuatl, Sleeping Woman, were two giants, paramours who roamed the world to finally settle in the paradise of the Valley of Anahuac. In that time colossuses, like mountains, moved and played. They lived there for thousands of years. One day, the Energies of the Eternities became angry and displeased. To be transfigured into peaks was their fate. They killed the woman, Iztaccíhuatl, for she was the greater transgressor, but the man, Popocatépetl, was condemned to eternal life facing his beloved for beyond time. There are times that, in his agony, he attempts to tear himself free to go to his *enamorada*, to hold her once more, for when he does she will rise from the dead and live to play in the Valley and roam the world with her faithful lover once again. But this will not happen until Popocatépetl understands the displeasure he caused the Energies of the Eternities. So, you see, part of his fate is to try to understand the reasons for his condition. Popocatépetl ponders his state and, often, in his monolithic intellectual and physical struggle to uncover the reason that will enable him to move and to touch his beloved, he shakes the Earth, avows with fearful groans and spits rage from his mouth. Smoke that spirals from the *fumaroles* is evidence of Popocatépetl's burning, loving heart that keeps the body of Iztaccíhuatl warm, awaiting his touch."

"The snow, what does it signify?" Vince pointed to the whiteness on the volcano.

"The Popo is forever covered with snow, the discipline and patience that lovers must possess to wait until they embrace again. Without the cold coat the Popo will surely convulse horribly and cause a great catastrophe."

The artist brushed more moonlight onto the painting; my vision followed each stroke, then I caught the shine leading the *cihuatita,* swiftly carrying the child on their journey to Xochitlalpan, *la Tierra de las Flores.* I followed the *cihuatita* as she sprinted through the door to a garden in Coyoacán, beyond the great city toward the Popo that I knew intimately. Like the grandmother in the park, the *cihuatita* held the child tightly against her breasts, as the *abuela* ran through green hills in dreams of her youth. Up familiar paths of the Popo, I ran after the *cihuatita* on the way to the Land of the Gardens, to the Tree of Lactations. I laughed as I passed by Amecameca and saw Sister Antonieta, my running partner, and Sister Cristina, *que en paz descanse.* I kept going, trying to keep up with the *cihuatita,* but soon I raced alone through a mythical painting populated with the faces and bodies of the people I loved. My mother and father jogged north to visit their newest *maquiladora* in Mexicali. Sara and Jennie together played the Mexican national anthem on the piano. I found myself going north chasing my parents and Sara and Jennie's music. Vanessa dashed by me, waving a gun and her Harvard degree. A shot flew in my direction, and Cassandra appeared, her body full of holes. She walked by, concentrating on her writing. "I have your notebooks," I shouted. She sailed away. I tried to reach her. I wanted to see how she was. I reached out to grasp Burciaga's hand. He pulled me toward him, held me and groped his way over me. I screamed. Sara and Jennie played the anthem *forte* while standing in a deep-green jungle clearing. Carlos, soaking wet with perspiration, listened intently and waved ten men back to the protection of the dense vegetation; I waved back, but he fled, turned, and fired several shots in my direction. I screamed, "It's me! Carlos! It's me!" I fell through the moonlight, which led to a small, intense lamp, illuminating a long poem, a tome held by deformed skinny hands, a hunchbacked man: clothes hanging on him as if on a hanger. He raised the volume toward me, the sleeves of his shirt slid down thin arms; he lifted his face toward me: my faithful Endriago, a skeletal countenance, severely emaciated neck, his eye protruding from one side of his face even more grotesquely. He read and smiled; he recognized me; he put the book down, picked up a coconut, and broke it

out with his fist and ended up inside the rolling bush. He panicked as he realized that the bulky dry bud was moving, and he with it. His pregnant mom ran to him and the rolling weed that headed for the old oak. The gust became furious at that moment as I moved to help the kid. Now, under the tree, the mother stopped the tumbleweed and broke its dry twigs, freeing her son's arm. She hugged him in the buffing wind when, suddenly, a series of cracks, like gunshots, got everyone's attention. The woman, still holding her boy, looked toward me, while Vince and Grandma focused upward to the high branches as they came crashing down with bright lights on electrical cords. Sparks and buzzing sounds marked the breaking of electric wire, charges popped, igniting the dried bushes crushed by tree limbs that had buried the expecting woman. The child ran to his grandmother, who was now hysterical, trying to gather and protect her grandchildren from the falling wood. I heard the expectant mother yell and saw her grabbing at the different colored lights, breaking branches to open a path out from underneath the timber. I ran toward her and, as I reached to help, she grabbed a broken light bulb and a torn high-current wire that supplied the electricity to the stage. Instantly, her clothing smoked, her hand and arm burst into smoldering flesh, she screamed and, like a large burning flag flapping in the violent wind, flames engulfed Tustin's landmark oak tree. Fire trucks and police units pulled up. They ran to the flaming tree and, next to each public officer, there came running a *cihuatita*. I looked about and saw even more trying to get to the pregnant woman. I understood that they had come for the child. Like the airstream, they moved about quickly, lusting to penetrate every space, to raise the flames even higher, but they never took their eyes off the pregnant woman. Like green hummingbirds, they darted in and out of the tree, waiting for the precise moment to extract the unborn child. My eyes followed their darting. My body burned with warmth and a glow. When I entered the blazing tree, hundreds of shouts followed from people watching me disappear under the fallen burning branches, like the dark muddy ocean of earth in which I walked. I moved toward the faint complaints of the pregnant woman. Like pesky mosquitos, I waved the flames from her face, her eyebrows, her hair almost gone. I looked into her eyes, caressed her uterus, and made her stand. Around us, the flames and the *cihuatitas* became frenzied and angered by my confidence. I fixed my eyes on every one of them.

"They are mine!"

Cihuatitas, like a thousand hummingbirds, darted toward the woman; they grabbed at her burning clothes, her arms, wanting her to fall back into the flames. They were not cruel; their concern was to save the child still wrapped in its warm womb. They watched the mother's smoldering flesh. As she staggered, I held her up against the wind and the *cihuatitas* who swirled around us.

"Walk, to save your child," I whispered softly.

Out through the blaze, the pregnant mother could see her other children holding Grandma. With the open flesh of her arm on my neck, she took a step out; she would not fall, she would not give up her child to the flames or to the thousands of hummingbirds that swirled in the fire. With a few more steps, we broke through the wall of flares to the cool air of the late evening. The wind had stopped blowing, while the fire devoured Tustin's landmark oak tree.

Standing alone, before the fire, still being licked by the flames, I watched the firefighters drape several blankets on the burning, expecting woman. They laid her on the grass, placed an oxygen mask over her nose, and started pumping her heart. She was horribly charred. Her eyes searched about until she found me standing there, watching her suffer. She knew I was aware that she would not give up. As long as she continued breathing, her baby would survive. While the *cihuatitas* transfigured themselves into women and multiplied within the crowd, people now voiced observations as to how I was not burned. The pregnant mother's clothes were scorched, the material had blended into her skin; yet I was not, my garments weren't even singed. Suddenly, a cry came from her: she stretched her blackened torso as water streamed out of her and settled underneath her; she pulled her legs to her chest and began to breathe rapidly. She understood exactly what to do. The stench of flesh and excrement ascended from her body. She labored to bring forth a child whom she would surrender to fire, even death. I broke through the circle of men and women aiding her and placed my hand on her contracted uterus that instantly opened like a watermelon, and from the red sweetness of skin and blood I withdrew an infant, a girl, and placed her on her mother's burned breast.

"What the fuck's happening?" a firefighter yelled.

"Her skin! It's changing!" a woman paramedic repeated.

As the officers swirled around, assisting the baby and her mother, Vince took me away.

"It's a miracle, a miracle!" Grandma cried out, holding her grand-children. "The lady who saved her—she did it!" I heard her say with a great joy in her voice.

The crowd scattered round, seemingly looking for me. Vince quickly took me back to the apartment. The faithful, who had been waiting there, had heard the commotion and joined the crowds in the park. That evening, as the word circulated about another miracle, long lines formed to pass by the site of the Miracle of the Wind and the Tree. Tustin's landmark oak tree had been reduced to ashes. People walked by and grabbed a handful of them, placed it in their pockets, purses, bags, rubbed it on their limbs and bodies. Some at the site of the charred trunk threw themselves on it, burning their skin, willing to suffer pain for a miracle or forgiveness. The police had to restrain the believers who came throughout the night, and the next day, until only a grayish ashen spot of the tree remained in the middle of the green grass. That evening, while Vince and I made love, an ongoing holy vigil continued outside his apartment in Old Town Tustin.

Several weeks later, after the excitement surrounding the Miracle of the Wind and the Tree, after the mother, who was miraculously saved by the lady known as *la Santa Ilusa de las Grietas*, appeared on national television, with her newborn miracle infant, the other children, and Grandma testifying "It was a miracle! I want to meet that holy lady and thank her, please, let me!" Southern California and Orange County fell back into the sphere of randomness, constant movement, ubiquitous change, pervasive surveillance, and capricious uncertainty, retreated into a domain where ancient spirits meander like rumors through modernity's heterotopia. Among the faithful keeping holy vigil outside Vince's apartment was an observer from the Los Angeles Catholic Archdiocese, accompanied by Father Cristóbal, a priest from México. The Church had again taken notice of the events that defined the life of J. I. Cruz.

The first contact Father Cristóbal made was through a church messenger who proposed a meeting with me at a place where we would be seen and unseen. I understood that he was unsure about whether or not I would see him. He must have thought that I still held his conduct with Sister Cristina against him. Images, memories of those days in Amecameca, of running on the paths of the Popo, and watching Sister Cristina slowly die while the Church denied her hospital care, angered me, yet I didn't blame Father Cristóbal. I recalled Sister Antonieta's explanation of his and Sister Cristina's quandary: It was a dilemma of love unrequited, and I accepted that explanation from my running friend.

Just outside the door of Vince's second-floor apartment in Old Town Tustin, a young nun asked to see *la Santa Ilusa de las Grietas*. I could hear every word she softly said, as I went to the door and stood alongside Vince, who wore a loose T-shirt. I held on to his hairy arms. The nun's eyes focused on his hair. Noticeably uncomfortable at my sudden presence, and especially watching me holding his arms and moving my hand up to his biceps, she stood as a poignant reminder of another corpulent woman, for she shared the same figure as Sister Cristina. Politely, she refused to enter the building.

"Father Cristóbal wishes an audience with you. He proposes tomorrow at three in the afternoon at El Palacio Real." The nun's bodily attitude indicated that she would not move from the doorway, would not leave without a reply.

I moved away, back into the apartment, while the nun inched forward not to lose sight of me. Vince motioned for her to enter. She held her ground on the threshold. For an instant, I felt like slamming the door literally in her face. What an impression that would make on Father Cristóbal! She took one more step forward.

"This request comes by way of Cardinal McCracken, who wishes you to accept." The nun raised her face and eyes smugly. How can you not accept—I imagined her thoughts—an invitation from a prince of the Church?

"Why do they want to meet with me? What have I done to attract their attention? As for Father Cristóbal, he should have stayed in México licking the wounds of his departed heart . . ."

Without my even finishing what I had to say, the nun turned and walked out to the stairs. Angered by her abruptness, I ran after her and caught her on the stairwell. "Hey, I haven't finished my reply!" I was furious.

"J. I.!" Vince called from the top of the stairs.

I grabbed the nun's arms, pulled her toward me, and beheld the anxious face of Sister Cristina. "Tell them *yes!*" I watched the nun lift her skirts and hurry out to the street. Suddenly, every face that I had left behind stared at me, and the past came crashing down to crush my heart. Weeping, I fought back and felt the coated arms and body of my lover holding me through the darkness.

The very next morning, the sun radiantly nudged me awake. I opened my eyes, remained motionless sensing the warmth of the thick natural light that fell through the window. Noises outside, from down below, street voices leaped and somersaulted to my ears to cascade, syllable by syllable, on my naked body. They waited, still wanting to see, hear, smell, touch, and violate my space. In God's name, they willingly used me to save themselves. I, *la Santa Ilusa de las Grietas*, had to respond to them by doing nothing, by not defending myself, by allowing to happen what would happen. I sat up and put on a loose linen dress, the delicate, wrinkled linen caressed the strength of my body. I had not bathed yet. I smelled like an exerted woman of labor. No lavender soap to linger, just me, God's creation, a flesh-and-blood Coatlicue with a mother's bouquet. I stood before the window and my son above. My double serpent mouth opened a smile to Vince, on the street, talking with his colleagues from the Tustin Police Department.

The chief, accompanied by a city councilman, who suffered from a palsied movement of the head and who never took away his gaze from me and the mayor, a tall pleasant woman who endeavored to be understanding despite obvious nervousness in my presence, spoke to us about money. "What has to be done? Impossible to guarantee your safety. Crowds are becoming unruly, harder to control," he said.

"We can't afford it. Police overtime. Miracle or not, we refuse to pay," the mayor added.

"Someboy has to act soon," the police chief said to Vince, as if I weren't present. They talked about me, but not with me: "Tomorrow we clear the streets. Neighbors, businesses are complaining, Vince."

The public, usually Anglo Americans, complained: "Get these religious fanatics out of here." "Mexican superstitions are insulting to intelligent individuals." "Miracles can't happen today. I, for one, don't believe in them. There must be a scientific or natural explanation for the strange events that have happened." "These people are congesting the street, making life difficult for everyone!"

"They must go!" a protestor screamed outside.

"And the city will bill you for the manpower," the mayor added. She had said what she came to say. Linen clung to my perspiring flesh.

She didn't wait for the two officials; she left, seemingly upset, and disgusted at my presence, at my smell, at my thinly covered naked body.

"It's the same in Santa Ana, Vince, the crowds in front of the Mayas' house. It's the same situation for the Santa Ana Police Department. The mayors talked. I'm sorry. There's talk about the Immigration and Customs Enforcement. I shouldn't be telling you this regarding the ICE. Just do something."

At the Mayas' house somebody shot into the crowd, wounding four of the faithful. "Go back to México for your miracles," the shooters shouted from the passing car.

The councilman, who had said nothing, bobbled his head. He said, confusingly, "I know have you important somewhere else to do." He turned and revealed a crooked back, a hump that I hadn't seen while facing him. Then the councilman turned and gazed at me one last time. His profile brought back a remembrance of someone I loved. I watched him slowly follow the police chief, Vince's boss, into the warm arms of Huitzilopochtli.

I believed in survivors, individuals who possess in life an aura of energy, like the Ekkersons, Mrs. Dougherty, and Endriago. Rebecca was a survivor; she was one of God's practical implementers of a divine intention, and she needed intention now more than ever. She resisted: she didn't want me to go. Manuel and Chucho tried their best to convince me to stay.

In Orange County, the anti-immigration movement changed its tactics, and the forced repatriation of Mexicans began, not only by the ICE but also by marauding, independent racist organizations that removed them from the streets and deported them to México. Rebecca had plans for me to be the Latina spokesperson against the xenophobia that plagued Southern California and now raised its specter over the area. According to her, my qualifications were ideal: born in the USA, educated, loving both México and the United States, speaking English and Spanish perfectly. Rebecca offered to raise my salary and, when that didn't seem to impress me, she offered me a partnership. "You don't have to leave. This miracle business will overdose on its own. Your followers will soon forget and you'll return to being just one straw in the broom again."

That night, Rebecca expressed more of her opinions. "The Latino population is growing and soon it will dominate the state. It represents a huge financial market with unlimited financial opportunities and political power. All we have to do is educate them to understand they can make money, they are capitalists and must stop saving their money at home or in a bank savings account and think about investing in housing, mutual funds, stocks, bonds, and other financial instruments. Get them to see that they have been a critical part in the economic development of Southern California and the world, and that their numbers and monetary strength equate to political power.

"That's why I found investors for the building of El Palacio Real. There I will help in the reeducation of the Latino population. And I want you, J. I., to be a part of this venture. I'm convinced that we will make money, and you will be able to help your people in Mexico."

"My family in México, as you well know, are very well off and don't need any financial help."

"I know your family is fine. Your father is back in the *maquiladora* business. I've heard he has opened a factory Mexicans call *La Maquiladora de los Sueños de la Imagen*. I don't quite understand the concept. But I do know that he is making bundles of cash."

Rebecca's knowledge about my parents, especially my father, amazed and bothered me.

"So, you see, J. I., I need you here. Your place is with us, helping the community find its power."

I was imagining the future shape of México and California on the morning of my meeting with Father Cristóbal.

Outside, Vince parked his car in the driveway. I watched him approach Rebecca's house, and I lost his image, but I heard him as he opened the door. He had been at his apartment and at the station, meeting with the chief and city officials. There had been no faithful followers walking or waiting in front of Rebecca's office. Patrol cars drove by approximately every ten to fifteen minutes. They stopped every person who walked or paused outside. Cops prevented everyone from worshiping out front. Fourth Street became a forced neutral dead zone. The panopticon forces prohibited my faithful from assembling to worship, to wait for *la Santa Ilusa de las Grietas* to come outside. "Police have cleared the streets in Old Town Tustin and Santa Ana officers have sent in their special units to prevent camping at the Mayas'. Nobody can gather in your name, J. I. If they do, cops invoke anti-gang ordinances and arrest innocent people. As for me, the chief has placed me on an indefinite leave of absence, with pay."

"If you work with me and drop the miracle business, be a regular person, they'll leave you alone, J. I."

"My God, Rebecca, have you turned into somebody I don't know? I can't do that. I have a calling: God, *la Virgen de Guadalupe*, Coatlicue, Frida, and oracle women who have gone before me speak to me. They guide me and I will not let them or my faithful down."

"Fine, but tell them that you will be a passive advocate who won't incite your faithful. That's why they are afraid of you. Not since the Vietnam War have so many gathered to support you and what you do. There is a presence among us that has not appeared on Earth for hundreds of years. Thousands of people are feeling that presence. You know what they want. You are needed here as much as in Mexico."

Rebecca picked up her briefcase. She went into Manuel's accounting office for a few minutes.

"I'll see you at El Palacio Real," she said.

Rebecca walked past Vince, who had taken a gun out of the trunk and adjusted his shoulder holster. While she buckled her seatbelt, in the rearview mirror she saw two police cars driving by in opposite directions.

The disbandment of the faithful had instigated a swarming of activity at El Palacio Real. Those who had gathered at Vince's apartment in Old Town Tustin, and those who had waited at the Mayas' house and been roughed-up, took their broken bodies and egos to El Palacio Real. There, they expressed their anger by equating the police to another vicious gang on the streets that tried to take away their constitutional right to worship, to gather, and to express themselves. Thousands of furious believers pushed their way into the immense building. They moved into the stores, rushed to the bars for food and drink, and simply took over El Palacio Real. Merchants, at first, were happy for so many potential customers, but as soon as they sensed the tenor of the crowd, they shuddered at what might happen if somebody lost their cool. Feeling both apprehensive and cautious, nobody—not the merchants or the customers—called for help; in fact, if a uniformed officer had shown up, that might have been sufficient to spark a riot. The crowd of religious believers, followers of *la Santa Ilusa de las Grietas*, was convinced they were safe at El Palacio Real. So they relaxed, drank coffee, beer, milk, juice, cokes, and water.

Food circulated first to the children, the sick and, then, to the adults. Words circulated like food, their sound nourished their imagination, inspired hope as they repeated the rumor that *la Santa Ilusa de las Grietas* was coming to the Miracle of the Mud Cafe to meet with church and civilian authorities.

El Palacio Real had become a success that surpassed the dreams of its investors, including Rebecca, who offered financial workshops for Latino men and women with constant, secure jobs. It didn't matter whether they were domestic help, gardeners, trash collectors, construction workers, masons, waiters, dishwashers, hospital or motel employees, mechanics, or professionals. What mattered was that most of them were earning a living, making a consistent salary and setting aside some of their earnings, saving it in the bank or hiding money at home. Rebecca's workshops introduced them to available investment options and financial instruments. They learned that they could invest in mutual funds, stocks, bonds, and property, and, eventually, could stop renting and purchase a house. Her weekly workshops were attracting large crowds, and many participants were on site the day of J. I.'s meeting with Father Cristóbal and city authorities.

J. I.'s believers crowded into El Palacio Real. Some others who doubted her miracles, even her existence, came to see if she would appear. To entertain the gathering, orchestras played and choirs sang. El Palacio Real offered the arena for the multitude of men and women to assure themselves that *la Santa Ilusa de las Grietas* was real and not a media creation or showbiz promotional character. In the crowd, there was a sense of public life, of a bonding, a sharing of the intensity in a belief, a faith in her coming appearance. By waiting and ritualistically participating, a sensual proximity flooded the venue; they were so close that their bodies rubbed against one another and made their blood flow joyfully because of the existence of such a woman, *la Santa Ilusa de las Grietas*. The meeting at El Palacio Real had become a spectacle of public life and faith and community, a location where the individual once again found roots and a sense of belonging to one unified body.

Suddenly, from outside, there advanced a roar, a cheer. The human sea opened a path for the arrival of Father Cristóbal, His Holiness

Cardinal McCracken, the police chiefs, one councilman from Tustin and one councilwoman from Santa Ana, and the mayors. Father Cristóbal's entourage was an extravagance of participation on the part of the *políticos* who dreaded losing the opportunity to, at least, meet *la Santa Ilusa de las Grietas*. It was as if revolutionary armies had marched victoriously into Santa Ana, California. Cameras focused on the leaders of one army, Father Cristóbal and Cardinal McCracken, and the members of their *Estado Mayor*, who took seats in the Miracle of the Mud Cafe. Reporters streamed live about the unusual events that unfolded at the unique cultural and shopping center in the heart of the city.

Rebecca had detailed for Vince a back-alley access to El Palacio Real, through the delivery entrances, that led to the Miracle of the Mud Cafe without anyone noticing. We had been waiting for two hours. During this time the poet/chef and his artist/chef wife, whose paintings decorated the walls of the cafe, had cooked up what they called *pollo borracho* and served the staff, Vince, and me. As I ate, a radiance came upon my body. I sensed it and became annoyed. Why does it have to be so obvious? I thought. Everybody in the kitchen noticed the glow around my head, but they kindly went on working, bringing no attention to my physical and spiritual states. They worked happily, at times glancing my way, smiling at the holy presence.

Meanwhile, outside, in the glorious halls of El Palacio Real, rumors, ideas, plans echoed from the army of believers. The poet/chef and the artist/chef's staff respected our surreptitious ingress. "Business as usual," the poet/chef announced as he invited us to sit at their workers' table. He offered a bottle of wine. After the second glass of red wine, I relaxed and let go of my worry of what was about to happen. I knew that I had to leave. The question was how. I wanted it to be on my terms. No airport.

"If they see me, the people will crowd into the cafe. It will be impossible to talk."

Vince spoke to our hosts. "Please," he said, "ask Father Cristóbal and His Holiness to come in with their friends. Bring them to your wonderful kitchen, to this workers' table to meet with *la Santa Ilusa de las Grietas*."

The artist/chef motioned to the sauté chef to prepare more food and to a waiter to bring more chairs.

"I'll tell them exactly that." The poet/chef pushed the kitchen door and held it open for a moment, just long enough to look back at me and smile.

In that moment, in the space the opening of the door offered, I perceived a perpetuity of images. I saw every face alive, every image possible, words thought and spoken I heard, an infinity of combinations of all possible signs that had existed, exists and will exist, held for an instant by my gaze. My weightless body swooned with pleasure, a gift from above I interpreted, as the door closed behind the poet/chef. The staff added tables, brought food and chairs for the guests whom I heard knock politely, and outside the private rented confines of the Miracle of the Mud Cafe, in the public spaces of El Palacio Real and beyond, a murmuring arose. The devoted knew what was happening. They understood that I was present and had invited Father Cristóbal and his group to meet.

One by one they entered: first the four *políticos*, followed by the two police chiefs, and His Holiness, dressed magnificently in his cardinal garb. Suddenly, a welcomed calm and a silence seemed to fill a minute gap of time, until Vince pushed the door open and stepped aside to allow Father Cristóbal to, at last, stand before me. He smiled, and his hands reached out to me. There was a feeling of sincerity, an authentic joy, to see me once again. He came around the table and embraced me and I, in return, warmly embraced him.

"Father Cristóbal, please, sit," I said, with conflicting emotions of joy and sadness, for he carried on his body and presence a profusion of memories that leaped at my eyes and mind. When he finally let go of my hand, he sat next to His Holiness Cardinal McCracken. The table was just about complete. There remained four spaces, and I pointed to the poet/chef to sit in one, to a young Chinese woman waiter, to a relative of the owners, and to a Black waiter to take a seat in the other places at the table. There was one more place at my left, where Vince stood watching over me. I indicated the chair. He took his place and whispered, "I will never betray you."

The artist/chef had caught the vision and quickly commenced painting the gathering and the meal with *la Santa Ilusa de las Grietas*.

I poured wine and we all drank. I broke bread and we all ate. As I prayed for them, I believed they accompanied me in their religious way. For half an hour the group chatted about mundane daily events, enjoying the gathering, until at one in the afternoon the Tustin Police Chief interrupted:

"We're here to talk about alternatives, not ultimatums!" He continued: "It is clear there is a problem with crowd control. We can't handle it. I know some of you are insisting that we bill Mexico for the massing of Mexicans who support *la Santa Ilusa de las Grietas*. No matter how crazy that might sound, there are people who are ready to charge Mexico, or deport you, lady."

"You are subverting the Latino population, especially the Mexicans, into believing that they are here for far more than just to pick our crops," the Santa Ana mayor stated.

"There is a clear case against you for sedition, for plotting against the city government and the national government," the Tustin mayor said.

"That's absurd. She has only helped people. She is not to blame for the following she gets. If you are honest and good to people, they will respond by supporting you. You should learn from her instead of accusing her!" the poet/chef shouted.

"The Church supports *la Santa Ilusa de las Grietas*. We desire to understand her good works. We are not here to accuse, but to seek more information, an absolute trustworthy sign."

"The ICE will deport you if you don't cease these ridiculous spectacles the people are calling miracles. They're more like witchcraft to me!" the Santa Ana mayor blurted angrily. "All you are doing is encouraging more illegals into the state. And we're sick and tired of paying for them. All they want is a free ride! As far as I'm concerned, you either stop this madness or take it out of the state!"

"I believe *la Santa Ilusa de las Grietas* has a gift from God; she has a calling. The Church proposes that she be escorted to a secluded convent or monastery where she can rest. It will appoint several observers, hearers, to follow and assist her in her every need. They will also log every word pronounced by her; these recordings will assist Church authorities to determine whether she has or has not a sacred calling, a special gift. For those of you who are ill informed, *la Santa Ilusa de las Grietas* was born in the United States, not far from here. She is a United States citizen. She was educated in México and at your finest U.S. universities. If she leaves, she will leave on her own terms, her own free will. You can't force her to abandon her faithful nor her country."

"Hey, I'll pay for the ticket back to Mexico!" the Santa Ana mayor offered.

"If she decides to take the Church's offer, we will take charge of the arrangements," His Holiness said sternly.

"Just remember that we won't guarantee your safety anymore," the Tustin police chief said.

"You're always going to be under surveillance. No matter where you go, *you* will be watched, and when you make a mistake, any little infraction, we will arrest you. I want you off the streets. I consider you a very dangerous person. You do great harm to the Hispanic community," the Santa Ana police chief added.

"I hope you stay, because we all support you," the Chinese waitress said. As if she had overcome a great obstacle, she sat back, satisfied at her participation.

Meanwhile, the artist/chef had worked at a frenzied pace and just about completed the last supper that I would have in the Miracle of the Mud Cafe at El Palacio Real. Nobody was happy at the end of this encounter. We solved nothing. It was up to me to decide to stay or leave, and as they walked out, not saying thank you or goodbye, I knew that they could make my life, and that of those that I loved, miserable. Father Cristóbal was the last to depart. I noticed that he spoke hurriedly with Vince.

Mrs. Dougherty's white wicker furniture, well kept, gleamed in the evening sunset at the Mayas' home. I sat in the garden at the back, next to the hothouse where the Mayas continued growing orchids the same way that Mrs. Dougherty had taught them. They never did business any differently; they were afraid if they did, the reality they lived would shatter. Rebecca, Lea, Rufino, and Chac had arrived at different times during the night and throughout the day. The police and the politicians kept their promise of surveillance, with Santa Ana and Tustin patrol cars driving by the house every hour or so. But they had also dispersed the crowds away from our sight. Where they had gone I didn't know, but if this was like what happened in México I knew they were waiting somewhere out there. We waited for Father Cristóbal. I heard Vince when they entered the house. I could hear the Mayas' excitement at having a priest in their house. Vince came into the garden first. He greeted me silently with his hand caressing my shoulder and hair. The Mayas held Father Cristóbal in the kitchen, offering him food and drink. Finally he appeared at the door with a glass of *horchata* in his hand. May ran after him and placed a dish of sweet bread on the table.

"Cualquier cosa que se le antoje, padre".

May ran back into the kitchen and watched from the window with Ray and the children. A priest in our house, she must have been excitedly thinking.

He was dressed like the first time I had met him in Amecameca: casual jeans, T-shirt, baseball cap, and white tennis shoes. It seemed as if we had lived this moment before. I recalled the theories of cyclical time, the stories and novels of Latin American writers I had read years ago. Watching Father Cristóbal pull out the wicker chair and sit before me was truly like living a fiction. "In my wildest dreams I never thought I would see you again," I said.

"If you keep doing what you do, the Church will always send me. I'm your best ally. I'm the person they turn to when they need to get you out of trouble. You made me the expert on you. Well, ever since Amecameca, the Church assigned me to learn all about you and your family. That's what I've been doing for as long as you've been here."

"Thank you, but I don't need any priest watching over me!"

"I'm sorry, but that is my sacred duty. I am assigned by the highest authorities in the Vatican. I am honored to be here."

"I'm not honored. I have plenty of surveillance! I don't need you or the damn Church! My calling is from God."

"I seem to recall that this is the same argument we had when I took you to Amecameca. Don't resist. You have a sacred calling. I have observed your regression into childhood as an *enfans*, babbling or speaking in tongues, eating only when fed by someone, and experiencing stigmata. I, along with many people, have witnessed your miracles. The celestial glow of your face and hands reminds us of the light of God shining through your humanity. I am convinced as well as the Church. We are worried about your safety."

"I'm fine, Father Cristóbal. No harm has come to me. I do God's will and He and His army of heavenly and earthly angels will protect me." I turned to Vince and motioned him to sit with us.

"Vince is aware of what is happening. There are radical religious sectors that see you as evil, and political groups that consider you extremely dangerous. These groups are plotting a deadly response as we speak. This place, the land of liberty, democracy, and religious freedom—believe it or not—for someone like you is more treacherous than México." Father Cristóbal drank a bit of his sweet *horchata*.

Vince placed an envelope on the table and poured some *horchata* for himself. He had been listening intently. I could see in his eyes and face that he was already convinced that I was in some kind of danger.

"I think this is a letter from Endriago." Vince started to open the envelope.

Father Cristóbal placed his hand over Vince's and said to me, "Before you open the letter, please, let me tell you what Endriago says and doesn't say. Maybe this will prove to you that I have great concern for you and those you love."

I didn't hesitate. "I'm listening."

Father Cristóbal paused and withdrew his hand, slowly, from Vince's. His countenance assumed a wayward, lost, and downhearted perspective. He could speak now, but he hesitated and drank his *horchata*.

"The letter contains a description of what he has done since he wrote you last. Mostly, he has been observing the patients going in and out of the pharmaceutical hospital. The experimentation going on there is shocking, Santa Ilusa de las Grietas. I don't understand how our government can allow North-American pharma to experiment with our Natives. Endriago concludes by asking you to go to Chiapas to help the native groups. You would expect this request. He has made it before. What he omits from his letter is his physical condition. He is withering away. His body is emaciated to skin and bone, but he eats well, never complaining about being tired. He keeps on working while he wastes away. The doctors can't find what's wrong with him. In spite of excellent medical care, he is literally fading away, being erased from our sight. I don't believe he has much time before he disappears into the greenery and moisture of the jungle."

As Father Cristóbal fell silent, I read Endriago's letter. It was difficult for me to imagine that he would allow himself to deteriorate physically. I believed he, strangely enough, was proud of who he was. As I read on I could not imagine a man of his physical stature and prowess poised to evaporate willfully into the mist of the jungle.

J. I., I have learned much during this time. The wealth of Chiapas is impressive. The earth's water provides electricity to light the streets and buildings of México and to run its machines. Oil is so plentiful and they say that Chiapas and Guatemala combined could produce more than Saudi Arabia. The area is rich with cattle ranches, meat on the hoof is plentiful, but, J. I., within this wealth our people here have no electricity, running water, and seldom taste meat. They are starving to death. Along with direct assaults, malnutrition is slowly killing the indígenas. Every day I see or hear of a baby dying. Chiapas is a land of children— more than half of the population is under the age of nineteen years—but before my eyes I have seen those kids who survive lose their teeth, wither away to old, feeble humanoids. For them there is no school—they don't know how to read or write. There is no future but their open starving mouths, their dusty sweaty bodies, and the grave (if they are lucky). Or the elements will consume their bodies wherever they may fall. Often I have been frightened, when, suddenly, in the jungle I stumbled into a bullet-riddled skull, or the naturally camouflaged sight of a green, decaying body, which seemed to have died walking and just before dying leaned against a tree to melt into the trunk. Many a time, I have been warned by the stench to avoid the sights of gross obscenity. Horribly, there is also an orgy of killing here.

Paramilitary and military forces, usually small patrol groups, wreak havoc on the Indigenous population. Most of the victims in the pogroms against the native chiapanecos are women and children. They are the easiest targets, the ones to get raped, beaten, and killed. Also, they are the ones taken, many times by force, to the pharmaceutical clinics and end up dying from some experiment, some injected substance. I have seen firsthand the hideous results when women, running and carrying their babies, are captured by the troops. There is evil here, and Satan is its leader. Only you, Santa Ilusa de las Grietas, can help and give us hope. I implore you to abide us in this, our most difficult hour.

Endriago

P.S. I cannot hold on much longer.

I returned the letter back to its envelope, thinking that I would read it later with greater detail. Father Cristóbal stood before me. Vince accompanied him to the door.

"You might want to visit your father in Tijuana. I understand he has established several new *maquiladoras* for his *gringo* business partners. You might want to see his good works. Here's the address of his new twin factories." Father Cristóbal tinged his suggestion with malicious irony. He quickly disappeared from my sight. In this manicured garden in the middle of Aztlandia, I contemplated my plight and Father Cristóbal's comments about my parents, my father's business activity. I was curious to know why he had returned to work and to Tijuana. Of course I knew the answer to my rhetorical question: for the money! After all, my father was still a Mexican venture capitalist. Clouds of dust—lots of it came to mind—, noise, and thousands of women working in an immense factory, so clean inside that its sparkle forced me to shut my eyes.

I had come to a standstill. My movements were constrained by political and disciplinary institutions. This, of course, had occurred before, but I elected not to make a stand here. I listened to the Mayas' commotion inside, saying goodbye to the good Father.

I remained in the garden until Vince came for me, and we walked into the Mayas' dining room. I remember that, throughout dinner, the children, excited by the priest's visit, talked about Father Cristóbal's easy-going demeanor. Jay and Fay had grown so much, and they seemed to really enjoy each other's company as brother and sister. All during and after dinner Vince had hardly spoken. I knew that he, like me, had to make a decision. I understood what I had to do, and wondered what Vince, my lover here in Aztlandia, would decide.

Later that week in Vince's apartment, in the late afternoon, I met a man whom I had known for some time, who loved me and who, forever, desired my body, a man God shamelessly covered with hair . . . I met the emancipated Vince Rodelo. He, excited like a child, walked up and declared his liberation.

"J. I., I have left my job. I was going to quit, but the chief talked me into taking a leave of absence. J. I., I will not let you go," Vince spoke. His face appeared worried, ready to confess every emotion he held toward me.

"Vince, it's not for you to tell me if I can go or not."

"J. I., I won't lose you. I want to be with you for the remainder of my life."

"It's simple: If I leave, just come with me."

A deep joy entered me and I gladly accepted his embrace and his kiss. That night we made love as more than mere lovers; we were not just bodies but a way of recreating and identifying our being. While inside me, I studied his face of perfect pleasure and, while he kissed me, I cried for the fear of the commitment that we had made to each other. When we finished, he sat on the side of the bed, his back covered with hair; he glistened, walked away like an ancient ape, and I was horrified.

I put the glass of Chardonnay on the white cotton tablecloth and wiped my mouth with the thick, green, cotton napkin of the Hotel del Coronado. I looked beyond, while several Mexican families played on the two green tennis courts just below, to the Pacific Ocean at Point Loma. I had read there was a Jesus-like statue of Juan Cabrillo overlooking the land and the bay he explored on his way north to the place Vince and I had left last night, as we meandered our way through the cities on the southern Pacific Coast of California. I had a sense, heightened by lack of sleep, of the thrill of an explorer trekking into unchartered waters, as Vince and I walked into the center garden.

The Hotel del Coronado, with its opulent shops, its rich dark mahogany lobbies, its view of the beach and San Diego Bay, made me feel as if I had returned to the beginning, to the source of my life. The hotel, according to my mother's explanations, was the place of the conception, not "immaculate" but one of love and passion, my origin. My construction had started here in one of the rooms facing the center garden, where a bride dressed in pure white had just then kissed her groom, to the approval of her parents and the applause of hundreds of guests. Vince and I walked through the wedding reception. Nobody asked who we were. We grabbed two plastic cups of champagne and made it for the door, but I literally bumped directly into the bride and the groom holding a crystal goblet each. As I caught a glimpse of what she saw, her eyes turned from expressing joy to the painful wideness of terror, for in a space occupied by no human body or member we both watched a sparkling glass rising through the air and suddenly stop, captured by the force of gravity pulling it down rapidly to the red tile floor. Her hands along with mine reached for the wedding chalice just before it shattered, then exploded upward into our faces a thousand tiny pieces. In the instant before screams, as witnesses observed the crystal roam through the atmosphere and fall, while I closed my eyes from the pain of the fragments, I reached for the newlywed face and held it for a second. She felt no pain from the crystal particles in her eyes.

"Oh God, it's broken!"

Then she screamed and reached for the large pieces, which I grabbed with her hands, four hands together.

"Oh, God, no it's not!"

I stood her up, stepped away from her and opened my hands to reveal the crystal goblet which—in the sight of the groom, the parents, and guests—had broken.

"It didn't break, beautiful bride. Here it is!"

I placed it in her hands. The bride noticed the radiance in my face and smiled.

Vince and I moved away quickly. The bride stepped toward us, wanted to follow, but the groom held her back. We reached the stairs and ran down to the ocean. When we stopped to sit on the beach, he noticed my eyes, red with blood.

"J. I., you're cut."

He wiped my blood tears, removed my soaked blouse and rinsed it in the ocean.

"No, I'll be fine." I walked into the Pacific. I carried the bride's pain of thousands of minuscule pricks in my eyes and neck into the water and bathed my body. I emerged naked and whole, like the ancient great white heron, with its magnificent ornamental nuptial plumes, that performed before me. From the Hotel del Coronado I could hear the wedding music, where, into the night, the bride in her white feathers danced and laughed with her groom.

That afternoon, as the sun went down, Vince and I drove to Dulzura, where he had arranged to stay at a beautiful bed and breakfast. In the evening, after Vince and I walked, literally, along the international border and observed United States Customs and Border Protection officers circle in white and green trucks like hawks scouting for prey, for human beings making a break for a better life, the owners of the bed and breakfast served a gourmet dinner. One of the guests was a man who described himself as a poet, a man who was very concerned with the handling of immigrants crossing the border, about the treatment these people received from Mexican *coyotes* waiting to victimize them, and from the CBP officers waiting to grab them and process them back to México.

"The border is a battle zone, becoming more militarized every day. Its victims are the poor from México," the poet said, while he enjoyed a medium-rare slice of prime rib.

"What is even worse are the *maquiladoras*. There they exploit human beings with impunity. Women are the primary victims of daily physical abuse. Abduction, beating, rape, mutilation, and murder are common events around the *maquila* zones along the border. They just built ten new twin factories, some old U.S.-México partnership start-ups. They built them right in the middle of Las Flores, one of the poorest and most violent zones in Tijuana. The poorer, the more frightened, the more desperate, the cheaper the labor."

The poet stopped and looked around. "I'm sorry. I get on my soapbox and get carried away. Hey, I'll make it up to you. Another bottle of wine here, please!"

Late that night I awoke to screams and the sound of revving engines from several trucks roaming the hills on the border nearby. Throughout the night, streams of light broke across the window and penetrated the darkness outside. I opened the blinds and saw half a dozen powerful spotlights centered on three people on the road leading to the bed and breakfast. I saw a man, and a woman holding an infant in her arms. Suddenly, the lights went out, and there was only blackness and the child's cry lingering in the dampness of the night. I climbed back and cuddled next to Vince, who slept soundly. I nestled into the thick hair of his back and remembered my family. I wondered about my father, his new factories. I could almost make out Sara and Jennie, my girls . . .

On the morning, we entered México, I barely ate breakfast, perhaps because of the restless night, the anticipation of crossing the border, of seeing my father, or the fear that someone would recognize me, or that somebody from the Church had followed us. Maybe Father Cristóbal knows where I am. It didn't matter. I knew he would find me and that I would go to Endriago in Chiapas.

A child's face appeared, a girl who perhaps worked at my father's new *La Maquiladora de los Sueños de la Imagen*. The *maquila* assembled components for cheap televisions produced, packaged, and distributed at his twin factory in Chula Vista. The girl: her face had tried to reveal itself throughout my restless night and while Vince and I were approaching the Mexican border. Driving at a stop-and-go pace, it took an hour and a half to reach the border station. A Mexican customs agent asked one simple question.

"¿Adónde van?"

"A Rosarito, a pasar el día," Vince answered in his best Spanish.

The agent waved us on. Vince drove onto the road that led us to downtown Tijuana. "Mexican air," I once heard a poet scream, reciting a poem about her Mexican mother. I was back in México, my mother country. I took a deep breath and for a moment felt liberated and proud.

From a restaurant overlooking avenida Revolución, we ate lunch. Vince had a dark beer, and we watched thousands of high school and college kids from the San Diego area meander along looking for booze, drugs, sex, and a good time. A man sitting at the next table opened his newspaper and narrated to his wife and two young daughters the contents of an article.

"Yeah, honey, the girl was the Maquila Beauty Queen. She was only fifteen years old. If I understand this right, her parents were ready to marry her to a much older man before she was kidnapped."

"It's horrible for those poor young women, those girls who work in those factories! They say they disappear frequently. Men, gangs, take them away, rape, and kill them. As if they were stray dogs, loose chickens . . . ," the woman said. She caressed her daughter's long blond hair.

"Who's a chicken, honey?"

"The girls who work in the *maquiladoras*. They're constant targets. I think that NAFTA, all that free-trade business just brought more desperate Mexicans to the border and has created more misery."

The man turned the newspaper pages.

"Oh God! This photo is horrible, honey! How can they publish such an attrocity?" I heard the man say, as Vince and I walked down to avenida Revolución.

The image of the child began to form when her parents decided to travel to Tijuana from Chihuahua, México. They feared Juárez: It was too dangerous, with many killings of poor workers by corrupted police and *narco* gangsters, they had heard. They went to Tijuana—it was near the cool ocean and sandy white beaches of Baja California Norte, and it was, after all, the gateway to the jobs of California. I made up this common story about the images that persisted in my thought, my mind's eye.

Vince turned the car on the street that would take us to colonia Las Flores, to my father's factory. I had not called him. What a surprise he will have, I thought. We arrived at the first *maquiladora*. The girl, her younger sister, and her mother worked six days a week in a foreign-owned factory making turn signals for automobiles. They made $4 a day. That was the average salary for *maquila* workers. The majority are young women always under the gaze of the owner's *gringo* administrators. One false move, one mistake, and they fire them. Many are abused. Many of the women are so afraid of losing their jobs that they allow the foremen, the supervisors, to have their way with them.

I often listened to my father discuss investments with his *socios norteamericanos*. It didn't bother me then. His business was profitable and made us rich. I understood that, but I do remember overhearing conversations among the men who ran the factories for him: They talked about the different women they had throughout the week. They laughed and would say those were the perks of the job.

The image at times turns horrible and I can make out the girl's crumpled figure on the rocky earth less than a mile away from my father's factory, her panties down around her ankles.

"*¿La Maquiladora de los Sueños de la Imagen?*" Vince asks a group of women standing outside a factory, buying coffee and donuts from a catering truck.

"¿Sueños de la Imagen?" he calls out again. An older woman approaches the car.

"Es una de las nuevas". The woman points straight ahead on the dirt road. *"Sigan ese camión. Por allí pasa".* The woman turns away and joins the group entering the factory.

We watch the bus, packed with women of all ages wearing distinct uniforms, the rocking motion from potholes in the road making them laugh. Two police cars, one with lights flashing, drive by and pass the bus that slows down even more to allow the patrol to move ahead. The bus stops at the side of the road at a large fence and gate. Here, red and white uniforms get off and start to walk to a distant building. The bus moves on. We follow.

In a matter of minutes, Vince and I have seen hundreds of women arriving, entering, and standing outside factories.

"There are no street lights here. We should leave before it gets dark," Vince suggests.

I remembered the man at the restaurant say, "Two hundred girls have disappeared in the last ten months." They travel for hours, get up early in the morning, some start at four and leave when it is dark. They are easy targets, I thought.

Vince pulls the car over to allow another police patrol to move ahead. Now, we follow the police. We drive for another ten minutes until it turns and goes around probably the biggest factory we have seen. Vince stops at the entrance. What a coincidence: *Los Sueños de la Imagen.* A small sign on the door announces that we have arrived at my father's factory. An arrow indicates "Entrance at back." Vince and I walk to the rearmost section of the building. At a distance of a football field away, I see police cars, a white van, a group of photographers hurriedly snapping shots of what seems to be a ditch. I start to walk toward them.

"Where are you going?" Vince grabs my arm.

"There will be no miracles here."

Vince let me go. I walked faster toward what I had already in my mind, the image becoming clearer with each step that I took. It moved from her innocent, beautiful face to the grotesque. As I neared, the police made a path toward her. The photographers ceased shooting as I stood over her. I smiled for I knew she had conquered death, she was beyond us all. There would be no miracles here. Her condition now would stand alone: a testimony to big profits.

"Big *tetas, buenota, horrendos crímenes,* pussy, fine fucks, *yo me las cojo con cariño, no soy malo con ellas si se portan bien. ¡Yo no soy matón!*"

I hear the police question what they call a prime suspect, hand-cuffed, against a car. He appeared absolutely demented, this man from the streets, dressed in black, filthy, speaking in nonsensical incoherent vocabulary, terms and acronyms in Spanish and English. I don't think he was Mexican. He appeared to be an Anglo strung out on drugs, crusted with dirt. He obviously had been beaten. He screamed: "*¡No la maté!* I fuckem, *¡es todo! Pero, como les digo, deben ser buenas conmigo, cabronas. Lo que está pasando no es culpa mía. ¡Esto es* free trade, *cabrones!* NAFTA y GATT *culo para mí y para los narcotraficantes y políticos*".

The crazed man looked over to me. He paused for a moment and let out a demented laugh. "*¡Ella entiende!* I've been doing it for years. It's easy. I love to fuck in the global . . . village. *¿Cómo que no prefiero a las chichonas? Son más alegres*".

One of the policemen's fists smashed the prime suspect on the mouth and pushed him back into the car, where he began to scream that he was innocent.

All the while, I stared into the girl's black-and-blue face, her taut skin pulled back, dried like cardboard, her lips stretched back revealing her white teeth. I saw her swollen stomach and chest, her pubescent breasts swollen larger, her nipples half bitten off, the muscle of her thighs ripped away from her bones, one leg severely bent behind her, her vagina grotesquely exposed, her flesh peeling away from her bones like boiled chicken, around one ankle her panties, her thick warm black socks still on her feet, her arms reaching above her head, her dress wrapped around her left arm. The putrid air unbearable, but I force myself to stay, to observe the hapless police and coroner examining the corpse for clues, evidence. They whisper as if standing before the sacred. One policeman turns and whimpers away. I look at the girl's countenance and see my own reflected there, screaming silently, asking, "What are you going to do about it?"

"¡Juana!" I hear a voice calling me back. *"¡Juana, soy yo!"* I look for Vince. He stands next to my father who is smiling proudly before one of the largest *maquiladoras* in Las Flores. Vince waves his hand, then points to me. Photographers resume shooting, police discuss her mortal wounds and, in the stench of her deteriorating body, my father runs toward me with open arms.

We embrace joyfully. Father, I thought, what have you created?

Alejandro Morales, the son of Mexican immigrants, was born in Montebello, California. He earned his Ph.D. from Rutgers University. Morales is professor emeritus in the Department of Chicano/Latino Studies at the University of California, Irvine.

Recognized by many as a pioneer of Chicano/Latino literature who writes in Spanish and English, Morales has authored several historical biographies in which he tells the fictional story of a character's life using historical personages and events, bringing together his love for both history and writing. His works are examples of Miguel de Unamuno's idea of Intra History, writing about the significance of the lives of ordinary people; of Linda Hutcheon's theory of Historiographic Metafiction, the practice of writing aware of theory, history and fiction as strategies to rethink and reevaluate the past; and Irving Stone's practice of writing biographical novels.

His research explores a variety of topics that concern the Chicano/Latino community including: history, immigration, race relations, ethnicity, family, labor, education, religion, memory, gender, power, border, borderlands, and the fantastic.

Recipient of the Luis Leal Award for Distinction in Chicano/Latino Literature, Morales was recognized for his contributions to Chicano/Latino literature and his accomplishments as a major American writer.